**Neve made a scoffing noise. "Of course somebody knows something, just a matter of whether or not they share it."**

"Why wouldn't they?" Mackenzie asked, her gaze narrowing.

Neve turned to her with a sympathetic gaze. "Small towns are weird," she explained. "There are some secrets that will become town gossip no matter how hard you try to keep them, and then there are others that should be public, but get buried so deep they might as well be part of the bedrock."

"That makes no sense," the girl argued.

Audrey's smile was grim. "Welcome to Edgeport."

Praise for

# Kate Kessler

## Two Can Play

"A smart crime novel that will engage readers."

—*Publishers Weekly*

"Readers can't help but enjoy solving the mystery along with Audrey right up to the final, unexpected twist."

—*RT Book Reviews*

## It Takes One

"Deliciously twisted and genre-bending, Kate Kessler's positively riveting *It Takes One* boasts a knockout concept and a thoroughly unique and exciting protagonist, a savvy criminal psychologist with murderous skeletons in her own closet." —Sara Blaedel

"A book that kept calling to me when I should have been doing something else. Hard to put down, compulsive reading."

—Rachel Abbott

"*It Takes One* is a gripping roller-coaster ride of shock and suspense.... Kate Kessler excels at creating an atmosphere of fear and suspense." —Kate Rhodes

"Kessler has created a kick-ass, heartfelt character in this lively, twisty thriller. Believe me—you'll enjoy the ride." —Sandra Block

"This first in a series combines an intriguing mystery with a terrific cast of characters. Fans of Nancy Pickard or Lisa Unger will find much to like in Kessler. Expect her to become very popular very quickly." —*Booklist* (starred review)

"[Audrey's] a likable heroine, and between her moxie and sense of humor, she'll soon become a favorite of those who like their suspense less dark and bleak.... Audrey is definitely a keeper."

—*Kirkus*

"Tense, fast-paced.... The action builds to a compelling and unexpected conclusion." —*Publishers Weekly*

# THREE STRIKES

By Kate Kessler

Audrey Harte Novels

*It Takes One*

*Two Can Play*

*Three Strikes*

# THREE STRIKES

## AN AUDREY HARTE NOVEL

KATE KESSLER

www.redhookbooks.com

This book is a work of fiction. Names, characters, places, and incidents are the product of the author's imagination or are used fictitiously. Any resemblance to actual events, locales, or persons, living or dead, is coincidental.



Author photograph by Kathryn Smith
Cover design by Wendy Chan and Crystal Ben
Cover images by Shutterstock


Redhook Books/Orbit
Hachette Book Group
1290 Avenue of the Americas
New York, NY 10104
hachettebookgroup.com

First Edition: October 2017

Redhook is an imprint of Orbit, a division of Hachette Book Group.
The Redhook name and logo are trademarks of Hachette Book Group, Inc.

The publisher is not responsible for websites (or their content) that are not owned by the publisher.

The Hachette Speakers Bureau provides a wide range of authors for speaking events. To find out more, go to www.hachettespeakersbureau.com or call (866) 376-6591.

Library of Congress Cataloging-in-Publication Data has been applied for.

Names: Kessler, Kate, author.
Title: Three strikes / Kate Kessler.
Description: First edition. | New York, NY : Redhook, 2017. | Series: An Audrey Harte novel ; 3
Identifiers: LCCN 2017025895| ISBN 9780316302555 (softcover) | ISBN 9780316302548 (ebook) | ISBN 9781478915362 (audio book downloadable)
Subjects: LCSH: Women psychologists—Fiction. | Police psychologists—Fiction. | Family secrets—Fiction. | BISAC: FICTION / Suspense. | GSAFD: Suspense fiction. | Mystery fiction.
Classification: LCC PS3611.E8456 T48 2017 | DDC 813/.6—dc23 LC record available at https://lccn.loc.gov/2017025895

ISBNs: 978-0-316-30255-5 (paperback), 978-0-316-30254-8 (ebook)

Printed in the United States of America

LSC-C

10 9 8 7 6 5 4 3 2 1

For my sisters, Heather, Linda, and Nathalie—just because.
And for Steve, always.

# CHAPTER ONE

Necromania is defined as an obsession with death or the dead. Most of humanity has it to some degree, being very much aware from a young age that life is a temporary and fragile thing. Psychologist Dr. Audrey Harte was familiar with the term, as well as the corresponding paraphilia that sexualized corpses. Fortunately, she'd never met anyone who suffered from the disorder.

*Un*fortunately, none of her academic or professional research had ever provided a label for those people who seem to have death obsessed with *them*—people like herself who had to have a grim reaper watching over them just as others claimed to have angels. It was an impossible theory to prove, but she wanted to name it, because if it *was* possible for death to stalk a person, she wanted a restraining order. Like, yesterday.

Since returning to the East Coast just five months earlier she'd been caught up in two separate murders and had a serial killer become obsessed with her. People always thought Maine was a peaceful state, and for the most part it was, but nothing *that* crazy had ever happened to her when she lived in California. It made a sort of karmic sense, however, that returning to the place where she'd once murdered someone would attract death's attention. If her life was one of those paranormal romances her sister liked to read (and Audrey too, occasionally), death personified would be a gorgeous guy with a lot of muscle and incredible sexual stamina, but her life was not a romance novel, and she was a little afraid death was actually a guy who lived in his mother's basement and had a shrine to her in his bedroom, along with thirty-two copies of *The Catcher in the Rye* and an autographed, framed photo of Ted Bundy.

She also realized that thinking she'd been singled out by death was somewhat egomaniacal, irrational, and paranoid, even if she had the scars to prove it. So she concentrated on her mother, who was recovering from a partial hysterectomy due to cancer, instead and told herself that death might back off if she didn't flirt quite so much.

"I'm going to lie down," her mother said, getting up from the table. Anne Harte was trim and youthful-looking for a woman in her sixties, who usually had a lot of energy, but fighting the cancer, and now the surgery to remove it, had slowed her. Audrey had taken time off from work to help out, which was ironic because just before her mother's surgery, she'd been shot in the left arm by a teenage psychopath, and consequently hadn't been as much help as she'd hoped.

"You need anything?" Audrey asked her, watching her tentative movements. Her mother was healing as she should, but she'd still been cut open, and was uncomfortable. If seeing your father vulnerable was scary, seeing your mother vulnerable was a lesson in impotent terror.

"Nope. Maybe a tea in a little while." Anne tucked her graying brown hair behind one ear. "You should rest too."

Audrey shook her head. "I'm good." It was true. It had been almost three weeks now and she felt okay. Her arm ached, but it was healing and that was all she cared about. Surprisingly, she'd done all the things her doctor and physical therapist told her to do to speed recovery. She'd be lying if she said she wasn't a little surprised to discover the practices actually *worked*.

"Wake me up in an hour or so, will you, babe? I want to make cookies for when Isabelle gets home from school."

Izzy was Audrey's five-year-old niece—a fabulous kid who had her grandparents wrapped around her little finger. "Aren't there any of the ones Jake made left?"

Her mother blushed. "No."

Audrey laughed—as much at her mother's sweet tooth as in relief that she was eating. "I'll ask him to make you some more."

"Don't you dare. That boy already feeds us more than he ought. I've probably gained ten pounds since the two of you started dating."

"Dating." That was such an insipid word to describe her relationship with Jake Tripp. Regardless, her mother needed the extra calories. The cancer and treatments had taken a lot of fat off her frame, and she was only now looking more like her usual self.

"He said he's bringing chicken potpie tonight. Gracie's recipe."

Anne smiled. "If he proposes, you'd better say yes."

Audrey started. She and Jake had only gotten together in June, but they'd loved each other since they were children. The idea of life without him was unfathomable, but she hadn't fantasized about marrying him since she was sixteen—and wasn't about to let herself start again. It wasn't like either of them was ever going to be free of the other, so why try to put expectations on it? "Have a good nap."

Her mother left the room and Audrey waited until she was gone to get up from the table and clear the remnants of their late lunch. Her weakened arm made the process take a little longer than it ought, but she eventually got everything put away. She took butter out of the fridge to soften for cookie-making later and carried her laptop into the living room.

Technically she was off work for the foreseeable future, recovering, but she needed to check her e-mail and make sure all was good with the Boston office. What she really wanted to do, however, was work on the proposal for a youth facility she planned to show her boss, Angeline Beharrie, a renowned psychologist.

The two of them had spent a lot of time recently discussing a remark Audrey made once about hoping to someday run a facility for troubled teens. Early next year, Maine was planning to close a couple of state-run properties, creating an opportunity she never would have thought would be available to her at this stage in her career. Angeline was interested, as having a private facility would greatly improve the efficiency of conducting research.

Over the years, Angeline had indulged her—spoiled her,

even—but she didn't want to count on that always happening. And she didn't want to always be in Angeline's shadow. Audrey wanted to earn her achievements. Still, she wanted this dream to become reality bad enough that if Angeline did want to indulge her, Audrey wouldn't try to stop her.

Lately, Jake had begun to show interest as well. She didn't know exactly how much money he had, but it was a lot, and his backing would allow her that much more control over the project. The proper phrasing and outlining was important, though. It all started on paper.

She was typing away, ignoring the slight ache in her arm, when her cell phone buzzed beside her on the sofa. She glanced at the screen; it was her friend Neve asking where she was and could Neve swing by? Audrey's reply was *Mum's & yes*. She hadn't seen the other woman in a few days, and she'd welcome the company. Working on the proposal didn't take the place of having a full-time job.

Neve's car—the familiar unmarked state police car—pulled into the drive a few minutes later. Audrey opened the door before she could ring the bell or knock. "Mum's napping," she explained in a low voice when her friend raised a brow.

Neve nodded. She and Audrey were the same age, and had chosen careers in which they could help people, but that was where the similarities ended for the most part, except maybe for resting bitch face. Neve was a tiny bit shorter, her complexion several shades darker, and her hair a riot of corkscrew curls that could be achieved only through genetics. "How's she doing?" she asked, as she crossed the threshold into the house.

"Better." Audrey closed the door on the cold November air. She hadn't re-acclimatized to it yet. Jake laughed at her every time she insisted that Maine was colder than it had been before she left. "Much better than we expected, to be honest."

The other woman toed off her boots and shrugged out of her coat. "And you? The arm doing okay?"

"Yeah, it aches a bit, but it's healing." Once Neve hung up her coat, Audrey gestured for her to walk ahead.

"Dad says you'll be tender for a while. He also said you must have the devil looking after you that it didn't tear through all the muscle."

"I'm sure he did," she replied dryly. Neve's father had arrested her and her best friend Maggie for the murder of Clint Jones—Maggie's father—almost nineteen years ago, and had been convinced ever since that Audrey was Public Enemy Number One. "He needs a hobby."

"Tell me about it."

They walked into the kitchen and Audrey put the kettle on. "Biscuit?" she asked.

"Your mom's or Jake's?"

Audrey reached for the plastic container on the counter and popped the lid. "Dad's actually, but he used Gracie's recipe. Mum was not impressed with him."

"I'll try one, sure."

"Molasses?"

"You know it."

They made small talk as Neve helped her set the table and

make the tea. Audrey asked about Neve's boyfriend, Gideon, and his daughter, Bailey.

"B's good. She mentioned that you came to see her last week. It meant a lot to her."

"I'm glad." Audrey felt responsible for Bailey's incarceration at Stillwater—a correctional facility for girls—and that responsibility was part of the reason she was working so hard on making her own facility a reality. Stillwater was where she had gone after killing Clint, and it was one of the properties that would be closing in the spring. There needed to be a place where girls like Bailey could get the help and support they needed while paying for their crimes.

"How much longer are you going to be around before you return to Boston?" Neve asked. "It would be nice if you could stay until after Christmas and not have to worry about driving back and forth."

Audrey hesitated.

"*Are* you returning to Boston?" Neve asked as they sat down.

"Probably. Maybe." Audrey shrugged and reached for the sugar bowl. "I don't know. I have some things to discuss with Angeline first. I've been thinking about what you and Jake both said to me about getting more involved with kids who need help rather than just studying and interviewing them, and the more I think about it, the more I think you're right."

"Had to happen sometime," her friend replied with a smile. She pulled a biscuit in half and slathered it with butter before reaching for the molasses. "You wouldn't think I was right if it wasn't what you wanted for yourself." She took a bite.

Audrey tilted her head in acknowledgment as she dressed up her own biscuit. That was true. "So, what's up?"

Neve swallowed and creased her brow. "I got a call from a friend of mine a couple of days ago. Before she was killed, Maggie registered with the state adoption registry. Did you know she had a kid?"

She had, and since the father of that child was also Maggie's father, it was a detail Audrey had kept to herself since finding out several months ago. She had thought about looking for the girl, but frankly, she couldn't bring herself to do it, knowing the problems the kid might have. The kind of problems that arose when your father was also your grandfather.

Just when she thought she couldn't despise Clint Jones more, he managed to make it happen from beyond the grave.

"I knew," she replied. "It was a few months after I went to Stillwater." The years there had been the worst and best years of her teenage life. Certainly the most life-changing. That's where she'd met Angeline for the first time, and where she decided that she wanted to be a psychologist too.

Neve winced. "Christ, she was that young? No wonder I didn't hear about it. Maggie probably wanted that secret to stay hidden. I don't think Gideon knew."

Gideon had been married to Maggie. Not a huge dating pool in small towns—it made it all very incestuous, for lack of a better term. "He probably didn't." She was fairly sure of that because she hadn't known either, until she read Maggie's journal. "Did your friend say anything else?"

"Yeah. So, someone requested Maggie's contact information, and the registry had to let them know she'd died."

Audrey's heart smacked against her ribs. "You think it was her daughter?"

"It was. My friend responded to the request personally, and offered to see if she could find any family. She knew I grew up here so she called me."

Audrey shook her head. "There's no one left. Everyone that I knew of is dead. There might be family in New Hampshire. That's where they lived before coming here."

"I checked. No one."

Audrey studied her friend carefully. Why did it feel like Neve wanted more than Maggie's family tree from her? "Is Gideon considering meeting her?" Talk about a strange situation—him meeting Maggie's kid after she'd done so much damage to his own daughter, Bailey.

"I haven't told him yet." Neve's hand on the table curled into a fist. "The only person I could think of who might be able to tell this girl who her mother really was is you."

*Oh, no.* "You do realize there's a good chance Clint is the kid's father." She let that—and all its implications—sink in.

Neve's jaw dropped. "Shit. I never thought." She looked panicked. "She's already on her way. She'll be here in fifteen minutes."

"Here?" Audrey echoed. "As in, *here*?"

Neve nodded. "She drove down from Calais."

She ought to be angry at Neve for making presumptions. She should be pissed, because she was sitting there in sweats, with no makeup, and still recovering from a gunshot wound to her left arm. Now was not a good time to meet a kid whose origins she couldn't possibly begin to explain in any way that wouldn't be upsetting to either of them.

But she *wanted* to meet the girl. God, she was almost excited about the opportunity. And it wasn't just because Audrey wanted to know if she was all right, or if she was loved, but because the kid was all there was left of the Maggie who had been her best friend. The Maggie she had loved and had killed someone to protect before she became... what she had become.

"What were you going to do with her if I hadn't been here?"

Neve shrugged. "I would have figured something out. You okay with this?"

She laughed. "I kind of have to be, don't I? She's going to be here any minute." She shook her head. "Asking first would have been nice, you know."

The cop didn't even have the decency to look apologetic. "If I'd given you warning, you would have found a way to avoid her."

"No, I wouldn't." She would have wanted to, but she wouldn't. "Maggie named her after me, did you know that?"

"Shit. No." She looked uncomfortable, which made Audrey smile a little. *Good.* "She told me her name was Mackenzie."

Weird as having the kid share her name would be, Audrey

was a little disappointed the girl or her parents had changed it. "Did she seem developmentally delayed when you spoke to her?"

"I haven't actually spoken to her. We've e-mailed and texted each other." Neve's brow puckered. "How bad are you talking?"

"It varies." She reached for another biscuit. "She could be okay. I'm not looking forward to telling her that I killed her grampie-daddy, but it will be easier if I know she can fully understand why."

Neve stared down at her cup. "Oh, right."

"Yeah," Audrey agreed. That little matter of murder. She sighed. No point in getting wound up.

They sat in silence for a long moment, and then the doorbell rang, startling them both. Audrey hadn't heard a car drive in. Her heart thumped heavily against her ribs as she walked to the entry way. The knob was cold beneath her palm as she pulled the door open.

Standing on the step in the cold was a young woman with long dark hair and big blue eyes. She had Maggie's nose and mouth, but she was taller and not as curvy. She smiled uncertainly and extended her hand. "Dr. Harte? I'm Mackenzie Bell. Detective Graham said you could tell me about my birth mother, Maggie Jones."

Audrey swallowed, fighting the tears that burned behind her eyes. "Hi, Mackenzie," she said as she wrapped her fingers around the girl's. "I'll tell you as much as I can." But she wasn't going to have to tell her that she'd killed her father, because there was little to no way the girl belonged to Clint Jones—she had no obvious physical or mental defects.

But if Clint wasn't her father, who was?

Incest didn't happen just in small rural towns, but the sheer happiness—the *relief*—Audrey felt realizing that Mackenzie probably wasn't both Maggie's daughter *and* sister made her feel like she was trapped in a *South Park* joke.

There was no denying who her mother was, and every time Audrey looked at the girl she saw another little heartbreaking reminder of Maggie—*her* Maggie—but there was someone else there too and she couldn't figure out who he was. It wasn't Clint—she knew this in her bones.

Audrey had taken her to the kitchen, where Neve waited, and made a third cup of tea. When the girl sat down at the table, after saying hello to the other woman, Audrey and Neve exchanged a glance over her head. The girl wasn't what they'd expected, and that only raised more questions.

"Thank you both for agreeing to meet with me," Mackenzie said when Audrey set a cup of tea in front of her. "I just turned eighteen in October. I went on to the registry that same day. I couldn't believe my birth mother died only months before I could find her."

Audrey shook her head. The emotion on the kid's face cut deep, even though a part of her was certain reality wouldn't have lived up to Mackenzie's hopes. "I can't imagine how disappointing that must've been."

Mackenzie glanced at Neve. "You knew her as well, didn't you? Maggie, I mean."

Neve nodded. "I've known both her and Audrey since I was young, but Maggie and Audrey were best friends."

Audrey shot the other woman a narrow look. What she said was true, but it was also throwing Audrey under the bus as far as explaining all of Maggie's issues.

The girl smiled, and there was Maggie again in her face. The good Maggie, before life had totally destroyed her. "What was she like?"

That was a loaded question, but Audrey found herself smiling fondly, despite all the baggage she and Maggie shared. "When Maggie moved here I thought she was so exotic. She came all the way from New Hampshire, and I had never been outside of Maine."

Mackenzie looked at her with delight. "Did you become friends right away?"

"Yeah, we did. The best of friends." She just let that hang there, uncertain of what else to say.

"Did you stay best friends even after you killed her father?"

Audrey blinked. "Well, that was... blunt."

"Sorry." There was no hostility in the girl's tone, no judgment in her expression, just simple curiosity. She should have known that Mackenzie would know who she was, and what she and Maggie had done. If their situations were reversed the first thing she would've done upon finding out her birth mother's name was a Google search. The records were sealed, but that didn't stop people from talking, and talking was what people in Edgeport did best.

"For a while. Then we grew apart."

"Did he really molest her?"

"Yes."

"She told you and you believed her?"

"Yes, but also I witnessed it."

Both women stared at her, their eyes wide. Had she never told Neve that part of the story? Hadn't her father? Everett Graham was the one who had arrested her, who came to the house that night and found Clint's bludgeoned naked body on the floor of Maggie's bedroom. Audrey had cracked his skull open like a bone piñata after finding him raping his daughter. There were times when she wondered if Maggie had planned for her to arrive during one of Clint's "visits" so she'd do exactly what she'd done.

"*Jesus*," Neve whispered.

Mackenzie's face was white—stark white. "Please tell me he isn't my father too."

Relief and remorse rushed through Audrey at the same time. She'd been so concerned about how she was going to explain to the girl the situation surrounding her birth, she hadn't entertained the idea that she would have already put it together. How long had she spent scared and dreading the truth before driving down to Edgeport?

"I don't think he is." Audrey braced her forearms on the table and leaned over them. "There are certain characteristics of children born of father-daughter incest that I don't see in you. I'm not a geneticist, but I have studied the psychological aspects, and I would be very surprised if you were the product of such." Though a small percent of such births did turn out perfectly healthy.

The girl made a tiny noise as her shoulders sagged. "Oh my God, you have no idea how happy that makes me. I was so scared." She wiped at her eyes. "How could he have done that to her?"

"I don't know. I'm not sure I want to." The thing was, she could try to explain it, but it wouldn't make sense, because most sane people couldn't wrap their head around the concept.

Her dark blue gaze locked with Audrey's own. "You killed him for what he did."

She wasn't completely comfortable discussing this in front of Neve, who might be a friend but was still a cop, but what the hell. She wasn't ashamed of what she'd done, and truth be told, if she could go back in time she'd probably do it again. Not like they could try her again for it. "Yes. I didn't want him to hurt Maggie anymore, or hurt anyone else."

Neve was watching her, because as far as the world was concerned, Maggie had been the one to put an end to Clint. That's what they had told the police—Neve's father.

*"You owe me."* She could hear Maggie's voice echoing in her head from a day long ago, just before Audrey left for college. *"I took the blame for you. Don't you ever forget that."*

Mackenzie reached across the table and touched Audrey's hand. "Thank you."

Her words struck like a kick to the sternum. It was foolish, really. After all these years, hearing those words from a stranger shouldn't have any effect. She knew at the time that Maggie had appreciated what she'd done, and she was certain Maggie must have thanked her several times, but after having so much judgment piled on her for that one act, hearing those words from Maggie's daughter meant more than she could ever articulate. In fact, she had to actually take a moment to compose herself before she could reply, and even then all she could do was nod. There was a band around her throat that made speech impossible.

"Will you tell me about her? Everything about her?" Mackenzie asked. "I'm staying at the Cove. I'd like to find out as much as I can about where I came from."

Audrey cleared her throat. "I'll tell you everything I can, but you should know that Maggie's life was not an easy one."

The girl laughed humorlessly. "Yeah, I kind of figured that out already."

"I'll bring you some of Maggie's things that Gideon has in storage," Neve said, but she looked at Audrey. Neither one of them would deny the girl the chance to know Maggie, but there were some things a daughter just didn't need to know, and it would be their job to weed those things out before letting her comb through Maggie's short life.

Mackenzie glanced at both of them. "Who killed her? I heard rumors..."

Neve grimaced. “Look, there’s a lot you don’t know—”

“And probably a lot I don’t want to,” the girl interjected. “I know. I don’t want either of you to think I’m judging. I just want to know the truth, no matter how bad it is.”

Audrey and Neve shared yet another glance, and both of them nodded. “Okay then,” Audrey said. “That’s what you get. I’ll give you as much truth about Maggie as I can.”

“Do either of you have any idea who my real father is?”

The girl was asking all the hard questions up front, and each one was like a slap. Audrey didn’t resent her for it, but she had had easier conversations with psychopaths.

“I don’t,” Neve told her. “I knew Maggie, but we weren’t that close.”

“She never said anything to me,” Audrey admitted. “Back then we told each other everything, or at least I thought we did. She always seemed to be in like with some guy, and she was... provocative for that age. Unfortunately, no single person stands out in my mind.”

“Well, maybe there’ll be some clue in her things,” Mackenzie suggested so hopefully Audrey’s heart twisted in an effort to get away from her vulnerability.

“Maybe,” she agreed. “It’s a small town, somebody must know something.”

Neve made a scoffing noise. “Of course somebody knows something. It’s just a matter of whether or not they share it.”

“Why wouldn’t they?” Mackenzie asked, her gaze narrowing.

Neve turned to her with a sympathetic gaze. “Small towns are weird,” she explained. “There are some secrets that will become town gossip no matter how hard you try to keep them, and then there are others that should be public, but get buried so deep they might as well be part of the bedrock."

"That makes no sense," the girl argued.

Audrey's smile was grim. "Welcome to Edgeport."

# CHAPTER TWO

A couple of hours after Mackenzie and Neve left, Audrey was in the kitchen, putting dinner together. Sometimes it felt like all she ever did in that house was get upset, laugh, and eat. Her sister, Jessica, was at the table with their mother. Jessica's daughter Isabelle lay on her stomach on the floor with a coloring book and colored pencils, while toddler Olivia drooled happily on her mother's lap. Audrey's smile lingered on Izzy, who favored her in looks and temperament, right down to the heterochromia that gave her one blue eye and one brown.

"Maggie has an eighteen-year-old daughter?" her mother asked, pressing her hand to her mouth. "God. How awful."

"At least Clint isn't the girl's father," Audrey remarked. "At least, I don't think he is." Really, a DNA test was the only way to tell for certain. Mackenzie, or Mac as she said they could call her, had already asked to take one.

"That's something, I suppose," Jessica agreed. She and Audrey had similar faces and dark hair, but Jessica had their mother's blue eyes. Jessica was also softer-looking, prettier. She didn't have the same hardness to her that Audrey had, even though Audrey was younger. It was easy to resent her for that. "But who *is* her father?"

"I don't know." Audrey set a pan of chicken in the hot oven and closed the door. "I'm not sure I want to know."

Both her mother and sister arched an eyebrow. Even the baby looked at her as if she was full of shit. Her nosiness was legendary.

"Okay, I do want to know," she amended. It was hard to properly articulate, but she felt like it was her duty to find out. "It's probably someone we know, and if it was anyone over the age of eighteen, it's statutory." She didn't say "rape" because she knew Izzy was listening. "Clint might have even profited from it."

Her mother winced. "What a vile man."

Jess shook her head and glanced at her sister. "You did a good thing where he was concerned."

Audrey didn't point out that her sister hadn't spoken to her for years because of that "good thing" she'd done.

"Are you sure Maggie never said anything to you, Babaloo?" Anne asked. "I can't believe Maggie carried that secret all by herself."

It was a ridiculous nickname—one that Audrey had no idea as to how she'd earned it—but it was her mother's pet name for her and she liked it more than she'd admit. It was also weird hearing her mother express sympathy for Maggie. "I'm pretty sure I'd remember if she had."

She didn't like Jessica's scrutinizing gaze. "That's what really bothers you, isn't it? That she kept it a secret from you." Little Olivia chose that moment to laugh. It was just a little hiccup of a sound, but for a second, it felt like mockery, which was completely ludicrous coming from a two-year-old.

Audrey hadn't kept anything a secret from Maggie—not even her feelings for Jake, which was why it had hurt so much when Maggie slept with him. Maggie knew everything about her, and Audrey had known so very little about her friend. Clint had been molesting her for almost a year before she told Audrey about it. Maggie had been very, very good at keeping secrets, or at least one of her alters had been. Perhaps that was an upside to dissociative identity disorder—compartmentalization at its finest. Not that she was making light of it—it was an unsettling thing to witness.

"I'm more bothered by the fact that I didn't *see* it," Audrey admitted. "I cursed this town for not believing what Clint had done to her, and I was just as blind."

"You were thirteen," her sister reminded her. She glanced at her oldest, who was being surprisingly un-nosy, before adding, "You K-I-L-L-E-D someone for her, Auddie. What more could you have done?"

"I don't know, but I can do something now." Audrey still couldn't articulate why, but she needed to find out who Mac's father was—for the kid, for Maggie, and for herself. There was a part of her that still believed she owed Maggie... something.

Jessica bounced Olivia on her knee. Chubby arms and legs waved with delight. "Auntie Audrey has a savior complex."

"You been taking psychology classes online?" she asked, her tone dry.

Jessica grinned at her. "I don't need a class to know that, brat."

No, probably not, Audrey allowed. As a kid she'd dragged home strays and tried to help people whether they wanted it or not—and that was long before she took a cheap door stopper to Clint Jones's skull. She'd never been a particularly nice or gentle kid, or adult for that matter, but she wanted to make things better for people if she could. And it usually didn't matter if she liked the person or not. Or if they liked her.

"Just remember, sweetheart, whoever this girl's father is, he might not even live here anymore." Her mother was ever the voice of reason.

Right. But really, how many people had left the area and stayed gone? Not many. And most of those who had left hadn't gone far.

She picked up her dishes and took them to the kitchen.

"Hey," came her sister's voice as she closed the dishwasher door. "Seriously, are you okay?"

Audrey turned. Jess had left Olivia with their mother, and while there was never much of what one might call privacy in the house, they had as much as they were going to get. "I'm good. Surprised. Relieved. Nosy—but good."

"I know how much Maggie meant to you." Her sister glanced away. "She was more of a sister to you than I was."

"Maybe once," she allowed. "But not after I came home. The psych hospital didn't do her any favors." If anything Maggie had come back from that worse than she'd been going in—or maybe she'd just be less inclined to hide it. Regardless, she hadn't been the same.

"I blame myself, you know." She'd never confided that in any of her family before—only Jake and Angeline. "If I hadn't killed Clint, she wouldn't have been sent to that place. Sometimes I think I did more damage than good as far as Mags was concerned."

"Maggie was damaged long before you ever showed up." Jess's tone was blunt to the point of leaving a mark. "You're not to blame for how she turned out. If anything, she probably would have been worse if not for you. Can you imagine if she'd been here when she had that girl?"

No. Audrey couldn't. "Fair point." Mackenzie certainly wouldn't have had the good upbringing she seemed to have enjoyed. "Thanks, Jess."

Her sister gave her a quick but tight hug. "I'm here if you need me." And then she walked away, leaving Audrey standing there with a tight throat and no idea what to do with herself.

Her sister and the girls stayed for dinner. Jessica's husband, Greg, joined them as well, arriving around the same time that John Harte got home. John—Rusty to many who knew him—was sober, and had been for at least a couple of weeks, but he'd made it that long before. Audrey was waiting for him to fall off the wagon. She wasn't being a defeatist—she wanted nothing more than for him to stay sober—but the odds were not in his favor. And she'd learned a long time ago not to get her hopes up.

Her father's hair was a mix of ginger and gray, shaggy and a little long. He wasn't overly tall, but he was built like an ox. He was well-liked in the community, for the most part—until he went looking for a fight. Then everyone with an ounce of common sense got the hell out of his way. One thing Audrey could never hold against him was his love for her mother. Sometimes he was a total prick, but he'd die for Anne, and that was all that mattered in the end. Mostly.

The girls went nuts with their father and grandfather there, and it wasn't long before John had one in either arm as Greg put Olivia's high chair together at the table.

"No Jake tonight?" Greg asked Audrey as he followed her into the kitchen. She liked Greg, and always had. He grew up a couple of towns away, and started dating Jess when she was a college freshman and he was a senior. Audrey had only really started to get to know him since she'd come home. His coloring was similar to Jess's—dark hair and blue eyes. There was a kindness in his face that was reflected in his youngest daughter. Izzy, unfortunately, was more Audrey than either of her parents.

"Gracie's is open tonight, so he's working," she replied. Gracie's was the town tavern, which Jake owned. He'd become quite the land baron, for lack of a better term. "I'll see him later." She handed him a bowl of mashed potatoes to bring to the table before taking the chicken out of the oven.

"Jess just told me you met Maggie's daughter today?"

"Yeah." She carried the pan to the dining room and set it on the trivets on the table. "Mackenzie. She's eighteen and lovely."

"God," he whispered. "Eighteen. How old would Maggie have been?"

"Fourteen. She had her when she was in the psych hospital after Clint's death." Audrey walked away, knowing full well that her brother-in-law had changed "death" to "murder" in his mind, even if he would never admit it.

Greg followed her a few moments later and got Olivia's sectioned plate out of the cupboard. It had Winnie the Pooh on it. "Is Clint the girl's father?"

"I don't think so. We won't know for sure until we do a DNA test." Maggie had already been pregnant when she had been sent to the hospital, so it had to have happened that spring—before the campground that Jake's grandparents owned filled up.

Greg shook his head, his brown hair falling over his forehead, making him look younger than he was. "That's crazy."

"I know. You want me to get Livvie's plate ready?"

He waved her away. "Nah, I got it." He glanced at his daughters, playing with their grandfather in the other room. "Fourteen."

Audrey nodded. "Still a baby herself. Makes me want to know who the son-of-a-bitch father was." She called the last part over her shoulder as she returned to the dining room.

"Language!" Jessica cried, just as Olivia chirped, "Bitch!"

Audrey cringed under her sister's glare as their father chortled—Isabelle joining in with unrestrained five-year-old glee. "Sorry."

Olivia grinned at her. Looked her right in the eye as her chubby cheeks eclipsed her gaze in a big grin. "Bitch."

Everyone laughed—even Jess. And then she tried to explain to the toddler that the word wasn't a good one, even though it made the adults laugh. Audrey wished her luck.

After dinner, she stopped by Gideon's. Neve had promised to have Maggie's belongings out of storage and ready for her to pick up there, and when Audrey walked into the spacious, modern kitchen, she found three large plastic bins waiting for her.

Gideon—tall, lean, and gorgeous with his ashy brown hair and gray eyes—opened the fridge and pulled out two bottles of beer. "Want one, Audrey?"

"Sure," she replied, seeing that he'd already reached for another. "Thanks for letting me take this stuff, Gid."

He shrugged, a lopsided smile tilting at his mouth as he handed her the frosty bottle. "I don't hold any sentimental value for it. I don't envy that poor kid, about to be introduced to Maggie for the first time."

"There was goodness in her once," Audrey said in Maggie's defense, albeit without much force. "A long time ago. I'll try to concentrate on that."

He eyed her for a moment, eyes like flint, as she took a drink. "Lucky for her you're the one doing the introductions."

"Yeah, I suppose I loved her as much as anyone could."

Gideon raised his bottle as though making a toast. "More than she deserved."

"Maybe." But she couldn't help but think of how most of Maggie's mental problems had started after Clint died. "Or maybe not enough."

He just looked at her. It was Neve who said, "Oh, get your

head out of your ass. You going to wear the guilt of Clint Jones for the rest of your life?"

Audrey raised a brow. "You know, I hope not." She smiled. "My head's not up my ass."

"It is a little bit," her friend amended with a grin. "Change of subject."

That was the end of the conversation about Maggie.

Audrey stayed long enough to finish the beer. She and Neve made plans to drive up to Stillwater to visit Bailey soon.

"I can't believe they're shutting the place down," Neve remarked.

Audrey agreed. The place had been around forever. "Any word on where Bailey will be sent?"

Gideon swore. "We're trying to work that out. Because of her circumstances, they're not eager to send her to a juvenile lockup, but there aren't that many private facilities around that have the psych staff to maintain her therapy."

Yeah, there wouldn't be too many who knew what to do with a bisexual teenager tormented with guilt over killing her stepmother/lover. The poor kid. "See if the judge will go with getting her into a private facility with therapy on the side. If necessary, I can treat her until you find someone else."

Both of them looked as though she'd dropped her pants.

"Can you do that?" Neve asked. "Ethically?"

"I think so. It's gray, sure, but we can say I was seeing her before I knew she'd killed Maggie." She had talked to Bailey a few times before she figured out the whole tragic event. "And I would only do it until a replacement could be found." She could help them find that replacement, and Bailey could help her reacquaint herself with clinical therapy.

Neve smiled—it was a very self-satisfied expression. "Look at you. Dr. Audrey Harte, ready to be an actual doctor."

Audrey made a face at her. Neve hadn't been subtle in her belief that Audrey would be happier treating kids rather than studying them, as she had been at her previous job in California. Audrey didn't want to give her the satisfaction of knowing Neve had figured it out before she had.

Gideon, on the other hand, wasn't happy with just a smile. He walked over and hugged her. What the hell was she supposed to do with that? Grateful fathers were strange things. Loving, open fathers even more so. Gideon was as odd and wonderful to her as a platypus.

Awkwardly, Audrey extricated herself from his embrace and his appreciation. She finished her beer in one deep swallow and picked up a container by the handles. Gideon and Neve grabbed the other two and brought them out to her Prius. They put two in the trunk and one in the backseat. Then Gideon went back inside.

Neve tucked her hands into her jeans pockets. "Good luck," she said. "I hope you don't find anything too awful."

"Yeah," Audrey agreed, opening the driver door. She turned to the other woman with a doubtful smile. "I hope so too."

Mackenzie had sent her a text with her cottage number at the Cove, so Audrey didn't have to check in at the office when she arrived at the Tripps' resort. Jake's sister, Yancy, managed the resort and was probably working that night.

She hadn't forgiven Audrey for her daughter, Alisha, being kidnapped by a serial killer who was trying to get to Audrey. Audrey couldn't blame her for that and didn't want to add to the conflict. There was also the fact that Yancy was part of the Network, the town's gossip matrix, and while news about Mackenzie would spread soon enough, Audrey would rather not contribute to it. Trouble found her readily enough, so why court it?

The resort, which was located about six miles back the well-maintained dirt road, consisted of a large main building, a couple of smaller outbuildings, and about a dozen cottages. Jake was considering expanding because summers had gotten so busy. It was early November—hunting season—and at least three-quarters of the cottages were occupied by men with rifles, bright orange gear, and the inexplicable desire to kill something that couldn't fight back. Audrey had eaten her share of deer meat—no one in Edgeport called it venison—when she was younger, but she didn't now, on principle. At least when she had killed something it had been a full-grown man, and she'd bludgeoned him to death. None of this hiding in the woods, eyeing up your prey through a scope.

Still, the hunters brought in money for the town, and that was a good thing. Jake let them hunt on his property, which was generally kept private from the rest of the town. His family had owned all the land back Tripp's Cove for generations. This provided the hunters with less competition, but it also ensured they didn't piss off any of the townsfolk. Nothing like a bunch of strangers firing guns behind your home to get the blood up. There was a rumor that back when they were kids, Jake's father, Brody Tripp, and a bunch of his friends had chased an out-of-town hunter around the field at night, illuminating him with the headlights of their pickup like they were jacking deer. They didn't kill him, but they did string him up by his feet for a bit. That was the price of getting too close to Tripp property with a loaded gun.

Audrey drove back the smooth, narrow lane that meandered from the main building through the woods. All of the cottages were kept fairly private by trees and scrub. Some had ocean views, while others were surrounded by forest. Number nine was one of the ones near the water. It would be a prime location in the summer, but in the fall the ones surrounded by foliage were more popular. Some stubborn leaves remained in the trees, their colors bold and bright.

She parked in front of the little white cottage, next to the Honda she recognized as Mackenzie's. She popped the trunk, got one of the bins, and carried it to the covered cement patio. She was setting the second one on top of the first when the door opened. Mackenzie came out in jeans and a sweater and started taking the bins inside.

When Audrey came in with the last of them, she shut the door with her foot and set the container on the wood floor.

The cottage was one of the smaller units—just one bedroom—and decorated in subtle colors with furniture that was both comfortable and durable. Jake employed a couple of local women to do all the cleaning, and judging from how spotless the place was, Audrey guessed he paid them well.

"This is all that's left of her?" Mackenzie asked, looking at the dull gray tubs with a disappointed expression.

Audrey didn't tell her it was more than she had expected. She supposed three storage bins wasn't much when she thought in terms of an entire life, but Gideon hadn't been keen on keeping much of Maggie around.

"Yeah, that's it. Most of her clothing and jewelry was donated." She had a journal of Maggie's, one that her old friend had kept in her teens and adulthood that had started out as a kind of therapy. All the entries were written as letters to Audrey. It was personal, and she had no intention of showing it to anyone. She'd shared bits of it with Jake, but not even he had looked at it for himself. She wasn't about to let Mackenzie see it either. There was only one entry that pertained to Maggie's pregnancy and it didn't have many details—nothing that would help figure out who the father had been.

"It's not much, is it?"

"Maybe not in terms of belongings, but the things in these bins were important to her. Those kinds of things stand a better chance of telling us who your father is than old clothes or furniture."

The younger woman nodded, ponytail bobbing. She looked older under the overhead light, tension pulling at the skin around her eyes. "Do you really think we'll find out who he is?"

"Maggie might not have told me everything, but someone knows who your father is, or at least has an idea. Hopefully they'll feel like sharing the information."

Mackenzie looked up and met her gaze. God, there was something so familiar about that expression.

"If we do find him, do you think it'll be okay if I ask him why he had sex with a thirteen-year-old?"

Well, at least she didn't have to worry about the kid having some kind of romantic notion about her father. "You know, he may have been a kid himself." She wasn't sure why she felt like defending the guy, but it wasn't uncommon for young girls to date older boys, especially in small towns with limited selection, and girls who seemed to grow up so much faster.

"He still should have known better."

It was obvious Mackenzie had strong feelings, and all of her training and experience demanded that Audrey didn't argue. The girl felt how she felt, and there was nothing wrong with that.

"Where do we start? I guess I should be glad there wasn't more than three bins."

"Have you eaten?" Audrey asked. She knew the resort had a small kitchen that provided a limited menu, but she didn't know how late it was open this time of year.

Mackenzie shook her head. "No. I came here after I saw you and got settled in. Then I called my mom. I fell asleep in front of the television. I just woke up a little while ago."

She probably hadn't slept much the night before, Audrey

thought. She would have been nervous about traveling to the town where her birth mother grew up, and conspired to kill her own father with one of the women Mackenzie planned to meet. Audrey didn't have the heart to tell her it was probably going to get more emotionally draining. And crazier.

"First thing we're going to do is get you dinner. Come on, I'll take you to Gracie's." The place served food, so the girl being under twenty-one really didn't matter. She'd also have to take Mackenzie grocery shopping so she'd have stuff to eat at the cottage.

"But..." The girl looked at the bins.

"They'll be here when you get back, and you'll need energy to go through them. Let's go."

Reluctantly the girl got her coat and put on her boots. After making sure she had her keys they left the cottage and got into Audrey's car. The drive to Gracie's wasn't very long. Once they reached the main road, it was a left turn and then maybe two more minutes, if that. They pulled into the parking lot shortly before eight. It was Friday night and the gravel lot was almost full. Audrey took advantage of being with Jake and parked in the employee parking section in the back.

"What is this place?" Mackenzie asked as they walked around to the front of the building. Seventies southern rock filled the cold night air.

"It's been a lot of things," Audrey told her. "When I was a kid it was a takeout and pool hall. Now it's a tavern." The structure of Gracie's was actually an old house that had been

Frankensteined over the years, as old rural houses often were. Jake had managed to morph it into something a little more appealing. The outside was done in cedar planks. A wide veranda wrapped around the front and both sides. In the summer, people would sit out there, but in the colder months it was a place to smoke or actually hear the person on your cell phone. Neon signs flanked the front door—most of them were liquor company logos.

Inside, Gracie's looked like any other small-town establishment, maybe a little nicer. The bar was to the right and the stools in front of it were filled. Scattered tables filled up the rest of the space, leaving room for a small stage and dance floor in the back left corner. There were people actually up dancing, one of whom was Albert Neeley, a town institution and an old friend/punching bag of Audrey's father's. Bertie's idea of dancing was to hoist his beer bottle in the air and bend his knees in time with the music. At least he squatted in sync with the beat.

Speaking of her father, she didn't see him there. He wasn't behind the bar, a position Jake paid him for on occasion, or in his usual spot where he liked to sit when the intention to get drunk struck. If he wasn't in one of those two places—or fighting with Bertie Neeley—he wasn't there. Her mother must be wondering if her husband had been replaced by a pod person if he was home with her on a Friday night.

Audrey pointed at a small table near the hall for the restrooms and Mackenzie made her way toward it while Audrey snagged the menu off the bar.

"Hey, good-lookin'," she said to the man pouring rum into a glass.

He raised his head and grinned. When they were younger, Jake Tripp had been a cute kid. As a teenager he'd been almost pretty with his high cheekbones and lean jaw. He'd grown into his looks, and while he retained some of that prettiness, there was a hardness to him as well. He had lines around his hazel eyes—caused by an equal measure of smiling and frowning—and faint brackets around his mouth. A couple of days' worth of stubble diminished the almost boyish way his brown hair fell over his forehead. The contrasting dualities of his nature was one of the things Audrey found most fascinating about him. That and the fact that he knew her better than anyone else and still wanted to be with her. Many professionals would look at their relationship as unhealthy, but it was the only thing in her life Audrey had ever felt was completely right.

"Thought I wasn't going to see you till later!" he shouted over the music.

She nodded her head toward the girl at the table against the far wall. "Got a hungry kid to feed."

Jake arched a brow, not bothering to hide his curiosity. "Not hard to tell where she came from."

"Really? Because I'm drawing a blank on the second contributor. You want me just to give her order to Donalda when we're ready?"

He shook his head. "I'll send her over in a few." Then he leaned over the bar, kissed her forehead, and went back to work.

Audrey smiled as she moved toward Mackenzie. Maybe it was silly, but Jake always made her feel centered, like everything was going to be okay—even if it wasn't. They'd met when Audrey was four years old and had been connected ever since, but it hadn't been until Audrey came home the past summer that they finally got together. He'd been one of the few to believe that she hadn't killed Maggie, and even though there'd been some hurt between them, he'd helped her find the real killer.

She hadn't quite forgiven herself for figuring that one out. Hopefully she wouldn't have as much regret over helping Mackenzie.

"Is that your boyfriend?" Mackenzie asked when she sat down.

Audrey set the menu in front of her. "I guess you could call him that."

"He's cute," the girl said with a grin. She opened the menu—it wasn't terribly extensive. Almost one full page of it was drinks. "What's good?"

"I'm partial to the cheeseburger. The onion rings are really good too."

Wide blue eyes lifted from the page to meet hers. "Split some with me?"

*Maggie.* How many times had Maggie asked her to split onion rings, or fries, or a beer—even a guy? Christ, looking at her daughter was painful. Audrey swallowed against the lump in her throat. She shouldn't eat anything, because she wasn't the least bit hungry after dinner with the family, but she could never turn down onion rings. "Sure."

True to Jake's promise, Donalda bounced up to their table a few moments later. She was in her early twenties, blond, and built like a swimsuit model. She'd been sleeping with Jake's older brother Lincoln over the summer, but now she was seeing some guy from Eastrock, a neighboring town. She was a sweet girl, though not terribly ambitious. Also, her taste in men was suspect.

"Hey, Audrey! Nice to see you. Who's your friend?"

Mackenzie smiled up at her, and Audrey's heart gave a sharp little tap against her ribs. There was Maggie again. This was going to be a lesson in self-torture, seeing her old friend—old enemy—every time Mackenzie's expression changed. "Mackenzie Bell."

"Nice to meet you, Mackenzie," Donalda enthused. "What can I getcha?"

The girl placed the order, and Audrey added a Diet Coke for herself. Normally she'd get some rum in it, but she wanted to stay sharp. There was a very good chance the girl's father was there, or nearby. She wanted to be able to see how people reacted to her, because those with more than just the usual curiosity probably knew something useful. But word wouldn't have gotten completely out just yet, so no one seemed to pay them much attention at all.

In fact, there was one guy who didn't look at anyone except Jake. Audrey frowned. She didn't know who the guy was—he wasn't local. She was pretty sure she would remember a six-and-a-half-foot-tall mountain with long hair and a beard. He was oddly attractive for a guy who looked like he could kill you as easily as shake your hand. For that reason, Audrey didn't like him paying such close attention to the most important person in her life.

She watched as Lincoln approached the man. Lincoln was just a bit shorter than Jake, which put him at around five-eleven or six feet, and he was as lean as a scarecrow. His long dark hair was pulled back in a ponytail, and he was dressed in his usual "rock star" fashion. Usually Lincoln had more attitude than sense, but he looked almost nervous as he spoke to the behemoth towering over him. Lincoln knew the guy, and while he might not have been afraid of him, he was wary. Anyone who could make a Tripp wary was someone not to be underestimated.

Who was he and what the hell did he want with Jake?

"Is everything okay?" Mackenzie asked. "You look pissed."

Audrey shook her head, pulling her attention back to the girl sitting across from her. "I've been told I always look pissed." She smiled. "I think a good place to start would be a DNA test. I want to rule out Clint as a secondary contributor first and foremost."

Mackenzie shook her head. "Thank you for referring to him by name and not a family title. Whenever I think of him—and I don't even know what he looked like—it makes me sick."

"We don't need to talk about him. Tell me about the people who raised you. Are they good people?"

The girl nodded, a big smile on her face. "They're awesome." Then her smile faded. "Most of the time. You know, they're parents, so sometimes they're annoying."

"Yeah, I know." Audrey grinned. Typical teenage response

for parents who were doing their job. Of course, it wouldn't take much to be better than the Joneses; the fact that Clint and both of his kids had been murdered was proof enough of that.

Audrey was prepared to ignore the fact that all three of them had been killed after an altercation with *her*.

# CHAPTER THREE

In school, Jake Tripp hadn't been the strongest kid, or the fastest, or the smartest. What he had been was observant. So, when a big jock tried to knock his head off in grade nine, Jake knew the kid's knee was trouble, and kicked it hard enough to make him crumple into a whimpering mess, benching him for the rest of the season. In junior year he knew his English teacher had lost her mother at a young age and had a thing for Poe. Every writing assignment he turned in to her was melancholy and had an element of tragic death to it. He got straight A's that year.

So, when he walked through the back door of Gracie's shortly after midnight, after tossing the night's take into the safe, he knew the Goliath who had been watching him all night was there before he actually saw him. He smelled him—beer, cigars, and Old Spice, mixed with leather and dust. There was no way Jake could take the man in a fair fight—but the point of fighting was to win, not to be fair. He hoisted the baseball bat over his shoulder as he stood just outside the floodlight's reach.

"You're upwind," he said, his voice low.

The man walked out of the shadows, just into the light. He was a big bastard. "You half bloodhound or something?" The voice matched the man.

"Something," Jake replied. He kept his attention on the stranger, while also listening and watching for any friends he might have with him. "We have business?"

"We do."

"Then come by in the morning."

Light played eerily on the big man's smile. "Not that kind of business."

"No," Jake allowed, flexing his fingers around the bat. "It never is. I'm going to guess that given your appearance, and the way my brother twitched whenever he was near you, that you're his friend who was in state lockup with Matt Jones."

The man lifted his chin, tilting his head at a defiant angle. "I am."

"You going to tell me your name, or do I have to ask my brother?"

"They call me Ratchett."

"Bet your mother doesn't."

He hesitated. "No, she doesn't."

"You can see then, Ratchett, that we have a problem. I can't do business with a man who won't give me his first name."

The man scowled. He was a scary-looking son of a bitch. Probably not used to people playing coy with him. "The only problem we have is you running your mouth off, acting like you're the one in control of this situation." He took a step closer. He leaned a bit to the right, which made Jake think that maybe he had trouble with his left leg. If he got the bastard off his feet he might gain an advantage. Of course, there was that bulge under the left side of his jacket--probably a handgun. Shit. He should have taken the shotgun from behind the bar instead of the bat, but shotguns made noise. No one would hear him beat the guy's head in.

"The way I see it, you're the one on my property, in my town. That does give me an advantage."

"How do you think your little town will react to finding out you had Matt Jones killed?"

He'd known getting rid of Matt would come back to bite him on the ass, but Jake still couldn't bring himself to feel the slightest bit of regret for putting an end to the man who'd raised his hand not only to his sister, Yancy, but to Audrey as well. His only remorse was in the fact that Matt hadn't died by his hand. "There's not a soul in this town that would be surprised to hear that. And not one who mourned that son of a bitch. If you came looking to blackmail me, you'd better have more than a rumor."

Ratchett shook his shaggy head. "It's not a rumor when I'm the guy who did it."

Jake blinked. This was a turn he hadn't expected. What had his cousin Kenny been thinking, hiring this goon? "Isn't it against your best interest to point fingers at me?"

"No. I don't care if I go back to jail, but all I have to do is make a call. Doesn't matter from where. Then you'll have the staties up in your business. Doesn't matter if I can prove it; once I name you, they'll be on you, and can you prove you *didn't* order the hit? And what about your friend Kenny, the guard who set it up? He'll be in all kinds of trouble. You know what they do to prison guards who get tossed into gen pop?"

The bastard was smarter than he looked. "All this talking and you haven't told me what it is you want. I assume you're looking to extort some kind of payment in return for your silence regarding my alleged involvement in your crime?" He wasn't admitting to anything, not even in the dark.

"Fifty grand."

Jake laughed. "No."

Ratchett seemed surprised. "It's not negotiable."

Jake took a step toward him. "I'm not paying you a damn thing."

"I'm not bluffing."

He shrugged. "Do what you have to do. If I did kill Jones, there's no guarantee that you'd take it to your grave once I did pay you. So you see, I have limited options."

"Options? You either pay me or you don't."

Jake smiled. "Or I don't." He looked the man dead in the eye as he lowered the length of the bat into his opposite hand. Ratchett's head dipped in an almost imperceptible nod. He understood that "don't" might have blood attached.

"You should probably leave Edgeport," he advised.

A scowl brought heavy blond brows together. "I'll be back. Maybe a night sleeping on it with that hot little piece of yours will make you reconsider."

Jake went very, very still. Something dark and cold unfurled in his stomach. "Who?"

"That tight little number with the freaky eyes. I saw the two of you. A man doesn't look at a woman like that unless he's fucking her. She's pretty. Be a shame if anything happened to her."

Jake didn't think, he acted. He swung the bat low and hard, connecting with Ratchett's left knee so that the bat vibrated in his hands, and into his arms. The big man barely made a noise—just a grunt—as he fell back against Jake's truck, all of his weight on his right leg. He was used to pain, obviously.

The end of the bat came up under Ratchett's beard, pressing into his jaw. Jake leaned close, no longer worried about the gun under that worn leather coat. A man didn't kill what he wanted to use. "You and I have business, motherfucker. She is *not* part of that business. Go near her and they will *never* find what's left of you." Then he gave the much larger man a shove before walking around the side of the truck and climbing in. He started the engine and put it in gear, tearing out of the lot so fast that gravel kicked up behind the back tires. In his rearview, he saw Ratchett raise his arm to protect his face from the spray.

Jake pulled out onto the road, turning east, but he wasn't going to go home to Audrey just yet. First he had other business to take care of.

He was going to find his fucking brother.

Her father was the last person Audrey expected to find waiting for her when she arrived at Jake's place after leaving Mackenzie. They'd gone through some of Maggie's things—an entire bin—but found nothing regarding the other half of the girl's parentage. Hopefully some of the photo albums would reveal a clue. For all of his faults, at least Audrey's father had wanted to be part of her life—even if he had been responsible for some of the less pleasant parts of it. He sat on the front steps, hands dangling between his knees. He looked... lost.

"What's wrong?" she demanded as she got out of her car. Her heart was in her damn throat. It was late—midnight or after. "Is it Mum?"

He rose to his feet at her worried tone, haloed by the porch light. "No, babe. She's good. She's good."

Audrey's shoulders sagged. "Oh, thank God. You scared the hell out of me. What are you doing here?" Gravel crunched beneath her feet as she approached him. How long had he been waiting? It had to be in the forties—her breath was puffs of steam in the night air.

He tilted his head—the same way she did when she wanted to be understood. "I wanted to talk to you about this thing you're doing with Maggie's girl."

"This 'thing' I'm doing?" She shook her head. "What do you know about it?"

His lips thinned. "I know I don't want you digging around in it. All that stuff that happened back the Ridge."

Oh, hell *no*. "Dad..." She had to force herself to draw breath. "Tell me you don't know who he is." She didn't suspect him. Her father was a lot of things, but a child molester wasn't one of them.

He shook his head. "I know what went on at some of those

parties back the Ridge, and I know other people won't like you digging it all up. Not one damn bit."

She stared at him, unsure of what she was even thinking, or supposed to be feeling. "Are you afraid someone will try to hurt me?"

"Yes. That is exactly what I'm saying." He ran his hand through his hair—hair that was too long and shaggy for a man his age, but suited him all the same. "I never wanted any of that stuff to touch you girls. It was a different world back then."

"Who?" she demanded. "Who do you think will try to hurt me?"

"God damn it, Audrey!" He looked away and took a breath. Then he turned his gaze to her once again. "I know you think you owe this girl something, and I get it. Hell, I respect it, kid. But you're my daughter, and I owe you more than you could ever owe Maggie's kid. Is there anything I can say to make you drop this?"

Did he even have to ask? "No."

"Yeah, I was afraid of that. Then, here," He reached behind his back and pulled something out of his waistband. When he offered it to her, it took a moment for her to realize that it was a handgun. She didn't take it. She just lifted her head to look at him.

"What the fuck are you afraid I'll find, Dad?"

He grabbed one of her hands in his big, rough one and forced her fingers closed over the gun. Christ, he was strong. "There was weird stuff going on that winter. I don't know if you remember, but they found a kid dead in the river."

Audrey didn't know what to do with the gun, so she just stood there, like an idiot, holding it in her outstretched hand. "I remember. He fell."

"Yeah," her father said with a puff of harsh laughter that fogged the air in front of his face. "Look, it's too cold to do this right now. Take the gun, and for Christ's sake, be careful. I've almost lost you twice since June and my heart can't take it. Maybe it's nothing. Maybe I'm just paranoid, but just... try not to piss anyone off, okay?"

Seeing him afraid unsettled her. Her father was never afraid of anything—except losing her mother. And now she supposed he was afraid of losing her. For a big part of her life all she wanted to know was that she was more important to him than a bottle, and now that she had an inkling of it, she didn't want it. She didn't want to trust in it, because someday the day would come when that importance was tested and he'd choose the bottle again. That would break her.

"Okay," she said. She put the gun in her pocket, knowing he'd already made certain the safety was on. "Did you bring me any ammo?"

His response was to pull a handful of bullets from his coat pocket and dump them into her cupped hands. Not even a box. "You couldn't put them in a Ziploc or something?"

"I was trying to be quick. I didn't want your mother to notice. She'd worry."

Their gazes—almost identical—locked. He didn't want to worry her mother—he was prepared to worry enough for both of them. He was already scared for his wife and her battle with cancer. It would be unfair of Audrey to make him fear for her as well.

She crammed the ammunition into her other coat pocket. "I'll be careful," she told him. "I promise. Mackenzie just wants to know where she came from."

He nodded, his expression resigned. "Whoever her father is, it's not going to be good, kid. You and I both know that."

"I do."

"When I first heard about what Clint had done—and knew that it was true, not just a rumor I wanted to be a lie—my first thought was, had that son of a bitch done anything to my baby girl? When I saw what you did to him, I thought he hurt you too, and I was so ashamed of myself for not being there for you. Not believing it when you came to me. I'm sorry, Auddie. You have no idea how much."

"Dad..." She reached out and touched his shoulder. What the hell was she supposed to say? She'd know what to say to anyone other than her own father.

"I was proud of you," he rasped. "I knew it was messed up, but I was proud of you for killing him—and I knew it had been you and not Maggie who did it. I knew my girl was loyal and brave, and that she wasn't afraid of monsters. I never worried about you after that. I haven't worried about you for years, but since you've come back here...Are you sure this is where you should be?"

"Yes." She didn't hesitate, and the answer surprised her almost as much as it seemed to surprise him. Six months ago she would have said she belonged anywhere *but* Edgeport. "This is exactly where I'm supposed to be—with you and Mum, and Jess, and Jake. I'm still not afraid of monsters."

John laughed. "Right. You never did have the sense God gave a moose. You got that from me, I guess."

Audrey smiled. "I guess so."

"There's no talking you out of this, is there?"

She shook her head. "No. It's not about what I owe Mackenzie. It's about what I owe Maggie."

Scowling, he shoved his hands in his pockets. "That tab closed the day she died."

"You'd think that, wouldn't you?" As well as he understood her, there was no way she could make him understand the way she felt about Maggie. "I'm going to do this, Dad, but I promise you I'll be careful." That was the best she could do. He had to know she wasn't going to back off—especially not after he got her curiosity up.

"Well," he said with a tilt of his head, "I guess I'd better get home. Your mother will be starting to wonder if I'm curled up with a bottle of the Captain somewhere. If you need anything, you call me. Okay?"

Audrey nodded, her throat too constricted to reply without embarrassing herself.

Her father kissed her forehead. "Night, kiddo."

"Night," she whispered. She watched him get into his truck. He backed the half-ton onto the road, pausing long enough to give her a wave before driving off. Audrey stood there a few seconds longer, until the dark and cold started to seep into her bones. She dug her keys out of her purse and let herself into

Jake's house. The warmth of the kitchen—which smelled of apple pie and something savory—instantly made her nose start to run. She sniffed as she hung up her gun-heavy coat, and slung her purse strap over the back of a chair. She went straight to the cupboard and got herself a glass, then some mix from the fridge. From another cupboard she took a bottle of rum and poured herself a drink so stiff she could have held a funeral for it. Her father not wanting to drink that night was a good thing—a very good thing.

She'd drink for both of them.

She leaned against the sideboard and took a long swallow, grimacing as the first rush of rum flooded her tongue. What had happened back the Ridge? What sort of secret would someone kill to protect? It didn't matter. She wasn't interested in those secrets. She wanted only to find Mackenzie's father, that was it. Maggie might have been worth killing for, but she sure as hell wasn't worth dying for.

# CHAPTER FOUR

Audrey was on the couch watching a movie when Jake came into the house. It was almost one thirty in the morning, and the buzz she'd gotten from her drink was beginning to ebb, but she was too lazy to get up.

He walked into the living room barefoot, a beer in one hand and another rum and Coke for her in the other. She took one look at him and wondered if there was something in the water, making the men in her life on edge. Was he going to warn her off the trail of Mac's father as well? His lean cheeks were flushed, and not just from the cold. His jaw had a tightness to it that meant trouble, and beneath his faded T-shirt, his shoulders were rigid. Something in that look spoke to a deep-down part of her that always seemed to be looking for a fight.

"What's wrong?" she asked as he sat down beside her.

"Just a second," he replied, setting the drinks on the coffee table. He leaned over her, taking her face in his hands. He kissed her like her mouth was the only thing that could possibly save a really shitty day.

"Got a head start?" he asked as he pulled back. There was no way he could have avoided noticing the rum on her breath.

"I needed a drink," she confessed, taking his hand in hers.

"What happened?"

"You first."

Jake took a long swallow from his bottle of beer. "Did you see the behemoth at Gracie's tonight?"

She frowned. "Looked like a biker? Yeah, I saw him. He didn't take his eyes off you. I was starting to wonder if I should be jealous."

He snorted. "He was waiting for me in the parking lot."

Most people with good intent didn't lie in wait in the dark, but the fact that Jake didn't have a mark on him didn't alleviate her anxiety. "What did he want?"

"Money. Turns out he's Linc's buddy from state. He also claims to be the guy who killed Matt."

"Fuck." Her stomach clenched. Jake had done what he did because Matt beat her up—and abused his sister. In his shoes she would have been tempted to do the same thing. Small-town justice, and no one in Edgeport would blame him for it, except maybe Neve. But then, she wasn't from there, not originally. That kind of moral compass was bred into the blood; it was in the groundwater. Still, it wasn't the kind of thing that ought to be made public knowledge.

He took another drink. "Said his silence would cost fifty grand."

"How did he react when you refused?" Because she knew

Jake, and there was no way he'd cave to someone trying to blackmail him.

"Badly. I had to persuade him to reconsider. He'll be walking with a limp tomorrow."

Her first instinct was to ask him why the guy was still breathing, but she caught herself. "What if he goes to the cops?"

"He's not going to do that. He wants money, not trouble." His fingers closed over the top of her thigh and squeezed. "Do me a favor and don't go anywhere alone for the next few days."

It wasn't the perfect segue, but it would do. "No worries. Dad was by earlier and gave me a gun, so I'm good." She sucked back a healthy amount of rum. The drink Jake had made her wasn't nearly as strong as the one she'd made herself, but that was okay.

"A handgun?" He looked stunned. "What the hell for? Do you even know how to shoot one?"

"I do, not that I plan to use it." Audrey leaned back against the overstuffed cushions. Jake followed her; he was frowning. "He's worried I'll stumble into something dark looking for Mackenzie's father. Kind of makes me all the more certain it's not Clint."

"Yeah, I didn't think she looked like the product of incest."

"Seen many of those, have you?"

He gave her a pointed look. "Remember? Anna Legere?"

"Really?"

"Her mother and father were half brother and sister, only they didn't know it because her father's mother never told him who *his* real father was."

"That was nice of her to let her son marry his own half sister."

"They weren't married. Their parents wouldn't let them marry—they just slept together."

"Oh, well, that makes it all right, then." She couldn't stop a snort of inappropriate laughter.

"Guess she thought that was better than revealing her secret."

"Not much of a secret if most of the town knew." She remembered Anna clearly. She'd been what the older generation referred to as "slow" and she had cystic fibrosis, both of which Audrey knew were linked to incestuous births.

"True, but she still tried to deny it. People will do just about anything to protect their secrets."

"Except pay off a blackmailer."

His lips quirked. "Touché." He took another drink. "Rusty's argument is a valid one. I'll feel better knowing you have some protection, the way trouble seems to find you."

Very few people in town referred to her father by his given name; Rusty was the name Bertie Neeley gave him forty years ago when his hair was more ginger than gray. "He said parties back the Ridge could get pretty crazy."

Jake nodded and drained his beer. "My old man used to go back there. I think my mother went a couple of times. I remember them coming home one night, he had a cut over his eye and she had a fat lip. I sneaked back one night when I was about twelve. Mona Martin found me and offered to take my virginity."

She stared at him. "Mona Martin? She's at least seventy."

"She wasn't then," he reminded her with a lopsided smile. "My father described her as 'one of the town bicycles.' I guess her husband used to rent her out on occasion when he needed drinking money."

"Jesus Christ." Audrey took another drink. "What the fuck is wrong with some of the people around here?"

He shrugged. Some of the tension had left his shoulders. "Gran used to say there was a bitter wind that came up every once in a while and got into some people's souls, turning them black."

"You know I'd never want to argue with Gracie, but I think it's the isolation. The police hardly ever bother with this place—makes people think they can do whatever they want, and makes selling your wife for booze make sense."

"Not sure he made a whole hell of a lot. Mona was a hard-looking woman, even then."

"So you didn't take her up on her offer? Get a little boom-chicka-boom-boom from Mona?"

He frowned, and she didn't think it was her poor attempt at bad porn music that irked him. "No. Back then I was saving myself."

This was news, but then she'd never heard the Mona Martin story before either. "For who?" she asked with a chuckle.

"Believe it or not, back then I thought when the time came you and I would probably be each other's first."

Audrey's smile melted off her face and landed somewhere in the vicinity of her lap. "You did?"

Jake's gaze locked with hers. "I couldn't imagine being with anyone else."

"Clearly that changed," she drawled, but her heart was

pounding so hard it hurt. Why did she have to go and be a bitch?

"Yeah, it did. Once I found out that it could hurt for a girl... well, that killed the romance. No way was I going to do that to you. Couldn't stand the thought of anyone else doing it either. Consequently, I have never been anyone's first. Thank God."

He hadn't wanted to hurt her physically, but he screwed Maggie to break her heart and make sure she actually went away to college? "God, you are one seriously twisted person."

To her surprise, he laughed. He had a big laugh, the kind that revealed the straight white lines of his teeth and creased the skin around his eyes and down his cheeks. It always had the same effect on her—she ended up laughing as well.

When he stopped, Jake leaned his head against the back of the couch. He smiled at her, his fingers twining with hers. "We can do some target practice tomorrow. Tell Rusty to transfer the gun to your name on Monday."

"You really think I need it?" As if on cue her left arm throbbed. "Don't answer that. What about you? Will you be safe?"

"I'm not worried. You can't get money out of a dead man." But he was worried, she could see it. He was worried about her. Had Lincoln's friend threatened her? The man really didn't know what he'd walked into, did he?

"Target practice sounds good."

"You know what else sounds good?"

Audrey smiled. He had that look in his eye that never failed to send a little thrill through her. God, she was so easy. "What?"

"You, me, and a bath."

"It's a little late for that, isn't it?"

"Woman, neither one of us has anywhere to be before noon."

"Then let's go."

He led her by the hand up the old, solid oak staircase and into the en suite. As the big claw-foot tub filled with water, Jake slowly undressed her, his lips brushing every inch of uncovered skin. Audrey pushed everything else from her mind and concentrated on him. It wasn't difficult. One thing she'd learned since coming home was not to court trouble.

It would find her soon enough.

Jake and Audrey were making breakfast Saturday morning when Lincoln arrived. He walked in the front door without even knocking, as though he had the right, wearing the same clothes he'd worn the night before. His dark hair fell in tousled waves around his shoulders, and he smelled like cigarettes and beer. Normally debauched looked good on him, but that morning he looked haggard and pale.

"I've been wondering when you'd show up," Jake remarked, getting eggs out of the fridge. "Should've known it would be in time to eat."

Audrey took two of the eggs for the pancake mixture she was putting together and tried not to stab Lincoln with a fork. It wasn't his fault that Jake was being blackmailed, but he shouldn't have let his brother face someone like Ratchett alone.

"I wanted to make sure you're okay," Lincoln said. "Did the bastard come after you?"

Jake cut open a package of bacon with a small, sharp knife. "I'm fine, and he did. Where were you last night?"

"Looking for him." The older Tripp frowned. "Why?"

"I tried to find you."

"I didn't see you'd called until this morning."

Jake didn't look so sure he believed it. "Little warning would've been nice, Linc. You should have told me about him when he showed up last night."

The older brother nodded. "Yeah. Sorry."

That was all he had to say for himself? He was either a cowardly piece of shit or he'd known exactly what Ratchett was about. "What's he got on you?" Audrey asked, hoping it was the former.

"Nothing." Lincoln actually looked indignant. "He's just a scary son of a bitch."

All the more reason not to leave his brother to face him alone. Audrey would never let Jessica face a situation like that by herself. "You should have stayed until closing," she told him.

"I had something to do," he retorted, not even looking at her. His attention was focused on his brother. "Not like I work at Gracie's anymore. Are you going to pay him?"

Something in his tone gave her pause. Audrey's eyes narrowed as her fingers tightened around the fork in her hand. He didn't work at Gracie's because Jake caught him stealing. "Why?" she asked. "You and your buddy Ratchett going to split it?"

Jake glanced at her, and she could see surprise on his face. He'd known Lincoln all his damn life and he hadn't thought of that? He had to know his brother was capable of that kind of deceit. This was the guy, after all, who had stolen money from him.

Lincoln's face flushed dull red. "You're a real bitch, you know that?"

"Yeah," she replied with a glare. "I do."

Jake stepped forward, the small knife still in his hand. "Answer the question, Lincoln. I find myself suddenly very interested in what you have to say."

Audrey had to hand it to Lincoln: The asshole had balls. He stood there, within striking distance, and looked Jake right in the eye. "Yeah, that was the plan."

She set the bowl on the counter and left the fork in it. She stepped up to Jake's side, wrapping her fingers around the wrist of the hand holding the knife. She didn't think he would actually stab his brother, but then she couldn't guarantee that she wouldn't do it either.

There were so many things she wanted to say to Lincoln at that moment. She wanted to slap him silly, but it wasn't her fight.

"So what changed?" Jake asked. "You wouldn't be here if you were trying to coach Ratchett in the best way to get me to pay."

"You fucked up his knee, Jake. He doesn't just want money anymore." His hazel gaze darted to Audrey. "He's looking for payback that's a little more personal."

The base of her skull tingled. "If he comes after me, he's going to end up with a bullet between the eyes. You tell him that."

"I did." Lincoln's gaze darkened. "But I don't think he meant you."

That awful buzz spread down her neck into her shoulders, down to her fingertips. Yancy had been at Gracie's last night. She and Alisha lived alone farther back the road. They were isolated.

Jake went to the phone. He picked up the receiver and dialed. A few seconds later he spoke, "Lish? Is your mother there? Put her on... Yes, you can come for breakfast. Now give your mother the fucking phone."

Audrey and Lincoln exchanged a glance. Alisha was terribly attached to her uncle Jake and never missed an opportunity to spend time with him. She probably wasn't even upset that he'd spoken roughly to her.

"Has a big bastard with a beard spoken to you?" Jake asked into the phone. "When...? He's what?" His fist tightened around the knife handle until his knuckles were white. "If he approaches you again, call me. Don't be alone with him... All you need to know is that he's trouble. Keep a gun with you, and don't let Lish go out alone. Someone will pick her up for breakfast... Yeah, she's here. Deal with it. I'll be by to evict Ratchett later." He hung up.

"Evict him?" Audrey asked, an invisible band tightening around her chest. "He's not staying at the resort, is he?"

Jake nodded. "Apparently he checked in yesterday. Yance said he flirted with her. He knew who she was." He looked at his brother. "After breakfast, you're coming with me to let him know he's no longer welcome."

Lincoln nodded. He might be an asshole, but Ratchett negated any deal the two of them had when he paid the wrong kind of attention to Yancy. Matt had probably told him all about her when they were locked up together.

Right before Ratchett took the contract to kill him. *Jesus.*

Jake turned to Audrey. "Do you think Mackenzie would pick up Alisha on her way here?"

Audrey nodded. Since she didn't have groceries at the cottage, Jake had extended an invitation to breakfast to Mackenzie. Audrey planned to take her to the store to get a few things later that morning. "I'll call her."

"Is that the girl you had with you last night?" Lincoln asked. He dragged his fingers through his long, tangled hair, primping.

She shot him a sharp glance. "She's eighteen, she's my responsibility, and she's Maggie's kid."

Lincoln's eyes widened in his pale face. "Maggie's? Fuck me."

"Yeah, speaking of that, you didn't happen to sleep with Maggie when she was thirteen, did you?" Audrey asked.

To her surprise, he looked horrified at the question. "I didn't even live here then."

"You visited." She remembered seeing him from time to time. He'd strutted around then too.

"Back then I preferred older women, not little girls. I never touched her. I would never."

Audrey believed him. The truth was in his gaze, his body language, and his voice. He was honestly appalled at the idea—and her suggestion of it. Apparently, she had just discovered one of Lincoln's few morals. "Do you know anyone who did?"

Lincoln shook his head. "I heard some of the guys talk about her." He looked at Jake. "You must've heard the same shit."

Jake nodded. "Some of it. But I didn't spend too much time back the Ridge, and you did."

"Yeah, I used to go back there with Duger. Old Jeannie would go back there to drink and work off her booze tab with Wendell, or anyone else who was willing."

Wendell Stokes was a local legend, bootlegger, and all-around piece of work who hosted many of those fabulous Ridge parties where violence and sex seemed to abound. Duger was Scott Ray, Jeannie's son. He never had been quite right in the head, but he was mostly harmless—unless he got riled up. Audrey had beaten him up as a kid for calling Maggie a slut. He was okay after that. His mother, on the other hand, was a first-class bitch.

"Doog used to say that he had sex with Maggie." Lincoln frowned. "I didn't believe him. He lied about everything. I mean, the kid used to say that Elvis was his father."

Audrey remembered that. She also knew that kids with developmental issues sometimes had sexual ones as well. Duger hadn't normally been violent, but he could be. If he'd had sex with Maggie, he could've thought it was consensual. It might *have* even been consensual. Maggie wasn't always picky. "Is he still living over in Eastrock?"

Lincoln nodded. "He's got a trailer in Happy Valley."

"Maybe I'll go talk to him. He might know something helpful." Trying to find Mackenzie's father was going to be difficult, so she'd take even the slightest shred of gossip or hearsay as a place to start.

Jake gestured toward his brother with the knife. "Don't go warning him."

Lincoln held up his hands. "I didn't warn you about Ratchett—you think I'm going to warn fucking Doogie about her?" He lifted his chin in Audrey's direction.

Audrey shook her head and reached for her cell phone. She called Mackenzie and got the girl just as she was leaving her cottage. She said it was no problem to pick up Alisha and that they would be there in a few minutes. By the time Audrey hung up, Jake had Lincoln frying bacon and the griddle heating for pancakes.

Brothers. They were even stranger creatures than sisters. She didn't think she could make Jessica pancakes after finding out her sister had planned to blackmail her.

"Dwayne Dyer used to hang out back there with Barbie," Lincoln commented as he turned sizzling strips of bacon with a fork. "The two of them have been off and on for twenty years."

Audrey nodded. She knew them both. Barbie was Wendell's daughter. Twenty years ago she'd been the prettiest girl in Edgeport. And last Audrey had heard, Barbie and Dwayne were on again.

"There was that kid who died," Lincoln continued. "I didn't talk much to him. And Aaron Patrick. Oh, and your brother-in-law. He used to stay at Aaron's camp with him, I think."

Of the guys he'd mentioned, Greg was the only one Audrey was certain couldn't be Mackenzie's father. He was the most decent guy she knew. But why hadn't he mentioned having known Maggie back then? "And those are just the young guys," she lamented.

Lincoln shook his head. He'd tied his hair back when Jake made him start cooking. "One night when Mags and I were together she told me there were two men she despised in Edgeport when she was a kid—other than old Clint. Those were Everett Graham and Bertie Neeley."

Everett Graham made sense—he was Neve's father, the cop who had arrested her and Maggie for Clint's murder—but what was up with Maggie and old Bertie? He was just one of those old guys who probably had a job once—and a family—but lost them both due to their love of the bottle. He always seemed to have money and get by, though no one seemed to have any idea how he earned his keep. Audrey had never been a big fan of the guy, who always seemed to be either in love, or picking a fight with her father, but he'd never done anything terrible that she knew of.

She hadn't known Maggie was pregnant, though, so what she knew amounted to shit. She added Bertie to the list of people to talk to. It had suddenly gone from no names to a slightly daunting list.

Mackenzie and Alisha arrived almost ten minutes later. There was less than a three-year age difference between them, so they were chatting up a storm when they walked in. Alisha had that effect on people. She was a bubbly, curvy blonde who seemed to find joy in almost everything, despite having a friend who had committed murder, and having been the target of a serial killer. Audrey hoped she never lost that joy. It would be a sad day if she ever did.

Alisha flew at her as soon as she crossed the threshold, wrapping her arms tightly around Audrey's waist and squeezing like she never wanted to let go. Audrey hugged her back, blinking away tears that threatened. It had only been a few weeks since she and Jake rescued Alisha from a killer, but it felt longer because after what happened, Yancy thought keeping Lish away from her was the best course of action.

"Mom says she wants to talk to you," Alisha said softly, for Audrey's ears alone.

Audrey arched a brow. "Do you think that's a good thing?"

Alisha nodded. A small smile curved her pink lips. "Uncle Jake and I have been wearing her down."

Audrey wasn't so sure that *was* a good thing, but she'd pop back to Yancy's place when she got a chance.

The five of them ate breakfast together. Lincoln was just a little flirty with Mackenzie, and managed to come off as only slightly skeevey. Mackenzie laughed it off but gave as good as she got. After they were done and all the dishes were in the dishwasher, Lincoln and Jake took Alisha home on their way to pay a visit to Ratchett. Audrey and Mackenzie left Mackenzie's car at Jake's while they drove to Eastrock, the next town over, to get the girl some groceries.

The Hannaford in Eastrock wasn't terribly big when compared to what Audrey was used to in LA, but it served the needs of Eastrock, Edgeport, and Ryme, the three small towns that made up the immediate area. Edgeport was in the middle. Each town had a school to serve the area, with Edgeport covering the middle school grades. Eastrock was the largest of the three, and had the high school, but even then it only had a population of approximately 1,900 people.

It was easy to tell Mackenzie hadn't spent much time on her own yet, because her small cart was full of things like Pop-Tarts, ramen, potato chips, and diet cola. Audrey was hardly in a position to criticize, but she was not going to let the kid leave the store without a few healthy choices.

They were in the ice cream section, where Audrey had decided to stock up, when they ran into Jessica, whose cart was decidedly more full. Audrey introduced the two of them, then Mackenzie excused herself to peruse the selection of Häagen-Dazs.

"No kids today?" Audrey asked her sister.

Jess shook her head. "Greg took them to visit his parents." It was no secret that Jess and her mother-in-law often butted heads, so it was not a surprise that she hadn't gone with them. She glanced at the girl, who was just out of earshot. "Wow, she really does look like Maggie, doesn't she?"

Audrey followed her gaze. "Yeah. She has quite a few of Maggie's better qualities."

"That must be a little sad for you."

Her throat tightened at her sister's astuteness. "Yeah, but kind of nice too."

"I know this horse has been beaten to death already, but are you sure it's such a great idea to go looking for her father? I mean, we both grew up here—we know there's a very good chance that whoever her father is, she's not going to be happy to find him."

"Probably not. But she wants to know where she came from, and I can't deny her that. I'm just hoping that it's someone around our age, not some pedophile."

"Wouldn't we know if he was? I mean, that's the kind of stuff that gets around."

"If he was pervy? Probably. Which makes me think it was someone young. He might not even know he has a kid. Maggie kept it pretty quiet. We might not find him, but I owe it to Maggie to try."

"I'm not sure you owe Maggie anything." Her sister had once suggested that Maggie manipulated Audrey into killing Clint. Audrey thought it was a nice try on her sister's behalf to excuse what she'd done, but she knew herself. Maggie might have pointed her in the right direction, but it had been Audrey who picked up that door stopper and took a swing.

Jessica grabbed two containers of ice cream that were on sale from the freezer and turned her attention back to Mackenzie, who hadn't found what she was looking for, apparently. "She's pretty."

"Yeah. I feel like I should know who else she reminds me of, but all I can see when I look at her is Maggie."

"Mm."

Audrey glanced at her sister. "Hey, Lincoln mentioned Greg used to hang out back the Ridge some when they were young."

Jessica turned, a slight frown between her brows. "Yeah, I think he did. He was friends with Aaron Patrick, who had a camp back there. Why?"

"I wonder if Maggie ever showed up at any of their parties."

"Probably. I remember her showing up at some of the parties I went to, but Greg and I didn't run with the same crowds back then. I don't imagine he knew her if he didn't bring it up."

"Aaron Patrick." Audrey ran the name through her head. "Maggie talked about him. I remember her telling some girl that he was a terrible lay. The girl turned out to be his girlfriend. Maggie claimed not to know."

The sisters shared a look that expressed what both of them thought of Maggie's supposed ignorance. "It turned into a bit of drama, with Aaron talking smack about Maggie being loose or something. He said she begged him for it. Mags laughed. She said she begged him to stop—like it was a joke." She frowned. "I wonder if she *was* joking after all."

"It was a poor excuse for it if she was. But then, Maggie never was right. It's this place, I think. There are some messed-up people in this town." Her cell phone buzzed. Jess pulled it from her purse and checked the screen. "Dad. I should get going. He's probably wondering where I am."

"Probably. You know, there are fucked-up people everywhere," Audrey reminded her. "It's just that we know all of the ones here."

Her sister smiled as she steered her cart away. "Know them? Sweetie, you're *one* of them."

# CHAPTER FIVE

Lincoln didn't want to go with him, and Jake wasn't entirely sure he could trust his brother, but after cracking Ratchett's knee the night before, he wasn't stupid enough to confront the bastard by himself. He just had to hope Lincoln was more afraid of *him* than of the ex-con. Especially now that he knew Jake had no intention of paying the blackmail money. Frankly, the fact that Linc was still so nervous about confronting the other man made him cautious. Gran used to say that a little caution was good for a man—made him think before he acted.

"I need a shower," his brother commented, sniffing under his right arm as they drove back the dirt road. It was in pretty good shape, but Jake would have to have it graded in the spring. "Can I use yours?"

"If you moved back into the apartment, you could use your own."

Lincoln snorted. "No. It would still be yours. Besides, you don't want me so close to your business. I might steal from you again."

"Don't talk to me like that was my fucking fault," Jake

retorted, his gaze on the road. "You're the one who decided you were entitled to something."

"I am. I should have gotten some of Gran's money."

"She left you money."

"She left you more."

Because she knew Lincoln would piss his portion away. "It's not like she loved me more."

His brother laughed. He knew what a lie it was. "Please. You were the golden child. Everyone knows you were her favorite."

"What's wrong with that?" he demanded as something snapped inside him. "Jesus, Linc—Dad doted on Yance, and Mom thought you could do no wrong. She gave me away, for fuck's sake! Let me have Gran, okay? Fuck off and stop trying to make me feel bad for the fact that she loved me. I needed someone to."

He felt the weight of his brother's stare. He shouldn't have said so much, but now that he had, he couldn't stop. "She didn't leave me the money so I could just sit back and enjoy it. She left it to me because she knew I'd build something with it. She wanted the Tripp name to leave a mark that was more than drugs and an old campground. If you want a piece of it, fucking step up and earn it. I'm happy to share it with you, but I'm not going to just hand it over because you don't want to do the work. And just so you know, if anything happens to me, it all goes to Alisha."

A breath of silence. "Okay," Lincoln said. He didn't seem insulted that Jake insinuated he might try to kill him for his inheritance. And then, "You know, Mom's love isn't all that great. Don't wish for it."

"I don't." Eyes on the road. Jaw tight. "I stopped that a long time ago." That's what he told himself, but it wasn't the complete truth.

The rest of the drive to the resort was in silence. Not like there was anything left to discuss.

Tripp's Cove was, in Jake's opinion, one of the most beautiful places on earth, even in November and with the threat of snow. The grass was a yellowish sage but in spring would turn rich green. The beach was rocky—from small pebbles to huge boulders worn smooth by the tide. The main building on the resort side of the road looked welcoming but elegant, the grounds around it meticulously kept. He had a landscaping crew that came in once a week in the warmer months, twice a month in the down season. Every spring the building exteriors were washed down and repaired. The interiors were thoroughly cleaned after each checkout and routinely checked for any touch-ups or fixing. Jake was proud of what he'd built—and what Yancy helped him run and maintain. If he could share something like this with Lincoln... well, that would be good. He knew better than to get his hopes up, but he still had some.

They stopped by the office. Yancy was with a guest, so Jake checked the computer and found which cottage Ratchett was in. Number twelve, back a little farther in the woods. He and Lincoln could drive to it, but it was faster to cut through the woods on foot.

"Any jacking this season?" Lincoln asked as they traveled the path. As if on cue, the sound of a rifle shot echoed through the cove.

A twig cracked under Jake's boot. The cold salt air turned his nose and cheeks red and carried with it the smell of snow. He glanced up through the fir and maples; the sky was a watery gray, and he didn't need to check the news to know they were probably going to get hit by a taste of winter later that day.

"Not yet." He hoped there wouldn't be, but every year there was at least one idiot in town who decided chasing deer in a pickup late at night with a bunch of his drunken buddies armed with lights and guns was a good idea. It was illegal, and barbaric. Jake didn't stand for it on his land, or anywhere else if he noticed it. He might not be a big fan of the cops, but he reported jackers. His father used to delve out hillbilly justice on them. One time when he was a kid a bullet had gone through a window of his father's trailer, scaring him half to death. It had just missed him. When Brody Tripp and his mother had found out who was responsible, they paid the man and his friends a visit. Jake wasn't sure what happened, but Salter deBaie was never able to shoot a gun again, on account of his mangled right hand.

"You're really not afraid of Ratchett, are you?"

Was that actual respect in his big brother's voice, or did Lincoln think he was stupid? "The only thing I'm afraid of is losing someone I care about. I'm wary of your friend." He shouldn't have admitted that much.

"He's not my friend."

He glanced at him. "Seemed to be when you first brought up what he knew about me."

Lincoln avoided his gaze. That was usually a sign he was

being sincere. He had no trouble looking you in the eye and lying. "Yeah, well, I was a dick. Has he gone after Kenny?"

Kenny Tripp, their cousin, was a guard at the state prison in Warren. He had been the one to facilitate the ending of Matt Jones. He was a good man who had owed Jake a favor, and Jake had taken advantage of the situation. Now he had to make this right before Kenny suffered for it.

Jake's jaw tightened. "He'd better not."

They came out of the woods—thinner for the lack of leaves—into a small yard. A beat-up half-ton sat in front of it. Jake wasn't much of a snob, but he was glad the ugly damn thing was well hidden from the rest of the cottages. It was a faded gray, with one burgundy door, a Confederate flag in the back window, and one of those ball-sack things hanging off the trailer hitch.

"Classy," Jake muttered as they walked around it. He gave the rubbery balls a sharp kick with the toe of his boot and watched them swing for a second before continuing to the cottage. He took the door key from his pocket. He should update to swipe cards—they were more secure than keys and their usage could be monitored. He didn't need to spy on his guests, but being able to would be convenient in this case. He made a note to look into the cost later that day.

He knocked. No answer. No movement inside, but the window didn't give him a full view of the place. He slipped the key in the lock and turned. The deadbolt thunked. He turned the knob and gave the door a careful push. Ratchett knew he owned this place, so Jake wasn't going to take the chance that the asshole wasn't waiting for him inside, just out of sight.

A leather jacket was slung over the back of one of the kitchen table chairs, and a big pair of biker boots, worn and scuffed, sat by the door. The faint, warm smell of woodsmoke clung to the air, though the fire in the small black stove had gone out.

"Ratch?" Lincoln called when Jake nodded at him. Silence. "Maybe he's in the shitter."

Maybe. Jake kept silent as they walked into the small hallway that led away from the living area. The bathroom door was open. A porn magazine—its pages curled from extensive viewing—lay on the floor by the toilet. The shower curtain was open.

He turned to the bedroom. This style of cottage only had the one, and it was the only room in which they hadn't looked. He half-expected to find the bastard sleeping, but the door swung open to reveal a bed that hadn't been slept in, though there was a large impression on the top blanket.

"He's not here."

"Outside?" Lincoln suggested. "Maybe he went to get more wood."

Jake shrugged. Unlikely that the big man would be hiding from them in the woodpile, but it was worth a shot. They went out again, this time circling around back to where the wood for the cottage was kept. On the ground beside it was a small scattering of chopped pieces—as though someone had gathered an armload and then dropped it.

"What's that?" Lincoln asked, pointing.

Turning his head toward the woods, Jake saw something big in the grass at the edge of the forest. Every step he took toward it deepened the feeling of dread brewing in his stomach, until he was finally just feet away and unable to deny what it was any longer.

Beside him, Lincoln choked. “Oh, fuck.”

Jake sighed as his brother turned, stumbled a few steps, and then puked up his breakfast. His own stayed put, despite the fact that the grass at his feet was stained a dark, sticky crimson, and in the center of it lay Ratchett with half his face and throat missing.

“What the fuck are we going to do?”

Jake glanced at his brother, who was still bent over, hands on his knees. “You’ve got puke on your chin.”

Lincoln swiped at his face with his sleeve, grimacing when he saw the stain. “Fuck. Christ, that stinks.”

Yeah, it did. Jake could smell the acrid sourness from where he stood. “Aren’t you glad you didn’t shower first? There’s a box of neoprene gloves under the sink in the bathroom. Go grab me a couple.”

Lincoln hesitated. “Why?”

“Because I want to do a little light cleaning,” Jake shot back with a scowl. “Just get me the gloves.”

He stomped off. A few seconds later, his brother threw the purple gloves in his face. “Anything else, lord and master?”

“Shut up.” Jake pulled on the gloves as he crouched beside

the body. Jake didn't want to touch Ratchett's corpse, but he wasn't going to call the cops before doing his own search. The guy being killed on his property was bad enough, but he wasn't going to leave anything incriminating on the body—or in the cottage. He reached into the pockets of the man's jeans and found a wallet, cell phone, and hair elastic. The wallet had a hundred dollars, three old photographs of the same little boy at different ages, and a condom. His driver's license said his real name was Ryan. The phone wasn't password protected and had a short contacts list. There were a few texts—a few of which were from Lincoln, giving him the address of the resort.

Stupid shit.

"Want to tell me why you were the last number he called?" he called out.

Lincoln appeared in the doorway, wearing a matching pair of gloves. "He called me last night before he showed up at Gracie's. I didn't answer."

"Did he leave a voice mail?"

"Yeah."

"Saying what?"

His brother looked annoyed. "I don't know. Something about wanting to talk."

"Did he mention me?"

Lincoln shook his head. "No. He didn't like to say much over the phone—or text."

Jake turned his attention back to the dead man. "Small fucking favors." He set the phone down and went through the rest of his clothing. Nothing. When he stood, Lincoln was gone.

He walked back to the cottage to find his brother sitting at the table drinking a beer.

"Where'd you get that?" he demanded, shoving the soiled gloves into his pocket.

"From the fridge."

"Jesus Christ." Jake glared at him. "Are you stupid? You want the cops to know you were here long enough to have a damn drink?"

Lincoln's eyes widened. "Cops?"

"Yeah. A guy is dead. I have to call the cops."

"I thought we were going to get rid of him."

Jake froze, an unwelcome thought easing into his mind. "You killed him."

His brother choked on a drink, but he didn't spit out the beer in his mouth. No, Lincoln wouldn't waste booze. He managed to swallow, then took another drink to set himself to rights. "I did not!"

He wasn't convinced, but it didn't matter. He wasn't going to dispose of a body he hadn't killed himself, and if Lincoln didn't own up to it, Jake wasn't going to try to protect him. He pulled his phone out of his pocket. "Did you check his bags?"

Lincoln nodded. "Truck keys and a pack of gum. Change of clothes."

"Good." He scrolled through his contacts. "He's an old friend of yours. That's what you're going to tell the cops."

"I'm not talking to the cops!"

His brother looked panicked and Jake didn't have time for it. "Linc, you're in his fucking phone, and your prints and DNA are going to be on that beer bottle. Better to admit to knowing him and play the shocked friend than try to play ignorant. You're not that good an actor."

Hazel eyes narrowed. "And you are?"

Jake hit Send and waited. "Hey. You better come to the resort. Cottage number twelve. And Neve? Leave the siren off."

*Nineteen years ago*

"You kinda look like her."

Maggie Jones looked up from the photo in the magazine and smiled at Mike LeBlanc, who sat next to her. She liked Mike. He was the only guy who didn't look at her like he expected a fuck or a blow job from her. He and Greg Andrews were two of the few decent guys who hung out back the Ridge. The grown men were the worst—just like her father. Well, except for Rusty. He was nice, but usually so drunk he wasn't any help. She wished he'd bring Audrey with him, but the one time one of his buddies suggested it, Rusty punched him in the mouth. Bertie was okay, but he was more interested in being buddies than a protector. She didn't trust that.

She escaped as often as she could. Most times she managed to sneak off with Barbie and her friends. Barbie was older and way prettier than Maggie ever hoped of being. Barbie was a guy magnet, but the guys wanted to impress her. No one ever really wanted to impress Maggie. Their big mistake, though, was treating her like she was stupid.

Maggie was *not* stupid. And she wasn't a gullible little twit who could be manipulated into having sex. At least with guys closer to her own age she could decide if she wanted their dicks in her mouth or not. God, they were so easy. Sometimes they even paid her for it. She'd hide the money away so her father wouldn't know about it. He'd beat her senseless if he knew she was holding out on him. Still, she'd rather be back the Ridge with him than at home with him. At least back the Ridge he had distractions. At home he'd get that look in his eye and she knew what was going to happen next.

"You think so?" She liked Courtney Love—she was such a fucking mess. But a cool mess.

"Yeah. If you bleached your hair like hers and wore makeup, you'd really look like her. Only prettier."

She narrowed her gaze. "You don't have to suck up to me. If you want me to go down on you, just ask."

Mike's mouth dropped open. "I'm not, and I don't! God. What are you, fourteen?"

She nodded, not bothering to correct him. She'd learned that summer that if guys thought you were older they were easier to manipulate. "That didn't stop your friend."

He made a face. "Aaron's not my friend. I told him to leave you alone."

She shrugged. "He's okay."

"He's too old for you. He knows better."

"What he knows is that I'm available," she retorted. "When I've decided I'm done, he'll know that too. Don't treat me like a little girl that needs protecting." Yeah, she hated being treated that way, but secretly, she liked it. Other than Audrey, no one ever tried to protect her, or stand up for her. She appreciated Mike at least speaking up.

Mike looked like he didn't believe her. "Okay, but if you want him to leave you alone and he won't, you tell me."

Maggie agreed. She turned the page in the magazine. There was a photo of Chris Cornell from Soundgarden. "He's so pretty," she commented.

"He's fucking hot," Mike amended.

She jerked back, looking up at him like he'd just announced he was the Easter Bunny. "You like boys."

Mike's cheeks flushed. He was so cute, like a bunny or a puppy. Sweet. "Yeah. Our secret, okay?"

"Okay." If there was one thing she was good at, it was keeping a secret. And then she told him one of her own: "I like boys and girls."

He gave her a strange look. "Really?"

She nodded. He smiled, and she smiled back. They were still smiling at each other when the door to the little shed opened and in walked Barbie, Dwayne, Lincoln, Greg, and Glen, all of them following Barbie like dogs in heat. Barbie was smart keeping them to herself. She always had her pick. Maggie didn't mind getting the castoffs.

"Speaking of pretty..." Mike's gaze latched on to Lincoln before it met Maggie's. She giggled. Nobody thought Lincoln Tripp was prettier than Linc himself.

"What are you laughing at?" Linc demanded, glaring at her. He never seemed to like her much. It was like he was afraid of her or something.

"Nothing," she remarked, smiling in a way she knew would make him squirm. "Nothing at all."

"I'm going to get a beer," Mike announced and rose from the couch, leaving Maggie there alone. She stared at Lincoln until he looked away, and then, with a little smile, she went back to looking at her magazine.

*Boys.*

# CHAPTER SIX

Jake's truck was parked at the main building when Audrey and Mackenzie arrived back at the resort. Audrey wondered if he had talked to Ratchett and what the outcome of that conversation had been. She couldn't imagine the man would just shrug and go on his way, but she also knew Jake—and he wasn't going to just give the guy what he wanted. She had to hope that Ratchett was bluffing. And if he wasn't bluffing, she had to trust Jake's ability to get himself out of just about any situation.

Audrey set the two DNA tests she'd grabbed at Walgreens on the small dining room table. There was a layer of dust on top of the boxes but the expiration date was still good. The clerk at the checkout had raised an eyebrow at her when she set them on the counter with her other purchases. Audrey just smiled and said, "Don't you just hate not knowing?"

"Do you really think we'll need more than one?" Mackenzie asked as she put a gallon of milk in the fridge.

She considered lying to the girl, but there was no point. "Yes." In fact, they would be fortunate if they only needed the two.

Mackenzie winced. "I guess it would be asking too much for him just to step up and claim me. I thought maybe, you know?"

Yeah, Audrey knew. She'd seen a lot of bad parents in her years of studying juvenile offenders. "He might not even know about you," Audrey offered, feeling oddly generous. "Maggie never told anyone—that I know of—that she was pregnant." She left out that Maggie might have truly believed Clint was Mac's father. "Let's go on that assumption and take it from there."

"Do you think badness is inherited?" the girl asked after a moment's silence. She stood in the middle of the floor, holding a container of yogurt, her expression contemplative and a little fearful.

"Sometimes, but if you are worried about it, it's probably not an issue." The girl gave no indication of having any kind of mental or emotional issues, and while Audrey's instincts weren't always what they ought to be, she had no reason to doubt them in this case. "No matter who your birth parents are." That said, if she were in Mackenzie's shoes she would have gone back to her adopted parents already and said a big fuck-you to Edgeport.

The younger woman nodded. "Thanks." She put the yogurt in the fridge. "Did you hurt your arm?"

She hadn't even realized she'd been massaging it. "I got shot a few weeks ago."

"Shot?" Blue eyes went wide in horror. "By that Scott girl?"

Of course she would have heard about it—it had been all over the news. "Yeah. It wasn't all that serious. It's mostly healed, it just aches a little."

There was that almost coy, Maggie smile. "I wouldn't have thought psychology would be a dangerous career choice."

Audrey set some apples and oranges in a bowl on the counter. She'd convinced the girl to buy some vegetables and fruit before leaving the store, which made her feel older than she wanted to contemplate. "It's not the job. It's me. I have a knack for attracting trouble."

Mackenzie turned to her. "Maybe you have a knack for fixing it."

She laughed. "The perfect clinical response, Dr. Bell. Well done."

That perfectly clear complexion turned pink. "I wasn't being condescending."

"I didn't think you were." Audrey went to the storage bins in the living area and picked one up. She carried it back to the table. "Let's go through some more of this stuff. We can't just run around town taking DNA samples of every man Maggie might have... known." It was the kindest way to put it, unfortunately.

Mackenzie put the last of the groceries away and then joined her at the table. Deep in the bin, beneath some old CDs and on top of a high school yearbook, was an envelope filled with old photographs. Audrey smiled at the one on top as she pulled them out of the paper. It was a photo of the two of them taken the Christmas before killing Clint. They stood in front of the tree in Audrey's living room, arms around each other, grinning like idiots. They looked like children—even Maggie, who had so much forced upon her. After Clint, neither of them would ever be that innocent again.

"Is that you?" Mackenzie asked.

"Yeah. Christmas Day." She couldn't help but smile, thinking about that day. Thinking about her first best friend. Then her smile faded. "The last Christmas we spent together."

Mackenzie glanced at her, and Audrey could only imagine what she saw. "She named me after you. I saw it when I got a copy of my birth certificate."

"I know."

"You must have really meant a lot to her."

Audrey's throat tightened. She swallowed. "I did. Once. She was my best friend." She tore her attention away from the photo and turned to the younger woman, whose face was so terribly familiar. "That's why I want to help you." Because she *needed* to find him. Maggie had suffered so much, so young. And she'd done it in silence. Yes, the fact that Mags hadn't told her drove her nuts, but it hurt too. Maggie was why she'd become a psychologist. What she had done for Maggie had sent her down that path. She needed to give Maggie a little justice if she could—and not just the vigilante kind.

The girl smiled. "Tell me what you liked most about her."

She didn't have to think about it. "Maggie was fun. She always wanted to go on adventures—that's what she'd call them. We'd explore the woods, the beach, people's property. She just wanted to see everything. She saw the world as something to be discovered."

"What did she want to do with her life?"

"Other than be a rock star?" Audrey grinned. "Later, she wanted to get into makeup. She owned a salon here in town." Of course, Gideon had since sold it to some of the girls who worked there.

"I like doing hair and makeup. I guess I get it from her. My mom—my adopted one—is pretty granola. She wears Chapstick and that's it."

"Maggie knew everything there was to know about the different brands." She didn't mention that Maggie stole the local drugstore practically blind. "She always had new eye shadow to try. She used to make me up all the time. Mum hated it."

"Because she did a bad job?"

"Too good of one," Audrey corrected with a rueful smile. "No mother wants her twelve-year-old looking like she's a high school student." It had been the tricks Maggie taught her that made it possible for her to get into bars long before her twenty-first birthday.

"No, I guess not. My mother didn't like me trying to look older either. She's always telling me not to rush growing up—that someday I'll wish I could turn back time."

Audrey grinned. "Some of us are still waiting to grow up." She'd be the first to admit that the growth of her inner child was horribly stunted.

Wide eyes sparkled. "So, it doesn't matter if I try to rush it or not?"

"Not really, no. I've tried to adopt the philosophy of just enjoying being an ever-evolving work in progress."

"That sounds nice."

"It is. In theory."

Mackenzie laughed. "Who are these people?" She offered Audrey another photo.

It was curled at the edges, with little holes that indicated it had been pinned to a wall at one time. It was of Maggie, Barbie Stokes, Dwayne Dyer, Duger Ray, her brother-in-law, Greg, and another kid who looked familiar. Aaron Patrick, maybe? He wore a huge grin on his face and had his arm around Maggie's shoulders. He wasn't a bad-looking kid, bit smarmy though, but then what teenage boy wasn't?

"Do you know them?" Mackenzie asked.

"Yeah. Barbie and Dwayne are still around. Duger—Scott—is in Eastrock. Barbie would be our best place to start." Audrey had known her better than she'd known the guys. Plus, being female she might be more inclined to give extra details rather than just answer questions, since there was no chance of her being the girl's father. One thing Audrey wanted to ask was who had taken the photo, because Maggie wasn't looking at the camera, she was looking at the person behind it, and her smile was a wide and beautiful thing.

Who had put that smile on her face? Who had given that kind of joy to her terrible life? And why hadn't she told Audrey about him? Why wasn't there any mention of this person in the journal Maggie had kept after Clint's death? She needed to go through it again. Maybe she missed something when she read it the first time.

Or maybe Maggie had wanted to keep this person to herself—her special secret. What made him so important?

And why, she wondered, hadn't Maggie asked *him* to kill Clint?

"A coyote or something has been at him," Neve observed as she squatted near Ratchett's corpse. "Looks like he was shot in the throat."

Jake stood a few feet away. "Lucky shot."

Neve's dark eyes bore into him. "Or a good one."

Jake arched a brow. In his chest, his heart kicked it up a notch, but he kept his features relaxed. "You think it was intentional?"

She shrugged. "Could have been an accident."

A fucking lucky one—for him. It had to have been an accident, though. Who else other than himself would want to see Ratchett gone? Unless someone had followed the bastard to town. He'd suspect Kenny, but his cousin would have come to him first. Kenny would blame him, and expect him to fix it. And Lincoln...well, Lincoln could have made that shot. But Jake didn't think he'd faked his reaction to seeing the man's body.

"Had he been in town long?"

He shook his head, propping one shoulder against the doorframe. "He was at Gracie's last night. Never seen him before that."

"I should have known this wouldn't be easy." Neve sighed and shook her head. "Well, I'll need to talk to Yancy and your guests."

"Why?" Why the hell was he asking? He knew why.

"Because someone might have seen something—or one of them might have been the one to shoot him. You let your guests hunt on your land, right?"

"Yeah." He did. Guests were the only people he allowed to hunt on his property. Christ, could this really have been an accident? It was a happy one if it was. No, a happy one would be the guy falling off a cliff and not being found for ten years. "I've got a couple of parties staying here."

"For now we'll treat it like an accident until we know otherwise. Shit, this is going to ruin somebody's vacation if it was a guest that shot him." She glanced from the body to him again. "You don't seem very shocked at finding him. Lincoln lost his breakfast, but you're cool as a cucumber."

Dumbfounded, actually. "I can go into histrionics if it would make you feel better. And I was surprised when I found him. The shock has worn off a bit."

"How long did you wait to call me?"

"I didn't." It wasn't that much of a lie. "Actually, I'm surprised to have found a body and Audrey not be around." Maybe a joke would make her stop looking at him like she thought he had something to do with Ratchett's death. She ought to know better, that he wouldn't be so messy.

The cop smiled. "Yeah. It does seem strange that she's not with you. Where is she?"

"Took the girl grocery shopping." She wasn't going to believe this when he told her. His grandmother used to say he had the luck of the shithouse rat. As a kid he hadn't understood, but he was starting to. What were the odds on a guy who'd come to town to extort money from him ending up dead? On his land?

Neve nodded. "Right. Okay, you don't need to be here. In fact, it would be better if you and Lincoln left so we can process the cottage."

"Sure. Call if you need anything."

"Will do. Can you have Yancy print off a guest list for me?"

He said he would and then went in search of his brother. Lincoln was on the porch, out of the way of the cops going in and out of the cottage. He still had the beer bottle in his hand. Neve had given him a hard time for it when she arrived, but he told her he needed something to settle his stomach. "Let's go."

His brother didn't argue, but followed him toward the main building. There was no one there who shouldn't be—not even curious guests. They were probably all out hunting still. When news did get out, hopefully it would sound like Ratchett died of a heart attack, or other natural causes. He'd lost guests when Maggie had been murdered on the nearby beach, and he really didn't want to lose more because of another corpse. Maybe it was cold, but he had a business to run.

"What the fuck happened?" Lincoln demanded when they were a safe distance from the cops. "Did she say anything? Does she suspect something?"

His brother was pale. Jake didn't like it. It made him look spleeny—or guilty. "Neve thinks it might have been an accident. Stray bullet from a hunter."

Lincoln snorted. "Right. Men like Ratchett often die *accidentally*."

"I don't care how he died so long as it doesn't touch me or anyone I care about." That wasn't necessarily true. He was curious. It was just that his protective instincts and self-preservation outweighed his nosiness—unlike Audrey.

"You're a stoic bastard—just like Gran. Nothing ever shook her either."

"Plenty shakes me." Like when Alisha had been used by a serial killer to get at Audrey. He'd thought he was going to lose the kid—and Audrey too. That had been enough to almost drive him insane. It was not a feeling he'd enjoyed or planned to repeat anytime soon.

"Well, you do a fine fucking job of hiding it."

"He was shot late last night or early this morning," Jake remarked, coming back to the unfortunate topic of the dead man in his cottage rather than his lack of feeling. "Maybe he pissed someone off after Gracie's—someone other than me."

"It should have been one of us," Lincoln remarked as they stepped out of the woods.

"With a bullet in our throat?"

His brother frowned at him. "What? No. It should have been one of us who killed him—at least then no one would have ever found the body."

"Mm. What would you have done with the truck?" he asked out of curiosity. He had contingency plans for almost any scenario, but he wondered if his brother shared his preparedness.

"Take it back the Ridge, hide it, and tear it apart for scrap.

Probably burn the rest. Or bury it in parts. I have a friend that has a scrapyard."

"That would do it." He opened the door and stepped into the warm interior of the reception area. His sister sat at the counter looking at a computer screen. Her face lit up at the sight of them.

"Hey, boys. Did I see the police drive back the lane?"

Jake leaned over the counter to kiss her forehead. Yancy favored Lincoln more in looks, and she favored their mother with her unfortunate taste in men, but she and Jake were the closest of the three. He'd been there when she gave birth to Alisha at age fifteen, even though he hadn't been many years older. He'd taken care of her and her kid for years, and he didn't mind the burden one bit. When he'd built the resort she'd asked to help him run it—and took a business course at the nearest community college so she could do a good job. She was always learning new things—studying up on tourism texts and websites. He didn't know what he'd do without her.

"That guy in Twelve—Ratchett—we found him dead outside his cottage."

Her face dropped. "Shit. The big guy that hit on me? Really?"

He nodded, and Lincoln did too. "Found him out back. Neve's taking a look now."

"Any idea who shot him?"

"None."

"At least you don't have to deal with him anymore," she remarked with a shrug. Maybe Linc would like to comment on her stoicism. "What did he want from you, anyway?"

Jake hesitated. There was no way he could explain putting a hit on her abusive former boyfriend. "No idea."

"Not likely to find out either," Lincoln joined in.

Yancy tilted her head. "No, I guess not." That was the end of the questions about Ratchett, thank Christ. "That girl who picked up Lish this morning, who is she?"

He looked at her. "I don't want you gossiping about it, Yance."

She frowned—all defensive. Yeah, she and Lincoln really did look alike. "I won't."

He looked at her a little longer.

"Jesus, Jake! I won't gossip!" She actually looked offended.

He hoped she was telling the truth. She hadn't been as bad lately, but goddamn, the girl had a hard time keeping a secret. Regardless, he supposed news would get out soon enough. "Maggie's daughter."

Her hazel eyes widened. "Maggie had a kid?"

He rubbed the back of his neck. God, he felt tired all of a sudden. "After she and Audrey killed Clint."

"Wow." Yancy shook her head, wisps of her fine, light hair brushing her cheeks. "And I thought I was a young mom. What's she doing here?"

"Looking for her father. Audrey's helping her." He watched to see if she grimaced at the mention of Audrey—she didn't.

"That's good of her. Tell her to talk to Dwayne Dyer. I remember a few years ago he came up to Maggie at Gracie's and said something to her she didn't like. She told me later they had a thing once—before she was sent to the hospital after what happened with her father. I hadn't really thought about how young she must have been until now."

Dwayne Dyer was an asshole. He used to be a real bully back in school, though he seemed to have mellowed since. Jake hated bullies. And he believed that was a trait that never really went away. "I'll tell her, thanks."

His sister shook her head. "Maggie had a kid and there's a dead guy behind one of our cottages. I swear, the longer I live in this town, the more messed up it gets."

Jake's gaze drifted to the door—Neve was coming up the flagstone walk. For the next little while, he expected the sight of her was going to set his teeth on edge. "Tell me about it." If he managed to keep the cops from digging too deep into his business it was going to be a goddamn miracle.

Audrey's phone buzzed as she got out of the car. She checked to see if it was another text from Jake, who had asked to meet her at the main building if she was still at the resort. He'd caught her just as she and Mackenzie were headed out the door. The text wasn't from him, however; it was from Angeline, her boss, asking when she might have a free moment to talk about her facility proposal. If Angeline was asking about it, then she was definitely interested. Audrey sent a quick text back with some times she was free and then walked into the resort office. All three Tripp siblings—and Neve—looked up at her arrival.

"What's going on?" she asked. Neve had her cop face on.

Yancy looked tense, Lincoln looked nervous, and Jake... Jake looked tired. It was an expression that made her want to protect him.

"Dead guy at one of the cottages," Jake explained, his gaze meeting hers. There was nothing secretive or discernible in his eyes, but she knew it was Ratchett who was dead, and she knew Jake hadn't killed him. Had Lincoln?

"One of the hunters?" she asked with a frown, easily pretending ignorance.

"We're not sure who he is," Neve replied. "And let's try to keep it quiet for now. We haven't spoken to the other guests yet."

"Mackenzie's in my car," Audrey informed her, jabbing her thumb in the direction of the door. "She never said anything to me about hearing any noises this morning, but you might want to talk to her."

"I will."

The four of them watched her go. Audrey resisted the urge to immediately start questioning Jake, but Yancy didn't know what he'd done regarding Matt, and he wanted to keep it that way, since part of his reason for having Matt killed was that he'd beaten Jake's sister.

"Any idea how it happened?" she asked.

Jake's lips lifted in an ironic twist. "Looks like it was probably a hunting accident."

Audrey raised a dubious brow. She didn't really have a reply to that. *Probably* a hunting accident?

Jake continued: "I know you've got stuff to do with Maggie's girl, but I wanted to tell you before the gossip got out."

Behind the counter, Yancy stiffened. “I told you I wouldn’t say anything.”

He ran a hand over his face. Yeah, he was tired. “I know you won’t, Yance. I meant I wanted to tell her about the dead guy.”

“Oh.” His sister actually looked a little embarrassed. “Well, I won’t say anything about that either.”

It was obvious that no one in the room was going to bet on that.

“You should go home,” Audrey told him. “Take a nap or something.”

He frowned. “Are you fucking crazy?”

Her shoulders straightened. “It’s obvious you’re exhausted, and the cops are going to want to talk to you more, and you’ll probably have to deal with press. You want to be on TV looking like hell?”

Behind his brother, Lincoln smirked. Jake fixed her with a narrow gaze. “Using your mind powers on me is low. My vanity’s a fragile thing.”

She snorted, then slipped her arm around his waist and gave him a squeeze. “Go get some rest. I’ll meet you at home later.”

Something shifted in his expression. It was the fact that she’d called his house “home.” She knew it. He was such a domestic animal. “I have to open Gracie’s. Donnie’s not in for a few hours.”

“Call Dad. He’d be glad to do it. Jess was taking Mum out shopping, so he’s probably bored.” Normally she wouldn’t suggest putting her father in temptation’s way, but Jake really did look wiped. "He and Donalda should be able to look after things."

That he didn't argue was proof of just how tired he was. "Okay." He kissed her forehead. "I'll see you later."

She started to leave with him and Lincoln, but Yancy stopped her. "Audrey, can I have a minute?"

Audrey and Jake exchanged surprised glances before Audrey turned. Jake and his brother kept going. Lincoln gave her a light tap on the shoulder as he passed. "Sure." She walked up to the counter. "What's up? Lish mentioned you wanted to talk."

Yancy looked uncomfortable. The Tripps weren't real big on appearing vulnerable. "Look, I'm not sure you're the safest person to be around, but my brother seems to think you're worth the risk, and my kid has barely spoken to me since I told her I didn't want her to see you."

"I haven't encouraged that." Just for the record, of course.

"I know you haven't." The younger woman had no trouble giving Audrey the benefit of the doubt. "I also know she's seen you behind my back."

"I haven't encouraged that either."

A casual shrug—not calling Audrey a liar, but not believing her either. "I'm not very good at this mother thing. I didn't have the best teacher, but I'm grown-up enough to admit that part of my problem is jealousy. I blamed you for that bitch taking Lish, but I was angrier that you got to be the one that saved her. You're her fucking hero. I can't fight that."

Audrey's stomach fell. "You're her mom." Like Yancy needed

reminding. And Audrey was nobody's hero—or at least she oughtn't be.

"Yeah, I know." God, sometimes she looked like Jake, and now was one of them. "What I'm saying is that even if I think you're trouble, I know you'll do anything for my kid—like risk your own life. That means something. So, if you don't mind her hanging off you, I'm going to stop trying to keep her away."

The relief Audrey felt at those words...well, it was more emotion than she'd been prepared to feel. It burned her eyes and clutched at her throat. "I don't mind at all. She's an awesome kid."

Yancy smiled—small and lopsided. "That's more Jake's doing than mine."

"You sell yourself short."

"I let her see me with a man who hit me. How can she respect me when I don't even respect myself?" Audrey opened her mouth, but Yancy waved her off. "Never mind. I'm not asking you to be my therapist. I'm trusting you with the most important thing in my life. I just need to know that you'll be there for Alisha if she needs you."

Audrey smiled, despite the weight of what Yancy was asking pressing down on her shoulders. "Always."

Yancy visibly relaxed. She'd been young when she had Alisha—forced to grow up way too early, like Maggie. But then, Audrey had grown up fast too. Too many kids became adults before their time in Edgeport. It was the way it had always been. Probably it would always be that way. Maybe Maggie had wanted to spare her daughter that fate. And yet the girl had found the place on her own. Mackenzie wouldn't be the same by the time she left. That was an unfortunate truth. Because no matter what had happened to Maggie, it didn't change the fact that she'd grown up to be a monster, or that she'd hurt someone as surely as Clint had hurt her. Mackenzie was going to learn a lot of ugly truths, and there was nothing Audrey could do to prevent it, just like she hadn't been able to save Maggie. It wasn't within her power to stop the girl from trying to find out where she came from.

"Hey, I found something I thought you might want." Yancy brought up her purse from underneath the counter and began digging through the huge fake-leather bag. She pulled a photo out of her wallet and held it out to Audrey between her index and middle fingers. "You guys look like babies."

Audrey took the picture. It was of her and Jake sitting on the front porch of his grandmother's house—the one he now called his own. They had their arms around each other and were grinning at each other, heads close together. She couldn't be any more than eleven or twelve in it. On the back, written in Gracie's neat script, was *Two halves of the same fool whole.*

She smiled. "We *were* babies." She raised her head to look at Yancy. "Where did you find it?"

"It was in her jewelry box. Jake gave all of her jewelry to me and Lish. Anyway, I thought you'd like to have it."

"I would, thank you." Out of the corner of her eye she saw Neve through the window. She'd already finished talking to Mackenzie. "I'd better get going."

"Can you come by the house later?" Yancy asked. "Maybe have a drink?"

Was Yancy wanting to bond with her? "I don't know..."

"Jake's coming by. I thought maybe we could all have dinner together. Like a family."

Jake might accuse Audrey of knowing just what buttons to push, but Yancy was pretty damn good at it herself. "Sure. What time?"

"I'm done at five. Any time after that."

"Okay. I'll give you a call."

"Oh, and you might want to talk to Dwayne Dyer. He and Maggie were close, I think."

Audrey nodded her thanks. Dwayne was in that photo she'd found in Maggie's things. There had to be someone in that crowd who knew what happened back the Ridge that spring. As she walked out, Audrey met Neve just outside the door. "Did Mac hear anything?"

Neve shook her head. "She told me you're going to see Barbie, though."

"Yeah. She and Dwayne were both in a photo I found of Maggie taken back the Ridge. Yancy said they used to date."

Neve's striking features were tight. "They still do. He hasn't knocked her up yet, which is amazing. He's got like fourteen kids scattered around the county. Sometimes things can get a little heated between him and Barbie. If there's trouble, call me. I'll be around all day sorting out this shooting."

Normally Audrey would insist that she could take care of herself, but given all that had happened since she came home—and the fact that she had a gun not registered in her name—she nodded. "I will." She meant it too. "Hopefully I won't need you."

Her old friend smiled. “Oh, it’s just a matter of time before you need police backup, Harte. You and I both know it. Try not to kill anyone before I can get there.”

Despite the ominous warning, Audrey grinned back. “I’ll try.” She started toward her car, tossing over her shoulder, “But I can’t make any promises.”

# CHAPTER SEVEN

Every Tripp who had ever lived and died in Edgeport was buried in the small family cemetery back Tripp's Cove road. More than a century ago, old Angus Tripp had a falling-out with the minister of the local church and decided to build his own. The old bastard probably would have started his own religion as well, if he'd thought he could get away with it.

The church wasn't very grand—just a small stone building in a field high on a cliff overlooking a tidal river—but it was one of Jake's favorite places in all of Edgeport. His family had built it by hand, stone by stone. They'd cut the trees and shaped the lumber into pews that could still be coaxed into a gleam when polished. Occasionally someone asked to hold an event there, and he still maintained the yearly Christmas service his grandmother had loved.

Hers was the newest grave in the gated cemetery, the twenty-first-century graves standing out against those that came long before. Angus was buried there—beneath a large stone slab weathered and worn by time. Jake had the older stones restored and fitted with Plexiglas sheets on the front to keep the writing on them from being forever erased. It was his own little Tripp museum.

He tended to the place more often in the warmer months, lingered longer during his visits, but he made sure he came by at least once every few weeks to check his grandmother's grave and pay his respects. It was a private ritual, so when he spotted his brother's familiar form as he approached the gate, he hesitated.

Lincoln stood at the foot of their father's grave, his hands stuffed inside the pockets of his long wool coat, hair lifting on the cold breeze. He glanced up and met his brother's gaze as Jake opened the gate.

"I haven't been here in a long time," Lincoln said by way of greeting. "Too long."

"Same."

Lincoln snorted. "I doubt it." He shook his head, as if trying to counter the wind's assault on his hair. "I had to look for him. I forgot where he was."

Jake knew where every body was buried in that plot of ground. He could recite dates and epitaphs. He knew exactly how many steps it was from where old Angus was buried to where he himself would one day be put to rest. "He doesn't care."

"No. I guess not. You ever miss him?"

"Sometimes."

"I do. Remember those awful fucking songs he used to sing?"

Jake laughed. "Yeah. I used to wonder if we should be afraid." Brody Tripp had favored songs about phantom truckers, dead kids, and one in particular about someone named Jeanie who was afraid of the dark.

"I have some of his old records," Lincoln revealed.

He arched a brow. "You don't listen to them, do you?"

"Sometimes. He liked some pretty maudlin shit. Some of it's not bad, though."

"If you say so."

Lincoln only nodded. Silence fell between them—not awkward but not comfortable either.

"I've been thinking about going back to school."

Jake had to frown in order to keep his eyebrows from leaping up his forehead. "Really? And take what?"

His brother's chin lifted. "Some hospitality courses."

Hospitality. As in restaurant and bar management. There was a lot that went unsaid with that announcement, and Jake figured he heard most of it. To some it probably wasn't much of an apology, but it made him feel things he wasn't ready to completely identify.

"Sounds good." The offer to help with tuition refused to leave his tongue. Later, he'd offer—like once Linc had actually been accepted to a school and decided to go. "You want to come back to the house for a beer?"

Lincoln smiled, and for a moment, Jake saw their father plain as day. "Yeah, sure."

"How'd you get here anyway?" Jake asked as they left the cemetery.

"I walked out from Yance's."

"I'll give you a lift back later if you want." And then, "You know, I think the rest of Dad's records are in a cabinet upstairs. You want them?"

You'd think he'd offered his brother bars of gold from the expression on his face. "Yeah—if you don't."

"Are you kidding? You couldn't pay me to listen to Red Sovine. You want his CB too? You might be able to find 'Phantom 309.' "

"Fuck off." But it was said with a chuckle, and Jake smiled almost all the way home.

Barbie lived in a small, prefab bungalow on the main drag just west of Tripp's Cove. The front lawn was bald in a few spots, and there were dead flowers still in their pots on the front step, but the yard was otherwise neat. A four-wheeler in need of a good wash sat beside a half-ton of indiscriminate age, and behind that was a blue Subaru, which Audrey suspected had become the unofficial state car of Maine, there were so many on the roads.

"Who is this again?" Mackenzie asked, peering through the windshield at the little house. She looked uncertain, nervous. Audrey wanted to hug her, or at least assure her she was safe with her, but she couldn't. First, she didn't want the responsibility, but also because the girl wasn't hers to reassure or protect, no matter how much she might feel like she had some sort of claim. She didn't have the right to make any promises that this was going to be okay.

"Barbie Stokes," Audrey replied, unfastening her seat belt. "She grew up back the Ridge where all the parties took place."

"The girl in the photo we found?"

"Yeah. Her father was the one who hosted most of the parties back there." "Host" made old Wendell sound sophisticated. He wasn't. Audrey remembered him mostly as a short, whipcord kind of a man in a dirty undershirt and workpants.

"Were she and my... Maggie close?"

"I don't know," Audrey replied honestly. Though, Maggie often tried to emulate Barbie when they were younger. "But Barbie lived there, and she would have been around most of the parties." Barbie was also in the photos of the kids who hung out at Aaron Patrick's camp. Frankly, if Barbie couldn't tell them anything, Audrey didn't know what to do next.

They got out of the car. As they approached the house, the front door opened, revealing a young girl who looked about ten years old, and a brown mutt of a dog with one ear that stood straight up while the other flopped to the side. Its tongue lolled out of its mouth as it panted.

"Who are you?" the girl asked, more curious than confrontational.

Audrey smiled at her. She was a pretty little thing, wearing a sweatshirt that had several Disney princesses on it and jeans that were getting too short for her. "I'm Audrey, and this is Mackenzie. We're here to see your mom." She wasn't going to ask if Barbie was home, because it made her feel like a predator trying to ascertain if the kid was alone.

"Is she expecting you?" the girl asked.

"I don't think so." Her response was met by an assessing stare. Audrey tried to ignore the gears turning in her head. Just because a kid was vigilant and seemingly protective of her mother did not mean Barbie had been abused by Dwayne or any other man, and it didn't mean Barbie might possibly have some kind of substance abuse problem. This child could just be a very careful kid.

In the end, it was the dog that decided their fate. The mutt—patches of brown, black, and beige—suddenly bolted from the doorway, leapt off the steps, and ran up to Mackenzie, tail wagging. Mackenzie crouched down and began loving on the dog with genuine delight.

"Okay," the little girl said as she watched her pet slobber over someone else. Obviously the dog's seal of approval was what really mattered. "You can come in."

"Thanks," Audrey replied. As she walked up the front steps, the dog trotted past her into the house, a chew toy in its mouth. She glanced over her shoulder to make sure Mackenzie was with her. She was—wiping her drool-wet hands on the ass of her jeans.

Inside, the house was much like the outside. It wasn't much, but it was neat and clean. There was a porch where dirty boots, coats, and the dog dishes were kept, and then the kitchen through a second door. Audrey and Mackenzie went that far and waited. The furniture was old but well looked after. There was a plant in the window above the sink, and the only dirty dish was a water glass on the beige sideboard. Paper turkeys made from tracing little hands decorated the fridge, a reminder that Thanksgiving wasn't far away. It was a far cry from the house Barbie grew up in, which had been almost constantly in a state of chaos.

"Mom!" the girl shouted, stomping through to what Audrey assumed was the living room. "You got company!"

A few seconds later there came the sound of footfalls on the basement steps. A door behind them opened and a woman in her mid to late thirties and wearing jeans, a sweater, and flip-flops walked through. She carried a basket of folded laundry that smelled warm and fresh from the dryer.

"Hey, Barbie," Audrey said.

The woman wasn't wearing any makeup. Her skin was clear, her green eyes bright. Her dark hair was pulled back in a high ponytail. At one time, Barbie had been one of, if not the prettiest girl in Edgeport. No one could explain it, but Wendell Stokes and his wife made beautiful kids. But Barbie hadn't had an easy life either, and that was evident in the lines around her eyes and mouth. She was still a good-looking woman, but there was a worn look to her. It wasn't defeat, but it was close.

"Audrey." Her surprise was obvious. She set the laundry basket on a nearby chair. "What are you doing here?"

Audrey gestured to the girl at her side. "This is Mackenzie Bell. Maggie Jones was her birth mother."

Barbie's mouth opened. Her eyes widened. "Oh. Hello." She paused—awkwardly. She looked surprised, but not shocked. Maybe she'd known Maggie better than Audrey had first thought. "Do you want tea?"

The universal answer to everything. "That would be great." Audrey slung her purse strap over the back of a chair and sat down. "Mackenzie is here to find her father. I was hoping you could help."

The other woman set an old black teakettle on the stove and turned the burner on. She glanced over her shoulder at them, her highly arched brows knitting together, deepening the lines between. "How?"

"Maggie got pregnant just before Clint died. I hear he used to take her to a lot of parties back the Ridge."

Barbie's slender shoulders slumped. Audrey watch her draw a breath before turning around. She leaned against the stove. "You mean at my house."

Audrey nodded. "Yes."

She folded her arms over her chest. "It's embarrassing to talk about that stuff, you know."

"I know." Of course she knew. "We're only interested in anything you can tell us about Maggie and who might be Mackenzie's father."

The slightly older woman looked from her to Mackenzie and back again. "She never told you? Weren't you guys like best friends or something?"

Or something. "I think Maggie was embarrassed by those parties as well." She arched a brow and hoped she didn't have to clarify any more. Barbie had actually been there, so she had to know exactly what went on, or at least some of it. Stuff no kid should have to witness, let alone be a part of.

"She was younger than me."

Audrey nodded, watching as Barbie's jaw tightened. She waited for her to put it all together in her head—what age Maggie would have been.

Barbie shook her head. "Fuck," she whispered. Then her

head snapped up, and she looked past Audrey and the perfectly silent Mackenzie, to the open archway that led into the living room. "Britney, are you eavesdropping again?"

"No," came a small voice. Audrey smiled. Mothers had some kind of built-in radar, she was sure of it. Her mother always seemed to know when one of her kids was doing something they oughtn't.

"How many times do I need to tell you that it's rude to listen in on people's conversations?" her mother asked as the girl stepped out into the open. "Go to your room."

"But, Mom..."

Audrey looked at the girl and saw the distress in her face—the distrust and unease as she looked at the two strange women sitting at her table. She knew her mother was upset, and young Britney took that emotion on as her own.

"C'mere, Britney," Audrey said. "I'll explain to you what's going on."

The girl hesitated, but only for a moment. She approached cautiously, staying just out of arm's reach. Audrey's stomach tightened. What had this sweet kid seen, or had happen to her, that she knew to stay out of striking distance?

Audrey kept her expression open. "My friend Mackenzie was adopted when she was a baby. Your mom and I both knew her mother when we were kids. We're here to find out if your mom might have known Mackenzie's father too. That's it. We're just going to ask a few questions and talk to your mom. It's nothing bad, but it is an adult conversation. Is that okay?"

Britney regarded her with that serious gaze for a few seconds before nodding. "Okay."

Mackenzie rose to her feet. "Maybe, Britney, you could show me your room, and we can hang out while Audrey and your mom talk."

Audrey shot her a surprised glance. "Yeah?"

The younger woman nodded. "I think we all might be a lot more comfortable with this conversation if I wasn't in the room for it." She gave Barbie a slight smile.

"Sure," Audrey agreed. It was good of her to consider Barbie's discomfort, but it was also obvious that even though she'd prepared herself for hearing things she didn't want to hear, Mackenzie wasn't sure she wanted to hear it firsthand. "I'll let you know when we're done."

The teakettle whistled as Mackenzie followed Britney from the room. A few moments later, Barbie set two cups of tea, some cookies, and milk and sugar on the table. She sat down in Mackenzie's vacant seat. "That was good of her to go with Britney. You'd think she was the mom the way that kid fusses over me." She laughed self-consciously.

"Did she see her father hit you?"

Barbie went still, freezing in the act of stirring milk into her tea. Then she slowly started up again. "I forgot. You went off to college and became a psychiatrist or something, didn't you?"

"Psychologist."

"What's the difference?"

"We're more about therapy and less about drugs." It was an

overly simplified answer, but she didn't think Barbie would be interested in all the particulars. "You don't have to answer my question, but my guess is that Britney's father hit you—and her."

The other woman nodded, the lines around her eyes tightening. "Yes."

Audrey continued. "I'm going to assume hitting her is why you aren't with him anymore. It's just been the two of you for a while, huh?"

Another nod.

"She looks out for you and you look out for her." Audrey smiled. "That's good. How's Dwayne with her?" It was no secret that Dwayne Dyer had been generous with his sperm over the years. Audrey had to assume he wasn't much of a partner, but apparently, he wasn't a bad dad. She knew he acknowledged and spent time with all of his kids—the ones who knew he was their father, at any rate. That was worth something, Audrey supposed.

"He's good, but she's not his, y'know? I mean, he's got so many already..." Barbie laughed and dunked a cookie in her tea. "God, that sounds so fucked up."

Audrey smiled and reached for a cookie. They looked like sugar cookies—big and fat. She loved sugar cookies. She was going to have to get a run in later that day. "Gracie Tripp used to say that 'life is seldom neat.'" She dunked her cookie and took a bite. "Oh my God, these are good."

Barbie's lips curved. "My grandmother's recipe. Thanks. So, what do you want to know? I don't remember much about Maggie at those parties. I used to take off as much as I could."

"What about Bertie Neeley?" Audrey asked—only because Maggie had seemed to dislike him so much.

Barbie shook her head, her expression resolute. "No. Bertie wasn't like that. He's good with kids."

Audrey didn't push it. "Do you remember seeing Maggie with anyone else?"

"She'd go off with some of the younger guys. One night I took her with me when I left. We went back to Aaron Patrick's camp. After that she'd make it back there on her own. I remember her flirting with Dwayne—not sure if anything happened. She spent a lot of time with Duger. Your brother-in-law was there sometimes, and there was that kid that died. I think his name was Mike. That's all I can remember. I mean, you guys killed Clint that May and she wasn't at any more parties after that."

Audrey almost laughed. She said it so casually, like Clint had moved to Florida. "Your father shut things down?"

Barbie shrugged. "I think he felt guilty that he hadn't seen—or he'd ignored—what was going on. They all did. You might not know this, but you and Maggie made this place take a good hard look at itself, and no one liked what they saw."

No, she hadn't known that, and it was good to hear it. "That Mike kid, did Maggie spend much time with him?"

"What's going on here?"

Audrey jumped, and turned her head at the same time Barbie did. She hadn't heard a car drive in, or the front door open. Standing in the kitchen doorway was Bertie Neeley. He looked irritated. Audrey wasn't used to seeing him sober, so she didn't know how he normally appeared.

How long had he been standing there? From the look on his face, Audrey suspected he might have heard more of the conversation than she wanted.

"Hey, Uncle Bertie," Barbie greeted with a smile. They weren't really related, or at least Audrey didn't think so, but all the kids who grew up back the Ridge referred to Bertie as their "uncle." "Audrey was just asking me about that boy who died the same spring as Clint Jones. Do you remember?"

Bertie looked Audrey in the eye. "You kill him too?"

She arched a brow. Bertie had never been mean to her face before, so something about the situation obviously didn't sit well with him. "Pretty sure I wouldn't be asking about him if I had."

He grunted. "I'm here for Brit. Told her I'd take her over to that little junk shop in Ryme."

Barbie stood up. "I'll go get her." She cast an uneasy glance in Audrey's direction, but Audrey just smiled. She'd never been afraid of Bertie and she wasn't about to start at this point in her life.

The second they were alone, he fixed her with his narrow gaze. It really was strange not to see his eyes bloodshot, or smell the booze rolling off him. A haircut and clothes that fit would make the world of difference in his appearance. "What kind of trouble you stirring up now, Audrey Harte?"

She shrugged. "No trouble. Just looking for some answers. You used to party back the Ridge, didn't you?"

"I done a lot of things," he replied. "None of which are your damn business. You might want to think on that before you go digging around in folks' affairs. Some don't take kindly to snoops."

"You know, warning me off only makes me want to look harder. I'm not sure if it's a Pelletier thing, or if I get it from the Harte side."

His expression didn't change. "It's going to get you into trouble one of these days."

"Already has." She said it with a rueful smile.

"Even your luck has to run out someday."

Was that a threat? She couldn't tell if it was said with regret, or with hope. "I'll keep that in mind."

"Uncle Bertie!" Britney cried.

He jerked back as though Audrey suddenly burst into flames, his face lighting up with joy. Whatever his faults, it was obvious he loved that little girl. Nothing about the way he looked at her made any warning bells go off in Audrey's head. There was nothing predatory or salacious in his gaze—just simple adoration that was obviously returned. "Hey there, peanut. You ready to go shopping?"

The girl held up a small denim cross-body bag. "Sure am."

Barbie smiled. "Have her back by supper."

Bertie agreed. He didn't even look at Audrey again as he and the little girl left. Audrey watched them go, intrigue and confusion dancing around her brain. What had that all been about? Did Bertie know something? He had to know being so strange and cryptic would only pique her interest. Maybe he wanted her to dig around. Maybe he wanted her to get hurt. But that didn't make sense. Bertie got into a lot of fights, but that was because he could be an idiot when he was drunk. He was never mean.

Once they were gone, and Mackenzie sat down at the table, Barbie got another cup of tea and the three of them chatted about what else Barbie could remember.

"Maggie talked to me some. I think she felt safe having another girl around. Sometimes the guys would flirt with her. Most of the regulars treated her like a little sister. I don't remember her spending time with any one guy. I'm sorry I'm not much help. I'm embarrassed to admit it, but I partied pretty hard back then. Dwayne might remember more. He was friends with that Mike kid, I think. He's working today, but I can get him to call you."

"That would be great, Barbie," Audrey said. "Thanks." A few minutes later, she and Mackenzie backed out of the driveway, headed toward Lower Edgeport.

"Did she tell you anything?" Mackenzie asked.

Audrey had to force her foot to go light on the gas pedal. She was still keyed up from her encounter with Bertie. "She gave a list of possibilities."

The girl winced. "A list. Wow."

"Not a long list." She really had to be more careful in her wording. "I told you this wasn't going to be pleasant."

"I know."

Audrey glanced at her. Mackenzie sounded hesitant—uncertain. "We can stop if you want." The last thing she wanted was to see this nice, innocent girl get hurt.

"No. I want to know where I came from."

"Okay, then we go forward. If you change your mind, you just say the word."

"I won't change my mind." The stubborn set to her jaw was yet another reminder of Maggie—bullheaded to her own detriment.

Audrey glanced at the dirt road that led back the Ridge as they sped past it a few seconds later. What had gone on back there? What had happened to Maggie, and why had she never shared any of it with her?

And what, if anything, could Audrey do about it now?

*Nineteen years ago*

"I don't know why you waste your time on Jake," Maggie said as she flipped onto her stomach on Audrey's bed. "He's so young."

"He's older than us," Audrey reminded her. She pressed Play on the CD player; Soul Asylum's "Runaway Train" started. "We're just friends."

Maggie smirked at her. God, Audrey was so transparent sometimes. "Right. You don't want to get in his pants at all."

Her friend made a face. "It's not like that."

"Twu wuv," Maggie teased. Audrey didn't even know what she was missing. Didn't know what kind of power sex gave a girl. "You saving yourself for your wedding night? You know he'll come before he even gets inside you, right? That's *so* romantic."

Audrey hit her in the arm. She hit hard, but Maggie had

been hit harder, so she barely noticed the pain. She was good at putting herself in another place when things hurt. "Shut up. I don't want to have sex with Jake. Not yet anyway."

"How nice for you that you get to decide who you have sex with." Shit. She hadn't meant to say that.

Her best friend went pale. Maybe she was naive in a lot of ways, but Audrey was smart sometimes. Too smart. "What are you talking about?"

"Nothing. It was just a joke."

"No, it wasn't." Audrey came up on her elbows, looming over her. "What happened?"

For a second, Maggie wondered what Dree would do if she kissed her. Would she let her? Could Maggie shut her up as easily as she did boys that talked too much? No. Kissing would just make this worse. Audrey was one of the few good things in her life. She couldn't mess that up, no matter how much she sometimes stupidly wanted to. "I told you, nothing." Losing Audrey was the one thing that scared her.

*"Maggie."*

Tears scorched the back of Maggie's eyes. She was not going to cry. She glanced out the window. "Someone's here." Then she saw whose truck it was and her tears dried up faster than the beach at low tide on a sunny day. "Fucking Bertie Neeley."

Audrey frowned. "What's your damage with Bertie? He's a drunk."

Maggie laughed. She said it like that made him harmless, but she knew Bertie wasn't just some sweet old guy.

Still frowning, Audrey put her hand on Maggie's arm. "Did Bertie do something to you?"

"Do something?" Maggie mocked. "Jesus, Dree, just ask me if he fucked me, don't go all after-school special."

The change in her friend's expression was... beautiful. Audrey's face hardened. Her weirdly pretty eyes brightened, and in that brightness Maggie saw something that actually scared her. For a second she couldn't even breathe. Maggie had seen a lot of monsters in her life, but this was the first time she ever felt like she had one of her own.

"Bertie never touched me," she admitted, before she could lie. It was tempting to say he had just to see what Audrey would do.

"If it wasn't him, then who?" Her friend slid her hand down Maggie's arm and took hold of one of her hands. Maggie couldn't remember the last time someone had touched her in a loving, nonsexual kind of way. Not even her mother, who spent most of her time in her room, bruised and staring out the window. Sometimes Maggie just wanted to hand her a bottle of pills so she'd get it over with.

The tears she'd tried to hold back rushed forward with a vengeance. She couldn't tell everything. Dree was her best friend. The only other real friend she had was Mike, and she couldn't talk about him either. He'd made her promise that they'd keep each other's secrets and not talk about what happened in the little shed on the hill. She didn't want Audrey to look at her like other people did—like she was garbage. Audrey loved her, and she wanted it to stay that way for as long as possible.

But there was one thing she could tell her—the thing that no one knew. The thing that was to blame for every other bad thing that happened to her. Audrey could help her stop it. Maybe. If anyone could save her, it was Audrey.

Tears trickling down her face, Maggie told Audrey what her father had done to her—what he made her do to him. Every painful, disgusting thing. She tried not to cry as she remembered these things—some of them were like they'd happened to another person, like she'd watched them on TV rather than experienced them. When she was done, she sat on the bed, her shoulders sagging, nose clogged with snot, and waited for Audrey's reaction.

"I don't know what to do," she whispered. And it was true. She knew how to survive, but she didn't know how to save herself, and she couldn't see anything at all that made life worth living.

Then Audrey opened her mouth. "We could kill him."

Maggie stared at her. "Are you serious?"

"Yeah. Yeah, I am."

"You'd kill someone for me?"

"I'd do anything for you."

Maggie threw her arms around Audrey's neck and squeezed her as hard as she could. "You're the best friend ever."

"I always will be," Audrey promised. "Always."

And Maggie believed it.

# CHAPTER EIGHT

Where had it gone wrong?

Talking to Mackenzie—looking at her—had brought up so many memories of when Audrey and Maggie had been best friends. She still couldn't believe Maggie had kept her pregnancy a secret. If it were anyone else she'd assume Maggie hadn't known, but she knew that wasn't the case.

All of her training insisted that Maggie probably hadn't shared the information because of shame. She'd always looked at Audrey as being "the good one" of the two of them. Shame, when Audrey thought about it, was what had ruined their friendship.

When Audrey was released from Stillwater, Maggie was already back in Edgeport. Audrey had been nervous about seeing her friend again—what if Maggie rejected her? But Maggie hadn't rejected her.

Audrey rejected Maggie. Somewhere during her incarceration, Audrey had become ashamed of what she'd done, despite the fact that her adult self had no regrets. She didn't blame Maggie—she took full responsibility for her actions—but every time Audrey looked at her, Maggie was a reminder of what she'd done.

So Audrey starting pulling away, and Maggie tried to hold on. The harder Maggie dug in, the more ashamed Audrey became, because it was so very obvious by then that there was something very, very wrong with Maggie. The hospital hadn't made her better, and Audrey took some responsibility for that. If she hadn't killed Clint, Maggie wouldn't have been sent away. She'd be okay.

Realistically, adult Audrey knew that wasn't how things worked. Maggie's mental issues would have eventually come to the forefront, and without that stay in the hospital, things might have gone a lot worse for her. None of that mattered when it came to her feelings. Inside, she owed Maggie for being ashamed of her, and she wasn't going to let that shame spread to Maggie's kid. That was the thought in her head when she drove down to her parents' house later that same day, Mackenzie in tow. She couldn't bear the thought of leaving the girl alone in that cottage, despite her own desire to go through Maggie's things. It didn't seem right.

Jess and the girls were there when Audrey arrived, so it was easy for her to corner her father in the kitchen and let Mac entertain the girls.

"Do you know of anything that happened that spring back the Ridge that involved Bertie Neeley?" she asked.

John frowned. She didn't take offense; her father frowned a lot. "You expect me to remember something involving Bertie Neeley that happened almost twenty years ago?"

"Yeah, I do. I ran into him at Barbie's and he warned me off digging around back the Ridge. He wasn't the least bit subtle."

Her father shook his head with a sigh. "Damned old fool."

"Did you give me that gun because of Bertie?"

He grabbed her by the arm and pulled her away from the door. "Lower your voice, you harpy." There wasn't any insult in his tone, however. "You want your mother to hear?"

No, she didn't, so she kept her voice a whisper as she demanded, "Is Bertie why you gave me the damn gun?"

He rolled his eyes, making her feel like an idiot. "Jesus, kid, do you know how much I was drinking back then? No, I don't remember anything that had to do with Bertie except I probably knocked him on his ass more times than I want to admit."

"Well, something happened. I don't care unless it has something to do with Maggie."

His expression softened. If she lived to be a hundred she would never understand the friendship that existed between her father and Bertie. Never. "Hey, now. Watch it. Bertie Neeley might be a weaselly son of a bitch on occasion, but he would never, *ever* hurt a child. He's always loved kids, and been good to them. You remember how he used to keep a tab at the store so you kids could put your candy on it."

Actually, Audrey had pretty much forgotten about that. She hadn't thought of it in years, but he was right. Back when there had been a small general store in Edgeport, Bertie could always be counted on to buy a kid a treat.

But why threaten her if he hadn't done anything? It didn't make sense, unless he thought she might dig up something unrelated to Maggie. She had no interest in what else went on back that road. Still, it would pay to be careful.

"Hey, did you transfer that gun to my name before you gave it to me?"

He didn't even blink at her change of subject. "Yeah. Do you think I just let *you* run around with an unregistered handgun? That would be like handing an arsonist a flamethrower and trusting that nothing bad would happen."

Audrey laughed. "Thanks, Dad. You're a real peach, you know that."

His lips lifted slightly. "Hey, apple, have you met tree?" His smile faded. "Is it true they found a body at Jake's this morning?"

God, she'd practically forgotten about that too. Myopic much? "Yeah. A guy that was at Gracie's last night. He was shot."

"Hunting accident?"

"I'm not sure." She wasn't about to tell him Ratchett had been in town to blackmail Jake. "The police had just gotten there when I saw Jake, so I don't know much."

Her father arched a brow. "You know the difference between a hunting accident and murder."

"Okay, stop talking like I'm a murder expert."

He stared at her. "You want to go down that road? 'Cause we can."

She shook her head, not really offended. "One murder doesn't make me an expert any more than one drink makes someone a drunk."

"It only took one drink to make me one," he shot back. At the sound of laughter, his gaze drifted over her shoulder to where Mackenzie sat with Anne and Jessica at the table. "Speaking of apples and trees."

Audrey didn't look; she kept her attention focused solely on her father. There was a tightness to his face that unsettled her. "I wish you'd tell me what you know."

"Yeah, well, I wish you'd stop talking so much." His scowl lacked any real censure, though.

"I'm going to find out."

His brown and blue gaze locked with her own. "Someone might get hurt if you keep doing all this digging. And I don't mean you. It's not all about you, kid."

Audrey's spine straightened. "Maggie was my friend. She told me about Clint, but she didn't tell me about her kid. There was a reason for that." She had to know what that reason was. She had to at least try to make it right.

"Yeah, like maybe she realized she'd already ruined your life enough."

"Oh, Dad. Maggie didn't ruin my life—I took care of that for both of us."

John was still for a moment, watching her face. For a second, Audrey thought he might hug her, then he nodded his head at the scene behind her. "Just take care that little girl's life doesn't end up ruined too." He grabbed a plate of cookies off the sideboard and shoved it at her. "Now, go visit with your mother and sister. I'll make tea."

She backed off, reluctantly taking the plate. Her father had a way of firing her up and making her doubt herself all at the same time. She went into the dining room and set the cookies on the table before sitting down. Mackenzie was on the floor with Isabelle and Olivia, laughing at something Isabelle said.

Jessica watched them with a strange expression on her face.

"You okay?" Audrey asked.

Her sister's head snapped up. "Hmm? Oh, yeah. I was just thinking. I heard there was trouble at the resort this morning. Some dead hunter?"

"Something like that. I don't know all the details."

Anne shook her head. "What a tragedy."

"There's been a lot of death around here lately," Jessica remarked.

Audrey's lips twisted. "Ever since the reaper came home."

Both of them groaned and scowled at her. "Don't talk so loose," her mother chastised. "It's got nothing to do with you."

The serial killer who abducted Alisha had everything to do with her, but she didn't remind them of that. Making herself the bad guy wasn't going to help anyone, so she dropped it.

"I have something for you," Jess said, taking her purse from the back of her chair and putting it in her lap. She searched through it for a couple of seconds before pulling out an old, dog-eared photograph. "Greg said you might want it. I told him you were trying to find out more about the kid who died and he found this. It's a photo from a party back the Ridge."

Audrey plucked it from her fingers. She'd looked at a lot of photographs in the last twenty-four hours.

"Is that Greg?" she asked, pointing at one of the two boys in the photo.

Jessica laughed. “Yeah. Skinny thing, huh?”

Audrey grinned. “He was. Cute, though.” The other guy was also cute, with a wispy goatee only a teenage boy could grow. She flipped the photo over. *Me and Mike LeBlanc.* She turned the picture again and looked at his young face. The photo wasn’t as sharp as digital, so it was hard to make out his eye color, but she supposed he could be Mackenzie’s father. She wasn’t the best one to ask, because every time she looked at the girl, she just saw Maggie. Regardless, it was good to have a clear image of him.

“Thanks. Can I keep it?”

Jess shrugged. “He didn’t say you couldn’t.”

“Great.” She’d call Neve later and ask her if she could look into the official report for when the kid died. Meanwhile, there really wasn’t much else to do while they waited to definitively remove Clint as a parental option. Audrey had no idea how long that would take, and there was no need for Mac to hang around waiting with Calais only a couple of hours away. She could take Maggie’s stuff with her if she wanted—no one else wanted it. If it turned out that Clint was Mac’s father, then there was no need to dig around into the parties back the Ridge. And Bertie and his secrets could relax.

And Audrey would have the distasteful task of revealing the truth to a sweet young woman.

They stayed for tea—to Isabelle’s delight. Audrey found herself unceremoniously dumped by her niece in favor of Mac’s new-and-shininess. Olivia wanted Mac’s attention as well and grabbed a fistful of the young woman’s hair to get it.

"Ow!" Mac cried.

"Olivia!" Jess rushed toward her daughter, who stood there, long brown hairs sticking out of her clenched fist. "Sweetie, I am so sorry she did that to you."

Mackenzie rubbed her scalp. "It's okay. No harm done."

"You don't pull hair, Livvie," Jess chastised as she picked up her daughter. "It's not nice." She pulled the loose hairs from Olivia's fingers before setting the child in Audrey's lap.

Olivia, unbothered and clearly unapologetic, took the opportunity to steal a bite of cookie off the plate in front of her. She turned to her aunt with wide eyes framed by impossibly long and thick lashes, and held up the piece of white chocolate-chip cookie.

"Ache's cookie?" she asked. "Ache make it?"

"Ache?" Audrey echoed. Then it struck her, and she grinned. "Do you mean Jake, Livvie?"

The toddler nodded, her entire face lighting up at the sound of his name. "Ache!"

Jess leaned over and tickled her daughter's chubby leg. "Do you like Jake?"

A very enthusiastic nod was her answer. "Yeah!"

"She talks about him all the time," Audrey's sister said with a smile. "I think she shares your taste in men."

Audrey almost apologized to her sister, but realized she had nothing to be sorry for. "He's pretty impressed by her too," she said. "He'll be all puffed up when I tell him about this."

"He's going to make a good dad someday," Anne remarked, shooting her a pointed look.

"We're not having the kids talk," she informed her mother. "Be happy with the grandchildren you already have."

"I am happy, but I would be happier with more."

"Talk to David."

"He's promised me one. I want a guarantee from you too."

Audrey laughed, but her laughter faded when she looked at Jess, who suddenly looked pale and a little nauseous. Her heart faltered. Her sister could not be sick. She couldn't handle that on top of their mother's illness.

Later, when Mackenzie had already gone out to get into the car, Audrey made her sister walk her to the door.

"What's going on?" she demanded. "Are you okay? I thought you were going to puke when Mum gave me a hard time about kids. And you had a weird look on your face watching Mac with the girls."

Jess chewed on the side of her thumb. She looked up and met her sister's concerned gaze. "Don't say anything," she whispered, "but I think I'm pregnant."

Audrey's eyes widened. "That's a good thing, isn't it?"

The older sister shook her head. "I don't know. Maybe. We hadn't planned to have any more. In fact, Greg has a vasectomy appointment next month."

"Ah. You're not sure he's going to want to have it."

"I'm not sure *I* want to have it."

She looked so tormented, Audrey couldn't help herself—she put her arms around her sister and hugged her. "You'll figure it out. I'm here for whatever you need." She meant it. She and Jess hadn't been close for years—in fact they had despised each other—but that didn't change the fact that they were sisters. Family mattered. Blood mattered.

Jess leaned into her for a second before pulling back. "Thanks. You'd better go before Mum comes out wondering what we're talking about."

Audrey did as she was told. Pulling her coat tight around her against the cold as she walked to her car, she thought about all the different reactions a woman could have to finding out she was pregnant. Her sister was a married woman in her mid-thirties and she wasn't certain she wanted a third child. Somewhere there was another woman overjoyed by the same news, or one sobbing because she couldn't have children at all.

Why hadn't Maggie had an abortion? Any psychiatrist or psychologist at the hospital would have certainly recommended it given the circumstances—unless it had been too late at that point. That had to be the case.

She glanced at Mac through the windshield. The girl was so sweet. Maggie had loved her. Loved her enough to carry her to term and then give her up so she could have a better life. Audrey doubted Maggie had ever had that selfless love for anyone else.

So it stood to reason that she'd loved Mac's father too. Maybe. With Maggie sometimes love got messed up, but she had a grasp of the emotion. That meant he probably wasn't someone who had abused her. He was someone Maggie chose for herself. Someone young.

She thought of Mike LeBlanc, with his sweet face and teenage facial hair. Maybe she could do a *little* digging while waiting on the test results.

She pulled out her phone and called Neve. "Hey. Can you see what you can find out about that kid who died back the Ridge? His name was Mike LeBlanc. Thanks." Before opening the car door she added, "And maybe you could find his next of kin?"

She was going to need some DNA.

"So, Neve hasn't made any connections between you and Ratchett?" Audrey asked around a mouthful of ice cream. They were back from dinner at Yancy's and had the house to themselves. The evening had been a little... odd, but not bad, considering. She and Yancy had a chance to just chat, and she thought they had a better understanding of each other. Regardless, she had Alisha back in her life, and that was what mattered.

Actually, what really mattered was time alone with Jake. It felt like forever since they'd connected. It was only Saturday night, and the last two days had been filled with enough drama for a month.

Jake leaned back against the couch and pressed pause on the remote. "Not yet. She probably will, but I'm going to maintain that I never spoke to the bastard. I went to Gracie's today and erased hours of the outside security footage. She didn't ask for it earlier, but she probably will. I'd rather explain a glitch than have her see me hit the son of a bitch with a bat."

He didn't look the least bit worried. Worrying wasn't something Jake did. He knew fear, and he got angry, and then he did something to fix the situation, but he rarely worried or fretted over things.

She shrugged, dipping her spoon into her bowl. "Well, it's not like you killed him."

"Maybe I should have. Neve wouldn't be asking questions if I had." He stirred his spoon around. "Has she said anything to you?"

"Not a word." But to be honest, she'd been preoccupied with her own mystery. Neve wouldn't discuss a case with her anyway.

He didn't start their show again. Instead he turned to her. "How's the kid holding up?"

"Better than I expected." She took another cold mouthful. "We're going to drive over to Eastrock and see Duger tomorrow."

"Good old Doog. Hopefully his mother won't be there when you arrive."

Audrey shuddered. Jeannie Ray was Duger—Scott's—mother, and she made Audrey seriously entertain committing murder again. The woman was a gossip and a menace. When Audrey had first returned to Edgeport, her mother and Jeannie had a bit of an altercation at church. Anne seemed to have something on the old crone, but she didn't share the information with her daughter. "If her car's in the drive I'll just keep on going."

"You don't really think he's the girl's father, do you?"

"He could be."

"She's too smart to be Doog's."

"Yeah, well, there's not an awful lot of my mother in me, but she's still there."

He conceded with a slight nod. "Did I tell you Linc's talking about going back to school? Says he wants to take a hospitality course."

She licked her spoon. "You think he was being sincere, or sucking up?"

"I think he was sincere."

There was just enough hope in his voice to tug at her heart. Lincoln had conspired to extort money from him and he still wanted to believe in him. "I hope he was." And then, because she felt compelled, "The three of you working together would make Gracie happy."

"It would." He ran a hand through his hair. "Gran would smack me upside the head for this Ratchett shit."

"Well, I wish she was here to help me figure out what happened to Maggie. She'd know exactly where I should look and who I should talk to. She'd probably tell me what happened to Mike LeBlanc the night he died." No one knew why or how the boy managed to fall over that bank into the icy river below. The circumstances of his death had no bearing on whether he was Mackenzie's father, but they might have something to do with Maggie, and there was a little voice inside Audrey's head that couldn't stop asking if maybe Clint hadn't been Maggie's first murder.

"You know, I own the land where he died."

Audrey hadn't known. "But I thought it belonged to Wendell."

"It used to. He sold the lot adjacent to his house to me last April."

"Why?"

"One of his grandchildren needed money for college or something. I didn't care and didn't ask. I just wanted the land. It buts up against some of my blueberry scrub and has easy access to the river. I put a hiking trail on part of it."

She really didn't want to know how much of the town he owned at this point. "Can we go there tomorrow?" Not like there'd be any clues after so many years, but at least she'd have a visual.

He nodded. "Okay, no more talking," he said decisively. "We're going to watch this movie and pretend we're normal for a while."

"I think this is normal—for us at any rate."

"Normal is whatever we want to make it, and I want to watch this ridiculous movie with you and then go to bed and spoon. I don't care if it's corny—that's what will feel normal to me."

It sounded good to her. She didn't even care if they had sex. She just wanted to curl up in his arms and fall asleep that way, knowing that everything was right with the world.

Because God knew it could all go to hell before dawn.

# CHAPTER NINE

Sunday morning arrived overcast and cold. Fat flakes of snow danced in the air as Audrey and Mackenzie headed out to continue their quest.

"I'm so not ready for snow," Audrey confessed, frowning at the delicate white drops melting on her windshield. Sometimes she really missed LA. If she was there she and Angeline could discuss her plans for a youth shelter face-to-face instead of messaging and playing phone tag. Of course, if she was still in LA, she wouldn't be with Jake, so maybe the cold wasn't so bad after all.

"I don't think it cares if we're ready or not," the younger woman remarked, rubbing the pads of her fingers against her scalp.

"Still sore where Olivia got you?" Audrey asked with a faint smile as they drove toward the main road.

"A little. I'm such a baby."

"Hey, she's gotten me too. It hurts like hell. All kids seem to do it, though."

"My mother says she thought I was going to scalp her when I was that age. I feel like I should call her and apologize."

Audrey smiled. "Mothers are some of the most abused creatures on the planet, and yet no one can understand why I'm in no hurry to become one." The confession made her think of her sister. She would have to call Jess later and see how she was doing. She and Greg were great parents, but she could understand not wanting to add to their already crazy lives.

"My mother once had someone tell her that she wasn't completely a woman unless she pushed out kids of her own. Can you imagine someone saying something like that to a woman who had adopted her kid?"

Audrey shook her head, trying to ignore how much Mac had sounded like Maggie. "Some people just don't think before they speak. The mother of the guy we're going to talk to is like that, but mostly she's just an old cow." Jeannie Ray was an Edgeport institution. She seemed to despise the town almost as much as it despised her. It was her son, Scott, who they were on their way to visit. Duger, as he was called, was a couple of years older than Audrey, but they'd been in the same grade for a while until Audrey moved ahead. He wasn't terribly bright, but for the most part he'd been okay. Except for that one time he and Audrey got into a fistfight over him calling Maggie a slut. Weird, because everyone she'd talked to seemed to have the idea that he had actually liked Maggie. She was curious to see which was the truth.

And hopefully he'd forgiven her for humiliating him by pounding the crap out of him.

One of the reasons Audrey had become a psychologist was to help with her own issues—it happened a lot in the field. One of those issues was her proclivity to hit first and ask questions later. She'd had a lot of anger at the world growing up—she still did. Sometimes she still wanted to punch first. She had it mostly in hand, but it was there, just waiting for her to let it out. Beating up Doogie had felt good. Getting into that fight with Matt Jones had felt good, even though she suffered for it later.

Maybe she should invest in a punching bag.

The Happy Valley Trailer Park, where Duger lived, was located fairly centrally in Eastrock. In the dirt parking lot at the entrance of the site, there was a small building with a huge sign on the front that read BIG SMOKEY'S in chipped and faded paint. It was a small convenience store and takeout that made surprisingly good hot dogs—not that Audrey was brave enough to eat one of them now that she was an adult.

The park was basically a square with one road that ran around the perimeter. The trailer they were looking for was situated on the northwest corner, about a quarter mile from the main drag. It was a dirty baby blue with rust-streaked cream trim. A rotting deck in need of painting leaned off the back, where a lonely old charcoal grill sat in front of a black smudge on the siding. A yellow half-ton with one blue door was parked in the front.

"Am I a terrible person for hoping my father doesn't live here?" Mackenzie said, staring dumbfounded at the scene.

"Nope," Audrey replied, unbuckling her seat belt. "I hope he doesn't live here either."

The girl stopped her with a gentle touch of her hand on her arm. "Can we just take a minute?"

"Sure." Concern overrode the idea of being seen lurking in Duger's driveway. "You okay?"

"I'm not sure."

"We don't have to do this."

"It's just..." Mackenzie turned her head to meet her gaze. "When I found out my mother had been a teenager, I had these fantasies about her and who my father might have been. Sometimes he was the jock, or maybe valedictorian. Once in a while he was president of the chess club."

"I don't think our school had a chess club," Audrey commented before she could stop herself. Thankfully, her companion chuckled. "Am I correct in guessing that you never once fantasized that he was—how to put it?—'challenged'?"

Mackenzie's shoulders slumped. "Never."

She nodded. "For what it's worth, he's not a bad guy. I'd be a lot more worried if anyone from our football team was up for consideration—for what it's worth."

They got out of the car. Gravel crunched beneath Audrey's boots. She shoved her hands in her coat pockets, cursing herself for having forgotten her gloves at home.

The front steps—painted the same dull brown as the deck—were bowed and splintered. They groaned under Audrey's weight, fragile with rot. There was a hole in the side of the trailer where a doorbell used to be, so Audrey rapped on the aluminum door instead. A few seconds later, the inside door opened, revealing a tall, skinny guy with a blond brush-cut and pale eyes. He blinked when he looked at Audrey, his fingers trailing absently over the front of his faded gray T-shirt.

"Hey, Doog," she said.

"Audrey?" He smiled when she nodded. "I knew there couldn't be anyone else with them eyes. What are you doing here? Come on in." He stood back, giving them access to the trailer as he smiled expectantly. He was missing one of teeth on the top left side.

She could feel Mackenzie's trepidation as they stepped over the threshold. The girl had been brought up in a decent neighborhood, by people who made decent money. She was still a teenager, and her acquaintance with the world was fairly new. Poverty scared her. Mental deficiency scared her. And the idea that her father might literally be a poor idiot terrified her despite Audrey's sincere assurance that there were worse possibilities.

God, there were way, *way* worse possibilities.

"I haven't seen you in years," Duger said as he shuffled toward the kitchen. Inside, the trailer was surprisingly neat. Still crappy, but tidy. "Remember that time you smacked me senseless? Come in, come in. I think I have tea. Who's your little friend?"

Before Audrey could respond, Mackenzie did: "My name is Mackenzie. Maggie Jones was my mother."

Duger froze. His back was to them as he stood at the sideboard, the cupboard to his right hanging open. Slowly he turned around, a tin of tea clutched to his narrow chest. "Maggie? Maggie was your mumma?"

Mackenzie nodded. "Nice to meet you."

He moved toward her, the tin still in his hands. His gaze was open and curious as it ran over her. "Maggie's baby." He smiled then, revealing teeth that, while stained from cigarettes and coffee, were surprisingly straight—except for that one gap. "I made a wish to meet you one day."

Audrey jerked back like he'd suddenly tased her. "Doog, you knew Maggie was pregnant?"

He barely glanced at her—all of his attention and wonder was directed at Mac. "I did. It was a secret. She said, 'Doog, you'll keep my secret, won't you?' and I did. Guess it doesn't matter so much now that she's dead. And here you are, my wish come true." He swiped a finger across his eye and went back to making tea. "Sit down why don't you."

They did. Mac sat on the other side of the table, while Audrey plunked herself down near the chair with the ashtray and comic book in front of it.

"You still reading *X-Men*?" she asked, glancing at the brightly colored pages. She needed to make conversation after his easy confession about Maggie. Needed a second to process everything. Maggie had told Duger she was pregnant, but not her? Why?

Shame was the only thing that made sense. Back then Audrey had been a fairly average young girl. Her feelings about sex and sexuality ran way more romantic than Maggie's had, and she'd held on to an idealistic view of the whole process. Maggie had been just the opposite and often teased Audrey for being a prude. Audrey had been judgmental of other girls for their behavior, and Maggie probably hadn't wanted to lose her best friend.

And, the cynical part of her added, she wouldn't have wanted to lose the person she hoped would help rid her of her abusive father. The horror of Maggie's situation would have been lessened by her promiscuity in Audrey's young mind. She hated admitting that about herself, but that didn't make it any less true.

"Mom says she's going to burn them all when I'm dead." He cackled. "Like I'm going to die before her. Doesn't matter, I'm leaving them all to my niece and nephew. They can sell them and pay for college."

Audrey turned to Mackenzie. "Duger—Scott—collects comic books."

The girl—still looking pretty much like a deer in headlights—smiled slightly. "My brother collects *Batman*."

"I'm a Marvel man," Duger said just as the electric kettle squealed. "But Batman's okay for a nonmutant. He's no Wolverine, though."

"You always wanted to be Iceman, didn't you, Doog?"

He grinned again. "You remember, Audrey?"

She nodded. His smile was infectious. "I do. Who was it you were always trying to get me to play?"

"Rogue." He nodded. "You'd make a really good Rogue. Though she doesn't have eyes like yours. She can hit hard, though." A few moments later, he carried a tray to the table with three cups of tea, milk, sugar, and a plate of store-bought pound cake on it. Funny, Audrey thought, how even he had it ingrained in him to feed guests. It was just what you did in small towns.

He moved the ashtray and comic book to the sideboard before sitting down and handing each of them a cup, a napkin, and a piece of cake. Audrey thanked him and reached for the milk. "Can we talk about the spring Maggie got pregnant, Doog?"

He'd been staring at Mackenzie, and Audrey actually had to touch his arm to get his attention.

"That was the spring you and her killed Clint."

She nodded. Okay, if one more person talked like it was nothing after the entire town made her feel like a pariah, she was going to pitch a fit. "It was."

He reached over and took her hand in his. He was strong for someone so thin. "Clint was not a good man, Audrey. He deserved to die. You did the right thing. Maggie loved you for it. She told me before she died. We was at Gracie's having a beer. She said, 'Doog, Audrey saved me and she doesn't know how much I love her.' You were her best friend."

He was smiling like it was a wonderful thing. Like it was something Audrey should already know. But Duger didn't know the subtext. Maggie had loved her as more than a friend, and she'd ruined whatever friendship they'd once had. Maggie's love was a bitter, sour thing. And part of her missed it.

"Thanks, Doog." She forced a smile as he took a bite of cake. "I didn't know the two of you were such good friends."

His smile faded. Golden crumbs stuck to his lips. "We

weren't always. I called her a horrible name once. That was why you beat me up. You remember, don't you, Audrey?"

She nodded. "I do." She wasn't going to insult either one of them by apologizing for it.

"I felt so bad about upsetting her that I made Ma drive me down to see her so I could apologize. She hugged me. First girl to ever hug me. She said, 'It's okay, Doog.' After that we were friends." He snapped his fingers. "Just like that. You were Maggie's best friend, but she was mine."

Audrey swallowed, but her throat was too tight. "Did Maggie tell you who the father of her baby was?"

Duger glanced at Mackenzie, who was watching him like a child watching a dog she wanted to pet but was afraid to. "No. She said she loved him, though. And he loved her, but if her father ever found out he'd kill them both." He shook his head. "Clint was so mean."

*Mean* was too gentle a word to be wasted on Clint. "Mackenzie wants to find her father. Do you have any idea who he could have been?"

He shrugged, a little smile tugging at his lips. "I wanted it to be me, but Maggie said it didn't work like that. She said you had to sleep together to have a baby. Later, I figured out she meant sex." He chuckled. "'Cause once we fell asleep together and I was afraid that I'd gotten her pregnant too and she just hugged me and explained how it really worked. We laughed."

Audrey smiled at him as he shook his head like it was all a joke. Inside, she wasn't smiling. How could Jeannie have kept him so ignorant?

Duger's mirth faded. "Maggie slept with lots of boys. Men too. Sometimes they didn't sleep long. People never believed me when I told them Maggie and I slept together. I guess they didn't know I didn't mean it *that* way."

Mac lifted her cup of tea to her mouth, but not before Audrey saw her expression. The poor thing was pale. Maybe this wasn't such a good idea. If she wanted to keep going, maybe Audrey would continue these chats alone.

"If I showed you a photo, could you tell me if Maggie slept with any of the boys in it?"

"Maybe."

She took the photograph from her purse and handed it to him. He took it, leaving a greasy thumbprint. A big smile creased his face. "I remember this! We had so much fun. Maggie and Barbie sometimes slept together. They would cuddle and whisper and giggle. Maggie and Dwayne would go off into the bushes. Sometimes she and Mike would hide under blankets, if Mike was there. She and Aaron liked to go for walks sometimes when Barbie and Dwayne went off. Greg and I would play cards. He always drove us all home if we didn't fall asleep at Aaron's camp. Sometimes we all just stayed the night. Sometimes Maggie slept alone, and sometimes she slept with someone. My favorite nights were the ones when she slept with me. We'd make up stories."

Greg hadn't mentioned any of this, but then, she hadn't really talked to him about it. He had probably been drunk, unlike Duger, who never really drank all that much. It made sense that

Doog would remember events more clearly—or differently. Still, Audrey made a mental note to ask her brother-in-law about it the next time she saw him.

"So, basically," Mac said, "Maggie slept with everybody."

Duger looked up at her and grinned. "Yeah. She did."

The girl sighed, and Audrey's heart went out to her. "Doog, would you give us a DNA sample to compare to Mackenzie's just so we can make sure you're not her father?"

His eyes lit up. "You mean like on *Criminal Minds*?"

If only this were a TV show and she could have everything wrapped up in less than an hour. "Just like."

"Sure! Though it's gonna come back negative, Audrey."

She believed him but gave him a swab for the inside of his cheek anyway.

"Was there anyone Maggie seemed to like more than anyone else? Someone she spent most of her time with?" she asked, putting the plastic tube containing the swab in her purse.

"Oh, yeah," he said, nodding. "That would be Mike. No one could make her smile like Mike. Everyone liked him."

A nice guy whom everyone liked. Maggie would have been both suspicious and drawn to anyone who was kind to her. Maybe Mike and she had started off as friends. Maybe they even dated, though he would have been at least seventeen or eighteen. It wasn't uncommon for that large an age gap in rural towns, as much as Audrey didn't get it. Maybe he hadn't known she was pregnant.

Or maybe Maggie's father had found out about them and

killed Mike LeBlanc for daring to touch what Clint Jones thought of as his.

“I want to see where she died.”

The request was sprung upon Audrey just as she helped Mackenzie put her suitcase in her car. She was going to return home for a few days to keep up on her university work, but since there weren’t any reservations, Jake allowed that he’d keep the cottage as it was—for free—until she returned, so she didn’t have to lug her leftover groceries and Maggie’s belongings back and forth.

“Okay. We’re not far. Follow me.” She wasn’t sure what the girl hoped to find, but there wasn’t anything left on the beach of Maggie’s murder. The tide had a lovely way of resetting everything, taking all the sins of the town away.

Audrey led the way in her car. They had to leave the resort and then take a right on the beach access road. They parked near the gate and walked onto the rocky beach.

Mac burrowed deep in her coat. It was a cold, windy day, gray and angry. Waves crashed toward the shore, frothing white and spitting icy spray. Audrey knew she ought to button up, but there was something about the wind that made her want to feel it down to her bones. It pulled at her hair, stung her cheeks, but she lifted her face to it regardless of its cruelty. She’d missed it.

Eventually the cold won, and she buttoned the top button on her coat and crammed her hands in her pockets.

"Just over here," she told Mac, nodding her head toward the beach wood that marked the area. Even if the old tree wasn't there, she'd know where to go. She'd never forget.

Gravel and sand crunched beneath their boots as they walked. Neither of them spoke. In the distance, battered by fierce waves farther out in the bay, was the little island known as Minerva's Folly. It had been in Jake's family for generations—they had camped there once as kids, in the remains of Minerva's old house, where she and her lover had supposedly been murdered by her jealous husband.

How much blood had the tide tasted over the years since Edgeport's founding?

"Here," she said, coming to a stop.

Mackenzie stood beside, her gaze fixed on the ground. "I'm not sure what I expected to find. Maybe one of those crosses like people put along the highway where there's been an accident."

"It wouldn't last long," Audrey told her. "The tide comes in past this point sometimes."

The girl nodded. "Who found her?"

"Some guests at the resort spotted her and called the office. Jake sat with her until the police showed up." She thought maybe that might be important for Mac to hear.

"She must have been pretty terrible for someone to kill her and just leave her here."

Audrey turned her entire body toward her, taking the full force of the wind to her back. Her impulse to defend Maggie bordered on irrational. She ignored it in favor of a more "professional" response. "She was a lot of things. In the end, she tried to do what was right. Unfortunately, the person who killed her wasn't in a rational state of mind."

"She seemed to inspire violence in a lot of people—either toward herself or someone else."

"Being one of those people, I can't argue that."

Mac's eyes widened. "Oh my God. I'm sorry. That was so mean of me."

Audrey smiled. "I didn't take offense. It's true. Maggie did have a way of bringing out strong emotions in people."

"I came here wanting to find out about her—wanting to find something we have in common, or something I got from her. I'm not sure I want to find it now, and I don't know what any of the stuff I have found out about her means for me. I don't like knowing half of me came from a woman so broken."

Audrey wasn't always good with displays of emotion, but when Mac started to cry, she didn't hesitate to put her arms around her and pull her close. Part of her felt responsible for the kid's distress.

She glanced up, over the girl's head, and saw her answer through the swaying pine boughs.

"Come with me," she said, and took Mac's hand, pulling her back up toward the road, but instead of going to their cars, she took an old path up the squat bank.

"What's this?"

"We called it the camp," Audrey replied. "Jake's family owns it. We used to hang out here as kids."

"Not back the Ridge."

"No." She walked to the rickety front steps and found the hidey-hole for the key. "Come inside. I think you need to see this."

There wasn't electricity, and it was getting dark already, the days progressively shrinking, but Audrey used the flashlight on her phone to illuminate the interior of the building. It wasn't much—an uneven floor, some old furniture, and a lopsided table—but that wasn't what she wanted Mac to see.

"Here."

The girl came to stand beside her, facing the wall near the old stove. Hundreds of Polaroids and old photos covered the rough wood and exposed beams.

"We used to take pictures every time we were here." The old camera was still there, collecting dust on the counter.

Audrey shone her phone on a photo. "That's me and your mother." It was a photo of them with their arms around each other—taken the summer after Audrey's release from Stillwater, when she had tried to be Maggie's friend again. "And here we are with Jake and some of his friends. Oh, and this one was taken after some fireworks..." She went on, highlighting every good memory she could find—there were more than she'd expected.

"What's that?" Mac pointed to a spot on the wall. "'M & A 4ever.' Is that you?"

Audrey didn't need to look, but she did anyway. "Yeah." Her throat was uncomfortably tight. "That's us."

"I'm sorry that after all the two of you went through, your friendship didn't last."

"I used to feel that way too, but the fact that I'm standing here with you tells me Maggie and I never actually ended. Part of me still loves her."

Those big Maggie-eyes widened, filling with moisture. "Really?" Poor kid was a regular rain spout.

"Really." She reached up and pulled the tack out of the photo of herself and Maggie with their arms around each other. She stuck the pin back into the wall and handed the photo to Mac. "Here. I want you to have it."

The girl stared at the white-framed photo. "I think I look like her in this one."

"You do. Keep it as a reminder of all the good that was in Maggie. That's where you came from."

Audrey was not prepared for the hug that engulfed her, sending her staggering backward. Laughing, she wrapped her arms around Mac's shoulders and squeezed. It was then that she realized Mac was crying in earnest. She sighed. The poor thing. There was nothing else she could do but what she'd done nineteen years ago when seized in a similar way—just stand there, hold her, and let her cry it out.

Like mother, like daughter.

Sunday was family dinner night at the Harte household. Jake made his grandmother's brownies—a favorite of Anne's—and Audrey fried up some chicken. Not the healthiest of choices, but she'd gotten a run in after dropping Mac off, and healthy was overrated. Alisha, of course, had come with them, because she seemed to genuinely adore every member of Audrey's family. She'd smiled her way into John's heart, that was for certain.

"She seems to be doing well," Jess commented to Audrey as Alisha played with Isabelle.

"She is. More since her mother told her she could see me again." Audrey shook her head. "I have to wonder how much of her depression was an act to manipulate her mother."

Her sister shrugged. "It worked, and everyone's happier for it."

"I'll remind you that you said that when Isabelle does it to you."

"Yeah, don't." They shared a smile.

"How are you feeling?" Audrey asked, keeping her voice low.

Jess gave her a warning stare. "I'm good." And that was the end of the conversation. For once, Audrey knew not to push it, regardless of how nosy she was.

When her sister left her to see to the casserole she'd brought, Audrey sought out Greg. She found him standing in the doorway to the living room, nursing a beer as he watched Olivia use Jake as a climbing gym.

"He's good with her," he remarked when she came to stand beside him.

"She's nuts and he loves it."

Her brother-in-law smiled at her. "Must run in the family."

She chuckled, and then waited a breath. "I need to ask you about something."

He must have heard something in her voice, because he turned his entire body toward her, a concerned expression on his face. "What's up?"

"I spoke to Duger today. I don't know how faithful his memory is, but he said you and Maggie were friendly the spring Mike LeBlanc died." That was so much nicer than referring to it as the spring she killed Clint.

Greg blinked. "Yeah. We all hung out."

"Why didn't you mention it before?"

He looked confused. "Because it's not like she and I were friends or anything. She'd come back to the camp and hang out with Barbie."

"That was it?" Her dubious tone made him frown, but what did he expect? He hadn't told her that he knew Maggie back then. It would have been one of the first things Audrey brought up in the same situation.

"Jesus, Audrey, she was what, fourteen? I was eighteen. That's statutory rape." He looked disgusted by the idea.

"Actually, it's gross sexual assault," she corrected. "Maggie was thirteen." She'd looked it up just to be certain. There was no statute of limitation on it either. When—if—they found Mac's father, charges might be brought against him. She liked the idea of thinking at least one person might have to pay for what they'd done to Maggie.

"That's even worse." He gave her a sharp look. "Do you really think I'd do something like that?"

Did she? No. Or rather, she didn't *want* to think it. Truth be told she could imagine anyone doing just about anything if she put her mind to it. "It surprised me when Duger made it sound like you were all really close. I had to ask."

"No, you really didn't. I didn't mention it, because it was

nothing." Starting to walk away, he hesitated, then turned back to her, his expression a mix of hurt and anger. "You want to know someone who was really close to Maggie? Talk to Aaron Patrick."

"Greg..." He walked away from her and went to sit on the sofa to watch Jake and Olivia play. Audrey didn't miss the questioning glance Jake sent her. She smiled at him before turning away. *That went well.*

"What was that about?" her father asked, startling her.

"What was what about?" she asked in turn, hedging.

Exasperation slackened his features. "Seriously? You're going to play it like that?"

She shook her head. "It was nothing. A misunderstanding." Hopefully Greg wouldn't hold it against her for long.

"Right." He tilted his head. "Be careful, kiddo. You just got your sister back. You want to lose her again?"

No, no, she did not.

"Should I just tell Mackenzie to give up?" She'd never forgive herself if she gave up now. And she didn't need to add any more regrets to the list that had Maggie's name at the top of it.

Her father's expression softened. "No. You shouldn't do that." He set his hand on her shoulder. "You should do whatever you feel is right. Just... be subtle."

"I'm trying, Dad, but I'm not very good at it."

"Dinner's ready," Jess called from the kitchen.

Everyone converged on the dining room. Audrey made sure she got close enough to Greg to whisper, "I'm sorry."

He looked surprised, but he nodded. He even smiled a little, for which Audrey was grateful, because as she sat down at the table, she took a good look at her big sister and realized just how much she loved her. Maggie might have been the sister she chose years ago—putting her above everyone else—but Jess was her blood. Jess understood her in ways no one else could, maybe not even Jake. Audrey would do anything for her sister, and she knew that Jess would do anything for her. You protected the ones you love.

She wasn't prepared to lose her sister. Not again.

# CHAPTER TEN

The road that Jake took to access the section of the river where Mike LeBlanc's body had been found ran immediately alongside Wendell Stokes's property line. As a kid, Audrey had thought Wendell Stokes had good taste in decorating—his house had been black with white trim. Now she knew the black was really just tar paper, and that white trim had been turned yellow by the elements. Weeds had overtaken what at one time had been a pretty flower bed. Now the small blooms looked out of place among the crawlers and vines. The lawn—also overgrown—was patchy; thick clumps of dead grass were dotted with areas of blueberry scrub and bare dirt.

Behind the house was an automobile graveyard. An old pickup from the forties, which had been there for as long as Audrey could remember, was more rust than anything else. With its hood pulled up and bent at a strange angle, Audrey could see a bird's nest sitting on top of the useless engine. Beside that sat a convertible, its cherry paint faded to dull pink. On top of the convertible someone had tossed an old Norton motorcycle.

"Is that the one Wendell used to ride?" she asked.

Jake nodded and turned the wheel to the left, steering them closer to the bank on the rutted dirt path. "Linc tried to buy it off him a couple of years ago. He won't sell it."

"But he'll let it sit there and rust?"

"Yup."

Audrey shrugged. "Makes perfect sense." If he couldn't ride it no one else was going to either.

He put the truck in park and they climbed out. A short distance away—still on Wendell's property—two black mutts, obviously part mastiff, sat on a barren patch of earth near two large doghouses. Thick collars attached to heavy chain circled their necks. They didn't bark, but they didn't wag their tails either. They just sat there and watched. Waited.

"That's not creepy at all," Audrey remarked.

Jake chuckled. "They're nice boys." He pulled a Ziploc bag out of his coat—inside were two good-sized steaks.

"Are you about to buy the friendship of two dogs?" she asked with a hint of a smile.

"No. I'm about to continue a friendship with two dogs who deserve better than a chain and not having their shit cleaned up."

She loved him a little more at that moment. He always had more compassion for animals than for people. She supposed it had something to do wanting to protect those who couldn't always fight back, because he often appointed himself the protector of local children as well. That's how they had met—when she cried over a lost ice cream and he got her another. She'd been four or so at the time.

He took the steaks to the dogs, both of whom lowered to their bellies as he approached, tails wagging, ears back. Jake crouched down, petting them both on their wide heads before giving them the treat he'd brought.

Audrey glanced toward the house. There was an open door stuck in the side of it with nothing but a drop beneath, the steps having been long since torn away. Standing in that doorway, behind the screen, was Wendell Stokes—the man, the myth, the legend.

She remembered Wendell as a tall man, but he seemed stooped now—maybe five-ten in his boots. He was beyond lean, reminding her of Iggy Pop with his whipcord frame of taut skin over muscle and bone, but with a face more haggard than old Iggy could ever aspire to.

She lifted her hand in a wave. He nodded, his expression wary, before closing the door again.

"He used to be friendlier," she commented, turning back to Jake, who had finished with the dogs and was standing again.

"He got sober. Come on, I'll show you the spot."

"How do you know where they found him?" she asked, following after him as he set down a narrow little track in the tall, dead grass.

"You'll see."

She didn't much care for being left in suspense. Her inherent curiosity bristled at it. She didn't want to be caught off guard. Wanted to know what she was getting into.

The river wasn't much of a river anymore. When they were young they used to swim in it, but it had shrunk considerably.

Now it was more like a raging brook, the clear, icy water racing over the rocks like it was trying desperately to escape to the ocean. A lot of people felt that way about Edgeport, herself included, at one time. Sometimes she still thought about running.

They walked along the rocks and smooth gravel for a few hundred feet before coming to a stop. Here there was a deeper pool and the cliff above it was at its highest point. Audrey had to crane her neck to look up. It was a good drop from the top. Her gaze followed the line all the way down, and then she stopped.

"See it?" Jake asked.

She did. It was small, almost hidden behind a couple of rocks, but she saw it. A small, weathered cross. It might have been white at one time, but the paint had long disappeared, making it blend into the landscape around it.

"Who put it there?" she asked. Whoever was responsible for it had probably known Mike, or could at least tell her something about him.

Jake shrugged, hands tucked in the pockets of his coat. "No idea. It just showed up one day that spring."

"Why didn't you mention this before?"

"Didn't think it was important. It's kind of like those crosses on the highway, you know?" He actually shuddered. "Things creep me out."

A crunch above their heads made both of them look up. High above, on the edge of the cliff, stood Bertie. He was dressed in a hunter-orange jacket and cap and had a rifle under his arm.

"What are you two doing down there?" he called, frowning.

"What are you doing up there?" Jake shot back. "You're on my land, Neeley."

Bertie glanced behind him, as though there should be a sign. "Forgot."

Audrey's eyes narrowed. He hadn't forgotten. Everyone in this town knew exactly where everyone else's property lines were. If they pretended they didn't it was because they were trespassing on purpose.

"This is a hiking path. I don't want anyone getting shot on it," Jake continued.

Bertie looked affronted. "I ain't going to shoot a hiker."

"Bertie, you found Mike LeBlanc's body, right?" Audrey asked, her voice echoing slightly in the stillness.

The older man shifted. "Ah-yuh."

"Do you know who put up this cross?"

He looked her dead in the eye with a gaze that she had no doubt would have smote her dead if he'd had the power. "I did." And then he turned back into the woods and disappeared.

Since Bertie apparently had nothing more to say about Mike LeBlanc, Audrey decided to take a drive over to Eastrock and see if Aaron Patrick would talk to her. She should have called first, but surprising Aaron would get the most genuine reaction out of him. Class was just about to let out when she pulled into the parking lot.

Eastrock High looked as original as its name. Red brick with white trim, it looked vaguely factory- or penitentiary-like, as buildings erected in the early seventies often did. Before she even started school they'd shut parts of the place down in the eighties to remove asbestos. Should have just bulldozed the place to the ground. However, the bales of hay and the scarecrow on the front lawn did look cute. The scarecrow looked like it might have had the crap knocked out of it a few times by vandals, but it still managed to look festive and seasonal. The Scarecrows was also the name of the school football team.

She climbed out of the car with a slight tingle of anxiety running down her spine. The brief time she'd spent inside those walls hadn't been completely terrible. She'd learned a lot and studied hard, but she'd also gone to school with a lot of assholes. Maggie had often been one of them. Jake had been one of her few friends. Weird, but even though Maggie had taken the blame for dealing Clint the killing blow, most people found it easier to forgive her than they did Audrey. Or maybe Maggie had just had more charisma. Charm had never been Audrey's strong suit. Maggie had been more of a frenemy by their senior year, with the result that Audrey had dreaded going to school because of her. She bounced back and forth between trying to keep Audrey all to herself and making her life hell. It wasn't until she started studying psychology that Audrey realized Maggie had been trying to hold on to her—control her. And the more Audrey fought, the harder Maggie did as well. Only Maggie got mean. It was an abusive relationship to be sure. One bred from insecurity and a twisted kind of unreciprocated love.

Audrey pulled her coat closed as they crossed the front parking lot to the front doors. The kids spilling out of the place, filing toward the buses waiting to take them home, paid little or no attention to her. Occasionally a lack of notoriety irked her, but not that day. She just wanted to talk to Aaron and get out of there. It would be bad enough that the teachers and staff would be old enough to recognize and remember her. She really couldn't take one more person casually mentioning her bashing Clint's head in. She almost liked it better when people looked at her like they thought she might kill them. This talking like they'd been in on it—that they'd supported it, when they all treated her like a monster—was fraying her nerves.

It was almost like stepping into a time warp. She half-expected to see kids she knew walk by on their way to the gym. Fresh paint, a little updating. The principal's office was still on the bottom floor, almost tucked beneath the stairwell. Audrey had to straighten her shoulders before walking through the door.

The woman at the desk wore a sweater with a Peter Pan collar and had her red hair up in a chignon. She lifted her head when Audrey walked in.

"Audrey Harte! How are you?"

Heather Pelletier. A distant cousin and classmate. Audrey forced a smile. "Hey, Heather. I didn't know you worked here."

"Just started. What brings you by?"

"I'd like to see Aaron Patrick if he's here."

"I think he is. Let me ring him." She picked up the receiver of the desk phone and punched a button on the front. It looked like the same system they had fifteen years ago. "Hi, Aaron? You have a visitor. Do you want to come down or should I send her up?"

She hadn't been asked to sign in. Hadn't been asked what her business was. Heather didn't even tell Aaron who was there to see him. She could be there to shoot the place up for all the other woman knew. God, small towns were terrifying. How could anyone ever think they were a safe place to raise their kids?

"Go on up," the redhead said with a broad smile. She rocked that red lipstick that would make Audrey look like a clown. "He's in 207."

"Thanks. Good to see you, Heather."

"You too, Audrey. We should get together sometime."

"Yeah, sure." But they both knew they wouldn't. And they were both okay with that. Audrey left the office and jogged up the two flights of stairs. Room 207 was halfway down the hall, on the right-hand side. Still the science lab. Audrey knocked before opening the door.

Another wave of déjà vu as she crossed the threshold. The floor tile had been changed, and the walls were white instead of dull yellow. All of the lab units were clean, with stools on top of them so the janitor didn't have to sweep around them. She'd sat two rows back near the windows. She could still smell the formaldehyde. An uncomfortable pinch seized her right beneath her heart. Anxiety. Of all the things she'd been through in the past few months, her *high school* was going to be what sent her into a panic attack?

She drew and exhaled a slow breath. No. She was going to be fine.

The classroom was empty except for the man at the desk. Dark hair like Mac's. He looked up when she walked in. Green eyes. Not bad-looking. He smiled at her as he stood. "Audrey

Harte?" He came toward her with his hand outstretched. He was tall. Lean. He could be Mac's father. "You're the last person I expected to see. To what do I owe the pleasure?"

She accepted the handshake, and the outdated greeting. "Good afternoon, Aaron. I hope you don't mind the intrusion. I'd like to ask you a few questions about Maggie Jones."

His easy smile faltered a little. "There's a name I haven't heard in a long time. She died earlier this year, didn't she?"

Audrey nodded. She didn't bother correcting him that Maggie had been killed. "She used to hang out back at your camp with you guys, didn't she?"

"Yeah," he said, with a nod. "How come you and that pretty older sister of yours never came back?"

Because Jessica had been too straitlaced and Rusty would have had a hemorrhage if Audrey had gone to a party at that age. She gave Aaron a smile. "You never invited us."

"Oh, it was an open invite. I couldn't believe it when Greg got together with Jess. Wow, she was one of the prettiest girls in school, you know. All the guys wanted to get with her."

Her sister? Really? "I didn't know that."

"Both of you look so much alike." He gestured to one of the desks. "Do you want to sit?"

She supposed that was a compliment. Audrey slid into one of the desks as Aaron leaned against the corner of his. "I have to warn you, I drank and smoked a lot back then. I don't remember much about some of those parties, or anyone who went to them. What do you want to know?"

She was willing to bet he remembered plenty. "Maggie had a

baby after our trial. She got pregnant that winter that she partied at your camp."

He blinked. "What?"

He was honestly surprised. There was no faking that shock. But was he shocked because he'd known Maggie, or because he was wondering if the kid was his?

"Her daughter found me a few days ago and asked me to help her find her birth father. Maggie didn't list him on the birth certificate."

Suddenly the pleasant expression slid from his face. "Why would you think I'd know anything about it?"

Well, that was a surprise. He sounded defensive. She didn't think she'd made any kind of insinuation. No one wanted to be accused of pedophilia. And very few men wanted to be saddled with the responsibility of a kid—even if they were already a father.

"Maggie told me there was someone she spent a lot of time with. A guy. I'm assuming he was Mac's father, but she never told me his name. We've been going through some of her things, but we decided talking to people who were there might be our best bet. Do you remember Maggie ever spending time with one guy in particular?"

"Oh." His shoulders relaxed marginally, but he still wore a wary expression. "I didn't spend a lot of time with her."

Audrey wasn't a body language expert, but that sure looked like a lie. "There must have been someone she gravitated toward more than others."

He thought about it. "She hung around with Mike a lot."

"Mike LeBlanc?"

"Yeah." Aaron's face brightened. "They hung around a lot. I asked him if there was something going on with them and he just laughed like it was a big joke."

"Did he." Not a question. Was it just a coincidence that Mike was the one out of that little group who wasn't around to defend himself?

"Yeah. They'd go off together sometimes. Said they were smoking, but I always thought there was something else going on."

"She was thirteen," Audrey reminded him. "Never occurred to you to tell the eighteen-year-old to keep his hands to himself?"

He looked surprised that she asked. Horrified, even. "No. She was older than that. Wasn't she?" His face was white. "Christ."

Now he looked like a man with something to hide. A man who was just realizing what he'd done. At that moment, Aaron Patrick became her number two potential for Mac's father. "Did Mike hang around with anyone else?"

Aaron shrugged. The motion pulled his shirt close to his body, drawing attention to his midsection. Beer belly? Or did his wife feed him well? "That old Neeley guy was around a lot."

Bertie. Did he know about Mike and Maggie? Audrey thought of the white cross by the river, where Mike had died. Bertie certainly seemed to have some guilt where Mike was concerned. "No one else?"

Aaron shook his head. He actually looked sorry. "It was a long time ago. I spent a lot of time trying to hook up with Barbie Stokes, you know? I didn't pay a lot of attention to what other people were doing. Or who." He chuckled at his own joke, but his cheeks were still pale and his gaze was troubled.

"Who was Greg interested in?" she heard herself ask. She could kick herself. She didn't know if he and Greg talked much anymore. And what if Aaron told her brother-in-law she'd asked?

"Oh, Greg never really seemed to be interested in any one person. There were a couple of girls he'd hook up with on occasion, but nothing regular. One of them was Julie Pelletier."

Audrey's cousin. At least Julie would have been of legal age. "Do you know Mike's family?" she asked. "Someone who might be willing to give us a DNA sample?"

He blinked. "DNA?"

"Yes. It's the only way to prove if he was or wasn't Mackenzie's father."

"Mike LeBlanc's mother, Carol, lives down by the Methodist church. Little blue house. Now, if you will excuse me, I don't mean to be rude, but I don't remember any of Maggie's guys, and I have papers to mark."

She was tempted to push it. Tempted to ask Aaron for his own DNA, but she knew she wouldn't get it. And since she might want to talk to him again, Audrey decided to drop it for now. If he shot them down completely she might never get a chance to get close enough to investigate him further.

Investigate. Like she was some kind of private detective. God. Solving two murders didn't make her Jessica Fletcher, though the old girl did know how to rock a tracksuit.

"Thanks for your time, Aaron," she said, standing. She offered him his hand. "I appreciate you meeting with me."

Aaron looked confused. It took him a moment to put his hand around hers. He looked as though he'd rather bite down on an electric fence than touch her, but he did. "Of course. I hope you find the young girl's father."

She smiled at him. "I'm sure I will. Thanks."

She left him standing there, by his desk. She could feel his gaze on her as she left the classroom. With the ghosts of the place closing in around her, Audrey quickened her pace until she practically ran down the stairs to the foyer and outside. She called Neve on her way to the car—to see if her friend might be able to expedite any DNA samples she collected. She told her about her meeting with Aaron, and that she was going to see Carol LeBlanc.

"Is it wrong that I'm hoping it's the dead guy?" Neve asked.

Audrey chuckled dryly. "Nope. I'm rooting for him too. Listen, I gotta go. Talking on your cell phone while driving is against the law."

"Ha. Aaron Patrick is one of Bailey's favorite teachers. I'm really hoping it's not him."

"Yeah," she replied, then added just before disconnecting, "I think he's really hoping it's not him too."

*Nineteen years ago*

"You look happy," Maggie said when Mike sat down on the sofa beside her. They were at Aaron's camp. There was a party going on—the place was full—but it was all teenagers, so she felt reasonably safe. Boys were easier to manipulate than grown men. "I am happy," he confided, giving her a coy glance out of the corner of his eye. "I think I have a boyfriend."

"What?" she squealed.

"Ssshh!" He glanced around to make sure no one was paying attention to them. "Keep it down! You think I want any of these Neanderthals to know I'm gay?"

Right. She should have known better. There were guys in that camp who would drag him out back and beat him stupid because they thought gay might be contagious. She scooted closer on the couch. "Who is it?"

He shook his head, grinning like an idiot. "Not telling. You don't know him."

He was lying. Jealousy shot through Maggie. Mike was her friend. A good friend, so who was this guy he wanted to keep secret? Secret from her? "Yeah, well, I have someone too." Two could play that game. She hadn't planned to tell anyone her secret—it was something special just for her—but she'd use it if she had to.

His expression turned to disbelief. "Who?"

She smirked. "Not telling."

"He's not here, is he?" He looked around the room.

"So what if he is?" Her smirk grew. "You want to confront him? Make sure he's treating me right?"

"I want to kick his ass. He's old enough to know better."

"Seriously?" That was a disappointment, and not the answer she wanted. "The fag's going to get all moral on me? Like I'd date anyone under seventeen." Save that for Audrey. Maggie couldn't be bothered with *little* boys.

He looked like she'd slapped him. "What did you call me?"

Maggie sat up, suddenly cold inside. Shit, she'd gone too far. She always went too far. "Mike, it was a joke."

"Yeah, right." He nodded. His cheeks were flushed a dull red as he stood up. "This is a joke too—you mean fucking slut." He walked away then, leaving her sitting there, feeling like she was going to cry.

"You okay?" came a familiar voice.

Maggie looked up. Tears were filling her eyes. She blinked them away as she shook her head. She couldn't find her voice. Of course that would be the moment when *he* showed up. Now he'd think she was weak. A stupid little girl.

He offered her his hand. "Come on."

Maggie knew what would happen when she let him lead her away, and she was okay with it. At least it was her decision.

She took his hand.

# CHAPTER ELEVEN

Tuesday morning arrived cold and gray. Audrey did not want to get out of bed, but she and Jake were going to look at the property back the Ridge that might suit her new business plan. She'd managed to catch up with Angeline again the night before, and her boss was definitely interested in the project she had in mind. Audrey knew better than to get too excited, but she was. More excited than she'd been about anything in a long time.

She needed to check in on her mother later too. Thank God her brother David would be arriving within the week to stay for a few days leading up to Thanksgiving. He only lived in New York, but his job made it hard for him to get home on short trips.

She also had to drop Duger's DNA sample off at the lab in Machias. There weren't many to choose from in the area, but Neve had a friend at this one who said their DNA workload was light at the moment and that results should only take three to five days to come back. Mackenzie was determined to travel back and forth between Calais and Edgeport for as long as it took, but Audrey was hoping it wouldn't come to that. By now the entire town knew why Mac was there, and no one had stepped forward to claim her, which meant her father either didn't want to be found out (Aaron?), had left town, or was dead (Mike). Regardless, it might never get sorted out.

Maybe she could do that thing they did in crime shows and steal Aaron's discarded coffee cup to get his DNA. She was going to be in the area again later that day, but this time to see Carol LeBlanc. The woman's eagerness to meet with her was almost sad. Audrey had found herself truly hoping Mike was the one, just so Carol could have the grandchild she so obviously wished she'd had.

Audrey dressed warmly in a sweater, jeans, boots, and a wool coat. Jake wore a similar outfit, though he managed to look rugged and casual in his. He needed to shave and he could stand a haircut, but she liked it when he looked rough around the edges. There was something that felt right about the two of them standing on the front porch—Gracie's old porch—with the air smelling of snow and woodsmoke, and a dreamlike quiet over the property. The only sound were the gulls swooping around the tidal inlet below the cliff across the road. It was low tide, and the birds were after a late breakfast. She stood on the wooden planks—they needed paint—and looked around her. The darkness of what had happened to Maggie that winter and spring didn't matter at that moment and for a few seconds she didn't wonder what secrets the townsfolk were trying to keep. She didn't even care who Mac's father was, because the girl was a good kid despite sharing his DNA.

"What?" Jake asked, glancing down at her.

"This," she said, shoving her gloved hands in her coat pockets. "It's pretty damn close to perfect."

"Thinking about running, Aud?"

She shook her head. "Thinking about staying." She only lifted her gaze to his after she said it.

He looked at her for a moment before putting his arm around her shoulders and pulling her close. "Keep thinking about it."

A car speeding back the road caught their attention, and then completely ruined the mood when it slowed and pulled into the drive.

"Oh, fuck," Jake muttered. "What did we do to deserve this?"

"I talked to Duger," she replied dismally as Jeannie Ray got out of her truck and slammed the door. If she wasn't reason to burn the entire town to the ground, Audrey didn't know what was. She was a scarecrow of a woman, skinny to the point of shapelessness. Smoking and bitterness made her look older than her early to mid sixties, but she was as formidable as an old witch could be as she stalked across the gravel toward the house.

"Audrey Harte," she called in her sharp, raspy voice. "You stay the hell away from my son."

"Jeannie Ray," Jake called back. "Get your bony ass off my land."

The woman stopped in her tracks and blinked. She hadn't expected that. "He's a good boy, so you leave him alone."

"Back off, Jeannie." Audrey slipped free of Jake's arm to walk down the steps. "I didn't do anything to Doo... Scott. We talked."

"You took that girl to his house. Now all he can talk about is Maggie's daughter, like she's some kind of damn unicorn."

Audrey tilted her head. "I'm sure he gave you some choice tidbits you were only too happy to share with the Network." The Network was made up of a small group of local women who formed the gossip nucleus of the community. Yancy had been part of it, but stepped back after Audrey and Jake got together. She didn't want to gossip about her brother, and if he was with Audrey, there was going to be gossip. Yancy probably didn't want to hear it either.

Jeannie didn't even have the decency to look guilty. "She never should have had that baby, poor thing. But it's not Scott's."

"She's not an 'it,' and I really don't plan to discuss her with you." She walked past Jeannie toward Jake's truck. He followed.

"Why'd you come back here?" Jeannie called after them. "Just to ruin our lives? That's what you do, girlie. You ruin lives!"

Audrey got into the truck and slammed the door. Jake put the key in the ignition. "You want me to run her over? I don't mind."

She laughed. "No. Then we'd just have to clean up the mess."

He shrugged and put the truck in reverse, leaving Jeannie standing there, giving them the finger. They backed out onto the dirt road, then headed toward the main drag. Jeannie was hot on their heels.

"Think she's going to follow us all the way?" Audrey asked.

Jake glanced in the rearview. "Doubtful. You know she's just afraid of one—or both—of us enough not to push it."

Sometimes, thought Audrey, being a murderer had its perks. But she believed Jeannie's reluctance to fully engage in a fight with her had more to do with whatever secret her mother had over the old crone. Anne still refused to divulge what it was she'd told Jeannie she'd reveal earlier that summer if she didn't leave Audrey alone.

Ridge Road was less than a quarter mile away on the right. It was also unpaved, but not quite as smooth as Tripp's Cove. The truck's tires kicked up gravel as they drove, bouncing occasionally through a pothole. True to Jake's prediction, Jeannie hadn't followed them.

There was an old house on the left that Audrey remembered visiting as a kid. It looked like it had been vacant for years, however. Grass grew high around its foundation, and several windows had busted panes—probably caused by kids throwing rocks. Its siding was dull gray with a hint of yellow, the wood rotting and brittle.

"I used to like that place," she commented.

Jake looked out the window. "I tried to buy it, but the current owner won't sell. Seems a shame to let the poor thing fall apart like that."

"What would you do with it?"

He shrugged. "Fix it up. Rent it. Tear it down and build something new. I'd figure something out."

She shook her head. "I never thought you'd become a real estate mogul."

"No?" There was amusement in his gaze when he glanced at her. "What did you think I'd become?"

"I don't know," she replied, honestly. "I never thought about it. I guess it never mattered to me what you did so long as you were still you."

His smile faded a little. He cleared his throat, and she watched his eyebrows lower. "I love you."

He didn't say it a lot, but it was like opening a window to the most beautiful day every time he did. "I love you too." And she did. There were people who would classify it as obsessive, probably enabling, but she didn't care. There was a peace inside her now that hadn't been there since the day she left Edgeport, and she knew he was the cause of it. If he kicked her out tomorrow she would still love him, and only him, until the day she died. Melodramatic as it was, it was also true.

They drove the rest of the way in silence. Audrey glanced out her window at Wendell Stokes's house as they passed. The other day she hadn't noticed there was a satellite dish attached to one tar-papered side. Priorities. There was an old dish—one of those as wide as a car—on its end behind the house near the river, where it had obviously been tossed.

The river led her to thinking about Mike LeBlanc again. What had happened to him? And why couldn't someone give her a hint as to who Maggie was close to? Yes, Maggie had been a little...*free* with her body, but she was still a kid, and young girls developed crushes on older guys that were hard to miss, even if they thought they were keeping it secret.

She pushed the thoughts away as they drove deeper back the

Ridge. Their destination was a few miles back—maybe five. Not too many people lived back there anymore, but at one time a large portion of Edgeport's population had owned and worked the blueberry and farmland among the rolling hills. Now it was mostly hunting camps and forgotten homesteads.

It had been back that road that Matt Jones had threatened to rape her back in June. Her grandmother Pelletier once said that she thought there was some kind of poison in the Jones blood, and Audrey used to laugh. But there had been something wrong with that entire family—a mental sickness she couldn't name or define.

"Here it is," Jake announced, pulling into a driveway.

"I remember this place," Audrey remarked. "It belonged to my great-grandparents."

"Yeah, it used to be in the Pelletier family." Her mother's people. He put the truck in park and cut the engine. "They sold it to the Hansoms in the fifties, and then their son sold it to me."

"Why would you buy this much land?" she asked. "There has to be a few hundred acres to this place."

"Five hundred and fifty. I bought it for the blueberry land—it borders scrub I already own. If you used this for your facility, the kids could help with processing the berries. I'd pay them, of course. Then some of the proceeds from sales could go back into the property."

"I like that, and it would definitely give the kids structure."

Jake opened the truck door. "There are plenty of opportunities for the place to partially fund itself. Come on."

She climbed out of the truck and followed him up the gravel drive to the main house.

"You've been using that place in Morrill as a model, right?" he asked as they walked.

Audrey nodded. "Sort of. They don't treat violence or major mental illness, while I'd be more open to that, depending on the staff we hire."

"Okay, well, this place has stables, and plenty of room for horses, dogs—whatever animals you want. Plus, the kids could work the land. It wouldn't take much to make this a viable farm again."

She took a look around. "Lots of maple trees too. We could tap them in the spring."

"Yeah. If it's allowable I'd like to start something where some of them could work for me. I'd pay them, of course—make them feel they're earning it rather than it being part of their therapy."

She stared at him. "You've put some thought into this."

He frowned. "Well, yeah. It's for you."

She could have kissed him then, but he kept going. "Think of how many local jobs you'd create—you'd need farm hands, cooks, cleaners. Teachers. You'd have to hire therapists from outside the area, but that's fine."

"And you have rental properties." Sweet God, he really had thought of things. This would benefit him as much as it would her. Excitement unfurled in her stomach. *This might work.* Because she wouldn't be the only one driving it to succeed.

"How many bedrooms in the farmhouse?" she asked, walking around the side of the building.

"Just six, but there's an old bunkhouse that the former owner used as storage space that could easily be used as a dorm, and another building that could be converted as well. They built an in-law suite onto the house that could be used as classrooms or a dining hall and offices. The stables are in good shape and could keep several horses. There's riding trails through the property. We could build anything else you need."

His enthusiasm was contagious. She'd never heard him talk with such animation—at least not since they'd been kids. This was his passion—making something abandoned into something new. No, it was more than that. It was turning Edgeport into something better that he loved. He saw her facility as something that would benefit the town—and them.

"Can we go inside?" she asked.

He pulled the keys from his pocket. "Of course."

Inside the farmhouse and the other buildings was no less impressive. Audrey took dozens of photos of the interiors and exteriors. It was gorgeous against the backdrop of acres of golden grass and leaves of red, gold, and orange. Angeline would have to love it. Audrey didn't know what she'd do if she didn't. Could she raise enough money on her own? She could get a loan, but would it be enough? She didn't have the clout behind her to open such a place.

God, she wanted this. She wanted it so badly she'd sell her story to Hollywood if she thought anyone would want to film it—and pay for it. Wanted it enough that she was going to take some additional classes that would help in running it, that would help in treating the kids who came there. She was going to change her focus to a more clinical one, and actually start treating kids. That was going to take work as well. She didn't care. She'd do the work. She had never been afraid of work, only afraid of failing, which was why she hadn't been afraid to push herself to her limits.

"I know where we could get some horses," Jake said as they toured the old stables. The smell of hay and horse clung to the air. "I read that dogs can play a big part in juvenile therapy. You could rescue some from a shelter. Maybe get some cats and rabbits too. What do you think of chickens? You could sell the eggs you didn't use."

"Maybe some sheep," Audrey added. "Oh my God, Jake, I hope Angeline goes for this."

He turned to her. "She can be an investor, or even a partner, but this is *yours*, Aud. I'll do whatever needs to be done to make sure you get it, if this is what you truly want. Is it?"

She nodded, not trusting her tight throat to let her speak. Tears burned the back of her eyes. She wanted it so very, very much.

"Okay, then." He gave a decisive nod. "You're going to have it."

She reached up and took his face in her gloved hands, pulling him down so she could kiss him. "You're amazing," she whispered.

He grinned. "I know. Ready to go home?"

The heat in his hazel eyes warmed her, chasing the chill from her fingers and toes. As much as she wanted to look around some more, she wanted to get him home and back into bed even more. And then she wanted to send the photos she'd taken to Angeline, and to Reva Kim, who she hoped would be interested in running the place.

She'd spent so many years chasing her dreams away from Edgeport, only to find everything she wanted tucked away in the remote town's little corners. It was crazy.

Somewhere—she had no idea where—Maggie was watching her, and laughing.

Her own facility. It was going to happen.

"Did you send the pictures to Angeline?" Jake asked as he walked into the living room later that same day. He handed her a beer.

"I did." She smiled. They had come home, had sex, and taken a shower. Now she was wearing a pair of his sweatpants and an old T-shirt and he was wearing something similar. It felt gloriously decadent and comfortable. He'd even massaged her wounded arm, and it felt so good. The beer would just be the icing on what was already an excellent day.

"Are you getting together with Mackenzie this week?"

"For a bit, yeah. We're going to see Mike LeBlanc's mother and finish going through Maggie's stuff."

"I thought she had gone through all of it."

"She has, but I haven't. She might have missed something." She snuggled up against him. "Any word on Ratchett?"

"Not yet, but I'm expecting Neve to show up soon." He

turned his head toward the window as they both heard a car pull in. "Speak of the devil."

Audrey's heart gave a nervous thump. What did Neve want? It took all of her willpower not to follow him to the door. She did, however, get up a few moments later and head out to the kitchen.

Neve was there in an official capacity; that was obvious by her posture and demeanor. She had her dark hair pulled back into a smooth bun. She was wearing her gun.

"Hey, Neve," she said. "What's up?"

"Hey, Audrey. I'm here because of Ryan Ratchett." She looked at Jake. "His brother, who goes by the name of Tex, told me Mr. Ratchett came to Edgeport to see you about some money."

Jake arched a brow. "Would have been nice if Ratchett had told me that. I told you I don't know the guy."

It was amazing just how good a liar he was. Most people had tells or tics, but not Jake. He stood there, drinking his beer, one hand in his pocket like they were talking about sports or the weather. Maybe because he managed to engineer some truth in everything he said.

Neve was obviously looking for signs of duplicity as well. "He was shot with a .270 rifle."

"That's a fairly common gun around here." Probably every household up and down the shore had one.

"Do you have any .270 hunting rifles?"

"One."

She nodded, her shoulders coming back like she was bracing for something. "I'll need to take it."

Jake didn't look surprised. "Okay."

"What about Lincoln or Yancy?"

"Would you let Lincoln have a gun?" Neve actually smiled at that. "Yance might, but I doubt it. She was never one for hunting."

"I'll go see her as well. Is she working today?"

Jake nodded.

"Seriously, Neve?" Audrey asked, her heart giving a worried thump. "You can't really think Jake did this. Or Linc and Yancy."

"No," her friend replied. "I don't. If Jake wanted this guy dead I don't think we'd ever find him. But I have an investigation to conduct, so I'm going to do it, and find out who really did kill him so Jake doesn't have to live with the suspicion."

Audrey couldn't argue that. She'd been all set to argue whatever the other woman said, but she ought to have known Neve would realize Jake wasn't the killer. It was too sloppy to have been him.

"Come with me," Jake said. "I'll show you the cabinet." He set his beer on the sideboard and left the room. Neve followed him. Audrey stayed where she was, hoping this all went away soon.

A few moments later, Neve and Jake reappeared. Neve carried a rifle case in her left hand. "I'll get this back to you as soon as I can," she told Jake. "The lab will run some tests."

He shrugged. "I don't hunt, so it doesn't matter."

"Don't hunt?" She looked surprised. Audrey supposed it made him a bit of a rarity. "Don't let Gideon hear you say that. He's made getting a big buck his life's mission."

"Yeah, well, he actually likes to eat it. I don't."

"You're getting soft in your old age," she teased, moving toward the door.

He smiled. "No, I'm not." Audrey also smiled. No, he wasn't soft. He was just, and sometimes capable of great tenderness, but not soft.

Neve turned to Audrey. "I'm sorry for making this awkward. Occupational hazard."

"I get it." And she did. Neve had a job to do—it was like her asking Greg about Maggie. Nothing personal. "Let's plan that trip to see Bailey soon." It would be amazing if she got her facility open in time for Bailey to be sent there. Maybe then she could make up for having the kid locked up in the first place—not that she was to blame, that fell on Maggie's shoulders, but still... She'd like to help the girl if she could.

Neve told her she would and left.

Jake picked up his beer and took a drink. "I'd really like to know who killed that son of a bitch," he remarked. "Just so I could slap them upside the head for the fun of it."

"Maybe it really was an accident," she suggested, hoping for the shooter's sake he didn't find them out.

"Maybe." He took another drink. "Maybe not."

"Let's just be glad he's dead. Whatever he knew obviously died with him if his brother didn't tell Neve everything."

He just nodded, and she knew he wasn't satisfied. Someone

had died on his land, and he wouldn't be satisfied until he made sense of it. Audrey was just glad whoever had killed Ratchett hadn't bashed his head in; otherwise *she'd* be the top suspect.

"You think the brother's going to be trouble?" she asked.

Jake gave her a pointed look. "I know it."

# CHAPTER TWELVE

Carol LeBlanc's house was blue, with an even darker blue star on the front of it and matching shutters. A child's coloring of Pilgrims having dinner with Native Americans was taped to the inside front door. Audrey smiled at the sight of it. Someone didn't care if they stayed inside the lines or not.

"I used to stick real feathers on mine," Mackenzie commented as Audrey rang the bell. She'd driven down from Calais and met her there. "Once I brought it home for Mom to put up. All my turkeys and natives had to have real feathers."

"Obviously you were a true artist," Audrey remarked.

The girl grinned. "Your tone says fun, but your words say OCD."

Laughter crawled up Audrey's throat. "I say everything with love."

"Mmm. Right."

God, she liked this kid. Maggie's kid. Something wouldn't let her forget that. Like it was important that she remember and be wary of an eighteen-year-old girl because part of her came from Maggie. Gracie used to say there had to be some kind of rot in the Jones family tree. Something inherently nasty in their blood. Maggie had never been a nice kid. Never sweet or light. But Audrey had loved her all the same, and part of her still did, even after Maggie made her a murderer. Even after all the terrible things Maggie had done. She supposed that was the benefit of understanding why Maggie had done them. Sometimes she wondered if the reason she'd become a psychologist wasn't to figure herself out, but to figure out Maggie.

The door opened, revealing a tiny woman in her late sixties with graying black hair and wide gray eyes.

"Mrs. LeBlanc?" she asked.

The woman smiled, looking from Audrey to Mac. "Dr. Harte. Miss Bell. Good afternoon. Please come in." She stood back to grant them entry into her little house.

Inside the house was tidy and spotless. The furniture was clean but well used, and the hardwood floors showed signs of having been trampled by kids and pets and a generation of adults. It was a welcoming house. A comfortable one, with the smell of tea and cookies greeting them.

"I hope you like molasses cookies," she said, guiding them into the kitchen.

"I think they'd kick us out of the state if we didn't," Audrey quipped. "You didn't need to go to so much trouble."

"Oh, it was no trouble. Molasses cookies were Mikey's favorite. When you said you wanted to talk to me about him I knew I had to make them."

Audrey glanced at the photographs lining the hall. One of them was a graduation photo. It was Mike, of course, with a big grin on his face. She noticed Mac stopping to study his cute, young face. Looking for herself, maybe?

They sat at the kitchen table, where Mrs. LeBlanc served them tea in mugs most people would say were better suited for coffee but Audrey thought were just the right size. She dumped milk and sugar into her cup and took a cookie when offered. She knew her manners.

Carol smiled at her. "You know, I knew your father, Rusty, back in the day. Your mother too. Oh, those Pelletier girls were always so pretty. You look a lot like her, but how wonderful that you have those striking eyes like your father. There was an old woman around these parts that said Rusty Harte's mismatched eyes let him see things other people couldn't."

"If they did, he didn't pass that part on to me." Audrey dunked her cookie into her tea. "I'm sorry I'm not as familiar with your family. Mike was a little bit older than me. Was he your youngest?"

"Yes. And certainly my sweetest. Such a sensitive little boy. He couldn't stand to see people upset. If you were sad he'd do everything in his power to make you smile or laugh. He was quite funny." She smiled in that wistful way that all people did when bittersweet memories took hold. "Annoyed the tar out of his father with his antics."

"Sounds like my brother," Audrey said, commiserating. "He's the clown of the family."

The older woman directed her attention at Mackenzie. "So, you think my boy might be your daddy, do you?"

Mac turned wide eyes to Audrey. "I... I don't know."

"Mike was hanging out with my friend at the right time," Audrey said to Carol. "Since we haven't found anyone who knows much, we thought maybe Mike was who she was seeing." When she'd initially called the woman, she'd left out how young Maggie had been at the time. There hadn't seemed to be any good reason to tell her.

Carol nodded. "I see. Well, it would be a blessing if you were to be his, my dear. A little piece of my boy come home."

Mac looked as though she might cry. Audrey felt for her. It was obvious the kid wanted to belong to this woman, and why wouldn't she? She was lovely and grandmotherly. Better option than Jeannie Ray.

"Would you consent to a DNA sample, Mrs. LeBlanc?" Audrey asked. "I have a test with me that we can send to the lab."

The woman looked startled. "I don't know if I have any. The family threw away a lot of his things. They thought they were helping me, you see. I wasn't... *well*, afterward. I suppose I had a bit of a breakdown."

What they used to term a "nervous breakdown" could cover a number of symptoms, of which anxiety and depression were only two. Basically it meant the person was unable to function in daily life for a period of time because of being overwhelmed by dysfunctional behavior. The death of a child was a credible reason, in Audrey's opinion. She gave the older woman a sympathetic smile. "I understand. We can compare Mackenzie's DNA to yours." It had been her intention all along. She hadn't thought that the woman might keep her son's hair or nails after his death. Obviously people did that sort of thing, but the idea of it always creeped Audrey out a little. Belongings, yes. Bits of the dead? Not so much.

"Oh, of course. How silly of me. You know I watch all those crime shows, you'd think I'd be a bit more sophisticated." She chuckled at herself, smoothing the tablecloth with hands riddled with arthritis. Her knuckles were permanently bent.

"Will you tell me about Mike?" Mackenzie asked. Audrey wanted to nudge her with her toe under the table—caution her against making her mind up before they had any evidence—but she couldn't do it. Besides, letting Carol talk about her son wasn't going to hurt anyone, except maybe Mac if the test proved he wasn't their guy.

"Oh, he was a love. Such a bright smile! He was terrified he was going to lose his teeth like his grandfather, so he was obsessed with dental care. But he loved music—had quite the collection. And he liked old movies. He and I would watch *Gone with the Wind* every Thanksgiving."

"I like old movies," Mac offered, eagerly. "My mother and I watch *My Fair Lady* together."

"Oh, that's a favorite of mine as well." Carol's eyes sparkled. God, the two of them were already in love with each other. Maybe she shouldn't have brought the kid with her after all. Or maybe she should just let them believe what they wanted and send Mac home thinking her parents were star-crossed lovers and her father died before he could do the right thing by Maggie. There was a certain poetry to it, she supposed.

Wouldn't it be kinder to let it go right there? Let the two of them have each other and forget about what might have happened back the Ridge? But Audrey didn't think she could let go that easily. She needed the truth, even if she didn't share it with Mackenzie. She had to know Maggie's secret, even if she had no idea what she was going to do with it.

"Why did Mike start spending time in Edgeport?" Audrey asked.

His mother looked surprised by the question. "Well, he went to school with kids from there, obviously." Then, to Mac, "Have you ever watched *Giant*?"

"Do you know who he hung out with?" Audrey pressed before Mac could reply.

"No, dear. I don't remember any names. Maybe he told me, but my mind's not what it used to be."

Audrey grabbed another cookie and sat back in her chair. So, his mother didn't really know who he hung out with, and the people who were around that summer claimed not to know him that well. So what the hell was Mike doing in Edgeport if he wasn't partying with good friends?

Maggie was the only explanation she could think of.

"Did any of the kids he hung out with come to the funeral?"

Both women seemed vaguely insulted by the question, but this was important. Wasn't it? Or was she the only one still interested in figuring out what happened that winter/spring?

"Well, yes. There was that nice Andrews boy." That would be Greg. "And Aaron Patrick. Oh, and a little girl with blond hair and big blue eyes. She was younger than Mike, but she felt like an old soul."

*Maggie.* Audrey's heart leapt in her chest, but she kept her expression neutral.

"Oh, and that nice Mr. Neeley was there. He even helped pay for the funeral. Said what a good boy Mikey was." There was that lost little smile again. "I still get cards from him on occasion."

"That's very nice of him." And it was. But the question was, why? Audrey understood that Bertie had found the boy's body, but paying for the funeral? Sending cards? And then there was the cross he'd erected on the riverbank. Why would he do that for a kid he didn't know, or at least hadn't known well?

Now, instead of simply the mystery of Mac's conception, she had the mystery of Mike LeBlanc's death on her hands. The two of them were connected, she was certain of it.

*Let it go,* a voice in her head whispered. *You know what happens when you poke your face in Death's business.*

Death always—*always*—poked back.

"Thanks for doing all of this," Mackenzie said later as Audrey stepped inside the cottage. "I know you're probably busy with work and your mom."

"Not that busy," she replied with a smile. Actually, she was going to check in on her mother later. They had plenty of leftovers from Sunday for their dinner so she didn't have to worry about feeding them—not that her father wasn't capable of putting a meal together. She had a small stack of books for her mother as well. The woman read like a fiend.

When she walked into the cottage, Mac stood in the middle of the kitchen. "I really liked Mrs. LeBlanc."

Audrey nodded. "I know."

"Do you think she's my grandmother?"

"I have no idea. The test will tell us for sure, however." Carol had swabbed the inside of her cheek for them with a smile. "I think she'd like to be."

"You think I'm grasping at the fairy-tale ending, don't you?" Blue eyes locked with hers in a challenging gaze that was all too familiar. "That I'm hoping for the dead kid because I can make him whatever kind of father I want. He won't disappoint me."

Audrey hung her purse on the back of one of the chairs. "Is that what you're doing?"

Mac's cheeks flushed. "I forgot you're a shrink."

She arched a brow at the harsh tone. "Psychologist. Look, Mac, I'm not sure what you want me to say here. I think you're doing what anyone in your position would. I don't think it's wrong to hope for the best scenario, but if you're looking for absolutes, I can't give them—even though I'd like to. It would be fabulous if the results came back and you could give that woman some happiness. It would be awesome if you gained another grandmother. I can't tell you that what you're feeling is wrong. I can tell you that I'm afraid you might be setting yourself up for disappointment. And that's not as a doctor, but as someone who cares about you."

The girl slumped into a chair. "I'm just scared he's going to turn out to be some old guy with no teeth who smells bad."

Audrey shrugged. "If he is, you don't have to know him. He's nothing to you, just a donor."

A flash of defiance in those eyes again. "You think I should just forget it and go home to the nice people who love me."

At that moment, was she a friend, or a therapist? She wasn't billing, so it had to be the former. "I can't tell you to stop because I wouldn't either. I would want to know, even if the news was bad, because the question would drive me nuts for the rest of my life. Can you go home and forget?"

She shook her head, dark hair falling around her shoulders. "No. I think it will drive me nuts too. I signed up on the registry on my eighteenth birthday. I've been wanting to know the truth ever since my parents told me I was adopted."

Only to find out her birth mother had died shortly before she was old enough to look for her. Talk about disappointment. "Then we keep going."

Mac gestured at the bins in the living area. "I've been through everything, but maybe you'll find something I missed. I can't believe she wouldn't have kept something of him if she actually liked him."

"Unless she was trying to protect him." Maggie might very well have kept reminders, only to get rid of them when she got older.

"Do you want tea?"

"God, no. I drank so much at Carol's I think I've got tea leaves in my veins." She grabbed a couple of hardcover books and three photo albums from the top bin and returned to the table.

"She made Mike sound really fun. Did Maggie have any fun in her life?"

"We had fun," Audrey replied. "At least, I thought we did." She remembered making Maggie laugh, the two of them being silly little girls. It hadn't all been a lie.

"Good. I hate the idea of her entire childhood being dark and bleak."

The first photo album was mostly photos of Maggie under age ten. Audrey went through it quickly. The second covered the early teens, so she gave it a more patient perusal. Nothing jumped out at her, except that she could pinpoint when Clint started abusing her. Maggie stopped smiling in photos; she lost some of her light.

Fucking bastard. She'd dig him up and kill him again if she could.

The next album didn't have anything in it either. Audrey slid it across the table and pulled the books closer.

"She was a King fan?" Mackenzie asked.

"Most of us were," Audrey replied. "Aren't you?" Really, he was a Maine treasure, wasn't he?

The girl shrugged. "I don't really like being scared."

She smiled. "Maggie loved it. She and I would stay up late telling each other ghost stories. The more ridiculous the better." She flipped through the pages of the battered hardcover of *Christine*. Nothing—not even a note in the margins. She even opened the dust jacket and checked in there. She put it with the albums before reaching for the second book.

"*Carrie.* This was her favorite. I remember she used to wish she could do things with her mind. She said there was a list of people she'd kill or hurt. I used to think she was just being dramatic." Sadness washed over Audrey as she ran her hand over the torn cover. She opened the book. Inside, on the title page, Maggie had written her name in her loopy script. Almost every page had something marked or underlined. There were notes too, but most pertained solely to the text. Nothing personal.

Maybe Maggie had honestly destroyed everything that gave a glimpse into who she really was.

Audrey was about to shove the book aside when she noticed that the dust jacket was taped to the back inside cover. The front one was loose—no sign of ever having been taped. The other book hadn't been taped at all.

She pushed her finger against the inside flap. There was something under it.

"What is it?" Mackenzie asked, her voice rising. "Did you find something?"

Audrey popped the tape, her heart hammering against her ribs. She reached inside and pulled out something wrapped in a smooth plastic sheet. When she picked it up, it unfurled like a window blind.

Negatives. Honest-to-God, old-school negatives. Negatives Maggie had hidden inside her favorite book.

"What are those?" Mac asked.

Audrey held them up to the light. There were people in the negatives. She couldn't make out features, of course, but the fact that Maggie had kept them secreted away got her anticipation up.

"Photographs," Audrey replied. "There's a place in Eastrock that has a machine to print them. I'll take them over tomorrow."

The girl crowded close, as though the murky images might actually become clear and perfect before her eyes. "Do you think he's in one of them?"

It was impossible to tell. They could be the negatives for photos they'd already seen in one of the albums, but Audrey didn't think so. "I don't know, but if he isn't, I don't know where else to look. I'm convinced it was someone she actually liked, so that leaves Dwayne, maybe." Or poor dead Mike.

Or Aaron.

"If we find him, will you come with me to meet him?"

The girl looked so apprehensive that Audrey reached across the table and took her hand in hers. "Of course I will. I wouldn't let you do that alone."

"Thanks. For everything you've done. You didn't have to do any of it. I'm sorry I was a bitch earlier."

If she thought that was being a bitch, Audrey had a few lessons for her. "I wanted to," she replied, but that wasn't true. Not entirely. She did have to do it. She had to do it for Maggie, and for the baby she'd loved and named Audrey. She had to do it for the friendship they once had and lost.

"There's something else in there," Mac said, staring at the book. "Underneath the flap."

There was. It looked like a photograph. Audrey grabbed the edge and pulled, sliding it out.

*Oh.*

It was a photo of Maggie—young Maggie. She sat in a

hospital bed cradling a small, wrapped bundle in her arms and smiling.

Something grabbed Audrey's chest and squeezed. Wordlessly, she slid the photo across the table to Mac. The girl picked the photo up. Audrey watched a tear fall onto the glossy surface.

"She loved you," Audrey rasped. "You can tell from the smile on her face." And from the fact that Maggie had given her up—tried to give her something better than the terrible legacy of the Jones name.

The girl began to cry harder. Audrey stood up and moved around the table to wrap her arms around her. She didn't say anything. She just hugged her and cried a little with her, but Audrey didn't cry for Mackenzie.

She cried for Maggie.

# CHAPTER THIRTEEN

Fast Time Photo was located in a small shop on Main Street in Eastrock, where it had probably been since opening in the fifties. Audrey was willing to bet the sign above the door was original as well. The door chimed when she opened it.

Inside, the place smelled like old carpet stained with the tang of chemicals. Several locked showcases held elaborate photographic equipment and cameras. A shelf behind the cash actually held boxes of film, and a faded sign proclaimed, WE DO PHOTO RESTORATION!

A man with graying dark hair and bright green eyes came out of the back room and greeted her with a smile. "Hi there. What can I do for you today?"

"Do you still print on-site?"

"I sure do."

Audrey took the negatives from her purse as she crossed the floor toward the counter. "I'd like to get these reprinted."

He picked up the sleeve and held it up to the light, examining each row. "Just one of each?"

"Yes, please."

"Four-by-six?"

She had no idea. "Whatever's standard."

He took a paper envelope from the bin behind him and scribbled on it with a black fine-point marker. "When do you need them?"

"As soon as possible." She'd wait if he could do them now.

He looked up. "The printer's down. I've got a tech coming either today or tomorrow, so it might be a couple of days. Is that all right?"

No. No, it wasn't all right. But she didn't know of any other place that still printed negatives in the area, and she didn't want to send them away. With her luck they'd get lost in the mail. She didn't really have a choice but to be okay with it. Really, what difference did a few more days make? "Sure. Can you call me when they're done? I'll give you my cell."

He wrote that on the envelope. "What's your name, sweetheart?"

Sweetheart? People still said things like that? Yes, in small towns that time forgot they did. He didn't mean any disrespect—that was obvious from the kind glint in his bright eyes. He thought he was being nice.

"Audrey Harte."

His hand paused over the envelope. He looked up and met her gaze with one of surprise. "You're not from Edgeport, are you?"

Oh, hell. Was he now going to mention the fact that she'd killed Clint like everyone else seemed to of late? "Yes, I am."

"Anne and Rusty's daughter?"

"Yeah." She waited for whatever was going to come next.

The man smiled. "I used to date your mother before that ginger stole her away from me. I heard she wasn't feeling too well. How's she doing?"

Sometimes Fate had a lovely way of reminding Audrey that it wasn't all about her, and she appreciated it. She smiled. "She's good, thanks. Recovering from surgery and doing really well. I'll tell her you asked about her, Mr. . . . ?"

"Mason. Rick Mason." His smile grew as he looked at her. "You remind me of your mom."

People rarely told her that. She had her father's mismatched eyes and "charming" disposition. Her mother was a sweet and sunny person, something Audrey could never be accused of being. "Thank you. Most people tell me I resemble my father."

"Well, the eyes, yeah, but you have your mother's smile." He shook his head, as though remembering something. "Okay, I'll have these ready for you as soon as I can and I will call when they are done." He ripped the top off the envelope and gave it to her. "There's your claim number."

Audrey folded it up and slipped it into her wallet so she wouldn't lose it. "Thanks so much, Mr. Mason. I'll be sure to tell Mum I saw you."

"Give her my best, will you? Tell her I've never forgotten lobster pie."

Both of her brows rose at that—especially when he didn't offer any further explanation. "I will."

Her phone rang when she stepped out onto the sidewalk. She didn't recognize the number, but it was local. "Audrey Harte."

"Hello, Dr. Harte. This is Joanne over at LabEx. I have those DNA results for you."

That was fast. "Great."

"A more detailed report has been sent to you, but I wanted to let you know that there is no paternal relationship between the samples you sent."

She hadn't really expected there to be. Maggie never would have slept with Duger—it would have felt like taking advantage of him, and Maggie really only liked guys—and girls—who were a challenge. "Thanks for getting back to me so quickly."

"Well, we had a pretty light load, so I was able to push it through."

Ah, the benefits of rural life. In LA she'd have waited at least several days if not a week or more to get the same results. Audrey told her she'd be sending her another sample that day, thanked her again, and hung up. Then she texted Mac and told her the news, and that it would take a few days for the photos. The girl was working on a paper for one of her college classes, so she didn't immediately reply. She had driven back to Calais that morning to work on it. That she was keeping up with her schoolwork made Audrey admire her even more, considering all the drama Mackenzie had stepped into since first arriving in Edgeport.

Audrey remembered spending every hour she could working while she was at Stanford. Gracie Tripp had paid most of her tuition, and Audrey felt the responsibility of that debt. She wanted to make something of herself and she worked hard to do it. It paid off—it had gotten her a position with Angeline, one of the most respected researchers in the field of juvenile forensic psychology.

At one time, Audrey had been one of the many kids Angeline interviewed at Stillwater. That's where they'd met, and when Audrey showed up at the college where Angeline taught years later, the older woman not only remembered her, but became her mentor. Angeline and Gracie had been the two most influential women in her life, and she wasn't prepared to let either of them down.

She went grocery shopping for her mother, and for herself and Jake after that. Jake got a lot of his produce and such through Gracie's, so there were only a few things she needed to get. Ice cream was at the top of both lists for must-haves. How could her mother eat grape-nut ice cream? It just wasn't right. She got some of the kind with peanut butter cups in it for Jake and one with toffee and chocolate for herself. Then she stopped by the post office and mailed the DNA test from Carol LeBlanc.

When she got home, she took her groceries into the house, including her mother's ice cream. Then she changed into running clothes before she could talk herself out of it and went for a run back the road, making sure she wore the bright orange windbreaker she found behind the door. It would be rare for someone to mistake her for a deer, but there might be someone out there who would love any excuse to end her, and she didn't want to make it easy for them.

She only went a couple of miles. It was cold and she had things to do, so she turned around and headed back. Her breath puffed little moist clouds in the cold air and a warm wetness clung to her spine. As she approached the house, she saw an unfamiliar truck in the drive, and a big bald man on the front porch. The damp on her spine turned to ice at the sight of him. He looked like trouble—tall and broad, a mix of fat and muscle. She knew even without a clear view of his face that he was there because of Ratchett.

Self-preservation told her to keep running, but that felt cowardly. She jogged up to her car instead, hitting the unlock button on her key fob. "Hi, there," she called. "Can I help you?"

The man had turned at the sound of the beep. He was an ugly man. It was obvious he'd lived a hard life, and that his face had been battered more than it had ever been loved. His leather jacket was open, and his bald head was bare. "I'm lookin' for Jake Tripp," he told her. "You his woman?"

His woman? Even if Audrey didn't have an idea who the man was and why he was there, she wouldn't give him any information he might use against her, or Jake. "No, he just lets me park here when I go for a run. Sorry."

He nodded, his gaze raking over her in a way that made her skin crawl. He didn't completely buy her story, and he gave no indication of leaving, so Audrey had little choice but to get into her car and start the engine. She locked the doors and took the gun from the glove compartment before fastening her seat belt. Her fingers trembled as she placed the weapon on the passenger seat. Hopefully she wouldn't have to use it, but she wouldn't hesitate if he came after her. She knew bad when she looked it in the eye, and this guy was no good.

She felt the weight and intensity of his gaze as she put the car in reverse and backed out of the drive. She dug her phone out of her purse as she drove out the road and dialed Gracie's. Jake picked up on the second ring. "Hey," he said.

Audrey glanced in the rearview mirror, relieved when there was nothing but road behind her. "Hey. We've got trouble."

Audrey drove to her parents' house. Her mother's ice cream was in Jake's freezer, but she'd say she simply forgot it. There was no way she was telling either her mother or father about the man on the porch. Her mother would worry, and her father would get in his truck and drive up to Jake's—not a worry she needed. Instead she was just going to enjoy the peace and safety of the house she'd grown up in.

Talking to Jake had made her feel better. He'd told her not to worry, that she'd done the right thing. He was going to give Yancy and Lincoln a heads-up, and see if Lincoln knew the guy. He seemed to think this was Ratchett's brother—the one who had talked to Neve. But she believed Jake when he told her it was going to be okay and tried not to think of all the bad things that could happen.

Her parents had a gorgeous view of the water normally, but today it was gray and lifeless. Gracie always said a calm tide meant rain. It was better than snow, but that was coming soon enough. The tide seemed particularly ominous after her encounter at Jake's, like a portent of things to come—impending doom. The rush of endorphins she'd gotten from her run was gone, leaving her feeling edgy and restless instead. Trouble, like snow, was coming.

Her father was making lunch when she walked in. He looked tired.

"Grilled cheese?" she asked, sniffing the air. She felt a release of tension—and a wave of hunger. "With bacon? Can I have one?"

John shook his shaggy head. Two days ago he needed to shave; now he was starting to look like a Civil War reenactor. "I swear to God you kids only come home to shit and eat."

Audrey arched a brow as she put the groceries on the counter. She fought a smile. "You should be glad we do that, you old curmudgeon."

He scowled. "Curmudgeon? What are you, eighty?"

She lost the battle and grinned at him. "All right, you foul-tempered bastard."

"That's better." He opened the Foreman grill and removed a perfectly toasted grilled cheese with the tongs. He popped it onto a plate and handed it to her. "Take this to your mother. Yours is next."

Her stomach growled as she carried the sandwich into the living room. Her mother was on the sofa, her tablet in hand, glasses perched on her nose. "Where's Jess?"

Anne looked up, a smile curving her lips. "Hey there, Babaloo. She left after your father got home. She had some errands to run. Did you get the ice cream?"

"I did, but I forgot it at Jake's. I'll bring it down later. Whatcha reading?"

"Harry Potter. Have you read them?"

Audrey shook her head. "I've seen the movies."

"I figure Isabelle will be getting into them soon—I want to be able to talk to her about them. It's not bad. Is that for me?"

"Oh, yeah." She gave her the sandwich. "So, I ran into an old friend of yours today."

"Oh?" Her mother took a bite of sandwich and raised her hand to her mouth. "Who?"

"Rick Mason."

Her mother's face lit up. "Really? How did he look?"

"Like an asshole!" her father yelled from the kitchen. "Same as he always looks."

Audrey shook her head in disbelief. "Did he get a bionic ear or something? His hearing never used to be this good."

Anne sighed. "He always hears what doesn't concern him. Thanks for the sandwich, babe!" she called.

Her husband grumbled.

"Were you at Rick's shop?" her mother asked before taking another bite.

"Yeah. I found some negatives in Maggie's things. I'm getting him to print them for me."

"He'll do a good job. He was always into photography. He used to take pictures of me all the time."

"Boudoir shots?" Audrey teased. Her mother just smiled. Yeah, she didn't want to know. "You two must have parted on good terms."

"Actually, I left him for your father. He was pretty upset, but I guess forty years goes a long way to cushioning a man's ego."

"Cushion, my ass," John announced as he entered the room. He shoved a plate at Audrey with a grilled cheese on it. She snatched it out of his hands like a vulture. "If he thought he could have you he'd leave his wife tomorrow."

"Oh, John." Anne made a face. "That's not true."

He grunted and walked out of the room.

"What's wrong with him?" Audrey asked in a whisper.

Her mother shrugged. "He hasn't had a drink in a while. Your sister and he had a chat outside, but I'm not sure it did him much good. This whole thing with you looking for Mackenzie's father has him on edge."

"Why would he care about that?"

"I think it's a reminder to him of what he thinks of as a personal failure."

God, she was so thick sometimes. "Because he didn't believe me that Clint was abusing Maggie." How could her father have gone to any parties back the Ridge and not have seen what was going on? If she asked it, then he had to as well.

"He feels he let you down."

He had, but Audrey didn't say that. "It doesn't matter now."

Her mother patted her leg. "It will always matter to him, babe."

She'd rather ride a bicycle with no seat than continue that conversation, so Audrey just nodded and took a bite of her sandwich. The last time she checked, time travel still wasn't possible, so there was no going back and fixing the past. They just had to go forward.

After finishing lunch, Audrey did a load of laundry for her mother and then headed back to Jake's. There was no sign of the bald guy or his truck anywhere along the road, which was good. She was going to take her gun into the house with her just in case he came back.

Her phone buzzed as she got out of the car. It was a text from Angeline. *Away from office. Will call you tomorrow. I'm excited about this.*

Audrey squealed. Out loud. As she approached the house, she noticed something stuck between the door and the frame. It looked like an envelope. Frowning, she climbed the porch steps.

It was actually a folded piece of paper. She opened it. Printed in Courier font, it said:

`Audrey, stop sticking your nose where it doesn't belong.`

She hated people who hid behind notes. Last month she'd gotten enough of them—from a psychopath—to last her a damn lifetime, and now this? It was pretty tame by comparison, but it still made her heart pound.

"You know what?" She crumpled the paper in her hand. "Fuck you." And then, turning around, she yelled, "Fuck you!"

A shot rang out. Audrey flattened herself against the door, her heart pounding hard and fast. For a second she was there in that cottage again, a gun pointed at her, a bullet tearing through her flesh.

But wait. The shot hadn't been close. She heard another. No, they were far away, back in the woods. It was the men hunting at the resort, not someone taking shots at her.

*Jesus.*

She laughed as she slid her key in the lock. Her hand trembled. It stood to reason that she'd have some trouble processing what had happened to her last month. Alisha had been seeing a therapist, and maybe Audrey should as well. It had been months since she'd talked to anyone in a professional capacity. And with the amount of times people had tried to harm her since June, she undoubtedly had things to talk about. To work through.

She'd look for someone in her insurance provider's network as soon as she got inside the house. If only she could get her goddamn key to work...The door opened and she practically dove inside, slamming it behind her and turning all the locks. She leaned back against the wood and closed her eyes, breathing deep through her nose and out her mouth until her heart slowed and the sweat at her hairline cooled. She really wanted a drink.

*"He hasn't had a drink for a while."*

No booze. Lately she'd been imbibing more than she normally did, and it had become something of a balm for anything that made her angry or nervous. It was a road she was *not* going to go down. She went for the ice cream she'd brought home earlier instead. If she was going to self-medicate, it was going to be with sugar and dairy products.

She threw the shredded note in the trash, grabbed the tub of ice cream and a spoon, and headed for the living room. It was a good thing she'd already gone for a run, because she was going to need a lot of medicating.

Business at Gracie's was slow in the fall, necessitating that it not be open full-time. That didn't mean Jake didn't spend almost as much time there, however. There still needed to be orders placed, inventory and cleaning done, and the accounting aspect of the business attended to, which was one of his favorite tasks. Or at least it had been until he discovered Lincoln had been skimming.

He sat at his desk in the office in the back of Gracie's, tapping at the keyboard, entering the totals from the weekend into the bookkeeping program he used. Not a bad take for November, but then hunting season often created a bump in revenue. There'd be another influx in December, when a few local businesses and groups rented the bar for their holiday parties.

He checked the clock in the lower right corner of the screen. It was after nine. When he'd talked to Audrey earlier he'd told her he'd be home by then. He stretched his neck as he reached for the phone, getting a satisfying pop. She picked up on the third ring.

"Hey," she said. "Running late?"

"Just finishing up. You need anything?"

"Just you," she replied. "I'm worried about you. I don't like you being out alone with that Mr. Clean–looking goon out there. Come home."

*Home.* He'd lived in that house for twenty-five years, and had always thought of it as his, but it hadn't actually started to feel like a home until he started waking up with Audrey lying next to him. Lincoln would ride him mercilessly if he ever said that out loud—for being such a cliché—but Jake couldn't even find enough shame to care. And Linc, who changed sexual partners like most people changed toothbrushes, was hardly a valid measuring stick for a relationship.

Audrey had been the one thing that mattered in his life for a long time. The one person he held above himself who wasn't a blood relation, and hell, he would run into a burning building to save her even before he would for Lincoln or his mother. She was the one thing—the only thing—he would never recover from losing.

"I'll be right there," he promised. "Wrapping up now."

Jake saved his work and exited the program. He shut down his computer and rose out of his chair. His ass was a little sore from sitting so long. His grandmother would say it was because he didn't have any more ass than God gave a biscuit, but since no one else ever complained about his lack of ass, he was going to say Gracie was wrong just that once.

Before he left he had to make one more phone call. He used a burner phone he bought with cash. He had six of them in his desk—just in case. He dialed the number and waited.

"Hello?"

"It's me."

On the other end, his cousin Kenny sighed. "What do you want?"

"Anybody been asking you questions about Ratchett?"

"No. Should they?"

"Depends on how much of a trail there is."

"There isn't one. I'm not stupid."

"Never said you were. You'll let me know if anyone comes sniffing around?"

"I will. But Jake, you need to start listening better. I said we were done."

Something in his tone pissed Jake off. "We're family, Kenny. We are never fucking done." He hung up. Christ, he just wanted to make sure Kenny didn't get in shit for doing him a favor. Granted, the favor was killing a man, but surely his cousin understood that he wasn't about to let him hang for it if it came to that?

He grabbed his coat and shoved his feet into his boots, hating the feel of them on his feet, even though they were broken in and half a size too big. They still felt like cages on his feet.

His fingers clicked the light switch as he walked out of the office. At the back door he set the alarm before stepping out into the cold night. Snow fell in sparse, big flakes. It wouldn't amount to anything, but it was still a reminder of what would soon come. He closed the door, listening for the click of the latch, before locking it with his keys.

He hadn't even completely turned around when something hit him hard in the side of the head. A two-by-four, maybe? The wood bounced off his skull, but the force of the blow sent him crashing into the side of the building. Knowing another blow was coming, he moved before his attacker was ready. He struck out, landing his knuckles into his opponent's throat. The big man coughed and sputtered, staggering backward.

Jake blinked, clearing his vision. He only needed one look to know that the man was family to Ratchett. Something in his height and the set of his brow. Fucker was huge—bigger than Ratchett even. He'd been too focused on getting home to Audrey to think of bringing the bat with him. He had no weapon except himself.

Something that felt like a car struck his ribs. It was a fist. Another hit him in the stomach, followed by a smash to the jaw that knocked him onto his back on the gravel. He tasted blood through the pain. He tried to get to his knees. Was his jaw broken? He tried to wiggle it a little but was interrupted by a kick to the ribs. One splintered and cracked. He couldn't hold back the cry of pain that it brought to his lips as he fell onto the ground once more.

"That was for my brother, you scrawny little faggot," the man informed him before kicking him again. Jake curled into himself in defense and was rewarded with a boot to the kidney. The bastard was going to kill him.

When the giant leaned down to grab the front of his coat, Jake kicked him in the face, knocking him back. The excruciating pain was worth the satisfaction of hurting the bastard. He struggled to his knees, then his feet, only to get a fist in the eye. He went down to one knee. A fist struck his other cheekbone. He drew back his fist and struck blindly, feeling something split beneath his knuckles. A lip, because the teeth beneath scraped his skin.

One. Two. Three. Those were the punches to his face and head that sent him sprawling. He didn't know if he could get back up.

He had to get back up. He was going to die there if he didn't. He couldn't die in the fucking parking lot. That was *not* how he was going to end.

Another punch, and another. Blackness fogged his brain. He was ashamed at how easily he'd been caught off guard. Ashamed that *he*, who had always been known as a scrapper, was going to be beaten to death. Was that irony or just cosmic payback?

Then he heard it—the sound of tires on gravel. Headlights swept the front of the building. It was probably just someone turning around, but the mountain beating on him wouldn't know that. Jake offered up a silent thanks to his grandmother, whoever was watching over him, as his attacker swore and ran for his vehicle. A big engine roared to life, and gravel spraying up from heavy tires pelted him in the arms and face.

He coughed. Tasted blood again. Numb fingers fumbled for his phone, struggling to free it from his coat pocket. He could barely see the screen through the blood in his eyes. "Call Audrey," he rasped as the darkness reached for him again.

It was cold on the ground. So cold.

"Hey. Are you on your way?"

He opened his mouth, but nothing came out except for a gurgle.

"Jake?"

His hand fell to the ground. The phone skittered across the rocks, but Jake didn't care. He didn't hear Audrey calling his name. He was already gone.

# CHAPTER FOURTEEN

She was wearing sweatpants and an old sweater. Her boots weren't tied and her coat was a red-and-black plaid one that belonged to Jake. Audrey didn't care. Her tires spat gravel that flew up and tinged off her car like little shots from a pellet gun. She barely checked for traffic when she pulled out onto the main road and pressed harder on the accelerator.

Her palms were damp on the wheel, her heart in her throat, but at ninety miles an hour, it took only a few minutes for her to reach Gracie's. She pulled into the back parking lot, the beams of her headlights settling on a figure lying on the ground. It was Jake. She knew it was Jake because she'd know him anywhere.

She jumped out of the car with the motor still running, leaving the door hanging open. Her boots skidded on the loose gravel, taking her feet out from underneath her. She fell hard to her knees beside him, rocks digging in through the fabric of her pants.

"Jake?" She didn't want to touch him—didn't want to hurt him any more than he'd already been brutalized. His face was covered in blood, one of his eyes swollen shut. Snow fell onto his skin, melting as soon as they met the warm redness.

Audrey pulled her phone from her pocket and dialed 911. There was an ambulance dispatch near Eastrock. She barely registered the operator's questions—her focus was on Jake. She didn't even realize she'd hung up after giving her the address.

She drew in a deep breath. She had to calm down. Had to remember this with clarity. Someone had beaten him up, and she needed to remember every detail. She pressed her fingers to Jake's neck—he had a pulse, and that was all that mattered at the moment.

"Can you hear me?" she asked.

Nothing.

The cold seeped through her sweater. She got to her feet and went back to her car, her battered knees protesting, loose boots threatening to trip her again. She opened the trunk and grabbed the two fuzzy throw blankets she kept there. She wrapped one of them around her shoulders as she returned to Jake, draping the other over as much of him as she could.

She knew he shouldn't be at Gracie's alone. Knew that big bastard had come to town with violence in mind. She should have been there with him. She should have had his back like he would have had hers.

Headlights washed over her—blinding. She held up her hand to cut the glare. She could barely make out the vehicle behind them, but she knew it wasn't her father. For a second, she wished she'd brought the gun he'd given her.

"Audrey?"

It was Neve. "He's hurt."

"Dispatch called me." She crouched beside her. "Do you know what happened?"

Audrey shook her head. "He said he was coming home. Then he called me back but didn't say anything. I knew something was wrong, so I came down and found him like this. There was no one else here."

"Okay. The ambulance will be here soon. Does Jake have security cameras installed?"

"Yes."

"Give me the keys. I'll go inside and watch the footage. See if whoever did this is on there."

Audrey went still. There was something in Neve's tone she didn't like. Just a touch of a push—insistence. She didn't doubt her old friend wanted to help Jake, but she knew Neve also wanted to help herself.

Neve wanted to go through the footage and see if Ratchett was on there. Even if Jake and his would-be blackmailer had only sat out in the parking lot and roasted marshmallows over an open fire while singing camp songs, Audrey wouldn't give Neve those keys. It didn't matter that the Ratchett footage had been deleted. She didn't know what had happened to Jake, and she wasn't going to hand that over to Neve without Jake's okay.

"I'm not letting you in without his permission," she replied.

"But his attacker might be on it."

Audrey turned to look at her. "And he'll still be on it tomorrow. Don't try to manipulate me, Neve. I don't fucking appreciate it. You want to see that footage, you get it from him like you're supposed to."

The other woman's face fell. Contrition and annoyance flashed across her features and then disappeared. "What can I do?"

"When the ambulance gets here, call Yancy and Lincoln. Tell them to meet us at the hospital."

Neve nodded. Didn't ask why Audrey wanted her to wait. She didn't want to deal with Yancy's and Lincoln's questions—not right then. Once they got to the hospital and the doctors got him cleaned up so she could have a better idea of how badly he was hurt, she'd deal with his family.

Her father arrived as she heard sirens in the distance. The ambulance.

"Audrey!" Her father ran over to them. He moved fast for an old guy.

"Dad!" She jumped to her feet and into his arms. Thirty-three years of not being able to depend on him evaporated in that moment. It would come back—it always did—but he'd come when she needed him, and that meant everything.

He hugged her—hard. "Neve called me. What happened?"

Audrey shook her head, tears burning her eyes. "I don't know. Someone beat him up." She knew it had most likely been Ratchett's brother, but her father didn't need to know about that.

"Pretty fucking bad," he commented, looking at the younger man on the ground.

Audrey sniffed and wiped at her eyes.

"Hey, hey. Kiddo, that doesn't mean he's not going to be okay. Jake's a tough son of a bitch. You and I both know that. He's going to be fine. This isn't any worse than what that little bastard Matt did to you."

But it was worse, Audrey knew it. And she could see it in the tightness around her father's eyes. She loved him for trying to lie to her, but sometimes she was too good at reading people, and her father was especially easy for her to read.

The ambulance arrived. The two EMTs were young but efficient. They were quick on their feet too, and they had Jake secured on the gurney within a few minutes. Audrey got into the ambulance with him.

"I'll go get Yancy and her girl," her father offered. "We'll meet you at Down East."

Audrey barely had time to nod before the EMT shut the door. A few seconds later they were on the road, the siren wailing.

"What happened?" the kid sitting next to her asked as he monitored Jake's condition.

She shook her head. "I don't know," she repeated, taking one of Jake's hands in hers. Until she talked to Jake—and it was until, *not* if—she wasn't going to say a thing.

Luckily, she didn't have to pray out loud.

A further benefit to small-town living: If you were lucky enough to have a hospital, chances are it wasn't going to be busy on a weeknight. The doctor was already behind the curtain examining Jake when the rest of the Tripp clan arrived.

Audrey—pacing—was able to fill them in on what little she knew before the curtain opened once more.

Dr. Stanfield was a tall, thin woman with short blond hair and bright blue eyes. "Are you the family?" she asked.

Lincoln nodded, stepping forward with his hand extended before Audrey could even think of moving. "I'm Lincoln Tripp, Jake's older brother. What can you tell us?"

Audrey had to fight her eyebrow to keep it from rising. Who the hell was this guy? He looked like Linc in his skinny jeans and flowy shirt, but he did not act or sound like the Lincoln she knew.

"Well, we're going to do some tests, but right now I think he has some broken ribs and a concussion. I want to make sure there isn't anything going on internally, so we're going to take him up for a scan and X-rays. If you just want to wait here, we shouldn't be too long."

The curtain was yanked open and two nurses pushed the bed—with Jake on it—out. Someone had wiped his face, but there was still blood smeared around his eyes and cheeks. Alisha took one look at him and choked on a sob. Audrey's heart twisted in her chest. Seeing him like that—so vulnerable—was the worst pain she'd ever felt. Her ribs felt too small for her body—like all of her organs were being squeezed in a vise.

Arms wrapped around her—Alisha. Audrey twined her own around the girl's shoulders. Yancy and Lincoln stood with their arms around each other as well.

"What's his name?" Audrey asked, because she could tell just by looking at Lincoln that he knew who had done this.

"Ratchett has a brother. His name is Tex."

"What kind of fucking name is Tex?" Alisha asked. "And who's Ratchett?"

Her mother looked at her. Didn't bother chastising her for swearing—like the rest of them weren't thinking the same thing. "He's the guy who was killed at the resort."

"Why would his brother want to hurt Uncle Jake?"

"Because he blames Jake for his brother's death," Lincoln replied. Audrey and Yancy exchanged a worried glance. "Now no more questions. Not here."

Audrey's father found them as they were sitting down to wait. He looked concerned as he walked up, carrying a tray of coffee cups and a donut box. It was probably the same expression Audrey wore. He also looked exhausted. She hadn't noticed it before this, but there were dark circles under his eyes. He handed out the coffees to Audrey, Yancy, and Lincoln and gave Alisha a hot chocolate. He had a coffee for himself as well, along with creamers and sugar.

"What do you kids need me to do?" he asked, dumping three packets of sugar into his coffee. Audrey had once read about the correlation between alcohol addiction and sugar addiction a long time ago. It made sense. Right then she didn't care if he dumped an entire bag of sugar in his cup. Right then he was exactly as he was supposed to be.

Lincoln licked the stirrer and tossed it in the garbage. "Gracie's is going to need someone to run it for a few days," he said, putting the plastic lid back onto his cup. "He wouldn't want that someone to be me."

John nodded. "I can do that."

Audrey glanced at him. "You sure?" He knew what she was asking. They'd been lucky so far that he hadn't given in to temptation any time he'd worked at Gracie's but the way he looked at that moment... well, she knew he wanted a drink.

So did she.

Her father met her gaze. "I'll be okay, don't you worry about it."

All right. She'd trust him, but mostly because there wasn't space in her mind to do otherwise. She was simply too scared and too worried about Jake.

He'd asked her the other day if she was thinking of running. At the time she hadn't been, but seeing him hurt made her want to pack her bags and jump the next plane to anywhere else. She wanted to run from the fear, from the realization of just how much losing him would break her, but she couldn't leave him. Wouldn't.

"You don't have to stay here, John," Yancy said. "Lincoln can drive Alisha, Audrey, and me home."

"I don't mind," he said.

Audrey patted his knee. Part of her wanted him to stay—use him as a crutch—but it was obvious he needed sleep. "You've done enough for one night, Dad. Go on home. Mum needs you. I'll call you later."

"Promise?" The look on his face told her there would be hell to pay if she didn't.

She smiled. "I promise."

He left a few minutes later. And shortly after that, a bored but anxious Alisha got up to go to the bathroom.

"Neve said this Tex told her that Ratchett came here to see Jake about money," Audrey said as soon as the girl was out of earshot.

"If she thought there was a connection between Jake and Ratchett before, this is definitely going to get her asking questions." Lincoln shook his head. "Fuck."

"I want to blame you for this," Audrey confided. "And I want to punch you in the face for it."

His gaze locked with hers, and for a second, the similarity to his brother was like a hand squeezing her heart. "Go for it, if it will make you feel better."

"I'm pretty sure it won't." To her surprise as much as his, she reached out and took his hand instead. "He's going to be okay."

"I know." He squeezed her fingers before pulling away.

"Look, this Tex guy is probably as much a criminal as his brother. Jake's a pillar of the community. Who are the cops going to believe?" This came from Yancy. Lincoln and Audrey stared at her. Pillar of the community? Was she high? Jake had done a lot for their town, but everyone who lived there knew the Tripps had a sordid and sometimes criminal past.

Still, Jake was one of them, and Tex was an outsider.

"Neve wanted to see the security footage from Gracie's," Audrey told them. "I think she wanted to check for Ratchett as well as his brother. Jake was going to erase the visit from Ratchett."

"It's not like Jake actually killed the bastard," Yancy said. "What did Ratchett want with him, anyway?"

Audrey looked at her, then to Lincoln, who replied, "He was in jail with Matt, who shot his mouth off about Jake having money. Obviously, the bastard thought he could come up here and help himself."

It was a lame excuse, but Audrey didn't have the energy to think of a better one. "So, if Neve questions Tex, the worst thing he can probably tell her is that his brother and Jake argued about money."

"I'll handle it," Lincoln announced.

The two women looked at him in surprise, then at each other, but neither of them said a word. Audrey had no idea what he could possibly do, but her concern was Jake, and she needed to concentrate on him.

Alisha came back from the bathroom and sat down between her mother and Audrey. She took turns resting her head on either of their shoulders. Then, when Audrey got up to pace, she moved to the chair between her mother and uncle. The poor thing—and Lincoln—was actually starting to doze off when Dr. Stanfield returned.

"Well?" Yancy demanded.

The doctor smiled. "It looked worse than it is." Audrey almost sobbed in relief. "I was right about a concussion, and he does have two broken ribs, as well as a bruised kidney. He's going to be sore and stiff for quite some time, but I don't expect there to be any lasting effects. We're going to keep him overnight just to be safe. He woke up before the scan and has been asking for all of you." She gave them his room number and then left them to process the news.

The four of them went up to Jake's room together, smiling and almost giddy with relief.

"It's about time," he growled when they walked in.

Alisha ran to his bedside. He winced when she hugged him but didn't say a word. He just let her hang off him, crying until her mother pulled her off. Yancy kissed her brother's cheek. Lincoln stood at the foot of his bed with his arms folded over his chest. "You all right?" he asked.

Jake glanced up at him and nodded. Something passed between them—something Audrey didn't fully comprehend, but understood as someone who had a sibling with whom she'd been at odds. It was a truce of sorts, she thought.

"Sorry I'm late," Jake said to her, trying to smile. His bottom lip was split and swollen. God, he looked like hell. Beautiful hell.

Audrey blinked to keep from crying. She didn't mind Jake seeing her tears, but she minded the other three witnessing them. "I forgive you this time."

He held out his hand and she took it, moving to stand at his side opposite Alisha. After a few minutes of telling them what happened, he told them all to go home. His head was killing him, and he didn't want them fussing over him. Plus, he'd realized he was repeating himself due to the concussion, and Audrey knew he didn't want to slip up and say something he'd regret. He also didn't want her spending the night in a chair beside his bed. Audrey promised she'd be back first thing in the morning so she could bring him home as soon as the doctor released him. Then she kissed his forehead like he often did her, and let his family say their good-byes. Alisha didn't want to leave.

They walked out of the hospital shortly after one a.m. It felt later. They walked across the parking lot as scattered snowflakes continued to fall. It still hadn't accumulated to any degree.

"You're driving a Mazda?" Audrey asked in amazement when Lincoln hit the unlock button on a remote and the lights on a red car lit up.

"You expected a Cutlass with mismatched doors?" he asked, voice as dry as a corpse in the desert.

"It's his girlfriend's," Alisha announced, getting in the back with her mother. "She lets him drive it."

"Shut up, brat," he growled, but he smiled when he said it.

Girlfriend, huh? Who did Audrey know who drove a red Mazda? "Are you dating Marnie Legere?"

Lincoln got into the car and shut the door. Audrey had no choice but to do the same. "What if I am?" he asked, giving her a challenging look.

She shook her head. "Nothing." Marnie Legere was at least ten years older than him, but that wasn't the shocking part. What was shocking was that Marnie had money and came from a good family. She'd divorced her husband several years ago and ran her own business in Ryme. She was good-looking and successful and smart.

What the hell was she doing with Lincoln? Audrey pondered that question for most of the drive home because it was better than worrying about Jake. Alisha chatted for the first ten minutes but then fell asleep, leaving the adults in thoughtful silence.

Lincoln dropped Yancy off first. He and Audrey went into the bungalow and checked to make sure no one had broken in before leaving.

"What's going on?" Alisha asked, groggily.

"Nothing, honey," her mother countered. "Go to bed."

"You never tell me anything," the teen complained, but she did as she was told.

"I'll call one of you if anything happens." She looked at Audrey. "You can stay here tonight if you want."

Audrey shook her head. "Thanks, but I want my own bed." Jake's bed. The bed that smelled of him.

When Lincoln pulled into the drive, he turned to her. "Do you want me to stay with you?"

She was more surprised by the offer than she probably ought to have been. "No. I'm fine. Come in and do a sweep with me, though?"

He did. Of course, they found nothing. Had she really expected to find something missing? Maybe Tex hiding behind the shower curtain?

"Set the alarm when I'm gone," he instructed.

"I will."

"You have a gun?"

She thought of the one her father gave her. "I do."

"Good."

She studied him, the tension in his posture and jaw. "You're going looking for him, aren't you?"

He nodded. "I am." He lifted his jaw, as if daring her to chastise him for it.

Audrey nodded. She thought of what Tex had done to Jake, and thought of her gun again. "Will you call me if you find him?"

Their gazes locked and held. She didn't know what he saw there, but apparently he liked it. His lips curved in a grim smile. "I will." And then he left.

For the first time in nineteen years, Audrey honestly wanted to kill someone. Thinking of Jake, lying beaten on the gravel, she knew she could do it without regret. She went to bed hoping Lincoln would call.

He never did.

*Nineteen years ago*

Maggie was in Bertie's trailer when Mike showed up. He walked in with a six-pack of beer and a couple of grocery bags. He looked surprised to see her there, but Bertie was one of the few adults in town who actually seemed to notice what was going on. Mike's eyes widened as Maggie pulled her hand out from beneath Bertie's, or maybe it was the bruise on her face that shocked him.

"What the hell happened to you?" he asked. They hadn't spoken much since that night a month ago when she called him a fag.

She shrugged. "Ran into a door." A door shaped like her father's fist. "I thought you'd be back at the camp."

He shook his head. "Aaron, Greg, Dwayne, Barbie, and Julie are back there playing strip poker. It's going to turn into an orgy."

Maggie smiled at him. "Get Aaron drunk enough, maybe you'll score."

He actually laughed at that. So did Bertie. "Not enough beer in the world—for me," Mike joked. "Thought Bert might want to play chess." He held up the grocery bag. "I brought stuff for pizza."

"Sounds like a fine idea," Bertie announced. "I have no plans. You want to join us, sweetheart?"

Maggie hated when he called her sweetheart. Her father called her that. Of course, she didn't say that to Bertie. She never told anyone. Except Audrey. Audrey, who actually thought she was a match for Clint Jones. She hadn't been spending as much time with her friend lately because she didn't like the way Clint was starting to look at her. Although, maybe she should have Audrey over. The minute Clint touched her, Rusty would beat him to death. Lately she'd been thinking that her father's death was the only way she'd ever be free.

"No thanks. Dad's at Wendell's so I think I'll go back to the camp." Lately, her father had taken up with Jeannie Ray and was obsessed with the woman. Maggie didn't get it, and she didn't care. If her father was drunk and with Jeannie, he didn't give a fuck about her, and that suited her just fine.

"You sure?" Mike asked. He looked worried. He knew what

would happen if she went back the camp. She wanted to tell him it didn't matter where she went. Lately she'd come to the conclusion that the only people who didn't want a piece of her were Mike and Audrey. They were the only two who didn't want something from her, whether it was sex or secrets, or whatever.

"Yeah. I'll be fine." Maybe if she was lucky Barbie would want to fool around. There was something so nice about being with a girl—all that softness. Nothing hard. Nothing that hurt.

She got up from the table. "See you guys later."

"Have a good night," Bertie said. "You need anything, you call."

Maggie smiled. They both knew she wouldn't call. Not him. And not when Mike was there. She pulled on her coat and stepped out into the cold night. She'd be glad when all the snow was gone and spring came.

Hard, icy gravel crunched beneath her boots as she walked back the road, humming to herself. When she arrived at the camp, the strip poker game was almost over. Dwayne wore his jeans and socks, Aaron was in his underwear, and Greg was in his T-shirt and boxers. Barbie was in her bra and panties and Julie was wearing panties only.

"You're late," Dwayne remarked as she took off her coat.

Maggie grinned, shifting to that part of herself that viewed sex as a social experiment. "Looks to me like I'm just in time."

# CHAPTER FIFTEEN

When Audrey walked into Jake's hospital room the following morning, Neve was already there, standing beside his bed. She had her coat off, so it was obvious she'd been there for a while.

"What are you doing here?" Audrey asked, warily.

Neve looked surprised at her tone. "I'm talking to Jake about the assault against him last night."

"You couldn't wait until he got home?" Didn't she know how close he'd come to dying? Tex could have killed him.

"It's okay, Aud," Jake said. His voice was rough. "Neve's just trying to help."

Audrey nodded stiffly. "Sorry. I didn't sleep well, and I guess I'm on edge."

Neve arched a brow. "You guess? Don't worry about it. If it was Gideon lying here I'd feel the same way."

That was nice of her, but it did nothing to alleviate the tension coiling in Audrey's muscles. Because of the situation with Ratchett she had started viewing Neve as the enemy, and it was difficult not to let it show. "Has the doctor been in yet?"

"Not yet."

"I'm going to go look for her." She turned to leave the room.

"Audrey." Neve came after her, looking concerned.

"What?"

Her old friend frowned. "I'm on your side, you know."

"No, I don't. I thought you were, but then you tried to take advantage of me last night—while Jake was bleeding on the ground. He's the victim here, and you looked at him like a suspect."

Neve didn't even flinch. "I'm sorry about that. It wasn't one of my proudest moments. I'm not trying to incriminate Jake. I am trying to find out if Ratchett's death was an accident, and if the attack on Jake last night is related. From the description Jake gave me, I'm fairly certain the guy who attacked him was Ryan Ratchett's brother, Tex."

Of course she knew who he was—she'd spoken to him about Ratchett. "Have you found him yet?"

The cop didn't look chastised. "We're looking for him. It would help if I had last night's footage from Gracie's so I could see for myself what happened."

Audrey's neck was starting to tighten up. "You'll need to ask Jake about that. I need to find the doctor." She didn't give the other woman the opportunity to reply, but turned on her heel and strode down the corridor. She went to the nurses' station and asked if Dr. Stanfield could come to Jake's room as soon as her schedule permitted, waited for confirmation, then headed back to Jake's room. She paused outside the door to pull herself together.

"Dr. Stanfield will be here as soon as she can," she informed him when she walked in. "Then we can get you home."

"Tell me you brought clean clothes."

She smiled. "Of course."

"I'll finish up and leave you to get ready," Neve announced. "So, you didn't recognize the man who attacked you?"

Jake shook his head. "Never saw him before. He was outside when I left Gracie's and he jumped me. If you think the security tape can help, knock yourself out. Rusty's looking after the place. He can give you access."

Neve glanced at Audrey, as though looking for a reaction. Audrey didn't give her one. "Thanks. So you can't think of any reason he would want to hurt you?"

"I can," came a voice from behind Audrey. She whirled around. Lincoln lounged in the doorway. He'd said he would take care of Neve, but she hadn't expected him to follow through.

"What's that?" Neve asked.

The older Tripp straightened and walked into the room. He was clean-shaven and smelled vaguely of soap. Marnie was obviously having a positive influence on him. "Because he thought Jake was me."

Audrey's jaw wanted to drop, but she kept it clenched.

"You?" Neve repeated. "Why would he think that? And why would he want to hurt you?"

Lincoln looked down briefly, as though he was ashamed. "Because I told Ratchett I owned Gracie's."

Audrey arched a brow. Lincoln was lying, of course.

"You what?" Jake demanded, wincing in pain as he tried to sit up. He sounded sincere. "You asshole." The two of them were wasted on Edgeport; they ought to be in Hollywood. Seriously, she'd seen documented psychopaths who weren't as good at lying as they were.

His brother shrugged. "I didn't think he'd come to town. Look, I borrowed money from the guy. I told him I could repay him quickly because I owned my own bar. But then you fired me and I couldn't pay him anymore. He came looking to collect. I assume his brother came looking for revenge and thought Jake was me."

Neve's brow furrowed. "Lincoln, where were you the morning Ryan Ratchett was killed?"

"At my girlfriend's," he answered, clearing his throat. "I'm seeing Marnie Legere."

Surprise flickered over her face. Audrey almost smiled at it. "So, if I ask Marnie, she'll verify this?"

He nodded. "I was with her all night until I went to Jake's the next morning. Look, I owed the guy money, but I didn't kill him. And even if I did, I wouldn't do it on Jake's land. That's just stupid."

Neve didn't look like she believed he'd think that far, but she didn't say that. "Do you own any guns?"

He made a face. "I don't like guns. Look, Tex is a six-and-a-half-foot-tall, bald fucker who drives a big black truck with a vanity plate that spells TEXASS. He should be easy enough for you to find."

"You have got to be kidding me." Neve's expression was almost laughable. "Does the horn play the first twelve notes of 'Dixie' too?"

Lincoln shrugged. "No idea if he's a *Dukes of Hazzard* fan

or not." Then, "Listen, Jake, I'm sorry. I had no idea Tex would show up looking to collect what I owe his brother, and I'm really sorry you got caught up in my shit."

"It's not the first time," Jake drawled. "You should have just come to me for the money."

Lincoln snorted. "Yeah, right. Like you would have given it to me."

"I would have."

"And lorded it over me." The secret to their performance was the undercurrents of truth and real tension between them, Audrey realized. Brothers were every bit as complicated as sisters.

"Okay," Neve said, closing her notebook. "I think we're done for now. Lincoln, I might have some further questions for you."

He nodded. "Sure. I'm usually at Marnie's. You have my cell number?"

Neve replied that she did. Before she left, she came over to Audrey. "We good?" she asked.

They weren't—not really. They wouldn't be as long as Neve kept digging. "We will be," Audrey replied.

"I can live with that." Then she said good-bye and left. Audrey actually went to the door and glanced out to make sure she had gone. Neve walked toward the elevators at the end of the corridor. Jake and Lincoln were still staring at each other when she came back in.

"If I could do it I'd give you both best actor Oscars," she told them.

"You just put your ass on the line," Jake said. "Why?"

His brother shrugged. "You would have done it for me."

"No, I wouldn't." But they all knew he would. "You could have turned me in, gotten your revenge for all the times you've felt I've wronged you."

Lincoln looked him dead in the eye. "I don't want revenge. If not for me, Ratchett wouldn't have come here. I have to own that, and this was the only way I could do it without implicating you."

"I appreciate it."

"I know."

Another long look. God, the two of them were kings of saying things without words. There was a lot of emotion packed into that stare.

Lincoln broke first. "I need to get going. Call me if you need anything."

Audrey murmured that they would and watched him leave. Again, she checked to make sure he was gone before approaching Jake's bed.

"You're paranoid, you know that."

She smiled. "I'm cautious." Her smiled faded. "Lincoln really stepped up."

"Yeah." He looked pensive.

"You think he's going to want something in return?"

His gaze met hers—his one open eye grim. "He will. Lincoln always does."

Alisha was a student at Eastrock High. Given that Tex might still be in town, the Tripp brood decided it would be a good idea to drive the girl to school and pick her up at the end of the day. Audrey went to pick her up that afternoon while Yancy sat with Jake and stayed close to the resort. The only thing that could get her to leave Jake's side was the fact that it was Alisha.

When Audrey pulled into the queue of cars outside the school, she spotted Alisha near the front doors, talking to a tall boy with long, light brown hair that was pulled back in a braid. It was obvious the kid was trying his best moves on her. Lish smiled sweetly at him, tilting her head slightly to the right. She was a natural flirt, the fabulous girl. The kid looked familiar. Now that she'd gotten a good look at him, there was no doubt the kid was Ben Patrick, Aaron's oldest son. Aaron and his first wife had married right out of college—because he'd gotten her pregnant. They divorced three years and two kids later. Ben was a good-looking kid and had a sweet face. Maybe it was just a coincidence that Alisha was talking to him. She was a cute girl. Cute girls and cute boys chatted together all the time. And it was a small school. Of course they knew each other.

The line moved, and she pulled up in front of the school. She pushed the button to lower the passenger window. "Hey, Lish."

The girl grinned at her and said good-bye to Ben. Then she got into the car. Audrey put the window back up before asking, "Tell me you were just flirting."

"I got his hair." She pulled a brush out of her backpack with long brown hairs in it.

"Oh, you did not." Audrey gaped at her. "Who do you think you are, CSI?"

Alisha looked surprised. "But now you can test it and see if Mr. Patrick is Mac's father."

"Sweetie, I'm pretty sure what you just did is illegal. Even if the results come back positive, we could get sued." Audrey wasn't completely sure of the legalities of the situation, and she wasn't sure she wanted to know. "How did you even get it?"

"I offered to braid his hair in gym class. He always pulls it back. I told him a braid would make his hair wavy, and offered to teach him how to do it. I used a new brush."

Audrey shook her head, fighting the urge to smile, even though she did not approve of Alisha getting involved, or her methods. She was not going to send that hair to be tested. Not right away, at any rate.

"Kid, your great-grandmother would be proud."

Audrey had to pop down to her parents' after dinner to help out with a few things. When she arrived, she found Jess and Greg and the girls there, having dessert. It had been Jess's turn to make dinner for them. They wouldn't have to do it much longer. Their mother was already complaining about not being an invalid, and their father didn't think either one of them was that good a cook. In fact, he made most of the meals he and his wife shared.

"I'm on laundry duty," she announced, and headed to the laundry room. She was folding the load that was in the dryer and waiting for the washer to fill up when Greg walked in.

"Can I help?" he asked, leaning against the door jam.

She arched a brow at him. "You want to fold Dad's underwear or Mum's?"

"Uh, neither?"

She smiled and tossed him a couple of towels instead. "Thanks."

He began folding the items with the finesse of a man used to laundry. "I heard you had a run-in with Aaron."

"Where'd you hear that?"

"Aaron."

That was unexpected. "I went to see him at the school. He ask you to call me off?"

Her brother-in-law set the folded towel on top of the dryer. "No. He wanted to talk about Maggie and those parties. I think he's scared it might be him."

She paused in folding her father's boxers. They were black with hearts on them. She didn't want to know. "Right now I'm thinking it was either him or Mike LeBlanc."

"Dyer was around a lot too." He reached for another towel.

"I haven't spoken to Dwayne yet." She wondered if Barbie had remembered to tell him to call her. "Carol LeBlanc gave me a DNA sample. I didn't ask Aaron. Now I'm thinking I should have."

"Calling me doesn't mean he's your guy."

"I got a note telling me to back off after I saw him."

His jaw tightened. "I'm sorry. Look. Aaron and I were friends a long time ago. We haven't hung out in years, but he wasn't a bad guy back then and I can't believe he's one now."

"I appreciate that. I know what it's like around here. I know how young kids start fooling around—and I knew Maggie back then. She was promiscuous. Most abused girls are."

He winced. "As a father, I hate hearing about that kind of stuff."

"Well, you're a good dad."

He looked pleased by her words. "I try."

Audrey sighed. She didn't want to have a confrontation with him, but she had to ask, "I've seen photos of you guys in Maggie's belongings. Looks like you were a fairly close bunch. You must have noticed something. *Did* Aaron sleep with Maggie?"

Her brother-in-law hesitated. Then he nodded as he folded the towel exactly the way her mother, Jess, and Audrey herself folded them. "Yeah. I know he had sex with her at least a few times. But it didn't seem wrong back then, you know? I mean, we all kind of forgot how young Maggie was. She seemed to be the same age as Barbie and Julie. I knew a lot of guys who dated younger girls. Aaron wouldn't have forced Maggie to do anything."

"I didn't think he had." And that was true—at least where the younger guys were concerned. Maggie had been a victim many times in her life, but at some point she became a predator. "Sometimes older guys are prizes. I knew several girls who lost their virginity to older guys and thought of them as trophies."

"I didn't know girls did that sort of thing."

She smiled sympathetically. "Girls do all kinds of things." And just because Aaron didn't force Maggie, that didn't make it right. He took advantage of a girl who thought trading her body for love and acceptance was how the world worked.

He frowned. "Shit."

Audrey might have laughed in other circumstances. "Your girls will grow up smart. And strong." That seemed to comfort him, so she didn't bother to add that the two of them would then proceed to do whatever the hell they wanted, just like every other teenage girl who came before them and would come after.

"I could talk to Aaron if you want—get him to give you a DNA sample."

She shook her head. "I don't want you involved."

"I was at those parties too. I'm already involved."

Audrey met his gaze and held it. "Did you sleep with Maggie?"

His cheeks turned pink. "There was nothing between me and Maggie."

"Then you're not involved."

He shook his head. "Okay."

"Good." And then, because she didn't want to have that discussion, she asked "Hey, do you remember when Mike LeBlanc died?"

"Yeah. I was there that weekend. It was a shock to all of us."

"Do you remember anything happening between him and Bertie Neeley?"

Greg frowned as he thought back. "Not really. Bertie was around a lot. I think he and Mike would sometimes drink together. They went snowmobiling a few times that winter. And sometimes they'd play chess. None of the rest of us knew how to play. Everyone liked Bertie."

"It was Bertie who found his body, right?"

"Yeah, which was weird because Mike and Maggie had gone looking for him. I guess he found him too late."

"Wait. *Maggie* was with Mike when he died?"

Greg frowned. "She left the camp with him, yeah. But she came back a little while later. When we asked where Mike was, she said he'd taken off. Next thing we knew, Dwayne came back from getting mix and said the cops were out at Wendell's and someone was dead."

Mike and Maggie had gone looking for Bertie, but Bertie was the one who found the body? No one else around. That was weird, even for Edgeport. Maybe her imagination was running wild, but something had happened that night. Something that ended with Mike LeBlanc's fall to his death. Something that involved Maggie. Audrey would bet that night began Maggie's dislike of Bertie too.

Greg helped her finish with the folding, and then she threw another load of clothes in the washer. Jess came and got her husband to go home as Audrey dumped detergent into the water. Her father wandered in as she was about to carry the basket full of clothes upstairs.

"You and Greg were holed up in here for a long time," he commented.

"We were talking about Mackenzie and Mike LeBlanc," she confided.

"You still thinking he was the kid's father?"

"Not sure." She shut the lid and the agitator kicked into motion. "But I am thinking Bertie Neeley knows more about his death than he's saying."

John rolled his eyes. "Jesus, kid. What does that matter now?"

"It matters because I might not be the only murderer in this town."

His gaze locked with hers. "Of course you're not the only murderer in this town. Just the only one to get caught." Thankfully he left out "stupid enough." "And what has murder got to do with Maggie's baby?"

Well, that she didn't know. Maybe nothing, but she had to find out. Maggie had kept all of it secret for a reason. "The night he died, Mike LeBlanc and Maggie went looking for Bertie Neeley."

"So?"

"Bertie found the body."

Her father nodded. "Makes sense if the kid was looking for him. Look, the boy died. It was a terrible accident, but it had nothing to do with Maggie."

"Unless Mike was the father of her baby."

"I wish to hell you would just leave it alone."

"Someone threatened me, Dad."

"Maybe you should listen."

"Would you?" she challenged.

It was a little standoff, there by the washing machine. Her father blinked first, shoulders sagging as he sighed. "No." And then, "If I can get you some answers about the LeBlanc kid, will you leave it alone?"

Audrey eyed him suspiciously. "So you do know something."

"I know someone who might."

"Why are you being so secretive?"

He shook his head. He actually looked disappointed in her. "You're as nosy as that goddamn Jeannie."

That was like a slap to the face. "I am *not* like Jeannie Ray."

"You're not *un*like her." There was actually a hint of a smile on his lips when he said it. Did he think he was being funny?

That was it. She kicked the basket of clean clothes toward him. "Do your own laundry." She stomped out without saying good-bye to him or her mother. She didn't care that it was childish. She was just sick of all the damn secrets, and she was still raw from the attack on Jake. She grabbed the bag Anne had packed and left for her on the sideboard and walked out. Let him explain it. Maybe he'd be more truthful with his wife than with his daughter.

# CHAPTER SIXTEEN

Audrey had just stepped through the door when the telephone rang. She grabbed it out of its cradle after turning the deadbolt. Maybe she was paranoid. "Hello?"

"Audrey? It's Dwayne Dyer."

Well, speak of the devil. That was a surprise. She tossed her purse onto the table. "Hey, Dwayne. What's up?"

"I was wondering if you could pop down tomorrow morning."

"To Barbie's?" It wasn't far. She could get Lincoln or Yancy to stay with Jake. "Sure. Has she remembered something?"

"No. I don't know. Maybe. She won't be home."

Audrey went still. "So it will just be the two of us?" As soon as she said it, she felt bad. She wouldn't be so wary if she was meeting Barbie by herself.

"Yeah. I thought maybe you might want to bring one of those test kits with you if you have one."

She had a very strong suspicion he wasn't talking about a pregnancy test. "I do." Jesus Christ, was Dwayne hinting at being Mackenzie's father? It seemed incredulous after running into so many walls.

"Good. I don't want to be who you're looking for, but I've never been the kind of guy to walk away from his responsibilities."

That was honorable. Kind of.

"I can come down around ten. Does that work for you?" If she could sleep in a bit, she was going to. With everything that had been going on the last few days, and being afraid of hurting Jake, she hadn't slept much.

"It sure does. Hey, I heard Jake got fucked up. How's he doing?"

What an eloquent way with words he had. She told him what Jake had instructed her to say—that he was sore, but he was fine, and thanks for asking.

Dwayne made a noise that sounded like a laugh. "You know, he's used that same BS since high school. Okay, I'll respect his privacy. Tell him I hope he stops pissing blood soon, and if he needs a hand with anything I'm around. See you tomorrow." He hung up.

Frowning, Audrey hung up and went into the living room, where she'd left Jake while she'd been gone. He was on the couch, watching TV. He looked gloriously stoned. She wished she was, because his face was painful to look at. His poor, pretty face. It was all puffy and battered. His left eye was swollen shut. In a few days he'd have those yellow and green bruises. Those were so ugly.

"Who was that?" he asked.

"Dwayne Dyer. He wants to know if there's blood in your urine. So do I."

He turned his head slightly, giving her a better view of that terrible eye. "Did he actually use the word 'urine'? If he did, call him back. I want to make sure he didn't take a blow to the head too."

She crossed her arms over her chest. "Be serious, stoner. Are you... pissing blood?" The very idea made her stomach feel hollow.

"It's better than it was this morning." She must have looked horrified, because the bastard actually chuckled—then groaned in pain. "Aud, it's common with a bruised kidney to pass some blood. That's why the doc told me to rest, and why she told you to make sure I rest. I just need to take it easy and drink lots of water and it will be fine. I promise."

She nodded. To be honest, the whole thing made her feel vaguely queasy. "Okay. But if it's not gone in a day or two, we're calling the doctor."

"Yes, we will. How was Mama Anne?" he asked. The pills made his voice low and thick. He was falling asleep.

"Good." She wasn't going to tell him about the rest of it. "She sent up some roast beef with potatoes and carrots for dinner." It was the first full meal her mother had cooked since her own hospitalization, and she'd cooked it with the express intention of feeding Jake. It was sweet, really. And stupid. Her mother shouldn't be overextending herself. Said the woman who kept forgetting she'd been shot just a few weeks ago.

"She's gorgeous."

"She sent apple crumb too."

"A fucking goddess."

She swallowed a chuckle. "Oh, and Livvie sent you this." She thrust a piece of drawing paper in front of his face.

He blinked. Then blinked again. She watched as he focused on the crayon strokes. "What is it?"

"Best I can tell, it's a portal to hell. She asked where you were and I told her you were sick. She immediately went to where Mum keeps the drawing and coloring supplies and drew this."

"It's a damn fine portal to hell. I like the yellow. It's cheery. Obviously she's an artist genius of the nihilistic school." He smiled drunkenly. "Will you put it on top of the TV so I can look at it whenever I want?"

Something in her chest snapped. *God, this man.* She had thought him sleeping with Maggie to push her away had hurt, but that hadn't been anything compared to the thought of losing him. It wasn't anything compared to what she felt at that moment. Her heart was so full and heavy with love that it hurt like a bastard and scared her more than anything ever had. But she wasn't going to run. She'd rather be afraid and with him than not.

So she put the swirling vortex of colored wax on top of the TV, and didn't argue that she thought the drawing couldn't be nihilistic if it was actually a depiction of a portal to hell. It could have just as easily been a drawing of Jake himself, or the secret of life. Maybe a bee?

"I want you to carry that gun your father gave you. Tex is still around, and I'm not much use in this condition."

He really was stoned to be this laissez-faire about the whole thing. “I wanted to take it with me last night and go find Tex with your brother.”

“You and Lincoln, now there’s a dangerous pair-up. You got your hopes up for nothing. He wouldn’t have killed Tex.”

“I think he might have if he’d found him. He was pretty pissed.”

“Yeah, well, Tex is still alive, isn’t he?”

Audrey could only assume that he was. “Is the lesson I’m supposed to take away from that the fact that were the roles reversed, you would not have stopped until you found Tex and blew his damn head off?”

“What do you think?”

“I think that you need to *re*think your priorities. Get some sleep.”

He yawned. “Okay.” Not even a minute later, he was sound asleep. Those pills had to be amazing. Maybe she should take a couple and bliss out for a few hours.

It was tempting. So tempting that it scared her. Instead, she went and got her laptop and sat in the big armchair, working on financial estimates for running a place the size of the old Pelletier farm and possible ways for it to sustain itself, so she’d be prepared when Angeline called later. The more information she could give her boss the better, and she needed to be clearheaded for that. She *wanted* to be clearheaded.

So she worked. And she fussed over Jake when he woke up, and when he needed a pill, she gave him one without taking one for herself. She watched him sleep for a bit, then texted Mac to see when the girl planned to return to town and filled her in on the fact that she was meeting with Dwayne the next day.

She checked her phone. Nothing from Lincoln. Nothing from Neve. Nothing from anyone. Even later that day, when she made plans for Angeline to come visit and look at the property, she didn't hear from anyone else. She thought her father might call—wanting to smooth things over—but he didn't. She thought about calling him to apologize. She called Jess instead.

"Hey," her sister said. "I can't talk right now. I'm at Mum and Dad's."

There was something in her sister's voice. "Is everything okay?"

"Yeah, I'm just trying to get some chores done up and keep an eye on the kids. I'll call you later." The call disconnected.

Audrey stared at her phone. What the hell? She was sure she'd heard her father's voice in the background, saying something to Jess. Were they talking about her? Was she paranoid much?

Maybe moving back to Edgeport wasn't such a great idea. She glanced at Jake's sleeping form. She needed to get this business with Mackenzie sorted and get back to what was important. Whatever happened to Mike LeBlanc, it probably had nothing to do with Maggie, and it had probably been nothing more than a sad accident. It didn't matter, and she didn't need to know everything. She had to find a way to be okay with it.

In fact, once she ran Dwayne's DNA kit, she was going to be

done with the search for Mac's father. And she wasn't going to use the hairs Alisha grabbed for her to run a comparison to Aaron. She hadn't said anything to Jake—or anyone—about the girl trying to help, and she wasn't about to get Lish in trouble. But she wasn't setting a good example, playing private detective like she was. It wasn't her job, and she sure as hell didn't want Alisha mimicking her by doing dangerous, stupid things. She didn't want to think about what might happen if Aaron ever found out Alisha had purposefully set out to collect his son's DNA.

She was catching up on e-mails when someone drove into the yard. It looked like Neve's car, so she went to meet her at the door. She had her cop face on.

"What's going on?" Audrey asked.

"Is Jake with you?"

"Of course. He's not allowed to go anywhere."

"Where were you last night?"

"Here."

"Anyone else with you?"

"Neve, what the hell is this about?"

"We found Tex Ratchett."

Audrey sagged against the door. "Thank God." No more worrying that the asshole was going to come after someone Jake cared about—or finish what he started with Jake.

Neve folded her arms over her chest. "We found him dead in the cab of his truck. Looks like he OD'd."

She didn't bother to hide her surprise. "So, it was an accident?" Just like his brother? Oh, *hell.* "You don't think..."

"I don't know what to think. I do know that there are no such things as accidents, not where you and your boyfriend are concerned."

Audrey straightened. "You making accusations, Officer?"

"I know the lengths you'll go to for someone you love." Of course she did. She'd been there when Audrey and Jake went to save Alisha. Her father had been the one to arrest her for killing Clint. The Grahams knew her too well.

"Not this time, Neve," she said.

"Two guys dead after tangling with Jake Tripp is one hell of a coincidence."

"Yes, it is."

Neve's dark gaze locked with hers. "Tell me you had nothing to do with it."

She shouldn't be so hurt. When she first came back to town, Neve had thought her a killer. Once a killer, always a killer. It was rock salt ground into an old wound. "What's the point? We both know you won't believe me."

And then she closed the door.

Jake was more himself the next morning. He was still in a fair amount of pain, because she saw him take the pills right on the hour that he was allowed to take more. The swelling had gone down some in his eye, but the bruising had gotten worse. He moved like an old man.

"Are you happy Angeline's flying out?" he asked.

"I am. I wish you were in better shape to help me show her the property. Thanks for getting beaten up just when I need you."

He smiled. Then winced. "I like to keep you on your toes. You'll do just fine without me, and I could be good by the time she gets here."

"Mm." That was all she had to say about that. She took a deep breath. "Tex is dead."

He looked surprised. "You waited long enough to tell me."

"I was waiting to see if Neve arrived here to arrest me. She thinks I did it."

One of his eyebrows rose—the other merely twitched above his swollen eye. "Seriously?"

"I think so. She made it pretty clear that she thinks something is going on, and she's pissed."

"Pride. She thinks she's being made a fool. She'll figure out you had nothing to do with it and apologize. You two will make up like you always do."

Audrey wasn't sure about that. Neve might have her pride, but so did she, and she didn't appreciate being accused of something she didn't do. She'd have more respect for Neve if Neve had come right out and asked her. "I guess we would have heard by now if they figured out Lincoln was lying." But really, who was going to dispute his story now, with Tex dead?

"He would have called." His compromised gaze slid over her. "You're dressed up. Where are you going?"

It was a sad day when "dressing up" was jeans and a sweater. Okay, so maybe she'd put on earrings and some makeup, but still. "I'm going to talk to Dwayne Dyer. He asked me to come to the house."

He shifted on the couch to see her better, hissing in pain when he moved the wrong way. "About Mac?"

"Yeah. He's offered to take a DNA test." It was random and unexpected. She hadn't even talked to him about Maggie before he'd made his offer.

"Do you think it's him?"

"It could be."

"You don't sound convinced."

"I'm not. Dwayne didn't leave me a note telling me to back off—not if he's offering up his DNA."

He looked at her. "You're still thinking Aaron?"

"Yeah. He's my number one." She stood up as a car pulled into the yard. "Yancy's going to stay with you until I get back."

"I don't need a babysitter."

She didn't argue. He was too grumpy, and it didn't matter. Yancy was going to stay with him whether he liked it or not. She just kissed him on the head and left the room.

"How is he?" Yancy asked when she walked in.

Audrey smiled. "Ornery and pretty much stoned."

"So he's Lincoln, then." The two of them shared a laugh. Audrey told her she wouldn't be long and left. Before starting the car, she checked her phone and found a text from Mac saying she'd be back in town that night. Maybe they'd have the photos to look at? Audrey responded that she didn't know, but that she'd see her later. Then she drove up the road once again and pulled into Barbie's driveway. Dwayne answered the door when she knocked.

Dwayne Dyer was a fairly good-looking man. He'd certainly attracted a lot of women in his lifetime. He was average height, with broad shoulders and a narrow waist. He had a hardness to his features that was common in those who'd spent too much of their lives partying, and nicotine stains on his fingers. His teeth weren't too bad, though. By Edgeport standards he was a catch.

"Hey, Audrey. Thanks for coming down. Come on in." He stood back to let her inside the house.

The dog was sleeping on an overstuffed dog bed in the kitchen and barely raised its head when Audrey walked in, but its tail thumped hard on the floor.

"Can I get you anything? Tea? Soda? Beer?"

He didn't sound like he wanted to make tea, and she didn't want a beer. "Soda's great."

Dwayne went to the fridge and got a can of no-name diet cola. "Glass?"

"No, the can is fine."

He grabbed one for himself too and joined her at the table. "Did you bring the DNA test thing?"

"I did. Are you sure you want to do it?"

He wrapped his hands around the can in front of him, the movement pulling his plaid shirt tight across his back. He had trouble meeting her gaze. "I like women too much, and I like to party, but I've never turned my back on any of my kids. My dad walked out on us when I was seven and I remember what it felt like to not have him in my life—to know that he left us, you know?"

Audrey nodded.

He fixed her with a direct gaze. "Maybe with all your education, you know why or how a man can just abandon his family. Maybe you understand it, but I don't. I could never turn my back on my kids. I'm not proud of being with Maggie. Back then she was pretty free with herself, and none of us knew what old Clint was doing to her. I mean, I guess some of the older men might have, but we kids, not so much. She liked to party, and she liked sex. She'd sleep with you and never expect you to call her or put any pressure on you. In fact, she was the one who would then just walk away and pretend like nothing ever happened. We didn't even think of her as being that much younger than us, 'cause she could party just as hard, you know?"

"Yeah." That didn't make it easy to hear.

Dwayne shrugged. His neck had turned a dull red, the flush spreading up his cheeks. "When Barbie asked me about it, I denied it, because I didn't want her to think less of me, but the more I've thought about it, the more I know it's just not right not to offer up my genes for you to compare, or however it works. If the girl's mine, I need to make it right."

That was respectable. As respectable as any of this was going to get. She could understand that he'd want to wish it all away. Audrey took the envelope and package containing the test swab from her purse. "All I need is for you to rub this on the inside of your cheek," she explained, offering him the swab.

Dwayne took it from her and did as she instructed. He

watched in silence as she popped it into the envelope afterward. "That's it?"

"That's it. We should get the results in a few days."

"You'll let me know?"

"You'll be the first person I tell," she replied. Even before she told Mac.

He nodded. "I'll have to figure out how to tell Barbie. She thinks I'm better than that."

Audrey felt genuine sympathy for the poor bastard. "She grew up back there, Dwayne. I don't think she'll judge you much. In fact, you doing the right thing is respectable."

"Hm." His lips twisted wryly. "Girl, you and I both know nothin' that ever happened back the Ridge was respectable. Your dad was the best of that lot, but I don't think he knew half of what they got up to back there."

She thought of the dead boy, and the mystery of him rushed to the front of her mind. "Like what?"

"Like Wendell and Bertie growin' their pot. Jeannie Ray selling herself to whoever would pay. Women getting beaten up and doing the beatin'." He shook his head. "It was a fucked-up place. Still is sometimes."

She was quiet for a moment, thinking on that. "What do you know about Michael LeBlanc?"

"The kid that fell down the bank?"

She nodded. "I admit, I've been a little obsessed with figuring out what happened to him."

Dwayne shrugged. "Don't know much. He was a nice guy. Liked to party. He hung out with Bertie a lot. No fucking idea why. He wanted to be a human rights lawyer or something." He took a cigarette from the package on the table and lit it, taking a deep drag. "Oh, shit. I'm sorry. Do you mind?"

So far he had told her more about Mike LeBlanc than anyone else. She didn't care if he chain-smoked the whole freaking pack. "No, it's fine."

He got up and cracked the window above the sink. "Barbie doesn't like the house smelling. I try not to smoke inside too much."

"So, Mike went looking for pot."

"Yeah." He tapped ash into the sink. "He never came back. Next thing we know, everyone's saying he's dead and Bertie found him."

"Do you think that's true? He just fell?"

"If he was local, I'd think it was weird, but he wasn't from here. I mean, his mom lived in Eastrock, but his dad lived up north. He wasn't like the rest of us. If he went stumbling around up there in the dark, I can see how he'd take a tumble."

"Do you know if Mike ever got together with Maggie?"

"Mike?" Dwayne laughed and took another hit off his dwindling cigarette. Absently, Audrey wondered how black his lungs were. "Doubt it. We all suspected Mikey didn't like girls."

And yet Greg had said Mike went off with Maggie on occasion. In his defense he also said he didn't know if anything happened. Aaron had intimated as much as well, hadn't he? "Did you ever see him with a guy?"

"No. Maybe he was straight after all. Maybe he just kept his mouth shut about it and was smart. Some of us learned the hard way that if you brag about banging a girl she might never let you in again."

Ah, small-town sexual vernacular. There was something so... euphemistically blunt about it. "Well, that's how most of us learn not to sleep with a guy who talks too much." She rose to her feet. "Thanks for the soda and the information. I'll send these results to the lab today and let you know what I find out."

Suddenly Dwayne looked very nervous. Was he going to rescind his DNA donation? Then he gave his head a brusque nod. "Yeah, okay. Not sure how I feel about it, but I'd rather know than not."

And that was what made Dwayne Dyer, despite some of his word choices and life choices, a fairly decent guy. Barbie could certainly do worse.

There was a knock on the door. Dwayne's gaze darted to hers. "Don't be mad," he said.

She frowned. "For what?" But he'd already gone to open the door. She found out what he meant a few moments later when Aaron Patrick walked into the room. Oh, *hell.*

Audrey stood up. "Don't you have classes to teach?" she demanded.

"I have a free period," he said softly, as though talking to a child, or growling dog.

"I told him I was going to meet with you," Dwayne explained lamely. "He said he was going to come by—said he'd tell Barbie about a girl I had a thing with a few weeks ago if I didn't agree."

"You've lived here your entire life," Audrey reminded him. "You know Barbie already knows, Dwayne." She'd probably known fifteen minutes after it happened. Then, to Aaron, "What do you want?"

"To talk to you," Aaron replied.

"You could have called me." Wariness made her take a step back.

He followed her. "I wanted to do this in person."

Her back was almost to the wall. She acted before she thought. All she knew was that she was cornered by two grown men. The last time one cornered her he'd beaten her up. She punched Aaron in the face as hard as she could.

"Fuck!" Aaron swore, staggering backward. He held his hand to his nose. Blood dripped between his fingers onto the item he had dropped.

"Jesus Christ, Audrey!" Dwayne cried. "He just wanted to talk!"

She held up her hand. "Back off." To her surprise, he did. She was shaking, thoughts of the beating Matt Jones had given her twirling in her head.

"I wanted to give you this." Gingerly, Aaron picked up the item from the floor and held it out to her.

Audrey's stomach fell. "A DNA test?" Oh, she really did need to look into getting a therapist.

He nodded, still holding his bleeding nose. "When Dwayne said he was going to, I knew I had to as well."

"Shit." She took the box with a grimace. "I'm sorry. I thought..."

"Yeah. I know. You got a Kleenex, man?"

She had to get out of there. "I'll let you both know what I

find out. Again, I'm so very, very sorry." She got out of there as fast as she could. Jesus, she was all kinds of stupid. What had this whole mess done to her? She was out of control. All of her professional training had gone out the window. She was nothing more than a backwoods vigilante running around punching anyone who looked at her the wrong way. That was not who she wanted to be. She'd send the tests in her bag off to the lab and then that was it. She would concentrate on getting her facility going and no more of this digging around in business that wasn't hers.

When she saw Mac that night she'd get fresh swabs from her and send both samples the next day. She'd explain to the girl that she had to be done as well.

She was going up the steps to the house when her phone rang. She had enough ice cream in her bag to feed a small army. It was better than rum, right? She glanced at the screen. It was her father. "Now's not a good time," she said as she fumbled for the house key.

"Bertie agreed to a sit-down with you."

That stopped her short. Her hand froze on the door handle. "When?"

"Tomorrow morning. He'll only do it if you come alone. No Mac."

"Okay." Her heart hammered with anticipation as she opened the door and stepped inside. "What did you have to do to get him to agree?"

"Nothing. He just called a few minutes ago. Only stipulation is that I come with you."

"I suppose I'm going to owe you if you come along?"

"Yeah, well, you can thank me with steak and a game night if this is the end of your Nancy Drewing where Bertie's concerned."

"Crib?" she asked, a smile tugging on her lips as she set her groceries on the sideboard.

"You know it. Maybe some forty-fives. Bring that hippie boyfriend of yours too if he's up for it. He probably cooks a better steak than you do."

"Sure. Okay, I gotta go. I just got in. I'll talk to you later."

"Yeah, call your mom. She wants to fuss over the boy for a bit."

Audrey promised she would and hung up. Why had Bertie decided to talk to her? It didn't matter. Soon the old man would tell her what he knew—and he knew something—and hopefully she would be able to put the mystery of Mac to rest and get on with her plans for the future. She'd talk to Bertie and then she was done.

Promise.

# CHAPTER SEVENTEEN

After dinner—which was shared with Alisha and Yancy—Alisha sat on the floor beside the couch where her uncle lay, gently spreading a thin layer of a mixture she'd made with Arnica and several essential oils, over his bruises. It smelled vaguely of lavender, which Audrey hated, but if it worked, she could get past it. She just wanted Jake to look like himself again.

"She made me take her to that natural place over in Eastrock to get the oils she needed," Yancy told Audrey as they put the plates in the dishwasher. "She spent hours researching online what oils were the best for bruising."

"She's such an awesome kid."

"Yeah, I know. I was worried how she'd handle this, after what she went through last month, but she's stronger than I gave her credit for."

"She's got Gracie's blood in her."

"More than I do."

Audrey shot her a pointed glance. "No, you've got plenty of your grandmother in you as well."

"Thanks." She shut the dishwasher door. "Someday soon she's going to leave me."

She still had a few years, but Audrey knew that wouldn't matter to a mother. "She'll come back. We always do."

Yancy smiled. "Even you."

"Yeah. The only person more surprised by that than my parents is me." She was rewarded with Yancy's laughter. It was nice getting along with her again. "Hey, did you hear about Tex?" They hadn't brought it up over dinner because Audrey had mentioned to Jake about Alisha trying to get involved in the hunt for Mac's father, and he passed it on to Yancy. Everyone was in agreement that the more "adult" discussions should be held when Lish wasn't around.

"I did. Heroin's a nasty thing. I used to date a guy who got addicted. He went from gorgeous to ghoulish in a few months. I heard it wasn't so much the amount he took, but the purity of it."

Audrey nodded. "Like Janis Joplin." Reportedly the singer had taken her usual dose, but it was incredibly potent and killed her.

Yancy glanced at her. "Is that how she went? I thought she died in a bathtub."

"Jim Morrison." She wasn't sure why she knew these things. "Neve doesn't think it was an accident—not with Ratchett dying like he did."

"Can't say that I blame her. Is she going to be trouble, do you think?"

"Yeah. I'm afraid so. She thinks someone is trying to make

a fool of her, and I'm not sure they're not. It's just not who she thinks it is."

"So, she'll look for someone to blame, and when nothing sticks she'll stop looking. She can't put it on Jake, at any rate." When Audrey was quiet, she continued, "Wait. She doesn't think *you* did it, does she?"

"I'm not sure. I think she's open to the possibility."

"Oh, that's just fucking stupid. When would you have time to kill someone?"

It was the most simple of questions—and one that Audrey hadn't even thought of. The perfection of it struck her as hilarious and she laughed out loud. "Oh my God. You're right!"

Yancy laughed too, cheeks pink and eyes bright. She looked just like Gracie at that moment, and Audrey felt a connection with her that she hadn't felt before. It was nice.

Her cell phone rang, interrupting their laughter. Audrey grabbed it on the second ring. It was Mac.

"Hey, kiddo," she said, channeling her father. "Are you back in town?"

"Audrey, I need you to come back to the cottage."

Audrey's smile faded at the fear in the girl's voice. "What's happened?"

"Someone broke in. It's trashed. And Audrey? All of Maggie's stuff is gone."

Whoever said nothing ever happened in small towns had clearly never been to Edgeport. Everything under the sun happened in small towns, and sometimes twice on Sunday. You just had to know where to look. Edgeport was no different. In fact, it seemed to invite activity, especially of a nefarious nature.

It was only because he'd taken his pills and was too stoned to argue that Audrey managed to avoid taking Jake with her when she went back the road. As it was, she took Yancy in his stead, and called Neve on the way. She hadn't forgotten that her old friend wasn't much of a friend at that moment, but she was still a cop and that was what Audrey needed.

The two of them arrived first and found Mackenzie pacing outside the cottage, in a heavy fleece jacket, leggings, and boots. All the lights were on.

"Are you okay?" Audrey asked as she shut the car door.

Mac came at her and Audrey instinctively opened her arms. "It's all gone!" The girl sobbed against her shoulder. "Everything of my mother's gone."

Audrey patted her on the back. "I'm just glad you weren't here. Come on, let's go inside. You're freezing."

"I didn't want to be in there alone."

The poor kid. Audrey kept her arm around her shoulders as they walked toward the cottage together. Neve had already gone inside. It was eerily quiet. She could hear music from farther down the road—probably some of the hunters—and the tide, and that was it. And while the moon didn't cast much light, the sky was a blanket of stars. So many stars. It was so peaceful and quiet, and cold. It was the sort of night best spent by a fire drinking something hot, not investigating the theft of a dead woman's meager belongings.

When she crossed the threshold, Audrey swore. The place wasn't destroyed, but it was trashed pretty hard. The glare of headlights lit up what was already made bright by electric light. Neve had arrived. Mackenzie went to step farther into the cottage, but Audrey stopped her. "Crime scene, sweetie."

Neve's boots clomped on the steps as she joined them. Audrey drew Mac just out of the way so Neve could see inside. "First Ratchett, then Tex, and now this," Neve remarked. "It hasn't been a good couple of weeks for Jake."

"No," Audrey agreed. "It hasn't." She looked around. "Nothing else is missing."

Neve shot her a glance. "Nothing but what?"

"The bins of Maggie's things. We had them right here." She gestured to the spot where they'd sat in the living area. "The TV is still here, the DVD player." Whoever this was, they came here with the intention of taking Maggie's stuff and that was it. Now that she really looked, Audrey could see that while things had been dragged out of cupboards and drawers, and furniture cushions had been tossed around, no real damage had been done. It was like someone had wanted to make it look worse than it was.

Did they think she wouldn't notice that Maggie's belongings were the only thing missing? That was desperate. And the act of someone not particularly skilled in the criminal arts. It was the act of someone who was afraid there was something in those bins that might incriminate them. But they'd had the bins since Mac arrived in town. Why take them now?

"Okay, let's take a look around and make sure nothing else is missing," Neve suggested. "I'll take some photos for evidence. Do you have somewhere else you can stay tonight?" she asked Mac.

"Yes," Audrey replied. Then to the girl, "Go put your stuff in your car."

Mac did what she was told.

"Any ideas?" Neve asked. "The kid's father?"

"I don't know."

Neve looked at the alarm pad by the door. "Did Jake ever get a call about the alarm going off?"

"Not when I was at the house. Yancy was at the house tonight and she didn't mention it either. Maybe Mac didn't set it before she left."

"Well, who'd want to break into a rental in sleepy little Edgeport, huh?"

Audrey shot her a dry look. "Anyone who lives here." God, breaking and entering used to be a professional sport for bored teens in the area. It was like a rite of passage, but she didn't think that's what had happened at the cottage.

"We can check for prints, but the place is probably full of them." Neve looked around. "Anyway, get out of my crime scene. I know where to find you if I need you. Where are you taking Mackenzie?"

"To Mum's. Call me if you find anything."

"Yeah. Sure."

That was noncommittal. "Look, Neve. I know you don't particularly trust me or Jake right now, but we didn't do this. You don't want to deal with me, fine. Call Jake if you find anything. It's his property, remember?"

The other woman's full lips thinned. "It's not that I don't trust you. I'd trust you to have my back, but I don't think you or your boyfriend has any respect for the law."

Audrey frowned. "Yeah, so little respect that you were the first person I called about this."

"I didn't say you didn't respect *me*."

Audrey just shook her head. "Whatever." She was tired. Too tired for this. She turned and walked away. She heard Neve on her radio calling for backup as she approached Mackenzie's car. Mac was in the driver's seat, looking pale and shaken. Audrey went over and knocked on the window.

"Can you drive?" Audrey asked when the glass lowered.

Mac nodded. "I'm okay. Where are we going?"

"My mother's." Normally she would have taken her to Jake's, but with him being laid up, and the threatening note she'd received, her parents' place was a safer bet. Plus, her mother and father could both fuss over the kid, which was what she needed.

"Okay. I don't think I could drive back to Calais tonight. I guess I'll go back tomorrow." She looked up. "Maybe we should just give up."

"Let's talk about it tomorrow, okay? You don't need to decide right now."

A little while later they pulled into the driveway of the Harte household. It was only shortly after nine, so lights were still on inside. Her parents were still up, and would be for an hour or two.

Audrey knocked before letting them both inside. Her father met her in the foyer with a concerned frown on his face. "What's wrong?" he demanded. "Is it Jake?"

Anne joined them and Audrey explained to them what had happened at the resort. "Mac needs a place to spend the night, and I knew you guys would take better care of her than I can."

Her mother smiled serenely. "Of course she can stay here. Rusty, go make some hot chocolate."

He actually did a little jig at the prospect of sugar. "Sweet. You like marshmallows or whipped cream, kiddo?"

Mackenzie smiled at him. "Both?"

"Right answer." He trotted off toward the kitchen.

"My room?" Audrey asked her mother.

"Yes, if the color doesn't turn her stomach."

Audrey rolled her eyes. "It's lavender," she explained to Mac.

"And black," her mother added.

"And black," Audrey echoed.

"I like lavender. And black."

Audrey shot her mother an arch look. Her mother pretended not to notice. Mac's luggage was only a computer bag and a small suitcase, but Audrey carried the suitcase up the stairs for her and put it in her old room. It really was hideous. She showed the girl where the bathroom was and got her a couple of towels, then told her to come downstairs when she was ready.

Both her mother and father were in the kitchen when Audrey walked in.

"She okay?" her father asked, stirring melting chocolate in a double boiler on the stove.

"I think so. It freaked her out, arriving at the cottage to find all of Maggie's stuff gone."

"Is that all they took?" He shook his head. "That's weird, isn't it?"

"Not if that's what they were after."

His mismatched gaze sharpened. "You sure?"

"As I can be, yeah."

He looked like he wanted to say something, but then he looked at her mother and his expression changed. "Well, that's definitely not the kind of guy she wants to know."

"I'm pretty sure she doesn't," Audrey told him. "In fact, she'll probably go back to Calais tomorrow and give the whole thing up."

Her father went back to his stirring. "That might be for the best."

"Maybe," she replied. She'd been ready to do the same thing, but now someone had scared Mac. It was one thing to threaten Audrey but another to threaten a teenage girl. After all that she'd been through since returning home, all the violence and pain, one would think that she'd do all she could to resist more conflict, but she couldn't let whoever had done this get away with it. She'd send Mac home the next day, but then she was going to find who had broken into the cottage and get Maggie's stuff back.

Maggie had lost enough already.

When her father pulled into the yard the next morning, Audrey was surprised. She half-expected him to bail on her. She answered the door to see his resigned but smiling face. "Hey, kiddo."

She stepped back, and when he moved past her, she caught a whiff of disappointment. "You've been drinking."

He didn't even try to deny it as he shoved his hands into the pockets of his baggy jeans. "I had a shot of rum before I left the house."

Rum, their shared poison of choice. "Needed a little courage, did you?"

John nodded. There was nothing left of his smile. "You still want to do this?"

Audrey felt a tug of conscience. "If Bertie is still open to talking to me, I would like to know what happened."

"Tell me this isn't just about you being nosy. Tell me you really think you're doing this for a good reason, because there are people who are going to get hurt, kid."

She hesitated. "Who, Dad?"

He shook his head. "Why won't you leave this alone?"

"Because Maggie kept this from me. She knew everything about me, but she had a secret. It's eating at me and I can't stand it. She said I owed her for her taking the blame for killing Clint. If I can find out who Mac's father is, maybe I can finally feel like we're even and let go of her. I can't carry her with me for the rest of my life." That was about as succinct and honest as she could be when she wasn't even completely sure of the why herself.

Her father stared at her for a moment. She could feel his gaze prodding inside her soul, weighing whether or not to believe her. "Go get a sweater. It's cold. I'll visit with Jake."

Effectively dismissed, Audrey ran upstairs and dug through the dresser for a sweater to pull on. When she came back down, her father and Jake were talking quietly in the living room. Jake was sitting up, his back supported by a pile of cushions. Their conversation ended when she walked in.

"You two plotting?" she asked, feeling a tiny bit paranoid.

"Nosy," her father stated, but there wasn't any censure in his tone. Once again she was struck by how tired and drawn he looked. His color was off. Normally his cheeks had some pink to them, but they were pale, and his eyes lacked their usual brightness.

Jake smiled at her with that little hint of amusement that was both endearing and infuriating depending on her mood. "We were talking about you, of course. Can't do that when you're in the room—wouldn't be seemly."

Was he making fun or telling the truth? Half the time she wasn't sure, and usually it didn't matter.

"You could just talk to me instead," she suggested.

This time his smile was more genuine—but not complete, as his battered face was too swollen and stiff to fully cooperate. "Sometimes it's like talking to the wind."

"Yeah, yeah. It's pick-on-Audrey day." She grabbed a coat from the hooks in the back hall. "Do you need anything before I go?"

Jake shook his head. "No. I'm good."

Audrey grabbed a scarf too, and was just about to head out to the kitchen to get her boots when he stopped her. "Aud."

Her father passed her. "I'll be outside."

She frowned. "What? Are you in pain? Do you need some pills?"

There was that amusement again. He held out his hand. "C'mere."

For a second, she stared at his abraded knuckles and thought about just walking away. Running—even though she said she wouldn't.

But she didn't walk—or run—away. She crossed the floor and twined her fingers with his.

"No matter what that head of yours tries to tell you, I am *always* on your side." He looked deep into her eyes as he spoke. "Even if it doesn't feel like it."

She nodded. "I know."

He squeezed her hand. "You're my reason."

Audrey frowned. "Your reason for what?"

Jake smiled. "Everything, woman. Everything."

God, he killed her. He knew just what to say to her. Anyone else and she'd wonder if he was trying to manipulate her, but Jake didn't need to use those tactics. "You're stoned." She crouched down and kissed him on the mouth—softly because she didn't want to hurt his lip. "I'll be back soon," she told him.

"Good, because I want to talk to you. It feels like we haven't had any time alone in days. At least, none that I've been lucid for."

"We haven't," she confirmed. "You've had too many people fussing around you. Even Lincoln."

"Yeah, it's a little late to play the protective big brother, but I'll enjoy it while it lasts. Now go. Rusty's waiting."

"He better not be behind the wheel."

"It was one shot."

She shot him a knowing look. "It's never just one. You and I both know that." Then she left, promising not to be long.

She armed the alarm, locked the door, and stepped out into the cold, gray morning. Her father was in his truck—on the passenger side. Normally Audrey would insist on taking her car, but Ridge Road was sometimes like a land mine of potholes and the half-ton was better suited for it. What the hell had she been thinking when she got that Prius? She'd thought she'd be driving it around Boston, where they had decent snow removal; that's what she'd thought.

She climbed into the driver's side. The key was already in the ignition. "Thank you for doing this," she said.

"Don't thank me. Let's just go get this over with."

"God, you are so dramatic."

He didn't say anything—just stared out his window, which worried her. Silent was not her father's usual mode.

Bertie Neeley lived in a trailer just before the Stokes homestead. It was painted a bright and cheery pale yellow with blue trim. It wasn't a look Audrey would have associated with Bertie, but the place was cute. There were even flower boxes, although they were empty for the winter.

A white curtain parted when they pulled in—Bertie's face through the glass. When Audrey climbed the front steps behind her father, Bertie opened the door. He looked freshly showered and wore a crisp but faded plaid shirt. With his hair slicked back from his face, there was a glimpse of the man he used to be. She remembered now, that Bertie hadn't been a bad-looking man when she'd been young. When had he gone to hell?

"I put the kettle on," he said by way of greeting. It was starting to whistle in the background.

John Harte simply nodded at him. Audrey made herself look him in the eye. "Thanks for seeing us, Mr. Neeley."

He raised an eyebrow. "Listen to you being all formal." He walked to the stove and turned off the burner. "Don't need to be so polite just 'cause you're intruding on my privacy, Audrey Harte."

It was said kindly, but she felt snugly put in her place. "Okay."

Inside the trailer was as much a surprise as the outside. Bertie wasn't much of a fashion plate, and sometimes his hygiene was suspect, but his house was tidy and neat, if a little run-down. An old chess set sat on a small table in the living area. He didn't have much money, if Audrey's memory served. Most of what he had came from a pension and doing odd jobs around the community. He'd been married once, she thought. Had a kid or two who had left with their mother decades earlier.

A sad little life, Audrey would have thought, but Bertie's place didn't reflect that. The cups that he put on the table in front of them were white with embossed flowers in the ceramic. Old, but in good shape. Elegant, even. Sugar and milk were in matching containers, and the teapot he placed on the table was part of the set as well. It looked as though the handle had been glued back on at one point. A plate of cookies followed.

Bertie sat down at the head of the table. Audrey and her father were across from each other. Audrey placed a napkin on the table and put a cookie on it. Molasses. She'd wait for the tea to steep before eating it.

Her father surprised her by speaking. "Bertie, I know my girl is going to ask you stuff that isn't any of her business, but I want you to know that she's not going to repeat anything you tell her. This visit is just so she'll leave you and the past the fuck alone."

Audrey started, her eyes widening.

Bertie nodded, his expression solemn as he gazed at Audrey. "She's got the Pelletier in her." He made it sound like a disease—or a parasite. "Won't lie—I wasn't going to tell you anything I didn't want you knowing, but I remembered what you'd done for that little girl, and it makes sense you'd want to do right by her daughter."

The two men seemed to expect her to respond to this, judging from the expectant way they watched her. Audrey raised a brow. "Thanks."

"Well, girlie, what do you want to know?"

Where the hell did she start? "You used to spend a lot of time back the Ridge with the kids that partied back there."

"Yup."

"Someone got Maggie pregnant. I think it was someone young. Do you have any idea who that might have been?"

Bertie glanced at her father. "There were several young men around that year who took a shine to little Maggie. My best guess is that it was one of them."

"What about Mike LeBlanc? Could it have been him?" It wasn't her imagination—Bertie stiffened at the boy's name.

"No, I'm pretty sure it wasn't Michael." Bertie's hands trembled as he poured the tea. It could have been nerves, or the DTs—delirium tremens. "He didn't chase skirt like those other boys."

She thought about what Dwayne had insinuated about Mike not liking girls. "How do you know?"

He stared at the cup in front of him, curving his big-knuckled fingers around it. "Because the only person Michael had sex with around these parts was me."

Tea sloshed over the side of Audrey's cup as she started. Of all the possible confessions Bertie could have made, this was not the one she had expected. "You?"

He nodded, peeking at her out of the corner of his eye. "I wasn't too bad-looking back then. I was in my early forties, divorced. Heavy drinking hadn't ruined me yet, and I did physical work, so my body was strong and lean. Michael was eighteen—almost nineteen. He was much more comfortable about his sexuality than I was. I admired that—no damn way was I letting anyone in this place know I liked men. Can you imagine?"

Unfortunately, she could. The locals were much more forgiving now, but back then they wouldn't have been. The kids probably would have been the worst too. Young, testosterone-riddled men often despised anything they saw as a threat to their own masculinity. Audrey nodded.

"So, we met in secret. He was here every weekend he could get down, him and those friends of his who didn't know how to hold their liquor and competed for the attention of Barbie and her friends." He smiled faintly. "Was like something out of one those romance movies—a perfect little world of our own—secret and just for us. We were terrified of anyone finding out, but we weren't going to stop. Your dad walked in on us once."

Audrey's gaze snapped to her father, whose cheeks had turned red. "I promised you I'd never tell, and I didn't."

Bertie nodded. "And I won't ever tell your secrets either, you old bastard."

Secrets? What secrets? One look from her father warned her not to ask. Did she really want to know? Okay, so Mike wasn't Mackenzie's dad. The kid was going to be so disappointed. But there was another mystery around Mike LeBlanc. "How did he die, Bertie?"

A flicker of pain tightened his features—intense enough that she regretted asking, even though she wanted to know. "One night the sweet little fool told me he loved me. I knew right then that I had to end things, even though I didn't want to. I was more than twenty years his senior and so deep in the closet I smelled of mothballs."

Audrey smiled at his choice of words. No one used mothballs anymore, did they? "So, you broke it off?"

"Not right then. See, I wasn't in any hurry to give him up, but then Wendell made some crack about Michael being my 'bum buddy.' Everyone laughed—thought it was a great joke—but I knew it would be only a matter of time before they figured out it was true. I started pulling away from Michael, made excuses not to see him. He knew what I was doing and he wasn't going to let me get away with it." He smiled a little. "He cornered me back at the shed one night—that's where Wendell and I grew our weed. Maggie was with him. She was all bristled up, telling me I couldn't just use her friend and toss him aside."

That sounded like Maggie. She could be very protective of

people she cared about—when she wasn't using them to her own advantage. "She left so the two of you could talk?"

"Mm. I told him it was over. He didn't want to accept it. I knew I had to hurt him to make him walk away, so I told him that while he was good to f... sleep with, he wasn't worth throwing my life away." Bertie swallowed. "I laughed at him."

Audrey couldn't help but think of her brother, and how brave David had been to come out to the people of this town. "Did it work?"

Bertie stared into his cup. "Yep. He started crying, and then he ran away. I knew he didn't know the woods and that it was dangerous at night, so I chased after him. When he heard me behind him he ran faster—didn't want anything to do with me. I yelled at him to stop—I knew he was getting close to the edge—but he didn't listen."

Audrey swallowed. "He fell."

A tear leaked from Bertie's eye. He brushed it away. "He did. Snapped his neck. I called the police and waited with him until help arrived—not that there was any help for him. I was too much of a coward to tell the truth, so I just told them I'd heard a shout, and that I'd found him on the bank. When they searched the area, they found evidence of kids drinking up there and assumed he'd been one of them. They never found the grow."

"And you never told anyone."

Bertie jerked his chin toward John. "He figured part of it out. I confessed the rest. I never told anyone else. Wendell and

I stopped growing, and I tried to numb my grief with drinking. I've been doing it ever since."

"You loved him." Her voice was hoarse. Oh, this was terrible. Her father had been right. She didn't want to know this. It was none of her business. Jesus, when was she going to learn?

He nodded. "I did. And I haven't loved anyone half as much since. He was good and sweet, and I lost him because I thought I could have both."

Audrey tore her gaze away. She stared at the cookie on her napkin. She hadn't touched it, and now she hadn't the stomach for it.

"So you see, my girl, Michael couldn't have gotten that poor little girl pregnant."

"No."

"And now you know why Maggie Jones hated me until the day she died. I tried explaining to her that I hadn't hurt him, but I don't think she ever believed it. Every once in a while she'd say his name in front of me just to taunt me. She asked me if I remembered him shortly before she died. As if I could ever forget the dear boy."

Audrey just stared at him. She pitied him. She really did. "You made that cross."

He nodded.

"Michael knew who Maggie was sleeping with." As he said this, Bertie looked her square in the eye.

"According to him she was sharing herself with all of them, including Barbie."

If he thought Maggie being into girls was going to shock her, he was wrong. She'd known that for a while now. And she wasn't surprised Barbie had left it out. It didn't matter. Barbie couldn't have gotten Maggie pregnant.

Bertie cleared his throat. "Now you have your answers, what do you plan to do with them?"

She looked at him—a haggard man, aged beyond his years. What would his young boyfriend think if he could see him now, ravaged by grief and alcohol? She wrapped her fingers around the wrist resting on the table closest to her. "Nothing," she told him, and it was a promise. "I'm not going to do a damn thing."

# CHAPTER EIGHTEEN

So, you got your truth. Happy?"

Audrey shot a glance at her father as they drove out the Ridge toward the main road. She was behind the wheel. "You know, if you'd been a bit more forthcoming I wouldn't have pushed it so hard." But it was a lame excuse and they both knew it. Truth be told, she felt a little ashamed of herself for suspecting Bertie of anything nefarious, despite his behavior.

He shrugged. "Wasn't my story to tell."

"And what a story it was." She shook her head.

"Too bad that kid died, though," he said eventually. "Bertie's never been the same since."

It was beyond sad. "You were right. I hate saying it, but you were right. I don't feel any sort of satisfaction in knowing."

"I know you don't. You wouldn't be the person I think you are if you did."

She wasn't entirely sure just what kind of person he thought she was, but she wasn't going to ask. "Your arm okay?" He was rubbing it.

"Yeah, just a little asleep. Had it propped on Bertie's table too long."

She fixed her attention on the road, wondering if she ought to continue. What the hell. "Dad, Bertie said Maggie was with everyone that hung out back the Ridge."

He glanced out the window. "Yeah."

"Does that include Greg?"

Her father's sigh filled the cab of the truck. "I don't know, kid. I suppose it does."

"He told me nothing happened between him and Maggie."

Rusty glanced at her. "Do you believe him?"

"I want to."

"Then you should."

He was right. If she went after Greg like she had the others, it would only cause trouble between herself and Jess, and that wasn't something she was willing to risk. "I do."

They arrived back at Jake's. Audrey put the truck in park and opened the door. When her father came around to get into the driver's seat, she put her hand on his arm—there was no give beneath her fingers. He might be in his late sixties, with a bit of a gut, but he was still as strong as an ox. "Thank you for coming with me and indulging my nosiness."

His expression softened. He ran a hand over the ginger and gray stubble on his jaw. "Shit, Auddie. I'd do anything for you kids. You know that."

She knew he'd do anything that liquor didn't get in the way of. For the moment, that was good enough. She put her arms around his waist and hugged him. He hesitated—for a second—and then he hugged her back. She leaned into his shoulder and breathed him in—still a slight hint of booze, laundry detergent, sawdust, and Old Spice. She'd once dated a guy who wore Old Spice. She had to break up with him because he reminded her of her father. He also drank like her father, so that helped end things.

Audrey pulled back. "Tell Mum I'll be down later to make dinner."

He shook his head. "I've got dinner tonight. You spend some time with Jake. Make a pie or something."

She laughed. "How did you know he planned to make a pie?"

"I'm not as dumb as I look."

"Jury's still out on that." She went to walk away. "Hey, Dad? What did Bertie mean...?"

"No." He pointed a finger at her. "That old fool made that crack about keeping my secrets. I don't have any secrets he or anyone else needs to keep for me, Audrey Elsa Harte. But that doesn't mean I'll stand for you snooping around. I have my past, you have yours. Leave it at that."

"Okay." She hadn't expected him to share, but she hadn't expected such an effective shutdown either. He was right. She wouldn't want him digging around in her past, so she was going to have to leave his alone too. She'd had enough digging into the past.

"I'll see you later," her father said and climbed into the truck. She lifted her hand in a wave before turning and jogging to the house. When she got inside, she found Jake in the kitchen, standing at the sideboard, rolling out pie crust.

"What are you doing?" she demanded. "You were supposed to wait for me so I could help."

He shrugged. "I got bored. There's only so many pills you can take and *Criminal Minds* you can glom before you need to get the hell up and think of something happy."

"Pie makes you happy?"

He gave her a "duh" look. "Pie makes everybody happy." He inclined his head toward the bag of apples. "Feel like peeling?"

Why not? She hung up her coat, pulled off her boots, and washed her hands. He'd already set out a sharp paring knife for her.

"How did the chat with Bertie go?"

"Fine."

"Did he give a DNA sample?"

"I didn't ask him to."

Jake stopped rolling and looked at her. "Why not?"

She removed the clip from the apple bag. "Because Bertie's gay." She knew Jake would never betray Bertie's secret, so she didn't feel guilty sharing it with him.

Both of his eyebrows rose—well, one did and the other twitched, held in place by stitches and swelling. "That was not what I expected you to say."

"Wasn't what I expected to hear."

"Explains a lot," he remarked, and went back to rolling. "Did Rusty know?"

"Yep. Apparently that's why he gave me the whole 'what happens when you dig into secrets' talk."

"So, who does that leave? The LeBlanc kid?"

The blade of the knife slid easily through the skin of the first apple. "This is where it gets fabulous—Mike LeBlanc was Bertie's lover."

He stopped rolling and stared at her. "Fuck off."

"It's the truth. I heard it from Bertie himself."

"Jesus." He draped the dough over the deep glass pie plate and slowly nudged it down as its weight did the rest. "So, Dwayne or Aaron, then?"

"I guess."

"Maybe it's someone you haven't talked to."

"Well, the whole town knows what we're doing. If the son of a bitch hasn't come forward by now, he really doesn't want to be found." She thought about Greg again and pushed it aside. He was a good guy. If he told her nothing happened, then nothing happened.

"That sucks for poor Mac."

"It does. I think she's given up."

"Maybe that's for the best."

"Maybe." She wasn't the best one to judge.

A car pulled into the dooryard as Jake laid pie crust cut out into shapes on the top of the apples, sugar, and cinnamon Audrey put in the pan.

"It's Neve," she said, peering out the window.

"If she's come to arrest me, she'll have to wait until this comes out of the oven. I'm not going to jail without a piece."

"You're not going to jail." Even as she said it, a little trickle of fear ran down her spine. There was a chance that Neve was there to arrest one of them—or at least question them some more.

She answered the door as Neve knocked. "Hey," she said, her tone cool.

Neve's expression was neutral. "I just wanted to come by and give you guys an update on the Ratchett investigation. Can I come in?"

She didn't act like a cop on the verge of arresting a murderer, so Audrey stepped back and allowed her inside. "Jake, Neve is here." He limped into view, wiping his hands on a dish towel.

"Hey, Jake." Neve rolled her shoulders, as if she was uncomfortable. "Your guns and the guns we took from Yancy came back clean—which I'm sure you're not surprised to hear." Was that suspicion in her tone?

"Not at all," he said.

"We're still looking into it, but so far ballistics doesn't match anyone who was staying here. However, there have been other people in from out of town, and locals hunting in the area as well. We're trying to track them down."

Of course she was.

"What about the bastard that fucked me up?" Jake asked.

Neve cleared her throat. She avoided Audrey's curious gaze. "His death has been ruled an accidental overdose."

Would it be bad manners if Audrey crowed? Probably.

Jake nodded. "Can't say I'm sorry he's gone."

"No." The cop looked like she'd bitten into something sour. It made Audrey both angry and sad, but she wasn't in the mood to defend herself, or to try to win back Neve's regard. Instead she took the pie from Jake and slid it into the hot oven. When she straightened, she turned to find Neve watching her. "I've got news for you too, Dr. Harte."

"Oh?"

"We dusted the cottage for prints. I was surprised we didn't get that many, but the crime scene guys said a lot of the surfaces had been cleaned recently—so good on your housekeeping staff. We pulled a partial print from the doorknob to the bedroom that didn't match Mackenzie's. Hopefully it will give us someone."

"But only if his prints are on record."

Neve nodded. "Well, I've taken up enough of your time. Have a good day. I'll see myself out."

Audrey followed her to the door and locked it behind her. It was rare for people to lock their doors during the day in Edgeport, but Audrey wasn't taking chances.

"You guys ever going to kiss and make up?" Jake asked.

"I'm not sure that's possible while she's convinced we're hiding something. Good news about Ratchett's brother, though." It might not have been the most subtle of topic changes, but it worked.

"Yeah." He frowned. "Wish I knew what the hell really happened. Somebody shot that son of a bitch, and I don't believe it was an accident. Maybe Tex's death was, but not that shooting."

"You may never know, just like I might never find out who Mac's father is. Some mysteries are never solved."

"I'll remember that, Columbo."

She arched a brow. "You better not be saying I look like Peter Falk, because you are never getting sex again if you are."

He grinned—then winced. "No, you don't look like Peter Falk. I suppose I can live with never knowing, and just be glad he didn't leave a better trail for them to follow to Matt Jones."

Folding a dish towel, she draped it over the stove handle before raising her gaze to his. "Something else is bothering you. What is it?"

"Lincoln. I'm waiting for him to collect on the debt I owe him for him saving my ass. He's going to ask for something big, I know it."

"Like what?"

"Like maybe part of Gracie's. Or money."

"You don't have to give him what he wants."

"That's not how owing someone in my family works."

"So change it. Do you know how ridiculous it is that Kenny put a contract on Matt just because he owed you? It was sheer stupidity, and you are not stupid, Jake. Let Lincoln ask for whatever he wants. It's not like you're his fairy godmother, or a genie in a lamp."

"No, but I'm his brother." He said it like the simple declaration explained everything. Maybe it did. What would she do for Jess or David? God, if she bashed a man's brain in for a friend, and took a bullet for her boyfriend's niece, what in the name of God would she do for family?

"I'm going to have more security cameras installed at the resort," Jake told her later that afternoon as they sat at the table eating warm apple pie with ice cream.

"Good idea." She was surprised he didn't have them all over the place, but then he liked his own privacy, so it stood to reason he'd respect that of his guests. "Too bad the ones you have didn't catch anything about the break-in."

"Mm. I'm still pissed about that." He swallowed. "When's Angeline arriving?"

"Saturday. Thanks for offering her a cottage."

"Might as well use them. Plus, she didn't balk at the price. I like that."

Audrey chuckled. "Well, hopefully she won't balk at the facility either."

He set down his fork. He'd already eaten most of the huge slab of pie he'd taken. How did he eat like that and stay so lean? Her jeans were getting snug. "Aud, she's flying from LA to the middle of butt-fuck nowhere to check it out. She's already interested. All you have to do is close the deal."

"I'm not sure I know how to do that."

"You know." He picked up his fork again. "And I can help if you need it."

"Thanks." She took another bite of pie. "I really hope she goes for it."

"She will."

She wished she had his confidence, but she didn't. There were just too many things that could go wrong, and then there was that part of her that didn't think she deserved to succeed.

In the past, she had worked hard, hoping it would cancel out the bad karma of murder. She didn't regret killing Clint, but she had always been very much aware of the gravity of what she had done. Part of her didn't think she was finished paying for it—that she would ever be finished. Why should she expect to get something she really, really wanted? She'd already gotten Jake, her mother's recovery, and a fresh start with her sister. Surely the universe wouldn't also allow her to achieve her dream of her own facility? And if it did, what terrible thing would happen to balance it?

She didn't really believe life worked that way, but the thought was still there, because the universe was a bitch.

"There's something I've been meaning to talk to you about," he said a few minutes later, when he'd finished his pie.

Something in his tone made her head snap up. "Is it about how much time I've been spending here? I can start staying with Mum and Dad more until I find my own place."

He frowned. "You're not getting your own place. And you're not living with your parents. You're staying here, where you belong. With me."

She half-expected him to thump his chest. She smiled at the image. "Okay. Do you want me to start paying half of the bills?"

Jake's frown grew. "Are you trying to insult me?"

Audrey held up her hands. "I'm not trying to, but you sound so frigging serious!"

He sighed, the lines in his face easing. "Sorry. I guess I've moved around too much today. My ribs are starting to hate me."

She started to get up. "I'll help you back to the couch."

"Not yet." He held up a hand. "First, come upstairs with me."

She arched a brow. "We're not having sex if your ribs are hurting."

"That's not why I want you to come upstairs, though it's tempting to try." When she didn't look convinced, he shook his head. "Look, humor me, will you?"

"All right, but after this, you're taking a pill and lying down. Got it?"

"Yes, Mother."

She let him lead the way up the stairs and followed his stiff and slow steps up the gently creaking boards. How many times in her life had she done this? When they were young she chased him up those stairs. Sometimes he chased her. Hell, they still chased each other. Gracie would yell at them that they sounded like a "horde of angry elephants," but she never tried to stop them. She trusted them together, didn't worry about what they might be doing.

At the top of the stairs, Jake took a right—away from the room they shared and toward the bedroom that had been his as a kid. Audrey followed him inside. It looked different than she remembered, but still the same. There weren't any posters anymore, but a few framed prints still hung on the walls. The bed was still in the same place, with the same quilt Gracie had made in shades of blue and gray on it. His guitar case was in one corner, an electric guitar on a stand beside it. There was a keyboard too, and a harmonica case on the dresser. She should get him to play for her more often. She used to get him to do it all the time when they were young.

He gestured to the bed. "Like we used to."

Okay, they were going to take a walk down memory lane. Audrey still had a feeling of slight dread in her stomach, but she went around to the left side of the bed while he stretched out on the right. Outside, day was already waning, but there was enough light in the room to see him clearly.

"Remember when we'd lie here and plan our futures?" he asked.

"No matter what one of us wanted to do we made sure the other was part of it—even if they didn't want to be."

He smiled, the lines around his mouth deepening. She wanted to kiss them. "You wanted to be a singer."

"We were going to have our own band. Then you decided you wanted to be an architect. What brought that on, anyway?"

"No idea. You were so pissed."

"Yeah. I couldn't draw to save my life. No way we could do that together."

"So then you decided to be a real estate agent so you could sell the places I designed."

She laughed. "God, I'm glad that didn't work out. I don't think I'm suited to sales."

"You told me about getting the acceptance letter from Stanford on this bed."

Audrey swallowed. "It was the first time you didn't have a plan to come with me."

He turned his head toward her as the fingers of his right hand twined with her left. "I wanted to, but I couldn't leave Gran. She was already getting sick. And I couldn't ask you to stay."

"I would have."

"I know. That's why I had to make sure you left."

And he had done that by sleeping with Maggie. It was still a sore point for her, but not so much as it had been when she first came home. She understood it now, even if she didn't like it.

Jake reached into his pocket. "We made a lot of plans and decisions on this bed."

"We did." She had thought she'd lose her virginity in it. She almost told him she loved him on it. Her heart had been hammering much like it was at that moment. "Why are we here now, Jake?"

His fingers tightened around hers. He lifted their hands, and then she saw what he had taken from his pocket. She made a noise that was something between a sob and a gasp.

Gracie's ring.

Jake slid it onto her ring finger. "What do you think, Aud? You want to marry me?"

# CHAPTER NINETEEN

The stone glittered, even though there wasn't much light in the room other than the grayness leaking through the windows. The metal was silver, or maybe platinum. The band was carved with intricate swirls that were dark and beautifully aged.

"I think it's a pink diamond," Jake explained. "Gran told me that one of my Tripp ancestors stole it a couple hundred years ago off some rich woman. I don't know if that's true, but Gramps gave it to her when they got engaged and she never took it off until the day she died. That's when she gave it to me and commanded that I wasn't to give it to anyone but you."

*Oh, Gracie.* Tears burned the back of Audrey's eyes. "I remember her wearing it. She used to let me help her clean it sometimes."

"I have the matching band too. If you want it."

Audrey turned her head on the pillow. Jake was watching her, his bruised face serious and... nervous? He was nervous. Afraid she might say no, even though he knew it wasn't possible.

"I want it," she whispered. "Even if it means marrying you to get it."

He laughed—which then made him groan in pain. She rolled onto her side and kissed him as hard as she dared. “You sure you want to do this? I’m a murderer, you know.” There was an edge of seriousness to her tone that she hated.

He reached up and smoothed the hair back from her face. “I’ve been sure since I was fourteen years old. Who else would be crazy enough to have us but each other?”

“You make a good point.” She grinned. “I lied earlier. We are going to have sex. Think you can handle that?”

Grinning, Jake nodded. “Be gentle with me.”

She was, though she was certain the experience caused him some discomfort. He claimed it was worth it afterward, as he downed two of his painkillers with a glass of water. He dozed on the sofa while she sat and watched her engagement ring sparkle under the living room lamps. She was practically giddy.

And she wasn’t going to think about what other shoe might drop while something so amazing was happening to her. No. Nothing—not even her own stupid imagination was going to dull that moment.

She wanted to tell someone her news. She wanted to scream it from the rooftops. Good God, she never would have thought she’d react like this. She laughed at herself—out loud.

But she couldn’t tell anyone before she told her family, could she? And they wouldn’t all be together until Tuesday, when David finally arrived. That meant she couldn’t tell anyone within a twenty-mile radius, or the gossip would eventually get back to her mother. The Pelletiers not only liked gossip, they attracted it.

So who could she tell? Angeline? No, she'd rather show her the ring in person.

Finally, she realized who she could share the news with. She mixed herself a light rum and cola and pulled on her boots, gloves, and coat. The day had gotten steadily more gray and cold, though it didn't feel like snow. Audrey wrapped a scarf around her neck and head as she started down the driveway. It was already getting dark, and it was only late afternoon. These short, dark days would eventually drive her to buy a UV light or drag Jake somewhere tropical for vacation. Maybe Jamaica. They could elope.

No, that wasn't an option. As she crossed the dirt road and walked a hundred or so feet up to an old lane, she kept her gaze on the little stone church set back in the field, still a good distance from the edge of the bank. The frigid breeze off the tide buffeted the inlet but had yet to erode it away. The Tripps had built a seawall decades ago to protect the land where their family had worshipped and been buried ever since old Angus Tripp had a falling-out with the local minister. Audrey had decided at a very young age she was going to be married in that church, knowing full well the only way to do that was to marry a Tripp. Of course, she'd already had one in mind.

She walked down the lane—hard tracks of mud in the grass that were so compacted even weeds couldn't poke through—and stopped to open the gate to the little cemetery. She hadn't visited in close to a month. She could shame herself for the neglect, but she didn't need to be by her grave to talk to Gracie. It was just that sometimes it made her feel closer to the old woman who had been her surrogate grandmother, mentor, and friend.

She sniffed as she crouched by the tombstone, nose running in the damp cold. "Hey, Gracie," she said. "If death works like I was told as a kid, you already knew that your grandson proposed today. And you already know I said yes, but I wanted to come tell you myself, just in case. He gave me your ring. I remember you telling me how Mathius proposed, and the way you'd smile when you thought of it. It makes me happy to wear your ring. I feel closer to you, and it makes me realize how much I've missed you." She sniffed again, but this time it wasn't from the cold. "I wish you were here to help me figure some of this stuff out, but whatever. I brought a drink with me so we can celebrate, and God, I hope you'd celebrate this, Gracie." She took a long, deep swallow of the drink, and then poured the rest on the grave.

She crouched there a moment, as though waiting for something to happen, but nothing did. "I'd better get back. I don't want to not be there if Jake wakes up." She touched her gloved fingers to the stone. "Good-bye, Gracie. I love you."

Audrey stood up and began the short walk back to the house. She had just closed the gate when the strangest thing happened. If it was a movie or a TV show, she'd scoff at the overly sentimental writers.

Two crows landed on the tombstone in front of her, their feathers dark and glossy. One looked at her and cawed. Gracie loved crows—she used to feed them table scraps. What was that old saying? *One crow, sorrow; two crows...joy.* The crow cawed again and then the two of them flew away, a matched pair.

Audrey grinned. She wasn't a religious person, but she didn't have to believe in God to believe in the power of Gracie Tripp. And after the week she was having, it was nice to believe in something.

Audrey had been promising to take Mackenzie to visit her mother's grave, and when the next morning arrived with sunshine, she decided that was the day to do it. It was also the best time to tell the girl she was done with the search for her father.

Audrey left her ring at home when she picked Mac up to go for a hike back the ridge and to visit Maggie's grave. She didn't want to explain the ring, in case Mac made a mistake and mentioned it to Audrey's mother. And she definitely did not want to explain it to Yancy, who was sitting with Jake while she was gone.

"I don't need a babysitter," he said sullenly.

"I'll feel better knowing someone's here." Then, to Yancy, "Don't let him bake anything. It wears him out."

"That wasn't what did it," he informed her with a grin.

Ten years ago she might have blushed. Instead she tapped the tip of her finger against his nose. "Poor, fragile little man." Then she kissed him. "I won't be long."

Mackenzie wasn't her usual sunny self when she arrived at the house, and Audrey hated adding to her glum mood. "So, I got a call this morning from the lab. The results came back on Mike LeBlanc's kit."

"It's not him, is it?" the girl asked. Her lower lip quivered.

Audrey shook her head. "No."

"I guess that was too much to ask." She brushed her hand under her eye. "Carol would have made a great grandmother."

Taking a deep breath to keep her own eyes from welling up, Audrey gave her a hug. "You can keep in touch with her if you want. I'm sure she'd like that."

Mac nodded against her shoulder. "You're right."

"Come on. Let's go."

They made the drive to the cemetery in relative silence, and when they stood in front of Maggie's grave, the girl said, "I think I'm done with this place. Whoever my father is, I don't think I want to know him."

Someone had sprinkled glitter on the headstone, Audrey realized when she spied twinkling. "I understand." Who could have done that? Who remembered that Maggie loved glitter? Someone who knew her as a kid, but Maggie hadn't been good at keeping friends. Maybe one of the girls from the salon. She smiled, regardless. Maggie would like knowing her grave sparkled in the light.

"I don't think you do," the girl challenged, her smooth cheeks flushed with more than cold. "Until a month ago, I didn't know anything about my birth parents. Then I find out that my mother was sexually assaulted not only by her father, but probably countless other assholes in this shitty town. He doesn't even want to know me."

Audrey stared at her. "We're still waiting on the results from two DNA tests."

"I know that! But it still hurts."

"I imagine it does. But you didn't do this for him, right? You started this for you, and if you're going to end it, make sure that's for you too."

Mac's shoulders slumped. "I wanted to know where I came from, but now I wish I'd never looked. My parents—the people who actually raised me—are amazing. They love me and support me."

"They wanted you."

The girl's eyes widened. "Yes."

"What you need to remember is that Maggie loved you. She could have terminated her pregnancy—and they probably tried to talk her into that. She decided to have you, and then she did the best thing she could for you—she gave you to people she knew would love you the way she wanted, but knew she couldn't. Maggie was a lot of things—mostly a mess—but she knew that. She didn't want you to grow up with that."

Mac blinked back tears, and Audrey realized that she no longer looked at her as Maggie's clone, but as her own person. "As for your father, he probably was a kid too. And even though he's not a kid now, coming forward and claiming you might land him in jail. If he was over eighteen, what he did to Maggie, even if they were dating, was sexual assault, and there's no statute of limitations on it. Regardless, he probably has a family of his own now, and he'd want to protect them."

"I guess the guys who did come forward were pretty brave, then."

Audrey shrugged. "Respectable at least."

"I think I'm okay with that." She smiled at Audrey. "I'd still like to go for that hike, if you're up for it."

Audrey returned the smile. "I need the exercise. Let's go." Then, absently, "Bye, Maggie."

Mac reached into the pocket of her coat and withdrew a small scrap of something. She bent down and placed it on the base of the headstone. Audrey's throat clenched.

It was a hospital bracelet—the kind they put on newborns.

"Good-bye, Mom," the girl whispered, and touched the stone.

Audrey turned away, throat so tight she could hardly breathe. She'd been more emotional the last couple of weeks than she had been in the previous six months. Part of her would be glad to see the back of the kid for that very reason, but another part was thankful for getting to know Mac—for seeing that something good had sprung from the Jones family tree.

They walked back to her car in silence. It was a short drive to Ridge Road and a few minutes later she pulled into the lane where Jake had taken her a few days earlier and parked.

According to Jake, the shack that Bertie had mentioned was on the land he'd purchased from Wendell. Not that she expected to find anything there, but Jake had also told her it was where some of the older kids used to go to make out or smoke up. Why had she never known this? Oh, right, she'd been in juvie for a good part of her teenage years. And then, when she came back, very few people had wanted anything to do with her. She scared them. Maybe that was why she was really there—to see what she had missed out on.

She made Mac put on a bright orange jacket she'd borrowed from her father, while she slipped the windbreaker from Jake's over her heavy sweater and turtleneck combo. People knew about the trail, so not many hunted in the area, but Audrey wasn't going to take the chance. If Bertie had wandered onto the land, others might, and if she got Mac shot she'd never forgive herself. Neve would lock her up for sure.

They entered the trail right at the road and began the slow, gradual climb up.

"It's pretty," Mackenzie remarked after a few minutes.

Audrey was starting to feel a little sweat forming around her hairline. "It is, isn't it? You know, when I was a kid, I thought this place was boring."

"It kind of is—for a place that always seems to have weird stuff going on."

She laughed. "Yeah, I guess. I forgot that it's beautiful too, though. And that alongside all those weird people, there are good ones too."

"There's always a trade-off." Mac shrugged. "That's what my dad always says."

"Smart man."

"He is. And a cynic." She laughed. "Which way?"

They had come to a fork in the path. The right path stayed close to the edge, while the left crept deeper into the woods.

"Left," Audrey said. The climb became steeper, and soon both of them were breathing hard and talking very little. Audrey stopped to take a drink of water from the bottle she'd brought. "Oh my God. I can't believe we used to climb all the way up here just to drink. Stupid kids." She hadn't gone there very often, but it hadn't seemed that hard a climb back then.

Mac laughed. "You were. We just went to an abandoned building."

They climbed farther, until they came to a spot that looked like it had been cleared at one time. The vegetation growing there was short and sparse on either side of the trail. On the right, about thirty feet away, was what was left of an old shack. It was standing, all four walls intact—the roof too—but the door lay on the ground in front of it, and the tar paper peeled in long strips off the sides of the building.

"There it is," Audrey murmured.

Her companion frowned. "What the heck is that?"

Audrey's lips twisted. "The Love Shack." That's what Jake had called it.

"What? Seriously?"

She nodded. "From what I've heard." She started walking toward it, making as much noise as she could.

"Why are you doing that?"

"Critters," she explained. "If there are any in there, I want them to clear out before I come in."

She was aware of Mac stopping several feet behind her. "Define 'any.'"

It wasn't really the right time of day for skunks, and it was a little late in the year, but there might be a family of raccoons or feral cats. "Nothing too dangerous." When she reached the shed, she kicked the side of it. She heard a thump and then a hiss before a huge tomcat ran out the open doorway and raced past them.

"Oh my God!" Mac pressed her hand to her chest. "I almost peed!"

Audrey laughed. She would never admit that her bladder had spasmed as well. She peeked inside the building. She didn't know what she expected to see, but she expected something. There was nothing within the rotting walls at all, except some boards, a few of which had been nailed together. If she were to guess, she'd say it had probably been the base of a cot at one time, but that some kids—or adults—had kicked it apart years ago.

She looked around. What had she expected? That Maggie's ghost would be standing there, ready to divulge all her secrets?

"Doesn't look like much," came Mac's voice.

"No," Audrey agreed. "It never was. Do you want to keep going, or turn back?"

"Let's turn back. I told your mom I'd have lunch with her before I left and I should get going. Mom says they're calling for freezing rain tonight."

"Then we'd better get you home." Audrey turned toward the door. Mac had stopped just inside the exit, her gaze fixed on the wall as her fingers reached out to touch.

"Audrey, look."

She stepped up beside the girl. There, carved into the grayed wood, was a crooked heart the size of an apple. It had been so weathered that it didn't even stand out from the wall anymore, it just blended in to the gouges and cracks. Inside the heart was carved MJ + PA.

Her heart gave a thump.

"Do you think that's her?" Mac asked.

"It's her," Audrey replied without hesitation. How many times had she seen Maggie carve that same heart? On desks, on rocks, on picnic tables. She never put anything inside it, but she always smiled when she made a new one, as if she had a secret. At the time, Audrey thought she just enjoyed vandalizing public, or private, property. She reached out and touched the wall as well.

"Who is PA?"

"I don't know." She took a photo of the heart. "I'll see what I can find out."

Mac seemed in better spirits on the walk down. Audrey told her stories about when she and Maggie were little—before Clint Jones realized his daughter was becoming a woman. About pretending to be superheroes and how many times they saved the world. Of digging clams and swimming in the ocean. Foolish stuff, mostly. Stuff even she had conveniently forgotten when she and Maggie became more enemies than friends.

"Frenemies," Mac quipped.

"Exactly. That's what Maggie and I became after we both moved back here. I tried to be her friend again, but she had changed. I guess I had too."

"It seems like such a shame, especially after what the two of you went through together."

"You'd think, but I've had to realize that Maggie went through most of it alone. I just thought I was there with her."

"Maybe that was her way of protecting you—just like you protected her."

Audrey looked at the kid. "Did you hear that?"

"Hear what?" She looked anxious.

"The sound of my head popping out of my ass. You just totally put everything in perspective for me."

Mac's laughter echoed through the forest. "Glad to help."

When they reached the car, Audrey unlocked it and opened her door. Just before she climbed in, she paused. The hairs on her neck stood up on end as a twig cracked above their heads.

She whipped her head up, just in time to see a figure disappear into the trees. The person was wearing a hunting jacket and a hat pulled down so low there was no way she could get a glimpse of their face. Probably just a hunter who lost his way, or Bertie.

She got into the car and started the engine. "What's Mum want for lunch?" she asked, doing a U-turn in the middle of the road.

"We made a boiled dinner last night. She said it would be even better for lunch."

"True. The vegetables will soak up all the flavor of the ham. I think I'll have to invite myself to stay." Audrey glanced at Bertie's trailer as they drove by. He was out in the yard with one of Wendell's dogs. He actually looked up and waved. She waved back out of instinct.

The person in the woods hadn't been Bertie. And she realized they hadn't been carrying a gun either. Not a hunter. But it had been someone, she was certain.

Someone watching them.

*Nineteen years ago*

"Asshole!"

Mike wasn't a big guy, but he was wiry, and he was sober—two things Aaron wasn't. Maggie watched in shock as her friend knocked the larger boy to the ground with a single punch.

Suddenly Greg and Dwayne jumped in to break things up, but not before the damage to Aaron's pride had been done. He'd been knocked on his ass by a guy he called a "little jack-off." It looked good on him, the prick. She touched her fingers to the spot where Aaron's palm had connected when she told him to fuck off. She didn't want to have sex with him. She never would have thought him to be a hitter. Maybe she shouldn't have gotten him all revved up and then told him his dick was too small.

When Mike saw the mark, he knew what happened. He went into the bedroom and pulled Aaron out.

"You okay?"

Maggie turned her head. It was Greg. He was always so nice. She smiled. "I've had worse."

The concern on his cute face deepened. Shit. She'd meant it to be a joke. Sometimes she forgot that there were "normal" families out there. Not everyone lived like she did. She put her hand on his arm. “I’m okay. Promise. He didn’t hit me that hard. It was my fault. I was a real bitch.”

Greg nodded. “Okay.” But he didn’t look convinced. “You want some ice?”

She said sure because she felt like he wanted to get ice for her. He got her a beer too, which almost made her laugh. She forgot he was normal and he’d forgotten she was only thirteen.

“I’m sorry Aaron hit you. Has he done it before?”

Maggie shrugged. “He’s always been kinda rough.” It was a bald-faced lie. Aaron had never touched her before—not unless she invited him to.

Greg paled. “I didn’t know.”

“Now you do. It doesn’t matter.”

“It does matter, Maggie. You shouldn’t let people treat you like that, especially guys.”

“You’d never hit a girl, would you?”

He shook his head as if the idea horrified him. “Of course not.”

She smiled and took a drink of the beer. “You’re a good guy, you know that?”

He actually blushed.

“Get off me!” Mike pulled free of Dwayne’s grip, but Dwayne put himself between him and Aaron.

“I want you out of here,” Aaron snared, wiping his split lip with the back of his hand. “You and your little slut can get the fuck out.”

“Aaron…” Greg started, but the other boy turned on him with a glare.

"You can leave too if you want. You can all just fuck off."

To Maggie's surprise, every one of them made like they were going to leave—Barbie, Julie, Dwayne, Greg, and Mike. They all grabbed their stuff and walked out of the camp, leaving Aaron by himself.

"Fucking prick," Barbie said as they walked out into the dark. "Good on you, Mike."

Maggie smiled as the others patted Mike on the back—literally and figuratively. "My hero," she said. The tiny bit of guilt she felt for setting Aaron up slithered to the back of her brain, where she buried it.

Mike turned and looked at her, giving her a faint smile.

"Do you need a drive home?" he asked her. "I have a stop to make."

Bertie? she wondered. He'd told her that he was seeing him. Personally, she didn't get the attraction, but whatever.

"I'll take her," Greg offered, clapping Mike on the shoulder. "You go do what you gotta do, slugger." He smiled.

Mike shied from the attention. Maggie watched him get into his car and back out onto the dirt road. There was a strange feeling in her chest—a tightness. It was jealousy, she realized. She was jealous of what he had with Bertie. Jealous of the older man for taking her friend away from her just like Jake took Audrey away. She didn't have anyone who felt that way about her. No one.

Dwayne and Barbie took Julie with them, so that left Greg and Maggie. She stepped up into his truck and closed the door. "You'll have to give me directions to your house," he told her.

Her father would still be out for a while. Going home was safe, but Maggie didn't want to go just yet. Her mother had one of her "spells" earlier and was acting like a crazy woman, and Matt could be such a little asshole. "Can we just drive around for a bit?" she asked. "I don't want to go home."

He glanced at her as he put the truck in reverse. She knew she'd kept her voice flat, but he'd caught something in her words or her tone. "Sure," he agreed. "You just tell me when you're ready, okay?"

She nodded. He pulled onto the road and turned left, heading farther back the Ridge. They drove for a while and had a couple of beers, and talked. Sometimes they didn't say anything. And when Maggie was ready, Greg took her home.

"Have a good night, Maggie," he said. He leaned over the bench seat and kissed her cheek.

Maggie jumped at the contact. It was so weird and foreign. No one had kissed her cheek since her grandmother died. "You too. Thanks again." Then she climbed out of the truck and climbed the rickety steps of the crap box of a house her father rented. Greg didn't leave until she closed the door behind her, but she stood there and watched him drive away. And she didn't let the tears fall until she was sure he couldn't see them.

# CHAPTER TWENTY

Jake was on the couch watching season two of *Downton Abbey* with a bowl of chips in his lap and a can of Moxie in his hand. He didn't drink the stuff very often, as it made him feel like a Maine cliché, but every once in a while he got a craving for the vermouthy, vaguely medicinal cola. It only took one to set him straight and then he'd be good to go for a few months.

He heard a vehicle pull into the yard and assumed it was Audrey back from her visit with Mac, but when someone knocked on the door, he realized that wasn't the case.

He set the chips and can aside and slowly rose to his feet. God damn it, he was still a mess. It took him forever to get to the door. When he opened it, he found his brother on the other side of the screen.

"Took you long enough," Lincoln remarked. "Still gimpy?"

Jake grimaced. "You're so classy."

His brother grinned, baring his teeth. "Can I come in, little pig?"

Tempting as it was to shut the door in his face, the company would be nice. He stepped back to allow Lincoln entry. His brother looked around the kitchen as he crossed the threshold. "Where's your woman?"

"Her mother's."

That seemed to please his brother. Eyes much like his own narrowed as they looked him over. "You look pretty happy for a guy who looks like he got hit by a train."

Jake shrugged. It hurt. Everything hurt. But Audrey had said yes. Only, he couldn't tell anyone that—not yet. Jesus, he was too happy. Every instinct in his body told him not to trust it, but he couldn't help it. She was his weakness. They'd let their families know on Thanksgiving, which they were going to host at his—their—place. "It's the pills."

Lincoln nodded, as though it made perfect sense. "Oxy?"

How the hell was he supposed to know? Lincoln was the drug expert in the family. He supposed his doctor had told him, but he couldn't remember. "Yeah. I guess."

"It's good shit. Mind if I grab a beer?"

"Knock yourself out." Jake headed back toward the living room and the warm cocoon of his couch, and made a mental note to count his pills after his brother left. He would be glad when he could stop taking the damn things. They made him feel soft in the head—like an idiot. Silly. That wasn't so bad when it was just Audrey, or even Alisha and Yancy around, but not so much where Linc was concerned.

Unfortunately, he reached the living room at the same time his brother did.

"Is that *Downton*?" he asked, lifting the beer.

*Ah, fuck.* "Yeah. Yancy made me watch with her and I got sucked in."

"What season?"

"Two."

"Episode?"

His brother's sharp tone and glance made Jake raise a brow. "Eight. I just started it."

Lincoln shrugged out of his coat and tossed it over the back of the recliner. "That's the one with the Spanish influenza. Play it up."

Jake didn't need to be told twice. Jesus, he hoped Audrey didn't come home and find him and Lincoln holed up in the living room watching *Downton Abbey* like old biddies with their "stories."

When the episode ended, he hit pause on the remote. "That was a downer. I wasn't expecting Lavinia to bite it."

Lincoln snorted. "She had to so Matthew can get it on with Mary."

Jake glanced at him. "Do they ever get together?"

"I am not saying, but let me go get another beer and we can watch the next episode. You want anything?"

He glanced at his half-full can of Moxie. "Grab me a Dr Pepper." He wanted a beer, but he wasn't about to mix alcohol and pain meds. When his brother returned, he said, "Thanks for what you did with Neve." No point in letting it dangle between them any longer.

Lincoln popped the soda can before handing it to him. "You would have done it for me. Besides, I owed you after what I did."

"And now I owe you." Why not just address the elephant in the room.

"Is that why you think I did it?"

"Isn't it?"

The darker-haired man scowled at him. "You're such a twat sometimes, Jay. I did it because I could, because it took the heat off you, and because it was partially true. Christ, you look like fucking death warmed over, and I played a part in that. The least I could do is try to make up for it."

Jake was glad he used the word "try" because they had a way to go before Lincoln made up for stealing, trying to blackmail him, and setting the Ratchett brothers on him. Still, it was as much of an admission of guilt as he was ever going to get. "Fair enough. Thanks all the same."

Lincoln squirmed under his gaze. "You're welcome."

Jake stared at him, looking at him as though he weren't his brother, but just another guy, assessing him. He always saw his brother as a bit of a screwup, but there was an edge to him—a bit of Gracie just under the surface. "Did you kill Tex?"

This time his brother met his gaze directly. "You think I have the balls to kill someone?"

At that moment, yeah. He did. But Jake couldn't bring himself to actually say it. If the situation were reversed, he wouldn't tell Lincoln, and he supposed he didn't want to know.

"Press play," Lincoln instructed, not seeming the least bit concerned that he hadn't answered. "It's the Christmas episode."

Jake chuckled, but he pressed Play and offered his brother

the chips as the intro started. As far as brotherly bonding experiences went, this one was pretty damn surreal, but he'd take it.

"How many episodes did the two of you watch?"

"Just two."

Audrey laughed as she set her laptop on the coffee table in the living room. "I wish I'd been here to see it." The idea of Jake and Lincoln getting sucked into the period drama was surreal. And somewhat adorable.

"It's a good show."

"I know it is." She plugged her power cable into the wall. "I've watched the entire series. By the way, Lincoln didn't take any pills. The right amount is in the bottle."

He looked relieved, and a little surprised. "How was the hike?"

"Good. I found 'MJ plus PA' on the wall of the old shed up on the Ridge."

"Who's PA?"

"No idea."

"This would be so much easier if I just had the names of everyone who slept with Maggie the spring I killed Clint."

"I don't think you'd want to see that list, even if you had it." He turned to her—his battered eye was open a little now. God, it looked terrible.

"As long as neither you nor my father is on it, I wouldn't care."

His smile turned sympathetic. "Yeah, you would." He

pushed himself upright. "What do we know about PA? Are we assuming he's Mac's father?"

"Maggie cared about him if she carved that—thought she was in love with him. So, he was either young, or youngish, and probably classically attractive. I'm assuming he was local, but maybe not from this town." Mostly because the initials didn't ring any bells for her either.

"I thought you were done with this business."

"I was until I saw that."

He stared at her, and for a second she wondered if he was having second thoughts about signing on for forever with her. "You know, all the yearbooks for the high school are online now."

"Really?" Audrey did a Google search for the site. It was the first one listed on the results page. "Okay, he could have been anywhere from fifteen to twenty at the time."

"Not fifteen."

"Why?"

"He had to get here somehow, and he probably couldn't always rely on his friends. Plus, I bet he sneaked out to see her through the week if he could. He probably picked her up."

That was true. Maggie might have been young, but PA had to be at least sixteen. But no one she had talked to mentioned anyone with those initials. No one. If the guy came around town, surely someone would know who he was. "Maggie always liked older guys." Before finding out that Audrey liked Jake, Lincoln had been Maggie's Tripp of choice. Once she saw Jake as competition for Audrey, however, she shifted her focus. Jake might have slept with Maggie so Audrey would go to college, but Maggie had done it just to show Audrey she could.

So, she began her search with looking at the yearbooks for Eastrock High that would include guys three to six years older than she and Maggie. She printed copies of every page that had a guy with the initials *PA* on it. By the time she was done, she had fifteen prospects.

"You know, there's a chance that PA was a girl and not Mac's father at all." Audrey's shoulders slumped. "Jesus, Maggie, you could have left me *something*."

"She thought Clint was responsible. She practically wrote as much in her diary, didn't she?"

He had a point. "If I could dig him up and kill him again, I would." She set her laptop aside and laid out the yearbook pages on the coffee table. She pulled a highlighter from her computer bag and began highlighting every PA on the pages.

*Phillip Aaron.*

*Paul Angenou.*

*Patrick Alexander.*

*Peyton Alexander.*

*Piers Abbott.*

*Prescott Aughtry.*

*Paul Amsdell.*

*Peter Andrews.*

Audrey stopped. She lifted the page to examine it more closely. In the center of the page, with shoulder-length hair and a scrap of hair under his chin that was very Eddie Vedder, was young Peter Andrews from Eastrock.

Peter Andrews who now went by his middle name, Greg.

Her brother-in-law.

Greg was an electrician with the school board, which meant that he got out of work at a decent time and was able to pick up the girls if Jess was still working. They lived just over the town line in Ryme, another little blip on a map of the eastern shore. Their house was a cute little yellow Cape Cod with periwinkle trim and shutters. Greg's car was the only one in the drive when Audrey pulled in. She expected this, because she had just seen her sister and the girls at their parents'.

Her brother-in-law was surprised to open the door and find her on the step. "Audrey. What's wrong?"

She couldn't bring herself to smile. "Can I come in, Greg?"

"Sure." He stood back and let her step inside. She didn't feel as though she was in any kind of danger as she crossed the threshold, but she wasn't looking forward to the conversation they were about to have.

"Jess is at your folks'."

"I know. That's why I'm here. I thought it would be best if she didn't overhear."

He laughed. "Jesus, Audrey. That sounds downright dramatic. You want a beer or anything?"

He sounded normal. Maybe he was just a good liar. "No." She pulled out her phone as she followed him into the kitchen.

"Does this look familiar?" She held up the photo she'd taken in the shed.

Greg squinted at it. His expression gave way to one of embarrassment. "I'd heard about it. I never actually saw it myself. Barbie told me, I think."

"Do you know why Maggie carved it?"

"Yeah." He grabbed a beer from the fridge. "I mean, she was a kid, so it was easy to tell she had a crush. Really, I think she just liked me because I wasn't one of the guys who took advantage of her." He took a swallow. "She used to follow me around a bit."

"You said you didn't know her well."

"I didn't. Haven't you ever had a crush from afar?" He asked it with a smile.

Jake was the only crush she'd ever really had.

"You're telling me Maggie never tried to get close to you?" Because that was *not* the Maggie she knew.

His eyes widened. "You don't think... fuck around, Audrey! How could you think I'd do something like that?"

"Because you didn't tell me about this when I first told you I was looking for Mac's father."

His expression was incredulous. "You've known me for years. You really think I'd sleep with a little kid?"

Not now, no. They hadn't known each other for years, not really. Greg only started dating Jess shortly after Audrey got out of Stillwater. By that point, Jess wasn't talking to her if she could help it, and was spending as little time at home as possible. Audrey had met Greg a few times, and he was always nice, but that was it.

"I don't know what you were like back then. I'm not accusing you of raping Maggie. I'm asking you if you ever had sex with her."

"I told you I never touched her."

"It's just the two of us here, Greg. You can be honest."

"You want my DNA? Give me a swab, I'll prove it. I am not that girl's father!"

"I'll have to pick up a kit." It was obviously the wrong thing to say. She knew it as soon as the words tumbled out of her mouth. She ought to have believed him. Trusted him. She didn't do either of those things easily with anyone, but she should have done it with him.

His face hardened. "Get out."

Oh, hell… "Greg—"

"Save it." He shook his head. "Look, I'm sure we'll be fine someday, but just leave, okay? I don't want to look at you. I won't tell Jess we had this conversation, but right now you have to get the fuck out of my house."

Audrey nodded. Talking would only get her into more trouble, so she was quiet. She showed herself to the door. What had she just done? She'd risked her relationship with her brother-in-law—with her sister—for the sake of a girl she hardly knew and who had decided she didn't want to know her father. She'd insulted a man who had always been good to her because Maggie had a secret that she never shared with her, and it pissed Audrey off. She might have just made one of the biggest fuck-ups of her life.

# CHAPTER TWENTY-ONE

Angeline arrived Tuesday morning. She was on her way to Massachusetts to spend Thanksgiving with family and made a detour to Edgeport to take a look at the Ridge property and visit Audrey.

It had been months since Audrey had seen her mentor, and the smile on her face when she greeted her was completely genuine.

Angeline Beharrie was average height, but liked to wear heels. She was always impeccably dressed, her white and silver hair loose and wavy, makeup perfect. She arrived wearing jeans, a sweater, a long coat, and boots. If Audrey knew her brands, the jeans and sweater were Lauren, the coat Gucci, and the boots definitely Prada. They shared a shoe size, so occasionally she ended up with boots and shoes her boss no longer wanted. They were always in near-perfect condition, and always designer.

But her shoes weren't why Audrey adored her. That was inspired by the fact that Angeline always accepted her for what and who she was, and then encouraged her to be the best she could be.

Audrey stepped into her Joy-scented embrace and hugged her hard. "It's so good to see you!"

"Yes, it is," Angeline said, her arms squeezing fiercely. "You look amazing. Being home agrees with you."

Audrey pulled back with a chuckle. "I've gained ten pounds. Jake feeds me too well."

"Ten pounds you needed." The older woman ran a hand down her arm. "You look happy. That makes me happy."

Those few words tightened around Audrey's heart like a fist. "Do you want to come in?" She gestured to the front door.

"Let's look at the property first. Then, you and I and Mr. Tripp can discuss business when we return."

"Sounds good. We'll take Jake's truck." Jake was sore enough that morning that he decided not to tempt fate, but Audrey also thought he wanted to give her time alone with Angeline.

If her boss had any misgivings about climbing into a dirty pickup, she didn't voice them. She simply tossed her purse on the seat and stepped up like she grew up on a ranch or something. She might wear high-end, but Angeline was pretty low-maintenance.

"It's been strange not having you around," Angeline remarked with a pat on the leg as they drove out the road. "I've missed you."

Audrey smiled. "I've missed you too."

"But I think spreading your wings was a good idea. Look at all you've accomplished since leaving LA."

"Angie, I've been a murder suspect and the target of a serial killer. I'm not sure either of those is an accomplishment."

Her boss smiled. "You've helped the McGann girl, and you assisted in the arrest of that same serial killer. Those are definitely accomplishments. And now you have a business plan for a facility that will service high-risk teens. I think it's amazing."

"You always did know just how to pat me on the head."

"I don't praise lightly. And I've felt some benefit from the things you've done. You certainly upped our public profile."

She laughed. "That's true. I know you've taken some flack for that as well."

Angeline waved a long, be-ringed hand. "Nothing I haven't been able to handle or smooth over. Though, I have to admit, there are some in the field who are aghast that I would work with someone who committed murder. There are also those who criticized me for working with a former subject. Others accuse me of wantonly taking advantage of you. I listen only to my own conscience. You've made my world an interesting place, Audrey. I regret nothing."

"Thank you for that. I'm not sure what I did to win your loyalty, but I'm glad I did it."

"Good girl. No questioning yourself—or me. You're learning." The older woman grinned as she spoke. "Oh my goodness. Does someone actually live in that little shack?"

"It has a rooftop patio," Audrey replied with a smile. "Of course someone lives there."

Angeline shot her a disbelieving glance. "On the way back

I have to take a picture. Tell me about the person who lives there."

So Audrey spent the next ten minutes relating the highlights—the ones she knew—of Rankin duChamps's life and career making moonshine.

"He sells it locally during the tourist season. I hear he makes pretty good money at it."

"But not good enough to buy a new house?"

"Plenty enough. He just doesn't want a new house."

"Fair enough. Fascinating."

They spent the rest of the drive catching up, with Audrey pointing out various places she thought her boss might appreciate along the way—such as Wendell Stokes's house and Bertie's trailer.

"My family used to own the property I'm going to show you."

"But your Mr. Tripp owns it now?"

"That's right. He owns the blueberry land surrounding it as well."

"He seems to be quite the real estate mogul."

"He's something," Audrey allowed with a proud smile. She pulled the truck into the driveway. "Here we are."

"It's remote," Angeline remarked, unbuckling her seat belt. She opened the door and stepped out. "My Lord, it's beautiful, though."

Audrey tried to see it through the other woman's eyes. She'd known about this place her entire life, but as she looked at it now, surrounded by golden grass, blueberry scrub, and multicolored trees, she had to admit it was nice. The rolling hills and clear blue sky didn't hurt.

They spent more than an hour walking through the old farm and its various buildings. Angeline took photos and made notes. She asked questions and made suggestions.

"I assume you've looked into federal funding opportunities?" she asked as they inspected the main house.

"I have, and there are a couple we could definitely apply for through the DOJ." The U.S. Department of Justice had several programs aimed at juvenile offenders, in fact. She had already researched what she'd have to do to be eligible.

"I'm sure there are others as well."

"There are. I have a list back at the house."

A pleased smile curved the older woman's lips. "I'm sure you do. Audrey, I must say that this is amazing."

"I've used another facility in the state as a model, but I'd really like for us to work more with the higher-risk kids to prevent competition."

"I'm sure there's room for both. Unfortunately, there always seems to be a need for juvenile facilities." She rubbed her gloved hands together. "Good God, it's cold out. Let's continue this back at your house."

For the first time, Audrey didn't say it wasn't her house. She was going to have to start claiming it if she was going to marry Jake.

Marry Jake.

*Jesus.* Shouldn't she be terrified? Why wasn't she thinking of all the things that could go wrong? She should be scared, but the only thing that scared her was just how happy she was.

Jake had water boiling for tea when they returned, and the table set for a light lunch of sandwiches and sweets, all of which he'd made himself, despite Audrey's protests that he rest and take care of himself.

Angeline shook his hand, studying him like he was a rare bird. Of course, she had heard stories about him over the years. "It's a pleasure to finally meet you, Mr. Tripp," she said.

"Jake," he corrected. "Apologies for looking like a patchwork quilt."

"None needed. Thank you for making such a lovely lunch. I hope you didn't go to much trouble."

Audrey only had to look at him to know he'd overdone it, but she wasn't going to wound his pride in front of someone he obviously wanted to impress. That he wanted to look good in front of Angeline was sweet. She knew all his effort had been for her. He'd even dressed up a bit in casual pants and a purple collared shirt that not only brought out the green in his eyes, but matched the bruises on his face. There was a sheen of sweat on his forehead, and the skin around his eyes was tight. He was in pain, but he'd be damned if he'd admit to it.

"None at all," he replied. "Please sit."

Over lunch they discussed costs, the available grants, and the potential of the property. Angeline seemed impressed when Jake told her he knew where they could get animals, and also that the kids could work the farm and his blueberry land. He explained to her the moneymaking opportunities that the property could invest back into itself. He also revealed how much of his own money he was willing to invest in the place. It was a sum that shocked Audrey, even though they had discussed his desire to help. She knew he had money, but not that he had *that* kind of money. Audrey mentioned local people who would be great to hire—and about offering a position to Reva Kim, who had been running Stillwater.

Angeline smiled. "I think Reva would be perfect. She hasn't accepted any other position that I know of."

Jake talked about having rental properties for teachers, or offering incentives to those who wanted to build a place, or buy an existing one. And then, of course, Audrey drove home how they could build Angeline her own cottage or apartment on-site so that she could come and do research whenever she wanted.

Afterward, Angeline leaned back in her chair, her fingers curled loosely around the handle of her teacup. Jake had used Gracie's favorite china for the meal. "I have no qualms about telling you both that I am definitely intrigued. More than intrigued, I'm interested in doing this."

Audrey almost squealed out loud.

"Let me talk to my financial adviser after the holiday. I want to show him all that you've given me. If he thinks it's a good idea, we can start on the legalities."

It was incredible to think that they might be able to make it work. Astounding, even.

"You're in charge of grant proposals," Angeline told her. "No one has as much passion for this project as you do. Consider making this place happen as your job from now on, though I'd like it if you could make the trip to Cambridge once a month until I can find someone to replace you there full-time."

"Replace me?"

"Well, yes. You're not going to have time to be my right hand if you're running the facility here."

Audrey frowned. "Are you firing me?"

Angeline laughed. "No, my dear. If we go through with this, you won't be my employee, you'll be my partner."

She hadn't thought of that. She really hadn't. Angeline's partner. Her equal. Unexpected tears scalded the backs of her eyes, but she refused to let them show. "That prospect is both exciting and terrifying."

Her boss patted her hand. "I planned for it to happen one day. I just didn't know it would be so soon. This is going to be an entire change of direction for you—a chance for you to really make a name for yourself. I can't wait to watch it happen."

Make a name for herself? As the psychologist who had killed someone. Who got herself into more trouble than she was worth. Maybe this place would finally make her grow the hell up and throw away the chip on her shoulder. Regardless, it was a fabulous opportunity. She wanted to do it, even though she was terrified of screwing up.

A little while later, she walked Angeline out to her rental car.

"Getting dark already," the older woman remarked. "I despise these shorter days."

"At least in LA you've got sunshine," Audrey reminded her.

"Yes, but you have something even more wonderful here. Love. You know, it's lovely to see you at peace with this place, Audrey. It really is."

"I'm not sure if 'peace' is the right word, but Edgeport and I are figuring each other out right now. Sometimes I want to pack up and go back to California, and other days I can't imagine being anywhere else."

"I don't think it's a coincidence that you found a way to stay." Angeline opened the passenger door and set her bag on the seat, then came around to the driver's side. "You mentioned you've been helping a young woman look for her biological father?"

She nodded. "Maggie's daughter. Not having the greatest luck. I'm not sure she wants to continue looking, and it's obvious someone else doesn't want us digging into it."

Angeline's expression took on an element of concern. "Please, be careful. I can't bear the thought of any more hurt befalling you."

"I don't like the idea either, trust me."

"Well, it's obvious whoever the father is, he wants to remain anonymous."

"Mm. Mackenzie has pretty much wiped her hands of it."

"But you plan to keep looking, don't you?"

Audrey shook her head under her assessing gaze. "I'm still waiting on some DNA results, but if Mac wants to be done, then I'll be done too." She still hadn't gotten the photos, and it would probably be after Thanksgiving for the lab results. It didn't matter. After her conversation with Greg, it wasn't worth it anymore. She wondered if he'd told Jess about it. She hadn't heard from her sister, but that wasn't necessarily a good thing.

"You've always been an avenger, haven't you?"

"My fatal flaw," she admitted with a smile. "But I'm not out to avenge anyone now. I just want to build something I can be proud of."

Her boss—partner—looked at her like she didn't quite believe her. "I have missed you."

They hugged again. Angeline said she might stop by again on her way back to LA, and assured her they'd talk about the facility again soon.

Audrey watched her drive away and didn't go back into the house until her car was out of sight.

"That went well," Jake remarked as he carried dishes to the sink.

She took them from him. "You should lie down."

"I need to be upright for a while." He turned, leaning against the edge of the sideboard. "You prepared to do the brunt of the heavy lifting tomorrow?"

"So long as you do the cooking, yeah. I'm sure everyone will pitch in."

"Will you be wearing your ring?"

She smiled stupidly. "Yes."

He kissed her again. "Good. I'm good at keeping secrets, but I don't want to keep this one anymore."

"Neither do I."

"Have you talked to David?"

She turned away to start filling the sink with water. Gracie's china did not go through the dishwasher. "Not since this morning, when he texted to say he was on his way." Her brother's flight had been delayed. His new ETA was that afternoon. Thanksgiving was the next day, but he'd be home for a couple of weeks to help out with Anne.

"Seth coming with him?"

"I don't think so. Jess and I both made sure he knows he's expected to have some alone time with Mum."

"In case she dies? You guys are a morbid lot."

"No! Because she doesn't get to see him that often."

"She sees him more than she used to see you."

"No more of that if you want me to carry stuff for your lame ass tomorrow." She smiled when she said it. Somehow they'd ended up offering to host everyone for Thanksgiving, and so they would have fourteen people there for the meal. Lincoln was even bringing Marnie, and apparently, sweet potatoes with marshmallows. It was all very bizarre.

Her phone rang. She dug it out of her purse and glanced at the screen. It was Jess. *Shit.* Her fingers actually trembled as she swiped her finger across the screen to accept the call. All the happiness from Angeline's visit evaporated, leaving her shaky and filled with dread. Was this when she lost her sister again?

"Hey." She tried to sound as normal as possible.

"Hey, you," her sister said perkily. "Listen, I need to run a few errands. Mum's not feeling so great. Can you sit with her for a bit while I pick up a prescription for her?"

"Sure. I can pick up the meds if you want."

"No, I'll do it. I need a few other things."

Audrey frowned. "Everything okay?"

"Yeah, no. It's good. I'm just distracted. You know."

The pregnancy, right. "Is Mum okay?"

"Yeah, she's got an ear infection of all things. The doctor called in some antibiotics. When can you come down?"

"I'll be there in twenty."

"Oh, one more thing. Neve was here today. She said she was checking in on Mum, but she asked Dad if he had a .270 rifle. You know what's up with that?"

Audrey's heart froze. "That's the type of gun that shot the guy back the Cove. She's probably checking everyone in town. What did he say?"

"That he had one, and showed it to her. Thing had a layer of dust on it so thick she laughed when she saw it. But if she was looking for one recently fired I guess that's the end of that."

"Yeah," Audrey agreed, but she had a sinking feeling that as far as Neve digging around into her business, it was only the beginning.

When their families began arriving for Thanksgiving dinner Thursday afternoon, Greg was distant, but he went through all the motions. Audrey hoped her questions hadn't caused irreparable damage. She didn't want to think about what that might do to her relationship with Jess. She was just glad he didn't seem to have told her sister what transpired between them. Was it for her benefit, or because he didn't want his wife asking questions he didn't want to answer?

Olivia did her little stomping, tripping run into the living room, where Jake sat talking to her grandfather over beer. "Ache!" she cried. "Achy!"

Audrey held her breath. Olivia hadn't seen Jake since before the beating from Tex. She might be afraid of his battered features. Jess came and stood beside her to watch what happened, ready to swoop in to the rescue.

Jake looked at the little girl as she careened toward him. "Hey, Livvie love."

She stopped right in front of him, her blue eyes wide as silver dollars. She raised a chubby hand and pointed at him. "Boo-boo?"

He nodded. "That's right."

"Mere."

He leaned down. Audrey saw him wince. His ribs were still sore.

Olivia came up on her toes and kissed him on the cheek. "All beddo."

"Oh," Audrey said on a sigh. "My heart."

Jess smiled. "I know. Kid kills me." And then she whispered, "Is there something up with you and Greg? He seems weird toward you."

Audrey shook her head. "Not that I'm aware of." Call her a coward, but she wasn't going to confess if he hadn't.

"Okay, good."

Time for a change of subject. "Has Dave said anything about the breakup with Seth?"

"Not a word." Her older sister followed her gaze to their brother. "He seems all right, though."

He did. He was just like he always was, fussing over their parents, doing everything he could to make life fun, making everyone smile. "How are you feeling?" Audrey asked in the same hushed tone.

Jess shrugged. She looked tired. "Like I have an impossible decision to make."

And then she drifted away to shoo her mother out of the kitchen. Audrey watched her go, her heart heavy with sympathy. She didn't know what she'd do if she found out she was pregnant. Part of her thought she would regret never having kids, but she couldn't recall ever actually *wanting* them. It was a talk she and Jake needed to have. Surely he wanted to continue the Tripp name?

Lincoln and Greg put the leaf in the dining room table. It would seat eight, with room for Olivia's high chair. Then they did the very classy but tried-and-true practice of two sawhorses with a slab of plywood on top of them to the end. When Yancy threw the tablecloths on top, you couldn't tell that the table wasn't actually that long—unless you looked at the legs.

Jessica and Alisha took on the task of setting the table, and Marnie and Lincoln carried in the plates, glasses, and silverware for them to place. Audrey kept an eye on the food, as she had been for several hours, with the occasional check-in from Jake.

Within thirty minutes they had everything ready and began bringing out the feast.

Isabelle was overjoyed to sit at the "big" table and asked if she could sit next to Alisha, who wanted to be near Audrey. Jake took his place at the head of the table and Audrey's father took the foot. Audrey sat to Jake's left. Across from her was Yancy.

"Jake, may I say grace?" Anne asked.

"Of course," he said, even though Audrey was certain he'd had no intention of saying it himself. In fact, grace probably hadn't been said in that house since his grandmother died.

It was strange, hearing her mother pray—or rather give thanks. They had never been a religious family, and this sort of thing only happened on rare occasions. Still, it was a nice touch, and they all said "Amen" together.

Audrey reached for the potatoes.

"Oh my God!" Her brother, David, cried.

Everyone jumped.

"What?" Lincoln demanded, a dinner roll in his hand. He stared at the potatoes as though he expected to find a severed finger in them.

David's eyes were huge as he stared at Audrey's hand. He looked so much like their mother with that expression on his face. "Audrey Harte, what is that on your finger?"

A flush swept up Audrey's neck and face as all heads turned in her direction. "It's Gracie's ring," she replied. They had planned to announce it at dessert, but she'd forgotten to take the ring off before they all arrived.

"Oh my goodness!" Anne pressed her hand to her mouth.

Lincoln gaped at his brother, the poor roll still clutched in his fingers. "Seriously?"

Jake nodded, a little grin curving his lips. Even with his face shades of green, purple, and yellow, he was still the prettiest thing she'd ever seen. "Well, there's no date yet, but yeah."

To say chaos erupted would have been an understatement. Suddenly everyone had raised their voice and was shouting their congratulations, getting up to hug them—even Greg. Audrey appreciated his hug the most, because it meant that things were okay between them even if she'd hurt his feelings. David and Alisha probably hugged Audrey the hardest and longest, but it wasn't until her father got up from the table that Audrey's heart rolled over. Beer in hand, he came up to where she and Jake sat. He offered his other hand to Jake.

"Welcome to the family, young fella. It's about goddamn time."

"Grampie!" Isabelle cried. "Don't swear!"

John apologized to his granddaughter. Then he turned to his daughter. "Congratulations, kiddo." He bent down and kissed her cheek, his ginger and gray stubble scratched her skin.

"Thanks, Dad," she whispered, her throat tight. God, it felt like she'd been on the verge of tears for a week. Her father, damn him, could reduce her in record time.

Her father went back to his seat and everyone started reaching for food again. Audrey and Jake shared a smile, then she felt a gentle touch on her arm. It was Alisha.

"You're going to be my aunt Audrey," she said. "I'm so happy."

That was all it took for a tear to escape down Audrey's cheek. She wiped it away as fast as she could and pulled the girl in for a hug. "I am too, sweetie."

"Can I see it?"

"Lish, let Audrey eat," her mother chastised. "You can look at the ring later."

The girl's smile faded a little, but Audrey let her look and flashed a smile at her soon-to-be sister-in-law. Yancy shook her head. "She has you so wrapped."

After the main course, they moved on to dessert. Audrey wasn't sure if she could eat anything else, but Jake had made coconut cream pie just for her, so she was going to give it one hell of a try.

As they all sat down—this time with a table laden with pies and cakes—they went around the table so each of them could say what they were most thankful for.

"I'm thankful for whoever decided to turn around in Gracie's parking lot," Jake quipped as he went first. And then, more seriously, "And I'm thankful that Audrey decided to come home for Anne's birthday this year."

Audrey smiled at him. "I'm thankful Gracie and I wear the same size ring." Everyone chuckled

They went around the table. When they got to John, he took Anne's hand in his. "I'm thankful I've had forty years with this woman, and I'm hopin' for forty more."

Anne leaned in and kissed him. Audrey, David, and Jess shared a glance.

"Oh God," David drawled. "Stop it. PDAs are so last year."

"What's a PDA?" Isabelle asked.

Her uncle turned to her. "Public display of affection, peanut."

"What's wrong with that?"

"Nothing," he said, blowing her a kiss.

They kept going. Finally it got to Greg. "I'm thankful for my wife, who believes in me no matter what, and for her family, who has always treated me like one of their own." He looked at Audrey. Point taken.

Little Isabelle grinned as all eyes fell on her. "I'm thankful for the same thing Grampie said he was thankful for this morning."

"What's that, sweetie?" her mother asked. Her grandfather shook his head.

Isabelle's grin grew. "That Auntie Audrey hasn't killed anybody yet."

Everyone started laughing. Audrey looked at her father. He shrugged. She looked at Greg, who was fighting a smile. That was what did it for her. If he was smiling, it was all okay. Finally, she shook her head and laughed as well. "So am I, Izzy," she said. "So am I."

The weekend passed in a food-laden blur. Audrey spent time with her brother, who was glad their mother was doing so well, and enjoying being spoiled by her while getting the chance to spoil her in return. And she took time every day to remind her father that she could snap at any moment and kill someone. And she ate. So much.

She texted Mac to see how she was doing and got a short reply that she was doing okay, along with a smiley face.

Jake was recovering well. He'd stopped taking the pills and was getting around much better. He still looked pretty rough, but he looked more like himself every day. And there hadn't been any more visits from Neve, which was something for which to be thankful.

Monday morning her phone rang. It was Rick Mason. "Audrey! I've got your photos ready."

For a moment, she wondered if she should even bother. But it would be rude not to pick them up. "I'll be over in a little bit. Thanks, Rick."

She'd just hung up when the phone rang again. She picked up. "Grand Central."

"Hey, kiddo." It was her father. He sounded a little out of breath. "I was wondering if you could come down this morning."

"I'm just about to run over to Eastrock. What do you need?"

"Nothing, never mind. Go do what you have to do." There was something off in his tone.

"I can come down after that."

"Sure, yeah. That's good."

Audrey frowned. "Is everything okay?"

"Yeah, it's great. No worries. I'll see you when you get here." He hung up.

Audrey stared at her phone. When had her father started using "no worries" in conversation? She shook her head and grabbed her purse and gloves. It looked like it was going to snow.

When she walked into Fast Time Photo, Rick was behind the counter. He looked up and grinned. "You weren't kidding! How was your Thanksgiving, my dear?"

"Fabulous. Yours?"

"Can't complain. Ate more pie than should be legal. Okay, so let me get your prints." He went to the bins behind him and picked through the alphabetized sections. He pulled out an envelope and handed it to her. "On the house. For your trouble."

"Oh, no. Let me pay you. It wasn't your fault the machine broke."

He held up his hands. "Please. I feel bad, and it was so nice to meet you. Just take them, and remember me if you ever have any other photographic needs."

She smiled at him. "I will. Thanks, Rick."

It was snowing when she left the shop. Her phone rang—it was Jess. She didn't pick up because she wanted to concentrate on the drive—and every time her sister called she was worried Greg had told her about their conversation. A few minutes later, Jake called. She'd stop by the house before going to her parents' to see what was up and see if he wanted to go to her parents' with her. By the time she got home the snow was already starting to stick to the ground. She ran into the house, shaking flakes out of her hair. “I think we’re about to get our first real snowfall of the year,” she said with a laugh as she tossed the photos on the table.

Jake met her in the kitchen, his face pale beneath his bruises. He had his boots on and his coat in hand.

“What happened?” she demanded, her stomach dropping.

“It’s your father,” he said. “He’s had a heart attack.”

# CHAPTER TWENTY-TWO

I've had just about enough of this hospital for a lifetime," Audrey said as they went through the front door of Down East.

Jake had a hold of her hand. He didn't complain that she was walking too fast, even though his ribs probably didn't like the pace. "Yeah, me too."

David had texted their father's room number just as they pulled into the hospital parking lot, so they headed straight for the elevator. Jake squeezed her fingers as the doors closed. "You okay?" he asked.

Audrey shook her head. That, with the motion of the elevator, made her head spin. "I will be, though. Thanks for coming with me."

"Like I'd make you do this alone."

"God, what I would give for a little boring in my life."

He smiled at her. "I'll give you fifty years of boring once this is done."

She returned the smile, despite being afraid for her father. "Only fifty?"

They found everyone already there when they walked into

the room. Everyone except for Greg, who was probably still at work, and the girls, of course.

"The gang's all here," her father quipped from the bed. He looked like shit.

Audrey blinked back a wave of emotion. He had told her in Jake's driveway that his heart couldn't take all the worrying about her. Her father was a bull, and a drunk, and sometimes a prick, but she was not prepared to see him vulnerable or fragile. In a hospital bed, hooked up to machines—looking like something death had chewed up and spit out—he was not her father, but some old guy with a weak heart.

"There are easier ways to get attention, you old whore," she said. She knew it wasn't her fault, but that didn't make it easier to see him like that.

David laughed. Jess shook her head. Their father grinned. "I like to do things with style."

"What happened?" She started to ask her mother, but stopped when she saw how pale Anne was. She turned to Jess instead. Jess, who always knew everything. Jess, who looked like complete and utter hell.

"He was outside, burning some stuff in the bin when he yelled for Mum."

"Felt like my goddamn chest was in a vise," John added, sharing a glance with his eldest child. Then, to Audrey, "You know, I can tell the story better than her."

Audrey pointed at him. "You need to be quiet and rest."

To her surprise, he didn't argue. That was scarier than the heart attack. He'd called her just before it happened. Jesus, if she'd only gone to see him instead of getting those fucking photos...

"What does the doctor say?"

Jess continued: "Doesn't seem serious, but they're going to run more tests to be sure. They've got him on blood thinners and they gave him something else to help blood flow."

*Nitroglycerin,* Audrey thought. She met her father's gaze. Years of drinking had probably taken a toll on his heart, but there was more to it; she could tell from the way he looked at her. Her looking for Mackenzie's father agitated him, but she couldn't take all the blame when he'd done so much damage himself. Her mother's illness had him scared. He was not the sort of guy to slow down unless he was forced to, and even then he growled about it. He thought red meat was one of the four major food groups. He was going to have to make some changes. They all were.

"You can't all be here," Anne announced a few minutes later. "I know you love him, but being stared at like a fish in a bowl isn't going to help. Either go to the waiting room or go home."

When Anne Harte gave an order, no one argued. They all cleared out and migrated to the family waiting room down the hall. Audrey took Jess aside.

"Any idea what brought it on?"

Jess looked worried and pale. She shook her head. "I was talking to him right before it happened."

"Before or after he called me?"

Her sister frowned. "He called you?"

"I was heading over to Eastrock to pick up photos I got

printed from some old negatives." Audrey shook her head in regret. "I should have gone to Dad. He wanted to see me and I blew him off."

"Photos of what?"

She shouldn't have said anything. "Nothing. Just a film from when we were kids."

David joined them. "What's going on?" he asked.

Audrey slipped her arm around his waist. "We're just trying to figure out if there was a trigger."

"He was distracted all weekend."

"He's been acting weird for a couple of weeks," Jess remarked. "Mom's surgery took more out of him than we thought."

Audrey agreed, but her father's mood had changed right around the same time she met Mackenzie and started looking for the kid's father.

Why had he called her just before it happened? Had something happened that was too much for him to handle? She couldn't imagine what that might be, but she couldn't help but assume some responsibility. It was her fault his heart had finally cracked under the strain. Her nosiness was why he was in that hospital bed. All that being thankful that she hadn't killed someone and she'd almost been the death of him.

Audrey didn't move far from the phone that night. Even though her mother kicked them out, she wanted to be able to get back to the hospital as quickly as possible if she was needed. She was tired, raw-nerved, and hypervigilant. So, when Neve's car pulled into the driveway just before suppertime, her fingers instinctively curved into fists.

"I'll get it," Jake said when she knocked on the door. "Don't want you getting arrested for assaulting an officer."

"It would be worth it," she argued, but she stayed in the kitchen as he went out to the entry. The porch light was on, and she could partially see Neve standing underneath it, hands in her coat pockets.

"Neve," Jake greeted dryly. "What a pleasant surprise. What brings you out?"

"Yeah," Audrey said, leaning against the kitchen door frame. "I really hope you're here to make this day even shittier."

"Can I come in?" the other woman asked. Jake stepped back to let her inside, and she stepped over the threshold. Outside, the ground was covered in a two-inch blanket of snow that the weather guy predicted would be gone the next day thanks to unseasonably warm temperatures. She wiped her boots on the mat, but her attention was on Audrey. "Actually, I wanted to see how your dad is doing."

Audrey crossed her arms over her chest. "You could have called."

"Thought it might mean more if I asked face-to-face." Neve looked her in the eye. There wasn't any accusation there, but Audrey thought she saw regret. She could only imagine what Neve saw in her gaze.

"Conscience bugging you?" Whatever else had caused it, she had to think that Neve's asking if her father had a rifle like the one that killed Ratchett had to add to his stress.

"I've asked every hunter in this town about their guns, but yeah, a little. I hope your father didn't think he was a suspect."

"I don't think it was himself he was worried about." When Neve only nodded, she continued: "He's doing as expected—charming the hospital staff and driving the rest of us nuts. He should be home in a couple of days if you want to pop by."

"Maybe I will. Is David sticking around?"

"For a little while." Then, she couldn't help but add, "He doesn't own any guns, in case you're curious."

"It's just a guess, Neve," Jake said, "but I think you've pissed her off."

"You think?" the other woman asked with a rueful smile. "Look, I didn't come here to make things worse. I wanted to apologize—to both of you."

Audrey straightened. She hadn't been expecting that. "Okay."

Jake leaned against the banister that led upstairs. "Go for it."

Neve shook her head. "Should have known you two wouldn't make it easy for me. Look, I couldn't believe Ryan Ratchett and his brother could have both died accidentally within hours of crossing paths with you, Jake."

He tilted his head. "To be honest, I'm having a hard time wrapping my head around it also."

"Yeah?"

"I don't like attention, Neve, especially the bad kind. You know that. I don't go for spectacles, and shooting someone is a spectacle. Regardless, neither of those boys gave me any reason to kill them."

She looked at the healing bruises on his face. "Oh yeah?"

Jake grinned. "I've had my ass kicked before and the victor lived to tell the tale."

"Ryan Ratchett came after Lincoln."

*Apology her ass,* Audrey thought. She was still digging. The woman didn't know when to give up.

God, they were so much *alike.* It was probably why they made good friends—and adversaries.

"You seem to think I look at killing as an easy thing. Killing is no more an effective way of dealing with trouble than an abortion is an effective form of birth control. Why kill someone on my land when I could have just paid what Lincoln owed and be done with it?"

It was obvious Neve saw his logic. The big hole in hers was Ratchett being shot on Jake's land. "I know you didn't kill Ryan—it was too messy. But something weird happened here, Jake, and your family is in the middle of it."

He nodded. "If you figure it out, let me know. I wouldn't mind having a talk with the folks responsible."

Whatever Neve saw in his eyes must have pleased her, because she gave a decisive nod. "Right." Then she turned to Audrey. "Gideon found this the other day. I thought you might like to have it." She held out a little plastic baggie.

Audrey took it. Inside was a charm bracelet she'd made for Maggie when she was eleven. There was a similar one in her jewelry box that Maggie had made for her. Of course Neve would put it together when she saw the "Best Friends" charm. As far as apologies went, it was a pretty good one. Her throat tightened as she shoved it in her pocket. "Thanks."

"That's some rock you've got on your finger. I'm sorry I had to hear about it through the town network rather than from you."

She met her gaze. "Yeah. Me too." But they both knew whose fault that was, and Audrey wasn't about to apologize for it.

Neve obviously understood that she wasn't about to forgive and forget, not yet. "Well, I'll let the two of you get back to your evening. You don't have to worry about any more questions or hassle concerning the Ratchett brothers." Audrey wondered if that meant she'd also stop looking for answers.

Jake stepped around her to open the door. "Thanks for stopping by."

The other woman smiled sheepishly. "I won't let the door hit me in the ass on the way out."

Once she was gone, Audrey went to Jake and put her arm around his waist. "Think that's the end of that?"

"No. I think she's going to be watching all of us pretty close for a while. I'm sorry for that. You two were becoming pretty good friends, though not that great if she thought you'd kill a guy just because he kicked my ass."

Audrey looked up at him, her expression dead serious. "No, she's right to have her suspicions. I'd go after anyone who tried to take you from me."

His eyes darkened. His hand came up and cupped her face. "Take off your clothes."

She didn't protest, but her fingers trembled as they reached for the button on her jeans. She didn't know what he had in mind, and she didn't care. He pulled off his shirt and took her to her hands and knees on the stairs, covering her body with his own. Everything else ceased to exist when he eased inside her. There was nothing but the two of them.

The way it had always been, and always would be.

"Have you looked at the photos yet?"

They were at the breakfast table. Audrey had bruises and carpet burn on her knees, and Jake had somehow chafed a patch of skin off the top of his foot. After the stairs they'd taken a break and then moved upstairs. Each time had been a little less frantic than the first, but still fraught with emotion. They were completely twisted, she knew that, and she didn't care.

The photos. After days upon days of waiting for them, she had forgotten all about them in light of her father's heart attack. "No."

"Maybe you should."

He was right, but then again, he usually was. She got up from the table where she'd been jotting down names for the facility while scarfing down French toast, and went to the counter where the Fast Time Photo envelope sat. She brought it back to the table, using her thumb to open the flap.

There was another, smaller envelope inside. Audrey withdrew that and took the stack of pictures from it, leaving the negatives inside. Jake pulled up a chair next to hers.

Some of the photos were grainy—taken at night with bad lighting. Mostly they seemed to be party pictures. There were some of a bonfire at the camp back at Tripp's Cove where they had parties in high school.

"Oh my God," Audrey said on a laugh. "Look at us!" It was a photo of the two of them sitting around a fire. Audrey's hair was really long, and Jake's hung to his shoulders. "We look so young." He might have been fourteen in the picture.

"We were. I was trying very hard to look cool."

"You succeeded."

"Only because I didn't want anyone to know I loved you."

She turned her head and kissed his cheek. "While everybody who looked at me knew how I felt about you."

"That just made it all the harder for me. Sweet Jesus."

Audrey had gone on to the next photo. It took her a second to realize what it was he was staring at. "That's me."

"In a bikini."

She'd never been much for little swimsuits, but that summer all the girls had them. Hers had been black, of course. The photo wasn't posed, but there was something overtly sexual about it. It was made all the more wrong by the fact that she only would have been thirteen.

"I forget that she sometimes felt more for me than I did for her." It was strange and uncomfortable to see evidence of it now. She whipped the photograph to the back of the pile.

A few more of parties, then one that made her pause. It was of Maggie and Greg. He had his arm around her while he held up a beer bottle in the other hand. They had their heads together and were both smiling.

"It doesn't mean anything," she said. "He told me they hung out."

"Probably nothing," Jake agreed.

She flipped to the next photo.

"Or something," he added.

Audrey could only stare. "That is him, isn't it?"

"Yeah. I see why Jess married him."

It was a teenage Greg. A teenage *naked* Greg. Taken in what looked like the little shed back the Ridge. He was posing for the camera, and right beside his head was the heart Maggie had carved into the wall.

"So, I guess he lied when he said he hadn't slept with her." Jake looked at her. "You okay?"

"I'm not sure." And then. "Son of a bitch." He'd looked her right in the eye and fucking lied to her.

Jake frowned when she turned her head toward him. "These photos don't mean anything except she caught him naked."

Audrey nodded. "You're right."

Obviously he could see how pissed she was—how conflicted. He sighed. "Bottom line, Aud: What would this news do to your sister?"

"Jess would be hurt."

"Is that worth calling him out?"

Was it? He would know she knew he'd lied. He'd have to acknowledge that. But sleeping with Maggie didn't make him Mac's father. How would Jess feel about all of this? She was pregnant and her father just had a heart attack—Audrey couldn't add this to it. It had happened almost twenty years ago. And there was always the chance that Jess would be upset with her. If Greg decided to cut ties with Audrey, her sister might take his side. She couldn't lose her sister again.

The back of her eyes burned as she gritted her teeth together. "No."

"Then the choice is simple, isn't it?"

Another nod. "You're right. I've just got to let it go." She tossed the photos aside. "I'll forget I ever saw these."

But they both knew she wouldn't.

# CHAPTER TWENTY-THREE

On Friday, Audrey went to pick her father up at the hospital while David stayed with their mother and made lunch. Of the three kids, he was the healthiest, and could be counted on to make something that wouldn't accidentally send John back to the hospital in cardiac arrest.

Her father was ready to go when she arrived, sitting on his bed and chafing to get out of the "damn place" and home where he belonged.

"You look good," Audrey told him. "Rested."

He shrugged into his coat. "Nothing to do in this goddamn hole but rest. I'm bored out of my ever-loving mind, kid."

"Well, let's get you home, then. You know you have to take it easy for the next few weeks." She drew a breath. "And Dad, no drinking."

"I know." He held up a stack of papers. "I have all the information right here."

She took it from him so she and her siblings and their mother could read it. He would try to sneak something past them if they didn't. "That means nothing but light activity, old man. I got you some puzzle and crossword books, and I made a Netflix queue for you. *Deadwood, Longmire*—bunch of stuff."

He gave her a curious look. "You're a good kid, you know that?"

She smiled. "I can be. Sometimes you're even a good dad."

"Christ, I wish someone had been here to witness that," he quipped, but he grinned. "Take me home, darlin'."

On the drive she decided to go ahead and ask what she wanted. It was just the two of them. "Dad, I don't want to upset you, but I need to talk to you about something that I promise won't go any further than this car."

John sighed. "You're going to ask me about Maggie, aren't you?"

She shot him a startled glance. "Yeah."

"It wasn't me. There's never been a time I was so drunk a child looked appealing."

"I know that." She was a little insulted that he thought her opinion of him might be so low. "But you know something, don't you?"

He glanced out the window. "Yeah, I do. But I'm not sharing it, kid. I'll take it with me to my grave."

"You almost did."

He turned to her, his eyes—so much like hers—tired and lined. "Yeah."

"Okay. I think I know something too, but I won't ask you again." To be honest, she was a little surprised to hear the words come out of her mouth, but it was true. She had planned to tell him about the pictures of Maggie and Greg. She had planned to question him about what he knew, but it wasn't worth his health.

"Good." He leaned back against the seat. "You happy, wearing Gracie Tripp's ring?"

How could he even ask her that? "Yeah. I thought you liked Jake."

"I do like Jake, but I love you, and the two of you have some kind of strange hold over each other. You always have. I remember that day he got you a new ice cream at the takeout because you dropped yours."

"Lincoln knocked it out of my hand."

"Whatever. That little fucker went inside and asked his granny for another cone for you and she gave him one. He came back out and gave you that thing like it was made of solid gold or something, and you looked at him like you agreed. Right then I knew there was something between the two of you that I'd never fully understand."

"What about when I kicked Lincoln for making me drop my cone in the first place?"

"That's when I knew you were my kid."

"Mum's word wasn't enough proof? My eyes weren't?"

"Oh, I knew you were partly me, of course, but when I saw that temper I knew you were more like me than Jessie. I had hopes for David, but he favors your mother too. Having that in you hasn't made your life easy at times, and I'm sorry for that, but I do like knowing that no one will ever push you around."

"Thanks, Dad." Her voice was rough. And then, "I'm glad you're okay."

"Me too, kid. I thought for a minute there that I was a goner. Tell ya what, it sure as hell gave me some perspective."

"Yeah? On what?"

"Life in general. I've been given a lot of great things—my family, some friends, a fairly hardy liver. Up until now I've taken most of them for granted, and I've always put them second to the bottle, even if I tried to tell myself otherwise. I figure it's time I stop doing that. This was God's way of slapping me to my knees, I think."

"Seriously?" she asked. "God? You haven't believed in God in years."

"Well, now, maybe He and I had a falling-out once upon a time, and maybe I've had a chip on my shoulder about it, but a man can't have his entire life flash before his eyes, be given a chance to fix it, and not wonder if it was a message."

"You know what? Whatever works for you is fine by me. I'm not going to argue with you."

He grinned. "See, now, that's a goddamn miracle unto itself."

David and Anne made dinner and the rest of the family brought sides. Jake made dessert and Audrey a salad. They arrived at five thirty, as it was getting dark. Jess and Greg and the girls were already there. Greg gave Audrey the stink-eye when she came in.

"What's his problem?" Jake asked.

She shook her head. "No idea." She wasn't in any hurry to ask either. It wasn't that she was in a bad mood, just that her father was more important at that moment than whatever Greg had going on. If he couldn't fake it for family's sake, then he could just go ahead and be as snarly as he wanted. She wasn't going to give him the satisfaction of acknowledging it.

It was a healthy meal—geared toward Rusty's new diet. Somehow David had managed to make all the lean protein and vegetables into a culinary masterpiece worthy of a cooking show. It tasted delicious.

"I need this recipe," Jake declared, pointing at the chicken with his fork.

David preened under the praise. "Of course. Now that we're going to be family I guess there's no harm."

"It's really good, Davy," Audrey added.

"Thanks, Aud. I've been thinking about writing a cookbook, *Cooking the Gay Way.*"

The adults chuckled. Isabelle looked up with a frown on her tiny brow. "What's 'gay'?"

"It means happy," Jess told her.

David sent her a narrow glance. "That's one meaning. The other meaning, sweetie, is that it refers to boys who like other boys."

His niece regarded him with a serious expression. Audrey could practically see the wheels turning in her head. "My friend Timmy has two dads. Is that gay?"

"Exactly!"

Isabelle turned to her mother. "I think you need to check your dictionary, Mummy."

More laughter. Jessica shook her head. "I deserved that." She looked to David. "Sorry, Dave."

He shrugged it off. "Like I'm offended."

"Are you gay, Uncle David?" Isabelle asked.

"Do bears poop in the woods?" he asked back.

She smiled, round cheeks appling. "Yeah."

"Then yes I am, Miss Izzy."

"I miss salt," Rusty lamented randomly, causing more laughter.

After supper, she helped tidy up in the kitchen. "Here," her mother said, handing her a box of garbage. "Go put this in the burn bin."

Audrey didn't argue. Her mother liked to burn most of their garbage because she liked to mix the ash with the garden fertilizer in the spring. She shoved her feet into her father's boots and clomped out the back door. The burn barrel was behind the garage. Her father had set up a light on the back of the garage to come on whenever there was movement, to scare away raccoons. It didn't appear to be all that effective, given the amount of stuff strewn across the ground near the barrel. As she approached, she saw that someone had left a bucket of stuff sitting on the dirt. That was what the scavengers had gotten into. Why hadn't they dumped it in the bin?

Then, she realized why. Her father been bringing stuff out to the barrel when he had his heart attack. It was very likely he had dropped the bucket then. Audrey set her own offering on the ground and reached for the other. She was just about to toss it into the barrel when something caught her eye. She frowned and stepped to the side, allowing the light from the building to better illuminate the inside of the barrel.

Her heart thumped hard as she reached inside and pulled the item out.

It was a copy of *Carrie.* Not just any copy. Scrawled on the pages inside were notes in a familiar hand. It was Maggie's copy.

She reached into the barrel and pulled out something else. It was the burnt remains of a photo album. She didn't have to look inside to recognize it. It was Maggie's too. Whoever had broken into the cabin at the resort had used her parents' burn barrel to dispose of all of it.

Her father? No. She was beginning to think seeing this stuff was what had triggered his heart attack. God knew she felt close to one herself.

The copy of *Carrie* was singed but still intact. Audrey stood there, holding it, unsure of what to do next. Her brain seemed to be stuck in a constant whir of noise.

"We need to talk," came a voice.

She jumped and whipped around. Greg stood there. He'd been smart enough to put on his coat. All she had was her sweater, and it wasn't thick enough for evenings in late November Maine. Under the glare of the light, his kind face had an almost sinister look to it, and Audrey wished she had the gun that was in the glove compartment of her car.

"Did you do this?" she asked.

His brow furrowed. "Do what? Burn an old book? No. I want to talk to you about this." He pulled an envelope out of his pocket and thrust it toward her. She hesitated, but then took it with her free hand. She had to hold it up to the light to read it. It was addressed to Jess, but at their parents' house number. It was from a lab.

"I don't know what this is."

"Open it."

She glanced at him. "Does Jess know you have her mail?"

His features tightened. "Look at it."

The seal had already been broken, so she withdrew the papers from inside. The words she read made her stomach clench, threatening to send dinner back up. It said that the probability of paternity with the samples provided was 99.96 percent. The names on the paper were Greg Andrews and Mackenzie Bell.

Disappointment hit her like a sack of rotten potatoes. She lowered the pages. "You said you didn't sleep with her."

"It was once, and I used a condom." He looked as ravaged by the news as she felt. "Did you do this and send it to your mother's for Jess to find?"

Of all the things she'd ever been accused of doing, that had to be one of the lowest. "No! I believed you when you said you hadn't slept with Maggie. If I'd stolen a DNA sample from you I would have confronted you. I wouldn't pull a stunt like this and hurt my sister."

"If you didn't do it, then who did?"

Audrey stared at him. "The same person who broke into the cottage and burned Maggie's stuff, you idiot." Realization dawned with a disappointed sigh.

Greg stared at her. She watched as horrified understanding dawned.

"Me," came a voice from behind him. *Jess.* "It was me."

Greg stepped to the side, allowing his wife to walk into the light. She looked pale and drawn under the harsh light. She stepped up to her husband. "Olivia pulled out some of Mac's hair one day. I knew as soon as I saw her with the girls that she was yours. So, I got a test and sent some of your hairs with it as well. I used Mom's address so you wouldn't see it."

He looked as though she'd punched him in the gut. "Why?"

She shrugged. "I know you honestly believed it couldn't be you, but I had to know. I had to know if you had another child before I decided whether or not to bring another one into the world."

His startled gaze fell to her stomach. "You're pregnant?"

She nodded.

Before they could get too wrapped up in each other, Audrey had to ask, "Why break into the cottage? Why didn't you just talk to me?"

Jessica turned her head to look at her. "You were so angry and determined that whoever had gotten Maggie pregnant would pay for it. You talked about rape and the fact that there isn't any statute of limitations on it and I panicked. I knew Maggie had photos or something of Greg because she taunted me with it one night at Gracie's. She told me she'd seen him naked and that she had proof. I thought she was just being foolish—mean. Then I saw Mac."

"You should have known I wouldn't have made trouble for Greg."

"You make trouble, Auddie. It's what you do." It wasn't said meanly, but it stung all the same.

Audrey straightened. "Dad knew."

Her sister nodded. "He suspected. He asked me if I thought it was possible. I told him I thought it was."

Now she was getting upset. "He was worried about you. That was why he kept warning me off."

Jess nodded. "And you just kept going."

"No, this is not my fault. You broke into a cottage—Jake's fucking cottage, Jess! You stole Maggie's things and you burned them on your parents' property!" She held up the copy of *Carrie.* "It didn't completely burn. Dad found the remains in the barrel. That's what caused his heart attack."

Her sister lurched forward, white-faced. "No." She grasped the rim of the barrel and looked in. "I was just trying to protect Greg. Protect us."

A bitter taste rose in Audrey's mouth. "If you'd just been honest with me, I would have dropped the whole thing. It was more pain than it was worth. God, Mac thinks her father is some asshole who wouldn't have loved her."

"If I'd known..." Greg began.

"I know," Audrey and Jess chorused. He would have done the right thing.

"All your talk about statutory rape and how angry you were." Jess cast a pained gaze at Audrey. "I was scared you'd tell Neve. You ruined my life once. I couldn't let you do it again."

Audrey stumbled back from her words like they were a punch.

"I'd never intentionally do anything to hurt you. Jesus, Jess, I found pictures of Greg and Maggie together and I wasn't going to tell you about them because I didn't want to fucking hurt you."

Was that remorse in her sister's expression? Audrey couldn't tell.

Greg ran a hand through his hair. "Christ. I acted so holier-than-thou, protesting my innocence. I'm that girl's father." He turned to his wife. "I have to tell her. I have to try to make this right. Don't I?" Now he turned to Audrey.

She was focused on her sister. Jess still gripped the blackened sides of the barrel. Her face had gone stark white, and there was something terribly off in her expression. "Jess?"

She looked up, eyes wide. "Oh, sissy." She hadn't called Audrey sissy since they were kids. "Call an ambulance."

Instinctively, Audrey looked down. The fine crust of snow at her sister's feet was dark with shadows, but in the light she could see a growing pool of crimson.

Jessica was having a miscarriage.

"How is she?" Audrey asked, handing Greg a coffee. They were in the family waiting room at the hospital. Again.

Rusty, Jake, and David had kept the girls while Audrey and Anne took Greg and Jess to the hospital—it had been quicker than waiting for an ambulance.

"Resting," he said. "Your mother's in with her. Did you know she had a miscarriage in between you and Jess?"

Audrey nodded. "We don't talk about it much." It had been a difficult time for her mother.

"No. Not exactly a pleasant topic," he remarked with a self-conscious chuckle. Then he closed his eyes as a wave of anguish washed over his features. "What are we going to do?"

She sat down beside him. "What do you want to do?"

"I want to go back in time and never touch Maggie, for one thing."

"Yeah, sorry, I can't help with that."

He smiled sadly. "I want to take responsibility. I want to know my kid. You think there will be charges?"

Audrey made a face. "Doubt it. Maggie's not around, so who's going to press them? The state? I gotta think they have better things to do, especially if you acknowledge Mac."

"God, what she must think of me."

"Hey, you honestly didn't think it was you. That's preferable to what she thought. Once she gets to know you it won't matter. She just wants to know where she came from."

"For what it's worth, I liked Maggie. She was messed up, but she could be really sweet."

Audrey couldn't think of a response that wouldn't sound taunting or sarcastic, so she only nodded. And then, "I'm sorry about the baby."

Greg's eyes filled with tears, but he blinked them back. "Thanks. Doesn't seem fair, really. I gain one child and lose another. Maybe it's my punishment. Jess's too for doing what she did." His eyes widened, like something horrible had just occurred to him. "Is Jake going to press charges for the break-in?"

She took his hand. "Of course not." She resisted the urge to add "idiot." Suddenly she knew what it was like to be her father. "If he'd known, he said he would have handed her the keys." Of course she had filled him in already. "He's going to talk to Neve, see if she'll drop the investigation." This would make the cop all the more suspicious of both Jake and Audrey, but Greg didn't need to know that. And there was always the chance Neve wouldn't drop it out of spite, but without Jake to press charges it would be difficult, especially if he then said it was all a big misunderstanding. Then again, that might make her all the more inclined to try to press charges against Greg. Who knew how the hell it would all play out?

"She didn't mean what she said, about you ruining her life again. She loves you. You know that, right?"

Audrey forced a smile. "Sure." But she wasn't sure he believed the words any more than she did.

Greg nodded, holding her fingers tight in his own. Audrey felt the warm drip of a tear on her hand. "It's going to be okay," she said, putting her arm around his shoulders. And maybe it would be.

Someday.

Instead of having them drive to Calais, Mackenzie decided to make a return trip to Edgeport. She asked Audrey to be with her when she officially met her father and was introduced to the girls as their big sister, so Audrey met her at Greg and Jessica's house.

It was awkward, but Audrey did it. Greg even dressed up a bit—collared shirt and dress pants. Olivia was too young to care, and Isabelle was happy to have Mac as her big sister, but it was obvious she didn't quite grasp what it meant, and that was okay. There would be plenty of time to explain it later.

"I owe you an explanation," Greg told his daughter. "Can we talk?"

Mac regarded him a moment. Audrey thought the kid was making him squirm—and she was okay with that. Greg didn't seem to get that the girl wouldn't have come if she didn't want to know him. Finally, she nodded. "Okay."

He took her into the living room so they could talk privately. Audrey and Jess sat in the kitchen and had tea. It was tense and awkward, and part of Audrey liked knowing her sister didn't want to be around her because it meant she at least felt bad for what she'd said and done.

"So?" Audrey asked.

"So, what?" Her sister sounded both defensive and depressed.

"How are you doing?"

She waved her hand. It was obvious she was on something for the depression that had followed the miscarriage. Knowing that she'd indirectly brought about their father's heart attack hadn't helped. Of course, Rusty told his daughter it wasn't her fault, but Jess and Audrey were a lot alike, and Audrey knew she wouldn't believe him if she was the one feeling guilty.

Not that she didn't have her own guilt. If she'd just kept her nose out of it, it wouldn't have blown up like it did. The therapist in her reminded her that there was no way she could have known, but that was a hard voice to listen to some days. That was why she'd made an appointment with a psychologist just outside Machias. She had her own issues to work through, and she couldn't do it alone.

"I'm not sure how we'll ever thank Jake for not pressing charges."

Audrey shrugged. Her fiancé would figure out something, someday, she was certain of it. "And Greg?"

"Nothing. Yet."

And there probably wouldn't be. Audrey and Mac had talked about it and then Audrey paid a visit to Neve and explained the situation. She had no problem using Jess's miscarriage as a way of softening the cop's disposition either. In the end, Neve had agreed to keep out of it since it would only make things worse. And how could Greg contribute to Mac's education and future if he lost his job over sexual assault charges?

Audrey frowned. "You don't seem very happy about it."

"I lost my baby."

"You gained a stepdaughter. A pretty awesome one."

"What am I going to tell people? Everyone's going to know."

"Oh, come on. So what? Lots of people slept with Maggie. He's one of a long list." It felt wrong to make light of it, but she had to, for her sister's sake. "Try being a murderer. Hey—at least no one will ever know you're a burglar."

Her sister actually chuckled at that. "I want to blame you for this. I don't know why, but I do."

"I know."

"It doesn't help you sitting there being all understanding."

"Probably not. You want me to blame you for Dad's heart attack again?"

Jess blinked back tears. "I should have trusted you."

"Yes."

"What I said..."

"Forget it."

Her sister's eyes widened. "You're not going to let me apologize?"

"I'm not going to apologize for killing Clint, so I don't expect you to apologize for holding it against me." Jess slowly nodded. "That's fair. I am sorry for hurting you, though. And for lying."

"I know."

A few seconds of silence passed. Jess trailed her finger along the handle of her cup. "Tell me something happy. Have you and Jake started making wedding plans?"

"Not really. We've talked about dates, but we're not in any hurry. We're already pretty committed to each other."

"Yeah, you two are creepy like that. You always were." She took a cookie off the plate between them. Her movements were slow—a side effect of the Xanax. "Mum said you got a call from Angeline, but she wouldn't tell me what she said."

Audrey raised a brow. "Really? That rains on Dad's theory about the Pelletier family's inability to keep news to themselves."

"Yeah. I think she refused to tell me for that very reason. He was in the room. So, what did the boss lady say?"

Butterflies danced in Audrey's stomach. "She's in. Jake and I are going to take a trip to LA after Christmas to finalize everything with her—and maybe take a vacation."

"You two could use one. I'm happy for you."

Audrey believed her. "I need to take some classes, get my Maine license to practice. I'm nervous. I'm not always good with people."

"If you want it bad enough, you'll figure it out."

"Yeah, I guess I will." She checked her watch. "I need to get going."

Her sister looked surprised. "What about Mac?"

Audrey smiled. "You've got this." Then she gave her sister a hug, albeit a slightly stiff one, said good-bye to her parents and nieces, and left. She didn't go straight home. First she drove back the Ridge, to the property that would soon house her dreams. From her trunk she took a small stake and a mallet. She drove the stake into the ground—not yet frozen—just to the side of the driveway. On the stake, printed in bold, red paint were the words GRACE RIDGE. It was the name she and Jake had decided on for the facility. She'd also decided to set up a couple of scholarships for kids who wanted to further their education—one in Maggie's name and the other in Mike LeBlanc's.

She smiled at the little marker. Someday there would be a big sign with the name on it, but for now, this would do. She was so happy. She was so terrified.

She threw the mallet back into the trunk and drove away. The sky was getting increasingly gray, and it looked like it might snow. Her next stop was the graveyard.

"Hey, Maggie," she said, crouching down near the tombstone. "So, Greg and Mackenzie are together right now. They're probably talking about you. Bet you love that, huh? You know, you could have made this easier on everyone if you'd just told me who her father was. You never were into making things easy, though." She took the charm bracelet Neve had returned to her out of her pocket and set it on the stone.

"I hope wherever you are, you've finally found some peace. God knows I could use some. I need to make peace with you, Mags. I think I'm finally starting to do that." Then she patted the stone and stood. One more stop to make before she could go home and get some work done. She was going to drive down to Cambridge next week and pack up her stuff in the condo, plus get some things out of storage to bring back to Jake's house. Their house.

She'd do some work for Angeline while there, check in on the staff and their projects, and get them to start asking some of their colleagues for referrals of professionals who might be interested in relocating to rural Maine. There might be a few willing to make the change, especially if the compensation was worth it. What she hoped for was to get a couple of veterans, someone in midcareer, and one or two newbies excited to be working in their field. Having Angeline's name associated with them would certainly help attract résumés.

She drove back Tripp's Cove, past her new home, and pulled into Yancy's yard. Again she opened her trunk and removed the item wrapped in a quilt and plastic bags that Audrey had hidden under her father's workshop the night Yancy asked her to come for a drink. She carried it up the front steps and rang the bell.

Yancy opened the door, looked at what she carried, and nodded. "It's all done, huh?"

"Yeah." Audrey offered her the bundle. "Officially ruled an accident. You know it's driving him nuts wondering what really happened."

"He'll get over it." Yancy set the package by the door. "He'd only give me a hard time for being sloppy."

"It was a damn good shot, from what I hear."

"It was, but I should have done what Jake would have done and just made him disappear, but no way I could have moved the son of a bitch on my own."

"I still think Jake would like to know that you did it to protect him."

Yancy gave her a look, and in that moment she looked so much like Jake it was unnerving. "He never told me he killed Matt to protect me. Besides, I don't want him to feel that he owes me like he thinks he owes Lincoln. I just prefer to think no one's keeping score."

"You sound like your grandmother."

"There are worse things, I suppose." But she said it with a smile. "Can I trust you to keep my secret?"

"I think I've proved my trustworthiness. Even when Neve questioned Jake I wasn't tempted to throw you under the bus. We're going to be family soon."

"We became family the day you took a bullet for my kid." Yancy opened her arms and Audrey stepped into her hug.

"We'll be family until we're both dead. If you ever need anything, I'm here for you."

"Same." She pulled back. "I'd better get going before your brother calls wondering where I am."

Yancy picked up the quilt and plastic-wrapped rifle. "I guess I can put this back in the cabinet now. When Gran left me this thing I never thought it would come in so handy."

Audrey smiled, said good-bye, and left. She had no remorse or guilt about hiding a murder weapon for her future sister-in-law. Maybe that made her a little psychotic. Or maybe it was just Edgeport justice coming around. Ratchett had threatened Jake, and there was no way she'd turn in his sister for making Ratchett go away. That wasn't how their world worked.

She went home. When she walked through the door, Jake was in the kitchen—barefoot as usual. He had a tub of ice cream in his hands. His face was almost back to normal now, and his movements weren't so stiff. Tex was lucky Audrey hadn't crossed his path, because she would have put him in the ground without a second's thought. She was going to marry this man, and God help anyone who threatened their life together.

Jake grinned, holding up the new tub of Rocky Road. "Want some?"

Audrey smiled back. "I do."

# ACKNOWLEDGMENTS

I really need to thank my editor, Lindsey, for the work she put into this book. Really, you went above and beyond. Thank you so much. Also thanks to Devi Pillai for helping me bring Audrey to life in the first place. To the fine folks of Maine who took the time to talk to me last summer as we undertook "Audreypolooza 2016" I offer my heartfelt appreciation. Thanks to my husband, Steve, for his endless patience and support, and for being the light I need when I'm done with the dark. You're my favorite person. Thanks to my friends for buying my books, sometimes several at a time (I'm looking at you, Lauralyn!), for gifting them and sharing them and growing Audrey's world. You all are so freaking fabulous. And finally, I need to thank the readers who have taken the time to let me know they've enjoyed the series thus far. You make it all worthwhile.

# MEET THE AUTHOR

*Photo Credit: Kathryn Smith*

As a child, KATE KESSLER seemed to have a knack for finding trouble, and for it finding her. A former delinquent, Kate now prefers to write about trouble rather than cause it, and spends her day writing about why people do the things they do. She lives in New England with her husband.

*April 26, 2017*

There were three words Officer Neve Graham hated to hear. They echoed in her ears as a twig snapped beneath the sole of her boot. *They found something.*

It was early April, but there were still patches of snow back in the heavily sheltered woods despite it being a sunny day. Another few rains and warmer temperatures and it would be gone soon. New shoots of life burst through the dirt, rotting vegetation giving way to something vibrant and green.

God, she hated spring. It smelled like death to her, all that decay laid bare by receding snow.

"You see it yet?" called a voice.

Neve turned. Coming along the path toward her was Charlotte de Baie, death investigator for the area. "Just got here," she replied. "Can I carry some of that?"

The other woman waved her away as they started along the rough path down the rocky hill. "Do you think it's her?"

"It's someone." When Neve had gotten the call earlier she'd been told that hikers had found human remains at the Edgeport State Park, commonly referred to by locals as simply "the falls." The area had only one missing person, but that was one too many as far as Neve was concerned. Part of her wanted to give the family closure, but there was no goddamn way she looked forward to making that visit.

Maybe it was a tourist. A lone hiker who hadn't told

anyone where they were going. It was possible—it happened occasionally.

Charlotte's boot skidded on a loose rock. Neve reached up to steady her. She really didn't want to be the thing to break the larger woman's fall at the bottom of the bank. Plus, the guys would make lesbian jokes for the next month, regardless of the fact that both Neve and Charlotte were in relationships with men.

When they finally reached bottom, they had to pick their way along the rocky terrain bordering the river to where the falls growled and splashed. There was a young man sitting partway up the steep incline. Neve recognized him as Gareth Hughes, one of the caretakers of the park. He was pale and perched on a rock about ten feet below the bridge that allowed hikers to cross over the falls.

"Climbed all that way down just to climb up again," Charlotte muttered, watching where she stepped. "Sounds about right."

Neve smiled slightly. "Better to come down the path than that." She pointed where Gareth sat. That was just an invitation for a broken neck, which was what had probably happened to the person Gareth found.

Finally, they reached the bottom of the falls where they were soon joined by Gareth's brother, Owen, and Neve's fellow state trooper Vicki Moore, who was in uniform and had been the first on the scene. There were others as well, but Neve was the primary officer since it was a female body. She'd been looking for Tala Lewis for months, ever since the girl went missing.

Neve and Charlotte suited up to preserve the scene and made their way fifteen feet up the side of the falls. The rocks and vegetation were wet from melt and rushing water, making it a slippery mess.

"Be careful," Neve cautioned as her own toe slipped on a slimy patch. Damn booties.

"Not my first rodeo, girlie," the older woman replied, deftly avoiding the same spot. Somehow, Charlotte managed to look cool and graceful while a tiny trickle of sweat ran down Neve's back.

Gareth reached down to give her a hand up the last couple of feet. Then, when Neve stepped to the side, he helped Charlotte as well. The bridge was only a few feet away—a good place for anyone else to stand so as not to contaminate the scene any more than it already was.

"Where is it?" Neve asked the younger man.

He pointed to a pile of rocks that looked as though it had been part of a landslide at one time. Behind them, Neve saw alders, more rocks, and a boot. A boot that looked as though it might still have a foot in it. She swallowed. She'd been doing this job for ten years now, and it never got any easier.

She and Charlotte approached in single file, Neve stepping on the hard rocks in an attempt to preserve the scene as much as possible. She paused on the top of the largest boulder and looked down.

Shit.

The body had been a young woman at one time. It was surrounded and still partially covered by rocks. Long black hair stuck to the scalp and tangled with debris on the ground. She wore a puffy purple jacket, ripped and stained with blood, and jeans stuffed into black boots. Her skin was almost the same color as her coat, with patches of red. *Freezer burn,* Neve thought. It wasn't the bloat that got to her—or even the smell. Thank God it was still too cool for bug activity and the rocks had kept her covered until the melt started. No, what got to Neve was the grimace, and there always seemed to be a grimace. It was the one reminder that what they were looking at used to be alive. The girl's revealed a slightly crooked eyetooth.

Charlotte began taking photos with her phone. "It's her, isn't it?"

Neve nodded, her throat tight. They both knew they'd have to compare dental records before they could say anything publicly, but there was no doubt in her mind. "It's Tala Lewis."

And it was obvious her death hadn't been an accident.

The moment Audrey Harte saw the unmarked police car pull into the drive, she knew something bad had happened. Detective Neve Graham was a friend, but things had been strained between them ever since Neve made it clear she didn't fully trust Audrey, or her fiancé, Jake. It wasn't that Audrey blamed her; Neve had every reason to be wary as a cop—but *not* as a friend. Audrey would never betray her that way.

So, if Neve was there, unannounced, then something bad had happened. Audrey turned away from the workers building an extension onto the old farmhouse that would soon be her Grace Ridge facility for troubled teens, and walked toward the spot where Neve had parked, under an ancient apple tree. There would be blossoms on the tree in a few weeks, toward the end of May, but for now it was thick with buds. It was obvious back here, on what locals referred to as "the Ridge," that spring had truly arrived.

Neve climbed out of the car and shut the door. She wore a black pantsuit and white shirt that indicated she was on duty. Was it Jake? Audrey's mother? No, someone would have called her or driven back—someone who wasn't Neve.

"What's wrong?" Audrey demanded, closing the distance between them with long strides.

Neve leaned against the car. Her dark hair was back in a tight bun, but curls had managed to escape regardless. They had met as children, and Neve had been the first black person Audrey had ever seen in person. Audrey was the first person Neve had ever met whose eyes were different colors. They'd been fascinated by each other.

Then Neve's father arrested Audrey and her best friend for murder and put an end to that.

Neve crossed her arms over the chest of her white button-down. "We found a body this morning."

Audrey's shoulders sagged. "Tala Lewis?"

The other woman nodded. She looked defeated. "Yeah."

"Shit. Alisha is going to be heartbroken." Alisha was Jake's niece, who'd been good friends with the girl who'd disappeared a couple of months ago. Alisha clung to the hope that her friend had taken off to New York or LA to pursue her dreams of becoming an actress. She was convinced that Tala would send word as soon as she was settled in, even though the girl was much more considerate than that, and would have never let people worry about her.

"I'm going to ask you not to say anything to her until we know for sure. I haven't talked to the parents yet."

"Of course." She didn't like keeping secrets from Alisha, but the girl couldn't be expected not to share the news with friends, and her mother—Jake's sister, Yancy—had a reputation as a gossip. It would be all over town before supper time.

Neve was silent for a moment, giving Audrey a chance to study her. She looked exhausted; there were dark circles under her wide eyes and tension in her brow. "What else?" She prompted. It was obvious now that Neve had sought her out, not because of Alisha, but because she needed to talk. "Is it Bailey?" Bailey was the daughter of Neve's boyfriend, and was currently incarcerated at a juvenile facility awaiting trial for the murder of her stepmother, Maggie. The same Maggie whose father Audrey had helped kill.

It all felt so very incestuous.

"No. She's good. The lawyers are optimistic." She shifted against the car, turning so that her back was against the driver's door. "The body we found had been stabbed. Multiple times."

*The body* rather than Tala. Neve was either being very diligent about not committing to the victim's identity or she was trying to be impersonal. "I don't suppose there's any way it could have been accidental?"

Neve gave her a sharp look, as if questioning her intelligence. "We found her back the falls. Someone had taken the time to cover her with rocks."

Audrey leaned against the car as well. "So now you have to tell the parents their daughter was murdered."

"By someone who seems to know the area, and had the thought to leave her in a spot where she was very unlikely to be found. If it wasn't for the park guys doing some work, we might not have found her. Once the warm weather hit..."

She didn't have to explain any further. Audrey had worked with the police—and watched enough TV—to have an idea what bugs and animals could do to a corpse.

"You're thinking it was someone local."

Again with the look. Audrey frowned. "Fuck off. It's what I do. I'm a therapist. I ask questions that have seemingly obvious answers, but you saying the answer is what's important."

Neve shook her head. "I'm sorry. You're right. I am thinking it was someone local. You saying it first makes me feel less guilty for thinking it." She sighed. "I thought when I left New York I was leaving this kind of stuff behind."

Audrey didn't know exactly what had happened, but she knew Neve had been shot and almost died, and that her parents had begged her to give up the city, because her father had almost been killed on the job years earlier. It was the reason they'd moved to Edgeport.

"It's been getting worse," Neve continued.

"Since I came home," Audrey supplied, because of course it was all about her.

"Shut up." Neve scowled at her. "You coming home didn't have anything to do with what Bailey did, and since then I've been much more aware, of when I'm investigating crimes that have to do with teenagers."

"Welcome to my world." Audrey had started into her career as a forensic juvenile psychologist because of her own background, but it soon became more than that. She wanted to help kids, but now her life was so full of wounded and even criminal teenagers that she sometimes wondered if she'd become desensitized to the very issues she wanted to help solve.

"No. You're trying to help these kids. I'm the bad guy. I had to arrest Bailey." She closed her eyes and leaned her head back. "I don't want to be my frigging father."

*Ah.* Audrey supposed she ought to have seen that one coming, but Neve didn't talk much about her father, or what she thought of him. Really, Audrey was the *last* person fit to comment on the mental and emotional health of Everett Graham.

"You're not your father any more than I'm mine."

Neve shot her an arch glance. *"Seriously?"*

"Hey, I might be like him, but I'm also like my mother at times, and I'm a fully grown woman capable of making my own decisions. I'm not my father, and you're a better cop than your father ever was. At least you care." That might have been overstepping, but Neve didn't seem to mind.

"She was stabbed to death, Audrey. I've never seen anything so brutal."

Audrey's lips compressed. "It was personal."

Neve nodded. "Very. If this was one of those criminal shows we'd be discussing overkill."

Audrey liked procedurals. "So, what are you going to do?"

The other woman sighed, tilted her head back as she met her gaze. "Wait for ID to be confirmed and the autopsy results to come in, and then I'm afraid I'm going to have to start looking for a murderer."

Audrey's smile was grim. "I've got an alibi."